The story is [...] young girl in [...] finishing scho[...] near her Yorkshire home she meets a young man, Gabriel Rockwell, son of a neighbouring baronet, who lives in a great mansion on the moors, Kirkland Revels. They fall immediately in love and marry, Gabriel taking his bride to live in the Revels. Few could have met with so chilly a reception as Catherine when reluctantly she was received by the extraordinary Rockwell family. Slowly, day by day and night by night, she sensed that she was in the grip of something mysterious, something evil—and the chill forefinger of fear was pressing on her. . . .

Available in Fontana by the same author

The Queen's Confession

King of the Castle

Bride of Pendorric

Mistress of Mellyn

Menfreya

The Legend of the Seventh Virgin

Victoria Holt

Kirkland Revels

Collins
FONTANA BOOKS

First published 1962
First issued in Fontana Books 1964
Fourteenth Impression April 1973

CONDITIONS OF SALE:
This book is sold subject to the condition
that it shall not, by way of trade or
otherwise, be lent, re-sold, hired out or
otherwise circulated without the publisher's
prior consent in any form of binding or
cover other than that in which it is
published and without a similar condition
including this condition being imposed on
the subsequent purchaser

© Victoria Holt 1962

Printed in Great Britain
Collins Clear-Type Press
London and Glasgow

Chapter 1

I met Gabriel and Friday on the same day, and strangely enough I lost them together; so that thereafter I was never able to think of one without the other. The fact that my life became a part of theirs is, in a way, an indication of my character, because they both began by arousing some protective instinct in me; all my life up to that time I had been protecting myself and I think I felt gratified to find others in need of protection. I had never before had a lover, never before had a dog; and, when these two appeared, it was natural enough that I should welcome them.

I remember the day perfectly. It was spring, and there was a fresh wind blowing over the moors. I had ridden away from Glen House after luncheon and I could not at this time leave the house without a feeling that I had escaped. This feeling had been with me since I returned home from my school in Dijon; perhaps it had always been there, but a young woman senses these emotions more readily than a child.

My home was a sombre place. How could it be otherwise when it was dominated by someone who was no longer there? I decided during the first days of my return that I would never live in the past. No matter what happened to me, when it was over I should not look back. Early in life—I was nineteen at this time—I had learned an important lesson. I determined to live in the present—the past forgotten, the future left to unfold itself.

Looking back I realise now that I was a ready victim for the fate which was awaiting me.

Six weeks before it happened, I had come home from school, where I had been for the past four years. I had not returned home in all that time, for I lived in Yorkshire and it was a long and expensive journey half-way across France and England; my education was costly enough. During my school years I had dramatised my home to some extent, so the picture in my imagination was different from the reality. Hence the shock when I arrived.

I had travelled from Dijon in the company of my friend, Dilys Heston-Browne and her mother; my father had arranged that this should be so, for it was unthinkable that a young lady should travel so far unchaperoned. Mrs. Heston-Browne had seen me safely to St. Pancras Station, put me in a first-class carriage and I had travelled alone from London to Harrogate, where I was to be met.

I had expected my father would be there. I had hoped my uncle would be. But that was ridiculous of me, for if Uncle Dick had been in England he would have come all the way to Dijon for me.

It was Jemmy Bell, my father's stable-man, who was waiting for me with the trap. He looked different from the Jemmy I had known four years before, more wizened, yet younger. That was the first little shock, discovering that someone whom I thought I knew so well was not quite what I had been imagining him.

Jemmy whistled when he saw the size of my trunk. Then he grinned at me. " By gow, Miss Cathy," he said, " looks like you've grown into a right grand young lady."

That was another reminder. In Dijon I had been Catherine or Mademoiselle Corder. Miss Cathy sounded like a different person.

He looked incredulously at my bottle-green velvet traveling coat with the leg o' mutton sleeves, and the straw hat which was tilted over my eyes and decorated with a wreath of daisies. My appearance startled him; he did not often see such fashionable clothes in our village.

" How is my father?" I asked. " I expected him to drive in to meet me."

Jemmy thrust out his lower lip and shook his head. " A martyr to gout," he said. " He can't abide the jolting. Besides . . ."

" Besides what?" I asked sharply.

" Well . . ." Jemmy hesitated. " He's just coming out of one of his bad turns. . . ."

I was conscious of a little tug of fear, remembering those bad turns which had been a feature of the old days. " Be quiet, Miss Cathy, your father's having one of his bad turns . . ." They had descended upon the house, those bad turns, with a certain regularity, and when they were with us we tip-toed about the place and spoke in whispers ; as for my father, he disappeared from view, and when he reappeared he was paler than usual, with deep shadows under his eyes ; he did not seem to hear when he was spoken to ; he had frightened me. While I had been away from home I had allowed myself to forget the bad turns.

I said quickly: " My uncle is not at home?"

Jemmy shook his head. " 'Tis more than six months since we've seen him. Happen it'll be eighteen more afore we do."

I nodded. Uncle Dick was a sea captain and he had written to me that he was off to the other side of the world, where he would be engaged for several months.

I felt depressed; I should have felt so much happier if he had been at home to welcome me.

We were trotting along roads which stirred my memories, and I thought of the house where I had lived until Uncle Dick had decided it was time I went away to school. I had endowed my father with Uncle Dick's personality; I had swept away the old cobwebs of time and let in the bright sunshine. The home I had talked of to my companions had been the home I wanted, not the one I knew.

But now the time for dreaming was over. I had to face what was—not quite what I wished it to be.

" You're quiet, Miss Cathy," said Jemmy.

He was right. I was in no mood to talk. Questions were on my lips but I did not ask them because I knew that the answers Jemmy would give me were not what I wanted. I had to discover for myself.

We went on driving through lanes which were sometimes so narrow that the foliage threatened to snatch my hat from my head. Soon the scenery would change; the neat fields, the narrow lanes, would give way to the wilder country; the horse would steadily climb and I should smell the open moors.

I thought of them now with a burst of pleasure and I realised that I had been a little homesick for them ever since I had left them.

Jemmy must have noticed that my expression brightened for he said: " Not long now, Miss Cathy."

And there was our village—it was little more. Glengreen —a few houses clustered round the church, the inn, the green and the cottages. On we went past the church to the white gates, through the drive, and there was Glen House, smaller than I had imagined it, with the Venetian blinds drawn down, the lace curtains just visible behind them. I knew that there would be heavy velour curtains at the windows to shut out the light.

If Uncle Dick had been at home he would have drawn back the curtains, pulled up the blinds, and Fanny would have complained that the sun was fading the furniture, and my father . . . he would not even have heard the complaint.

7

As I got out of the trap Fanny, who had heard us arrive, came out to greet me.

She was a round tub of a Yorkshire woman who should have been jolly, but was not. Perhaps years in our house had made her dour.

She looked at me critically and said in her flat-vowelled accent: "You've got thin while you've been away."

I smiled. It was an unusual greeting from someone who had not seen me for four years and who had been the only "mother" I could really remember. Yet it was what I expected Fanny had never petted me; she would have felt it "daft," as she would call it, to give any demonstration of affection. It was only when she could be critical that she believed in giving vent to her feelings. Yet this woman had studied my creature comforts; she had made sure that I was adequately fed and clothed. I was never allowed any fancy frills and what she called falderals. She prided herself on plain speaking, on never disguising the truth, on always giving an honest opinion —which often meant a brutal one. I was by no means blind to Fanny's good points, but in the past I had yearned for a little show of affection however insincere. Now my memories of Fanny came rushing back to me. As she studied my clothes her mouth twitched in the way I well remembered. She, who found it difficult to smile in pleasure, could readily smirk in contemptuous amusement.

"Yon's what you wear over there, is it?" she said. Again there was that twitch of the lips.

I nodded coolly. "Is my father at home?"

"Why, Cathy . . ." It was his voice and he was coming down the staircase to the hall. He looked pale and there were shadows under his eyes; and I thought to myself, seeing him with the eyes of an adult for the first time: He looks bewildered, as though he does not quite belong in this house, or to this time.

"Father!"

We embraced but, although he endeavoured to show some warmth, I was aware that it did not come from the heart. I had a strange feeling then that he was not pleased that I had come home, that he had been happy to be rid of me, that he would have preferred me to stay in France.

And there in our gloomy hall, before I had been home five minutes, I was oppressed by the house and the longing to escape from it was with me.

If only Uncle Dick had been there to greet me, how different my homecoming would have been!

The house closed in on me. I went to my room, where the sun was shining through the slats of the blinds. I pulled them up and light flooded the room; then I opened the window. Because my room was at the top of the house I had a view of the moor, and as I looked I felt myself tingling with pleasure. It had not changed at all; it still delighted me; I remembered how I had exulted to ride out there on my pony even though I always had to be accompanied by someone from the stables. When Uncle Dick was at the house we would ride together; we would canter and gallop with the wind in our faces; I remembered that we often stopped at the blacksmith's shop while one of the horses was shod—myself sitting there on a high stool, the smell of burning hoofs in my nostrils while I sipped a glass of Tom Entwhistle's home-made wine. It had made me a little dizzy and that had seemed a great joke to Uncle Dick.

"Captain Corder, you're a caution, that's what you are!" So said Tom Entwhistle many a time to Uncle Dick.

I had discovered that Uncle Dick wanted me to grow up exactly like himself; and as that was exactly what I wanted to do we were in accord.

My mind was wandering back to the old days. To-morrow, I thought, I'll ride out on to the moors . . . this time alone.

How long the first day seemed! I went round the house into all the rooms—the dark rooms with the sun shut out. We had two middle-aged servants, Janet and Mary, who were like pale shadows of Fanny. That was natural perhaps because she had chosen them and trained them. Jemmy Bell had two lads to help him in the stables and they managed our garden too. My father had no profession. He was what was known as a gentleman. He had come down from Oxford with honours, had taught for a while, had had a keen interest in archæology, which had taken him to Greece and Egypt; when he had married, my mother had travelled with him, but when I was about to be born they had settled in Yorkshire, he intending to write works on archæology and philosophy; he was also something of an artist. Uncle Dick used to say that the trouble with my father was that he was too talented; whereas he, Uncle Dick, having no talents at all, had become a mere sailor.

9

How often had I wished that Uncle Dick had been my father!

My uncle lived with us in between voyages; it was Uncle Dick who had come to see me at school. I pictured him as he had looked, standing in the cool white-walled reception room whither he had been conducted by Madame la Directrice, legs apart, hands in pockets, looking as though everything belonged to him. We were much alike and I was sure that beneath that luxuriant beard was a chin as sharp as my own.

He had lifted me in his arms as he used to when I was a child. I believed he would do the same when I was an old woman. It was his way of telling me that I was his special person . . . as he was mine. " Are they treating you well?" he said, his eyes fierce suddenly, ready to do battle with any who were not doing so.

He had taken me out; we had clip-clopped through the town in the carriage he had hired; we had visited the shops and bought new clothes for me, because he had seen some of the girls who were being educated with me and had imagined they were more elegantly clad than I. Dear Uncle Dick! He had seen that I had a very good allowance after that, and it was for this reason that I had come home with a trunk full of clothes all of a style which, the Dijon *couturière* had assured me, came straight from Paris.

But as I stood looking out on the moor I knew that clothes could have little effect on the character. I was myself, even in fine clothes from Paris, and that was somebody quite different from the girls with whom I had lived intimately during my years in Dijon. Dilys Heston-Browne would have a London season; Marie de Freece would be introduced into Paris Society. These two had been my special friends; and before we parted we had sworn that our friendship would last as long as we lived. Already I doubted that I should ever see them again. That was the influence of Glen House and the moors. Here one faced stark truth, however unromantic, however unpleasant.

That first day seemed as though it would never end. The journey had been so eventful, and here in the brooding quietness of the house it was as though nothing had changed since I had left. If there appeared to be any change, that could only be due to the fact that I was looking at life here through the eyes of an adult instead of those of a child.

I could not sleep that night. I lay in bed thinking of Uncle Dick, my father, Fanny, everyone in this house. I thought how strange it was that my father should have married and had a daughter, and Uncle Dick should have remained a bachelor. Then I remembered the quirk of Fanny's mouth when she mentioned Uncle Dick, and I knew that meant that she disapproved of his way of life and that she was secretly satisfied that one day he would come to a bad end. I understood now. Uncle Dick had had no wife, but that did not mean he had not had a host of mistresses. I thought of the sly gleam I had seen in his eyes when they rested on Tom Entwhistle's daughter who, I had heard, was " no better than she should be." I thought of many glances I had intercepted between Uncle Dick and women.

But he had no children, so it was characteristic of him, greedy for life as he was, to cast his predatory eyes on his brother's daughter and treat her as his own.

I had studied my reflection at the dressing-table before I got into bed that night. The light from the candles had softened my face so that it seemed—though not beautiful nor even pretty—arresting. My eyes were green, my hair black and straight ; it felt heavy above my shoulders when I loosened it. If I could wear it so, instead of in two plaits wound about my head, how much more attractive I should be. My face was pale, my cheek-bones high, my chin sharp and aggressive. I thought then that what happens to us leaves its mark upon our faces. Mine was the face of a person who had had to do battle. I had been fighting all my life. I looked back over my childhood to those days when Uncle Dick was not at home ; and the greater part of the time he was away from me. I saw a sturdy child with two thick black plaits and defiant eyes. I knew now that I had taken an aggressive stand in that quiet household ; subconsciously I had felt myself to be missing something, and because I had been away at school, because I had heard accounts of other people's homes, I had learned what it was that young child had sought and that she had been angry and defiant because she could not find it. I had wanted love. It came to me in a certain form only when Uncle Dick was home. Then I was treated to his possessive exuberant affection ; but the gentle love of a parent was lacking.

Perhaps I did not know this on that first night ; perhaps it came later ; perhaps it was the explanation I gave myself for plunging as recklessly as I did into my relationship with Gabriel.

But I did learn something that night. Although it was long before I slept I eventually dozed to be wakened by a voice,

11

and I was not sure in that moment whether I had really heard that voice or whether it came to me from my dreams.

"Cathy!" said the voice, full of pleading, full of anguish. "Cathy, come back."

I was startled—not because I had heard my name, but because of all the sadness and yearning with which it was spoken.

My heart was pounding; it was the only sound in that silent house.

I sat up in bed, listening. Then I remembered a similar incident from the days before I had gone to France. The sudden waking in the night because I had thought I heard someone calling my name!

For some reason I was shivering; I did not believe I had been dreaming. Someone *had* called my name.

I got out of bed and lighted one of the candles. I went to the window which I had opened wide at the bottom before going to bed. It was believed that the night air was dangerous and that windows should be tightly closed while one slept; but I had been so eager to take in that fresh moorland air that I had defied the old custom. I leaned out and glanced down at the window immediately below. It was still, as it had always been, that of my father's room.

I felt sobered because I knew what I had heard this night, and on that other night of my childhood, was my father's voice calling out in his sleep. And he called for Cathy.

My mother had been Catherine too. I remembered her vaguely—not as a person but a presence. Or did I imagine it? I seemed to remember being held tightly in her arms, so tightly that I cried out because I could not breathe. Then it was over, and I had a strange feeling that I never saw her again, that no one else ever cuddled me because when my mother did so I had cried out in protest.

Was that the reason for my father's sadness? Did he, after all those years, still dream of the dead? Perhaps there was something about me which reminded him or her; that would be natural enough and was almost certainly the case. Perhaps my homecoming had revived old memories, old griefs which would have been best forgotten.

How long were the days; how silent the house! Ours was a household of old people, people whose lives belonged to the past. I felt the old rebellion stirring. *I* did not belong to this house.

12

I saw my father at meals; after that he retired into his study to write the book which would never be completed. Fanny went about the house giving orders with hands and eyes; she was a woman of few words but a click of her tongue, a puff of her lips, could be eloquent. The servants were in fear of her: she had the power to dismiss them; I knew that she held over them the threat of encroaching age to remind them that if she turned them out, there would be few ready to employ them.

There was never a spot of dust on the furniture; the kitchen was twice weekly filled with the fragrant smell of baking bread; the household was run smoothly. I almost longed for chaos.

I missed my school life which, in comparison with that in my father's house, seemed to have been filled with exciting adventures. I thought of the room I had shared with Dilys Heston-Browne; the courtyard below from which came the continual sound of girls' voices; the periodic ringing of bells which made one feel part of a lively community; the secrets, the laughter shared; the dramas and comedies of a way of life which in retrospect appeared desirably light-hearted.

There had been several occasions during those four years when I had been taken on holiday trips by people who pitied my loneliness. Once I went to Geneva with Dilys and her family, and at another time to Cannes. It was not the beauties of the Lake which I remembered, nor that bluest of seas with the background of Maritime Alps; it was the close family feeling between Dilys and her parents, which she took for granted and which filled me with envy.

Yet, looking back, I realised that it was only now and then that the feeling of loneliness had come to me; for the most part I walked, rode, bathed and played games with Dilys and her sister as though I were a member of the family.

During one holiday when every other pupil had gone away. I was taken to Paris for a week by one of the mistresses. Very different this, from holidaying with the light-hearted Dilys and her indulgent family, for Mademoiselle Dupont was determined that my cultural education should not be neglected. I laughed now to think of that breathless week; the hours spent in the Louvre among the old masters; the trip out to Versailles for a history lesson. Mademoiselle had decided that not a moment was to be wasted. But what I remembered most vividly from that holiday was hearing her talk of me to her mother; I was "the poor little one who was left at school

13

during the holidays because there was nowhere else for her to go."

I was sad when I heard that said of me and deeply conscious of that desperate aloneness. The unwanted one! The one who had no mother and whose father did not want her to come home for the holiday. Yet I forgot quickly, as one does when a child, and was soon lost in the enchantment of the Latin Quarter, the magic of the Champs Elysées and the shop windows of the Rue de la Paix.

It was a letter from Dilys which made me recall those days with nostalgia. Life was wonderful for Dilys, being prepared for the London season.

"My dear Catherine, I have scarcely a moment. I've been meaning to write for *ages,* but there's always something to prevent me. I seem to be for ever at the dressmakers being fitted for this and that. You should see some of the dresses! Madam would *scream* her dismay. But Mother's determined that I shan't go unnoticed. She's making out lists of people who are to be asked to my first ball. Already, mind you! How I wish you could be here. Do tell me *your* news. . . ."

I could imagine Dilys and her family in their house in Knightsbridge—close to the Park with the mews at the back. How different her life must be from mine!

I tried to write to her, but there seemed nothing to say that was not grim and melancholy. How could Dilys understand what it was like to have no mother to make plans for one's future, and a father who was so preoccupied with his own affairs that he did not even know I was there.

So I abandoned my letter to Dilys.

As the days passed I was finding the house more and more intolerable and spent a good deal of time out of doors, riding every day. Fanny smirked at my riding-habit—the latest from Paris by the bounty of Uncle Dick—but I did not care.

One day Fanny said to me: "Your father's going off to-day." Her face was tightly shut, completely without expression, and I knew she had deliberately made it so. I could not tell whether she disapproved of my father's going away or not ; all I knew was that she was holding in some secret which I was not allowed to share.

Then I remembered that there had always been those times when he went away and did not come home until the next day ; and when he did come back we still did not see him because he shut himself away in his room and trays were taken up to him. When he emerged he looked ravaged and was more silent than ever.

"I remember," I said to Fanny. "So he still goes . . . away?"

"Regular," Fanny answered. "Once in t'month."

"Fanny," I asked earnestly, "where does he go?"

Fanny shrugged her shoulders as though to imply that it was no business of hers nor of mine; but I believe she knew.

I kept thinking about him all day, and wondering. Then it suddenly came to me. My father was not very old . . . perhaps forty, I was not sure. Women might still mean something to him although he had never married again. I thought I was worldly-wise. I had discussed life with my school friends, many of whom were French—always so much more knowledgeable in such matters than we English—and we thought ourselves very up-to-date. I decided that my father had a mistress whom he visited regularly but whom he would never marry because he could not replace my mother; and after visiting this woman he came back filled with remorse because, although she was long since dead, he still loved my mother and believed he had desecrated her memory.

He returned the following evening; the pattern was the same as I remembered it. I did not see him on his return; I only knew that he was in his room, that he did not appear for meals, and that trays were taken up to him.

When at length he did appear he looked so desolate that I longed to comfort him.

At dinner that evening I said to him: "Father, you are not ill, are you?"

"Ill?" His brows were drawn together in dismay. "Why should you think that?"

"Because you look so pale and tired—and as though you have something on your mind. I wondered if there's anything I can do to help. I'm not a child any more, you know."

"I'm not ill," he said, without looking at me.

"Then . . ."

I saw the expression of impatience cross his face, and hesitated. But I decided not to be thrust aside so easily. He was in need of comfort and it was the duty of his daughter to try to give it to him.

"Look here, Father," I said boldly, "I feel something is wrong. I might be able to help."

He looked at me then and the impatience had given way

to coolness. I knew that he had deliberately put up a barrier between us and that he resented my persistence and construed it as inquisitiveness.

" My dear child," he murmured, " you are too imaginative."

He picked up his knife and fork and began paying more attention to his food than he had before I had spoken. I understood. It was a curt dismissal.

I had rarely felt so alone as I did at that moment.

After that our conversation became even more stilted, and often when I addressed him he did not answer. They said in the house that he was suffering from one of his " bad turns."

Dilly wrote again, complaining that I never told her what was happening to me. Reading her letters was like listening to her talking; the short sentences, the underlining, the exclamation marks, gave the impression of breathless excitement. She was learning to curtsy; she was taking dancing lessons; the great day was approaching. It was wonderful to have escaped from Madame and feel oneself no longer a schoolgirl, but a young lady of fashion.

I tried again to write to her, but what could I say? Only this: I'm desperately lonely. This house is a melancholy one. Oh, Dilys, *you* congratulate yourself because you have left your schooldays behind, and I am here in this sad house, wishing I were at school again.

I tore up that letter and went out to the stables to saddle my mare, Wanda, whom I had taken for my own on my return. I felt as though I were trapped in the web of my childhood, and that my life was going on in the same dismal way for ever.

And the day arrived when Gabriel Rockwell and Friday came into my life.

I had ridden out on to the moors that day as usual and had galloped over the peaty ground to the rough road when I saw the woman and the dog; it was the pitiful condition of the latter which made me slacken my speed. He was a thin pathetic-loking creature, and about his neck was a rope which acted as a lead. I had always had a special feeling for animals, and the sight of any one of them in distress never failed to rouse my sympathy. The woman, I saw, was a gipsy; this did not surprise me for there were many wandering from encampment to encampment on the moors; they came to the house selling clothes-pegs and baskets or offering us heather which we could have picked for ourselves. Fanny had no patience with them. " They'll get nowt from me," she would say. " They're nobbut lazy good-for-nothings, the lot of 'em."

I pulled up beside the woman and said: " Why don't you carry him? He's too weak to walk."

" And what's that to you?" she demanded, and I was aware of her sharp beady eyes beneath a tangle of greying black hair. Then her expression changed; she had noticed my smart riding-habit, my well-cared-for horse, and I saw the cupidity leap into her eyes. I was gentry, and gentry were for fleecing. " It's not a bite that's passed me lips, lady, this day and last. And that's the gospel truth, without the word of a lie."

She did not, however, look as though she were starving, but the dog undoubtedly was. He was a little mongrel, with a touch of the terrier, and in spite of his sad condition his eyes were alert; the manner in which he looked at me touched me deeply because I fancied that he was imploring me to rescue him. I was drawn to him in those first moments and I knew that I could not abandon him.

" It's the dog who looks hungry," I commented.

" Lord love you, lady, I haven't had a bite I could share with him these last two days."

" The rope's hurting him," I pointed out. " Can't you see that?"

" It's the only way I can get him along. I'd carry him, if I had the strength. With a little food in me I'd get back me strength."

I said on impulse: " I'll buy the dog. I'll give you a shilling for him."

" A shilling! Why, lady, I couldn't bear to part with him. My little friend, that's what he's been." She stooped to the dog, and the way in which he cowered betrayed the true state of affairs, so that I was doubly determined to get him. " Times is hard, ain't they, little 'un?" she went on. " But we've been together too long now for us to be parted for . . . a shilling."

I felt in my pockets for money. I knew she would finally accept a shilling for him because she would have to sell a great many clothes-pegs to earn as much; but, being a gipsy, she was going to bargain first. Then to my dismay I discovered that I had come out without money. In the pocket of my habit was one of Fanny's patties, stuffed with meat and onions, which I had brought with me in case I should not return for luncheon; but it was hardly likely that the gipsy would exchange the dog for that. It was money she wanted; and her eyes had already begun to glisten at the thought of it.

She was watching me intently; so was the dog. Her eyes had grown crafty and suspicious, and the dog's were more appealing than ever.

I began: "Look here, I've come out without money . . ."

But even as I spoke her lips curled in disbelief. She gave a vicious jerk at the rope round the dog's neck and he gave a piteous yelp. "Quiet!" she snapped; and he cowered again, with his eyes on me.

I wondered whether I could ask the woman to wait at this spot while I rode home to get the money, or whether she would allow me to take the dog and she could call at Glen House for it. I knew that was useless, for she would not trust me any more than I would trust her.

And it was then, as if by chance, that Gabriel appeared. He was galloping across the moor towards the road, and at the sound of a horse's hoofs the woman and I turned to see who was coming. He was on a black horse which made him seem fairer than he actually was, but his fairness made an immediate impression; so did his elegance. His dark brown coat and breeches were of the finest material and cut; but as he came nearer it was his face which attracted my attention and made it possible for me to do what I did. Looking back afterwards it seemed a strange thing to do—to stop a stranger and ask him to lend me a shilling to buy a dog. But there he was, I told him afterwards, like a knight in shining armour, a Perseus or St. George.

There was a brooding melancholy about his delicate features which immediately interested me, although this was not so apparent on our first meeting as it was to become later.

I called to him as he came on to the road: "Stop a moment, please." And even as I said it, I marvelled at my temerity.

"Is anything wrong?" he asked.

"Yes. This dog is starving."

He pulled up and looked from me to the dog and the gipsy woman, summing up the situation as he did so.

"Poor little fellow," he said. "He's in a bad way."

His voice was gentle, and I was immediately exhilarated because I knew that I should not ask for help in vain.

"I want to buy him," I explained, "and I've come out without money. It's most annoying and distressing. Will you please lend me a shilling?"

18

"Look here," whined the woman. "I ain't selling him. Not for no shilling, I ain't. He's my little dog, he is. Why should I sell him?"

"You were ready to for a shilling," I retorted.

She shook her head and pulled the dog towards her; and I again felt that twinge of compassion as I saw the little animal's reluctance. I looked pleadingly at the young man, who smiled as he dismounted, put his hand in his pocket and said:

"Here's two shillings for the dog. You can take it or leave it."

The woman could not hide her delight at so large a sum. She held out a dirty hand for the money which, with a fastidious gesture, he dropped into her palm. Then he took the rope from her, and she moved away quickly as though she were afraid he would change his mind.

"Thank you," I cried. "Oh, thank you."

The dog made a little whimpering sound which I felt to be pleasure. "The first thing to be done is feed him," I said, dismounting. "Fortunately I have a meat patty in my pocket."

He nodded and, taking the reins from my hands, led our horses off the road while I picked up the dog, who made a feeble attempt to wag his tail. I sat down on the grass and took the patty from my pocket; I fed the dog, who ate ravenously while the young man stood by holding the horses.

"Poor little dog," he said. "He's had a bad time."

"I don't know how to begin to thank you," I told him. "What would have happened if you hadn't come along is unthinkable. She would never have given him to me."

"Don't let's brood on that," he said. "We have him now."

I was drawn towards him because I knew that he cared as much about the dog's fate as I did; and the dog, from that moment, became a bond between us.

"I shall take him home and look after him," I said. "Do you think he'll recover?"

"I am sure he will. He's a tough little mongrel, I imagine, but hardly the dog to spend his days on a lady's velvet cushion."

"He's my sort of dog," I replied.

"You should feed him regularly and often."

"It is what I intend to do. When I get him home I shall give him some warm milk—a little at a time.

The dog knew we were talking about him, but the effort of eating, together with the excitement, had been exhausting, and he lay very still. I wanted to get home as quickly as possible and begin looking after him; but at the same time I was loath to say good-bye to the man. His melancholy expression, which I believed might well be habitual with him, had lifted when he had bargained for the dog and had presented him to me, and I was anxious to know what could have happened to a young man, who was clearly blessed with a goodly share of the comforts of life, to have produced that melancholy. I was curious about him, and it was stimulating to discover this curiosity in myself at the very time that I had acquired my interest in the dog. I was torn between two desires: I wanted to stay and learn more about the man, and at the same time I wanted to take the dog home and feed him. I knew, of course, that there must be no question what I did, for the dog was dangerously near death by starvation.

"I must be going," I said.

He nodded. "I'll carry him, shall I?" he replied; and without waiting for my reply, he helped me to mount. He gave me the dog to hold while he mounted; then he took the little creature from me and, tucking him under his arm, said: "Which way?"

I showed him and we set out. In twenty minutes we had reached Glengreen, scarcely speaking on the way there. At the gates of Glen House we paused.

"He's really yours," I said. "You paid for him."

"Then I make a gift of him to you." His eyes smiled into mine. "But I shall retain rights in him. I shall want to know whether he lives or not. May I call and ask?"

"Of course."

"To-morrow?"

"If you wish."

"And for whom shall I ask?"

"For Miss Corder . . . Catherine Corder."

"Thank you, Miss Corder. Gabriel Rockwell will call on you to-morrow."

Fanny was horrified by the presence of the dog. "Happen there'll be dog's hairs all over t'place. Happen we'll be finding whiskers in t'soup and fleas in our beds."

I said nothing. I fed the dog myself . . . on bread and milk in small quantities, at intervals all through the rest of the day and once in the night. I found a basket and I took him to my bedroom. It was the happiest night since my return, and I wondered why I never thought of asking for a dog when I was a child. Perhaps it was because I knew that Fanny would never have allowed me to have one.

What did it matter—I had him now.

He knew I was his friend right from the start. He lay in the basket too weak to move, but his eyes told me that he understood what I was doing was for his good. Those eyes, already loving, patiently followed me as I moved. I knew that he would be my friend as long as he lived. I wondered what to call him; he must have a name. I could not go on thinking of him as the gipsy's dog. Then I remembered that I had found him on a Friday and I thought: He'll be my Dog Friday. And from then he had his name.

By the morning he was on the way to recovery. I waited for the coming of Gabriel for, now that my anxieties about the dog were over, I began to think more of the man who had shared the adventure. I was a little disappointed because he did not come in the morning, and I felt sad because I was afraid he might have forgotten us by now. I did want to say thank you to him, because I was sure Friday owed his life to his timely arrival.

He came in the afternoon. It was three o'clock, and I was in my room with the dog when I heard the sound of horse's hoofs below. Friday's ears twitched and his tail moved as though he knew that the other one to whom he would be for ever grateful was near.

I looked out of my window, standing well back so that he could not see me if he should chance to look up. He was certainly handsome but in a somewhat delicate way, not as we expected our men to be in Yorkshire. He had an aristocratic air. I had noticed this on the previous day but I had wondered whether I had imagined it because of the contrast he made with Friday's previous mistress.

I went downstairs hastily because I did not want him to be ungraciously received.

I was wearing a dark blue velvet afternoon dress—my best —because I was expecting him, and I had wound my plaits to form a coronet on the top of my head.

I went out into the drive just as he came up. He swept off his hat in a manner which I knew would be called "daft" by Fanny, but I thought it elegant and the height of courtesy.

"So you came!" I said. "Dog Friday will recover. I've christened him after the day on which he was found."

He had dismounted and at that moment Mary appeared. I made her call one of the stable-boys to lead his horse round to the stable, and water and feed him.

"Come in," I said, and when Gabriel came into the hall, the house seemed brighter for his presence.

"Let me take you up to the drawing-room," I said, "and I will ring for tea."

He followed me up the stairs while I told him how I was treating Friday. "I shall bring him down to show you. You will see a great improvement."

In the drawing-room I pulled back the curtains and drew up the Venetian blinds. Now it seemed more cheerful—or perhaps that was due to Gabriel. When he sat in one of the arm-chairs and smiled at me, I was conscious that in my blue velvet with my neatly plaited hair I looked very different from the girl in the riding-habit.

"I'm glad you were able to save him," he said.

"*You* did that."

He looked pleased and I rang the bell, which was almost immediately answered by Janet.

She stared at my visitor and, when I told her to bring tea, she looked as though I were asking for the moon.

Five minutes later Fanny came in; she had an indignant air and I felt angry with her. She would have to realise that I was now mistress of the house.

"So it's visitors," said Fanny ungraciously.

"Yes, Fanny, we have a visitor. Pray see that tea is not long delayed."

Fanny pursed her lips; I could see that she was trying to make some retort, but I turned my back on her and said to Gabriel: "I trust you did not have to ride far."

"From the Black Hart Inn in Tomblersbury."

I knew Tomblersbury. It was a small village, rather like our own, some five or six miles away.

"You are staying at the Black Hart?"

"Yes, for a short while."

"You must be on holiday."

"You could call it that."

"Your home is in Yorkshire, Mr. Rockwell? But I am asking too many questions."

I was aware that Fanny had left the room. I could imagine her going to the kitchen or perhaps to my father's study. She would consider it most unseemly for me to entertain a gentleman alone. Let her! It was time she—and my father—understood that the life I was called upon to live was not only exceedingly lonely but one unsuitable for a young lady of my education.

22

"No," he replied, "please ask me as many questions as you like. If I cannot answer them, I shall say so."

"Where is your home, Mr. Rockwell?"

"The house is called Kirkland Revels, and it is situated in the village—or rather on the outskirts of the village—of Kirkland Moorside."

"Kirkland Revels! That sounds joyous."

The expression which flitted across his face was enough to tell me that my remark made him uncomfortable. It had told me something else; he was not happy in his home life. Was that the reason for that moodiness of his? I ought to have curbed my curiosity regarding his private affairs but I found it exceedingly difficult to do so.

I said quickly: "Kirkland Moorside . . . is that far from here?"

"Some thirty miles perhaps."

"And you are on holiday in this district, and you were taking a ride on the moors when . . ."

"When our little adventure occurred. You cannot be more glad than I am that it happened."

I felt reassured that the temporary awkwardness was past and I said: "If you will excuse me, I will bring Friday down to show you."

When I returned with the dog, my father was in the room. I guessed Fanny had insisted on his joining us and that even he had been conscious of the proprieties. Gabriel was telling how we had acquired the dog and my father was being charming; he listened attentively and I was pleased that he manifested an interest even though I did not believe he really felt it.

Friday in his basket, too weak to rise, made an effort to do so; his pleasure was obvious at the sight of Gabriel, whose long, elegant fingers gently stroked the dog's ear.

"He's fond of you," I said.

"But you'll have first place in his heart."

"I saw him first," I reminded him. "I shall keep him with me always. Will you let me pay you what you gave the woman?"

"I wouldn't hear of it," he told me.

"I should like to feel that he is all mine."

"So he is. A gift. But I admit to an interest. If I may, I shall call again to inquire after his health."

"It is not a bad idea to have a dog in the house," said my

23

father, as he came to stand beside us and look down into the basket.

We were standing thus when Mary brought in the tea wagon. There were hot crumpets as well as bread and butter and cakes; and as I sat behind the silver teapot, I thought this was my happiest afternoon since I had returned from France; I was as contented as I had been when Uncle Dick came home.

I did not realise until later that this was because I now had something in the house which I could love. I had Friday. I did not think at this stage that I had Gabriel too. That came later.

During the next two weeks Gabriel called regularly at Glen House; and at the end of that first week Friday was fully restored to health. His wounds had healed and good food regularly taken had done the rest.

He slept in his basket in my room and followed me wherever he could. I talked to him continuously. The house had changed; my life had changed because of him.

He wanted to be not only my companion but my defender. There was adoration in those limpid eyes when they looked into mine. He remembered that he owed his life to me; and because he was the faithful sort, that was something he would never forget.

We went for walks together—he and I. Only when I rode did I leave him behind, and when I returned he would fling himself at me in the sort of welcome I had only ever had from Uncle Dick.

Then there was Gabriel.

He continued to stay at the Black Hart. I wondered why. There was a lot I could not quite understand about Gabriel. There were times when he talked freely about himself, but even at such times I always had the impression that there was something he was holding back. I felt that he was on the verge of telling me, that he longed to tell me, and could never quite bring himself to do so; and that which he held back was some dark secret, perhaps something which he did not entirely understand himself.

We had become great friends. My father seemed to like him—at least he made no protests about his constant visits. The servants had grown used to him, and even Fanny, as long as we were properly chaperoned, made no complaints.

At the end of the first week he had said that soon he would be going home ; but at the end of the second he was still with us. I had a feeling that he was deceiving himself in some way, that he was promising himself that he would go home, and then making excuses not to.

I did not ask him questions about his home even though I longed to learn more about him. This was something else I had learned. At school I had often been made uneasy by searching questions about *my* home ; I had determined not to inflict the same discomfort on others. I would never probe, but always wait to be told.

So we talked about me, for Gabriel had no such reticence where I was concerned, and strangely enough, with him I did not mind. I told him about Uncle Dick who had always been a kind of hero to me, and I made him see Uncle Dick with his sparkling greenish eyes and black beard.

Gabriel said once when I had talked of my uncle: "You and he must be somewhat alike."

"There is a strong resemblance, I believe."

"He sounds like the sort of person who is determined to get the most out of life. I mean, he would act without first weighing up the consequences. Tell me, are you like that?"

"Perhaps I am."

He smiled. "I believe you are," he said ; and there came into his eyes what I can only describe as a far-away look, by which I mean that he was seeing me, not as we were together at that moment, but in some other place, in some other situation.

I thought he was about to speak, but he remained silent and I did not press him, for I was already beginning to feel that too much probing, too many questions, disturbed him. I must wait, I knew intuitively, for him to tell me without prompting.

But I had discovered that there was something unusual about Gabriel, and that should have warned me not to allow myself to become too deeply involved. I had been so lonely ; I found the atmosphere of my home so depressing ; I longed for a friend of my own age ; and the strangeness of Gabriel enthralled me.

So I refused to see any danger signals and we continued to meet.

We liked to ride on to the moors, tether our horses and

stretch ourselves out in the shelter of a boulder, looking up at the sky, our arms behind our heads, talking in a dreamy, desultory way. Fanny would have considered this the height of impropriety, but I was determined to adhere to no conventions; I knew this attitude delighted Gabriel and I learned later why it did so.

Each day I would ride out and meet him at some agreed spot because I could not bear the sly glances Fanny gave him when he called at the house. In our small and sheltered community it was not possible to meet a young man daily without causing a certain amount of speculation. I often wondered, during the early period of our acquaintance, whether Gabriel was aware of this; I also wondered whether he felt as embarrassed about it as I did.

I had not heard from Dilys for some weeks, so I supposed she was too immersed in her own affairs to have time to write. I did feel, however, that now I could write to her because I had something to tell her. I explained about our finding the dog, and how fond I had become of him; but what I really wanted to talk about was Gabriel. My affection for Friday was uncomplicated, but I could not quite understand my feelings for Gabriel.

He interested me, and I looked forward to our meetings with something more than the pleasure of a lonely girl who has at last found a friend; I realised that this was because I was constantly expecting some revelation which would startle me. There was certainly an air of mystery about Gabriel and I believed that again and again he was on the verge of confiding some secret which he longed to share with me and could not quite bring himself to do so. I had a conviction that he, like my father, was in need of comfort; and while my father repulsed me, Gabriel, when the time came, would welcome my desire to share whatever it was that was troubling him.

It was impossible, of course, to confide all this to the lighthearted Dilys, particularly when I was not at all sure of it myself. So I wrote a chatty, superficial letter, and felt pleased because something had happened to me which was worthy to be written about.

It was three weeks after we met when Gabriel seemed to come to a decision; and the day he began to talk to me about his home marked a change in our relationship.

We were lying stretched out on the moor and he pulled up handfuls of grass as he talked to me.

26

"I wonder what you would think of Kirkland Revels," he said.

"I am sure I should find it attractive. It's very old, is it not? Old houses have always been absorbingly interesting to me."

He nodded, and again there was that far-away look in his eyes.

"Revels," I murmured. "It's such a lovely name. It sounds as though the people who named it were determined to have a great deal of fun there."

He laughed mirthlessly, and there was a brief silence before he began to speak; then it was as though he were reciting a piece he had learned by heart.

"It was built in the middle of the sixteenth century. When Kirkland Abbey was dissolved, it was given to my ancestors. They took stones from the Abbey and with them built a house. Because it was used as a house in which to make merry . . . I must have had very merry ancestors . . . it was called Kirkland Revels in contrast to Kirkland Abbey."

"So the stones which built your house were once those of an ancient abbey?"

"Tons and tons of stone," he murmured. "There's still much of the old Abbey in existence. When I stand on my balcony I can look across to those grey and ancient arches. In certain lights you can imagine that they are not merely ruins . . . in fact it is difficult to believe they are. Then you can almost see the monks in their habits moving silently among the stones."

"How attractive it must be. You love it, do you not?"

"It has a fascination for all who see it. Don't all things as old as that? Imagine, although the house is a mere three hundred years old, the stones of which it is built date back to the twelfth century. Naturally everyone's impressed. You will be when . . ."

He stopped and I saw the slow smile curve his delicate lips.

I am forthright and had never been able to hedge, so I said: "Are you suggesting that I shall see it?"

The smile about his lips expanded. "I have been a guest in your home. I should like you to be one in mine."

Then it came bursting out: "Miss Corder, I shall have to go home soon."

"You don't want to, do you, Mr. Rockwell?"

"We are great friends, I believe," he said. "At least I feel we are."

"We have known each other but three weeks," I reminded him.

"But the circumstances were exceptional. Please call me Gabriel."

I hesitated, then I laughed. "What's in a name?" I asked. "Our friendship cannot be greater or less, whether I call you by your Christian or surname. What were you going to say to me, Gabriel?"

"Catherine!" he almost whispered my name as he turned on his side and leaned on his elbow to look at me. "You are right, I don't want to go back."

I did not look at him because I feared my next question was impertinent, but I could not prevent myself from asking it. "Why are you afraid to go back?"

He had turned away. "Afraid?" His voice sounded high-pitched. "Who said I was afraid?"

"Then I imagined it."

Silence fell between us for a few seconds, then he said: "I wish I could make you see the Revels . . . the Abbey. I wish . . ."

"Tell me about it," I said and added: "If you want to . . . but only if you want to."

"It's about myself I want to tell you, Catherine."

"Then please do."

"These have been the most interesting and happiest weeks of my life, and it is because of you. The reason I do not want to go back to the Revels is because it would mean saying good-bye to you."

"Perhaps we should meet again."

He turned to me. "When?" he asked almost angrily.

"Some time perhaps."

"Some time! How do we know what time is left to us?"

"How strangely you talk . . . as though you thought that one . . . or both of us . . . might die to-morrow."

There was a faint flush in his cheeks which seemed to make his eyes burn brightly. "Who can say when death shall come?"

"How morbid you have grown. I am nineteen. You have told me that you are twenty-three. People of our ages do not talk of dying."

"*One* evidently does. Catherine, will you marry me?"

I must have looked shocked by this unexpected outburst because he laughed and said: "You are looking at me as though I am crazy. Is it so strange that someone should want to marry you."

"But I cannot take this seriously."

"You must, Catherine. I ask with the utmost seriousness."

"But how can you speak of marriage after such a short acquaintance?"

"It does not seem short. We have met every day. I know that you are all I want, and that is enough for me."

I was silent. In spite of Fanny's attitude I had not considered marriage with Gabriel. We were the best of friends and I should be desolate if he went away; but when I thought of marriage he seemed almost like a stranger. He aroused my curiosity and interest; he was unlike anyone I had ever known and, because of that certain mystery which shrouded his personality, he attracted me very much; but until this moment I had thought of him mainly as a person whom good fortune had sent my way at an important moment. There was so little I knew about him; I had never met any of his people. Indeed when they, or his home, briefly intruded into our conversation I was immediately conscious of Gabriel's withdrawing from me, as though there were secrets in his life which he was not prepared to share with me. In view of all this I thought it very strange that he should suddenly suggest marriage.

He went on: "Catherine, what is your answer?"

"It is No, Gabriel. There is so much we do not know about each other."

"You mean there is so much you do not know about me."

"Perhaps that is what I mean."

"But what do you want to know? We love horses; we love dogs; we find pleasure in each other's company; I can laugh and be happy with you. What more could I ask than to laugh and be happy for the rest of my life?"

"And with others . . . in your home . . . you cannot laugh and be happy?"

"I could never be completely happy with anyone else but you; I could never laugh so freely."

"It seems a flimsy structure on which to base a marriage."

"You are being cautious, Catherine. You feel I have spoken too soon."

I knew then how desolate I should be if he went away, and I said quickly: "Yes, that is it. This is too soon. . . ."

"At least," he said, "I do not have to fear a rival. Do not

say No, Catherine. Think of how much I want this to be . . . and try to want it a little yourself."

I stood up. I was no longer in the mood to stay on the moors. He made no protest and we rode to the village, where he said good-bye to me.

When I reached the stables Friday was waiting there for me, He always knew when I had gone out riding and never failed to be in the stableyard watching for my return.

He waited patiently until I had given Wanda to one of the lads, then he flung himself at me, making sure that I was fully aware of his pleasure in my return. Many dogs have that lovable quality, but in Friday it was stronger than usual because it was touched by an extreme humility. He stood aside while my attention was given to others, waiting patiently until it was his turn. I believed that the memory of early wretchedness always remained with Friday, and that was why in all his exuberant affection there was that touch of deep humility and gratitude.

I lifted him in my arms and he sniffed my jacket with ecstacy.

I hugged him. I was growing more and more fond of him with every day, and my affection for him enhanced my feelings for Gabriel.

Even as I turned into the house I was wondering what marriage with Gabriel would be like. I was already beginning to believe that it was a state which I could contemplate without abhorrence.

What would my life in Glen House be like when Gabriel went away? I should ride Wanda, walk with Friday, but one could not be out of doors for ever. The winter would come. Winters were harsh in the moorland country ; there were days at a stretch when it was impossible to venture out unless one wanted to risk death in the blizzards. I thought of long dark days in the house—the weary monotonous round. It was true that Uncle Dick might come home ; but his visits could not be of very long duration and I could remember from the past how life seemed doubly dull after he had left.

It occurred to me then that I needed to escape from Glen House. A way was being offered to me. If I refused to take it, might I not be regretful for the rest of my life?

Gabriel came to dine with us occasionally. My father always roused himself on such occasions and was a tolerable host. I could see that he did not dislike Gabriel. Fanny's lips would curl in a sardonic smile when Gabriel was in the house. I knew that she was thinking that he was making use of our hospitality while he was in the neighbourhood, and that when the time came for him to leave he would do so and promptly forget us. Fanny, who was determined to give nothing, was always afraid that people were going to take something away from her. There were sly references to my "hopes" regarding Gabriel. She had never married and believed that it was the woman who desired that state in cold blood because it meant that she must be fed and clothed for the rest of her life. As for the man who had to provide the food and clothing, he would naturally seek to "get what he wanted"—Fanny's expression—without giving more than he could help. Fanny's values were material. I longed to escape from them, and I knew that with each day I was withdrawing myself farther and farther from Glen House and feeling closer and closer to Gabriel.

May was with us and the days were warm and sunny; it was a joy to escape to the moors. Now we talked of ourselves and there was a certain feverishness about Gabriel. He always seemed to me like a man who was looking over his shoulder at some pursuer, while he was desperately conscious of passing time.

I made him tell me about his home, and he was willing enough to do so now. I felt this to be because he had already convinced himself that I would marry him and that it would not be only his home but mine.

In my imagination it was a hazy, grey edifice comprised of ancient stones. I knew there was a balcony because Gabriel talked of it often; I pictured the scene from that balcony, for Gabriel had described it to me many times. The balcony was evidently a favourite spot of his. I knew that from it it was possible to see the river winding its way through the meadows; the woods, which in some places went down to the river's edge, and a quarter of a mile from the house those ancient piles of stone, those magnificent arches which the years had not been able to destroy; and across the wooden bridge, away beyond the river, the wild moorland country.

But what were houses compared with the people who lived in them? I learned by degrees that Gabriel, like myself, had no mother, she had been advanced in years when he was conceived, and when he came into the world she went out of it. Our motherlessness was a further bond between us.

He had a sister, fifteen years older than himself—a widow

with a seventeen-year-old son; he also had a father who was very old.

"He was nearly sixty when I was born," Gabriel told me. "My mother was forty. Some of the servants used to say I was 'the afterthought'; others used to say I killed my mother."

I was immediately angry because I knew how such careless comments could hurt a sensitive child. "How ridiculous!" I cried, my eyes flashing with anger as they always did over what I considered injustice. Gabriel laughed, took my hand and held it very tightly. Then he said seriously: "You see I cannot do without you. I need you . . . to protect me against the cruel things that are said of me."

"You are no longer a child," I replied somewhat impatiently; and when I analysed my impatience I found it grew out of my desire to protect him. I wanted to make him strong enough not to be afraid.

"Some of us remain children until we die."

"Death!" I cried. "Why do you harp continually on death?"

"It's true that I do," he said. "It's because I am so anxious to live every minute of my life to the full."

I did not understand what he meant then; and I asked to hear more of the family.

"Ruth, my sister, rules the household and will do so until I marry. Then of course my wife will do that, because I am the only son and the Revels will one day be mine."

"When you speak of the Revels you do so in a tone of reverence."

"It is my home."

"And yet . . ." I was going to say, I believe you are glad to have escaped from it. "You are not eager to return."

He did not notice my interruption. He murmured as though to himself: "It ought to have been Simon . . ."

"Who is Simon?"

"Simon Redvers. A sort of cousin. A Rockwell through his grandmother, who is my father's sister. You won't like him very much. But then you'll rarely meet. There isn't much communication between Kelly Grange and the Revels."

He was talking as though there was no doubt that I would marry him and that one day his house would be my home.

Sometimes I wondered whether there was not some subtlety in Gabriel. He gradually built up pictures in my mind, so that his home and family somehow came alive for me, and as

32

the picture grew clearer in my mind it brought with it a fascination which was not altogether pleasant and yet no less impelling because of that—but rather more so.

I wanted to see that pile of grey stones which had been made into a house three hundred years ago; I wanted to see those ruins which from a balcony of the house would have the appearance, not of a ruin but an ancient abbey because so much of the outer structure remained.

I was caught up in Gabriel's life. I knew that if he went away I should be desperately lonely and dissatisfied with my life. I should be continually regretful.

And one sunny day, when I had walked out of the house with Friday at my heels, I met Gabriel on the moor; and we sat with our backs against a boulder while Friday crouched before us on the grass, his eyes going from one to the other, his head slightly cocked as though he listened to our conversation. This was complete happiness for him and we knew it was because we were together.

"There's something I haven't told you, Catherine," said Gabriel.

I felt relieved, because I knew that he was going to tell me something now which he had been trying to for a long time.

"I want you to say you'll marry me," he went on, "but so far you haven't said that. You don't dislike me; you're happy in my company. That's true, Catherine?"

I looked at him and saw again those lines between his brows; I saw the puzzled frustration there and I remembered those occasions when he had seemed to forget what it was that made him so melancholy, when he threw off his moodiness and became gay. I felt a great desire then to chase the gloom out of his life, to make him happy as I had made Friday healthy.

"Of course I don't dislike you," I said, "and we're happy together. If you go away . . ."

"You'd miss me, Catherine, but not as much as I should miss you. I want you to come back with me. I don't want to go without you."

"Why are you so eager for me to go back with you?"

"Why? Surely you know. It's because I love you—because I never want to leave you again."

"Yes, but . . . is there another reason?"

"What other reason should there be?" he asked; but he did not meet my eyes as he said that, and I knew that there was a great deal about him and his home that I had to learn.

"You should tell me everything, Gabriel," I said on impulse.

He moved closer to me and put his arm about me. "You are right, Catherine. There are things you should know. I cannot be happy without you and . . . there cannot be long left to me."

I drew away from him. "What do you mean?" I demanded sharply.

He sat up and looking straight ahead said: "I cannot live more than a few years. I have received my sentence of death."

I was angry with him because I could not bear to hear his talk of dying. "Stop being dramatic," I commanded, "and tell me exactly what all this means."

"It's perfectly simple. I have a weak heart—a family complaint. I had an elder brother who died young. My mother died at my birth, but it was due to the same heart condition, aggravated by the strain of bringing me into the world. I could die to-morrow . . . next year . . . or in five years' time. It would apparently be extraordinary if I lived longer than that."

I yearned to comfort him and he knew how his words had affected me for he went on wistfully: "It would not be a great many years, Catherine."

"Don't talk like that," I said harshly; and I stood up, so overcome by my emotions that I could say no more. I started to walk quickly and Gabriel fell into step beside me. We were both silent, and Friday kept running ahead of us to look back at us anxiously, head on one side, while his eyes implored us to be gay.

That night I scarcely slept at all. I could think of nothing but Gabriel and his need for me. This was what had made him seem so different from any other person I had ever known, for I had never before known a person who was under a sentence of death. I kept hearing his voice saying: "I could die to-morrow . . . next year . . . or in five years' time. It would be extraordinary if I lived longer than that." I kept seeing those melancholy eyes and remembering how at times he could be happy. And I could make him happy for what was left to him—I alone. How could I forget that? How could I turn away from someone who needed me so much?

At this time I was so inexperienced that I did not know how to analyse my emotions. But I was sure that if Gabriel went away I should miss him. He had brought a new interest into my life, making me forget the gloominess of my home; it was so pleasant to be with someone who was really interested in me after my father's indifference, someone who admired me, after Fanny's criticism.

Perhaps I was not in love ; perhaps pity was at the very root of my feelings for Gabriel ; but by the morning I had made up my mind.

The banns were read in the village church and Gabriel went back to Kirkland Revels, I presumed to inform his family, while I began preparing for my wedding.

Before leaving, Gabriel had formally asked my father for my hand, and Father had been rather bewildered by the proceedings. He had hesitated, reminding Gabriel of my youth and the short time we had known each other ; but I, who had been expecting he might do this, burst in on them and assured my father that I had quite made up my mind to marry.

Father looked worried and I knew that he was wishing that Uncle Dick were at home so that he could consult him ; however, I had no real fear of opposition, and after a while Father said that as I seemed determined, he supposed I must have my way. Then he asked the conventional questions about Gabriel's standing which Gabriel was able to answer to his satisfaction ; and it occurred to me for the first time that I must be marrying into a wealthy family.

I longed for the presence of Uncle Dick, because it seemed unthinkable that he should not be at my wedding. I believed that I could have talked to him of my feelings and that he would have helped me to come to a better understanding of them.

I told Gabriel how much I wanted Uncle Dick to come to the wedding, but he was so full of despair at the thought of postponement that I gave way. That desire in Gabriel to make the most of every hour touched me so deeply that I would let nothing stand in the way of the comfort he was sure I could bring him. Besides, although it was possible to write to Uncle Dick, one could never be sure when letters would reach him ; and when I heard from him—he was not a good letter-writer and this was rarely—his letters never seemed to answer mine and I always wondered whether he had received them.

I could not resist writing to Dilys. "The most extraordinary thing has happened. I am going to be married! How strange that this should happen to me before you. It is the man I wrote to you about—the man who helped with the dog. He lives in Yorkshire in a wonderful old house near an abbey, and it has all happened so quickly that I don't quite understand how it has come about. I don't know whether I'm in love with him. I only know that I couldn't bear it if he went away and I never saw him again. Oh, Dilys, it's so exciting, because before it happened I was so wretched here. You've no idea what my home is like. I myself had forgotten during all those years I was away. It's a dark house . . . and I don't mean that there's just an absence of sunshine. . . . I mean the people in it live dark lives. . . ."

I tore that up. Was I crazy, trying to make Dilys understand what I did not myself? How could I explain to Dilys that I was going to marry Gabriel because, for some reason which I could not fully understand, I was sorry for him and I knew he needed my help; because I wanted desperately to love someone who belonged to me; because my father had repulsed me when I had tried to show affection and had mutely asked for a little in return; because I wanted to escape from the house which was now my home.

Instead of that letter I sent a conventional little note inviting Dilys to my wedding.

Fanny was still sceptical. She thought it was a queer way to go about getting married. There were references to proverbs such as " Marry in haste, repent at leisure "; and she talked about " supping sorrow with a long spoon." Still, the thought of future disaster seemed to cheer her considerably and she was determined that my grand in-laws, if they came to the wedding, should have no complaints about the wedding feast.

Gabriel wrote regularly and his letters were ardent, but they spoke only of his devotion to me and his desire for our union; he did not let me know anything about his family's reactions.

I heard from Dilys that I had not given her enough notice of my wedding. She was so full of engagements that she could not possibly leave London. I realised then that our lives had taken such entirely different turnings that the intimacy which had once been ours was over.

Three days before our marriage was to take place, Gabriel came back and put up at the King's Head less than half a mile from Glen House.

When Mary came to my room to tell me that he was in the first-floor sitting-room waiting to see me, eagerly I went down. He was standing with his back to the fireplace watching the door, and as soon as I opened it he strode towards me and we embraced. He looked excited, younger than he had when he had left, because some of the strain had gone from him.

I took his face in my hands and kissed it.

"Like a mother with a precious child," he murmured.

He had summed up my feelings. I wanted to look after him; I wanted to make what life was left to him completely happy; I was not passionately in love with him, but I did not attach great importance to this because passion was something I knew nothing about at that time. Yet I loved him nonetheless; and when he held me tightly against him, I knew that the kind of love I had for him was what he wanted.

I withdrew myself from his arms and made him sit down on the horsehair couch. I wanted to hear what his family's reactions were to the news of our engagement and how many were coming to the wedding.

"Well, you see," he said slowly, "my father is too infirm to make the journey. As for the others . . ." He shrugged his shoulders.

"Gabriel!" I cried aghast. "Do you mean that none of them is coming?"

"Well, you see, there's my Aunt Sarah. Like my father, she's too old to travel. And . . ."

"But there's your sister and her son."

He looked uneasy and I saw the frown between his eyes. "Oh, darling," he said, "what does it matter? It's not *their* wedding is it?"

"But not to come! Does that mean they don't approve of our marriage?"

"Of course they'll approve. But the ceremony itself is not all that important, is it? Look, Catherine, I'm back with you. I want to be happy."

I could not bear to see the moody expression returning to his face, so I tried to hide my uneasiness. It was very strange. No members of his family at the wedding! This was most unusual; but when I looked back, everything that had led up to this wedding of ours was somewhat unusual.

I heard a scratching at the door. Friday knew that Gabriel had come, and was impatient to see him. I opened the door and he bounded straight into Gabriel's arms. I watched them together; Gabriel was laughing as Friday tried to lick his face.

I told myself that I must not expect Gabriel's family to

behave conventionally, any more than Gabriel himself did; and I was relieved that Dilys had declined my invitation.

"Happen they think you're not good enough for 'em." That was Fanny's verdict.

I was not going to let Fanny see how the behaviour of Gabriel's family disturbed me, so I merely shrugged my shoulders.

After the wedding Gabriel and I were going to have a week's holiday at Scarborough, and then we were going to Kirkland Revels. All in good time I should discover for myself what his family thought of the marriage; I must be patient until then.

My father gave me away, and I was married to Gabriel in our village church on a day in June about two months after we first met. I wore a white dress which had been made rather hurriedly by our village seamstress, and I had a white veil and a wreath of orange blossom. There were very few guests at the reception, which was held in the drawing-room at Glen House: the Vicar and his wife, the doctor and his, and that was all.

Gabriel and I left immediately after our health had been drunk. It was a quiet wedding; and we were both glad to leave our few guests and be driven to the station, where we took the train for the coast.

I felt that when we were alone together in that first-class compartment that we were like any bride and groom. Previously the unconventional manner of our marrying—at such short notice, so few guests and none of the bridegroom's family being present—had given the entire proceedings an unreality for me; but now that we were alone together I felt relaxed.

Gabriel held my hand, a smile of contentment on his face, which was gratifying. I had never seen him look so peaceful before and I knew then that that was what he had always lacked: peace. Friday was with us, for it was unthinkable that we could go away without him. I had procured a basket for him, for I was not sure how he would travel; I had chosen a loosely woven one so that he could see us, and I talked to him explaining that it would only be for a short time that he was thus confined. I had taken to talking to him, explaining everything, which had set Fanny's lips twitching. She thought I was "real daft" talking to a dog.

And so we reached our hotel.

During those first days of our honeymoon, I felt my love for Gabriel growing because he needed me so desperately to lift him out of those dark moods of melancholy which could quickly descend upon him; there was a wonderful gratification in being so important to another human being, which I think at that time I mistook for being in love.

The weather was glorious, the days full of sunshine. We walked a good deal; the three of us— for Friday was always with us. We explored the glorious coast from Robin Hood's Bay to Flamborough Head; we marvelled at those delightful little bays, the grandeur of the cliffs, the coves and glimpses of moorland beyond; we both enjoyed walking and did so frequently, and we hired horses and rode inland to explore the moors and compare them with our own of the West Riding. On that coastline there are occasionally to be found the crumbling walls of an ancient castle, and one day we found the remains of an old abbey.

Gabriel was attracted by the ruins; indeed I soon discovered that the fascination they had for him was morbid, and for the first time since our marriage I saw a return to that moodiness which I had determined to abolish. Friday was quick to notice that Gabriel was losing some of his honeymoon happiness. I saw him, on one occasion when we were exploring the abbey ruins, rub his head against Gabriel's leg, while he looked up appealingly, as though to implore him to remember that the three of us were together and therefore should be happy.

It was then that I felt little pin-pricks of alarm stabbing my pleasure. I said to him: " Gabriel, does this abbey remind you of Kirkland Abbey?"

"There's always a similarity in old ruins," was the noncommittal reply.

I wanted to ask more questions. I was certain that there was something which disturbed him, and it was in Kirkland Abbey and the Revels.

I blundered on: " But, Gabriel, you would rather not have been reminded."

He put his arm about me and I could see that he was desperately trying to break out of the mood which had fallen on him.

Rapidly I changed the subject. " It looks as though it might rain," I said. " Do you think we should be getting back to the hotel?"

He was relieved that I was not going to ask questions to

which he would want to give evasive replies. Soon, I told myself, I should be in my new home. There I might discover the reason for this strangeness in my husband. I would wait until then; and when I had made my discovery I would eliminate whatever it was that troubled him; I would let nothing stand in the way of his happiness for all the years that were left to us.

Chapter 2

The honeymoon was over. During the last day we had both been a little on edge. Gabriel had been silent and I had been a little exasperated with him. I could not understand why he could be gay one day and moody the next. Perhaps I was—although I would not admit this—a little nervous of facing the Rockwell family. Friday sensed our mood and lost some of his exuberance.

"There are three of us now, that's what he's telling us." I said to Gabriel; and that did seem to cheer him.

The journey across the North Riding was long because we had to change; and the afternoon was over by the time we reached Keighley.

A carriage was waiting for us—rather a grand one; and when the coachman saw me I fancied he was startled. I thought it rather strange that he should not have heard of Gabriel's wedding and surely he had not, for if he had why should he be surprised when a bridegroom arrived with his bride?

Gabriel helped me into the carriage while the coachman dealt with our luggage, taking covert looks at me as he did so.

I shall never forget that drive from the station. It took about an hour and before we reached our destination dusk had fallen.

So it was in the half light that I first saw my new home. We had passed over the moors which were wild and eerie in this light; but these moors were very like those which had been close to Glen House, and I felt at home on any moor. We had climbed high and, although it was June, there was a sharpness in the air. The peaty smell was in my nostrils and I felt my spirits rise in spite of my growing apprehension. I pictured myself riding on these moors—Gabriel and myself together. Now we were descending and the country was less wild although there was still the moorland touch about it. We were coming near to the hamlet of Kirkland Moorside, close by which was my new home, Kirkland Revels.

The grass was more lush; we passed an occasional house; there were fields which were cultivated.

Gabriel leaned towards me. " If the light were better you might be able to see Kelly Grange from here—my cousin's place. Did I mention him—Simon Redvers? "

" Yes," I said, " you did." And I strained my eyes and thought I saw the faint outlines of a house away to the right.

On we went over the bridge; and it was then that I caught my first glimpse of the Abbey.

I saw the Norman tower, the outer shell of which was preserved; the walls clustered about it, so that it was impossible to see at this distance that it was a mere shell. It looked grand yet forbidding—although I wondered in that moment whether it was really so or whether the moods of my husband had made me imagine there was something to be feared.

We were driving along a road which was bordered on either side by massive oaks, and suddenly we were in the clear and there before me was the house.

I caught my breath, for it was beautiful. The first thing that struck me was its size. It looked like a massive oblong of stone. I discovered later that it was built round a courtyard, and that although it was of Tudor origin it had been restored through the later centuries. The windows were mullioned and about them were fantastic carvings of devils and angels, pitchforks and harps, scrolls and Tudor roses. This was indeed a historic baronial hall. I thought then how small Glen House must have seemed to Gabriel when he had visited us.

About a dozen stone steps, worn away in the centre, led to a great portico of massive stone carved in a way similar to the space round the windows. There was a heavy oak door decorated with finely-wrought iron; and even as I began to mount the steps the door opened and I met the first member of my new family.

She was a woman in her late thirties or early forties and her resemblance to Gabriel told me at once that she was his widowed sister, Ruth Grantly.

She looked at me for a few seconds without speaking, and her glance was cool and appraising before she forced some warmth into it.

" How do you do? You must forgive us if we're surprised.

41

We only heard this morning. Gabriel, it *was* perverse of you to be so secretive."

She took my hands and smiled; although it was a baring of the teeth rather than a smile. I noticed that her eyelashes were so fair that they were almost invisible. She was just that little bit fairer than Gabriel; and what struck me at once was her coldness.

"Come along in," she said. "I'm afraid you'll find us unprepared. It was such a surprise."

I said: "It must have been."

I looked at Gabriel questioningly. What could have been the point in not telling?

We stepped into the hall in which a log fire was blazing, and I was immediately struck by the air of antiquity about the place. I could see that this had been preserved and was cherished. The walls were hung with tapestry which doubtless had been worked by members of this family centuries ago. In the centre of the hall was a refectory table and on it were laid utensils of brass and pewter.

I looked round me.

"Well?" said Ruth.

"It's so . . . exciting to be here," I said.

She seemed a little gratified. She turned first to Gabriel. "Gabriel, why all this secrecy?" Then to me as she spread her hands deprecatingly: "He seems to have no reason for keeping us in the dark until this morning."

"I wanted to surprise you all," said Gabriel. "Catherine, you'll be tired. You'd like to go to your room."

"Of course you would," put in Ruth. "And meet the family later. I can tell you we're all very eager to make your acquaintance."

Her eyes glittered as her somewhat prominent teeth were bared once more. Friday barked suddenly.

"A dog too?" she said. "So you are fond of animals . . . Catherine?"

"Yes, very. I'm sure everyone will be fond of Friday." I was aware of a movement high in the wall and I looked up quickly to the gallery.

"That's the minstrels' gallery," Gabriel explained. "We sometimes use it when we have a ball."

"We adhere to old customs here, Catherine," said Ruth. "I hope you're not going to find us too old-fashioned."

"I am sure I shall enjoy old customs very much."

"I hope so. When there are traditions . . ."

I fancied her voice was a little sardonic and I wondered whether she was suggesting that I could not possibly understand the traditions which belonged to a family such as theirs.

Ruth's cool welcome was increasing my apprehension and I wondered afresh what Gabriel's reason had been for withholding the news of our marriage.

A manservant appeared, to ask about our luggage, and Gabriel said: "Take it up to my room, William."

"Aye, master," was the answer.

He mounted the stairs with my trunk on his shoulder and Gabriel took my arm and we followed him. Ruth came after us and I could feel her eyes on my back, taking in every detail. I was never more pleased with Uncle Dick than at the moment. My smart travelling costume of dark blue gaberdine gave me confidence.

At the top of the flight of stairs was a door and Gabriel said: "That's the door to the minstrels' gallery." I hoped he would throw it open and that I should see whether someone were there, because I was certain that I had seen a movement in the gallery, and I wondered what member of the household had preferred to hide there to take a glimpse of me instead of coming down to welcome me.

It was a wide staircase of great beauty, but in the light of oil-lamps it seemed full of shadows. I had an uncanny feeling as I went up that all the members of this family who had lived in the house over the last three hundred years were watching me with disapproval—the girl whom Gabriel had brought into the house without consulting his family.

"My rooms," Gabriel told me, "are at the top of the house. It's a long climb."

"Will you keep those rooms now that you have a wife?" asked Ruth from behind me.

"I certainly shall. Unless of course Catherine does not like them."

"I feel sure I shall."

"There are others to choose from if you are not satisfied," Ruth told me.

We had climbed to the second floor when a young man appeared. He was tall and slim and very like Ruth. He had cried: "Are they here yet, Mother? What's she . . ." before he saw us. He paused, not in the least embarrassed, laughing at himself, while his eyes went to me.

"This is Luke . . . my nephew," said Gabriel.

"My son," murmured Ruth.

"I am delighted to meet you," I said, and held out my hand.

He took it and bowed over it so that a lock of his long fair hair fell forward over his face.

"The delight then is mutual," he said with a faint drawl. "It's amusing to have a wedding in the family."

He was very like his mother, and that meant that he was like Gabriel too. The same rather prominent, aristocratic features, the delicate fairness, the almost languid air.

"What do you think of the house?" he asked eagerly.

"She has been in it less than ten minutes and has not seen a tenth of it—and what she has seen has not been in daylight," his mother reminded him.

"To-morrow I will take you on a tour of inspection," he promised me, and I thanked him.

He bowed once more and stood aside for us to pass; but when we went on he joined the procession and accompanied us to the rooms on the third floor which I gathered had always been Gabriel's.

We came to a circular gallery, and the feeling that I was being watched was stronger than ever; for here were the family portraits, life-sized; three or four roze-quartz lamps were burning and in this dim light the figures had the appearance of reality.

"Here we are," said Gabriel, and I felt the pressure on my arm; I heard Friday in his basket then; he whimpered faintly as though reminding me of his presence. I believed that Friday sensed my moods and knew that I felt as though I were being enclosed in an alien prison, and that I was resented here. Of course, I reminded myself, it was due to the fact that we had arrived in the twilight. It would have been quite different if we had come on a bright and sunny morning. There was too much atmosphere in these ancient houses; and at nightfall the shadows came to plague those whose imaginations were too vivid. I was in an extraordinary position. I was eventually to be the mistress of this house, and three days ago no one in it had been aware of my existence. No wonder I was resented.

I shook off the uncanny feeling, turned my back on the portraits and followed Gabriel through a door on the right and into a corridor. We went along this until we came to a door which Gabriel threw open. I gave a gasp of pleasure for I was standing on the threshold of a charming room. The

44

heavy red damask curtains had been drawn across the windows; a fire was burning in the big open fireplace and, on the mantelpiece which was of beautifully carved white marble, candles in gleaming silver candlesticks were burning and throwing a soft light about the room. I saw the four-poster bed with the curtains to match those at the windows, the tallboy, the chairs with tapestry backs worked in gold and red; there were red rugs which seemed to be flecked with gold, and the general effect was of warmth. On a table was a bowl of red roses.

Gabriel looked at them and flushed. Then he said: "Thank you, Ruth."

"There was too little time to do much."

"This is a beautiful room," I said.

She nodded. "It's a pity you can't see the view from the window."

"She will in an hour or so," put in Gabriel. "The moon will be up then."

I felt my fears evaporating.

"I'm going to leave you now," said Ruth. "I'll have hot water sent up; and could you be ready to dine in three-quarters of an hour?"

I said we could; and she and Luke left us. As the door shut on them Gabriel and I looked at each other in silence.

Then Gabriel said: "What's wrong, Catherine? You don't like it, do you?"

"It's so magnificent," I began. "I didn't imagine . . ." Then I could not restrain my resentment. "Why on earth didn't you tell them you were getting married?"

He flushed and looked distressed, but I was determined to know the truth.

"Well, I didn't want any fuss. . . ."

"Fuss!" I interrupted. "But I thought you went back to tell them."

"So I did."

"And you found you couldn't . . . when it came to the point?"

"There might have been opposition. I didn't want that."

"You mean they wouldn't have thought me worthy to marry into their family?" I knew that my eyes were flashing; I was both angry and miserable; this was such a disappointing beginning to my life in this house. I was hurt with Gabriel, and very depressed because I was realising that the fact that

45

my marriage had to be kept a secret until it was a *fait accompli* meant I was not going to live on very easy terms with my new family.

"Good heavens, no!" cried Gabriel emphatically. He caught me by the shoulders, but somewhat impatiently I freed myself. "They'll be delighted . . . once they know you. They don't like change, though. You know what families are."

"No," I retorted, "I don't. And they are distressed, which is natural. The idea of having me suddenly produced as a new member of the family! I can understand how they feel."

"But you don't understand, Catherine," Gabriel said pleadingly.

"Then tell me," I flashed at him. "Explain. Why does there have to be this mystery?"

He looked very unhappy. "But there is no mystery. It's simply that I didn't tell them. I didn't want fuss and bother. I wanted to marry you as quickly as possible so that we could be together and make the most of all the time that's left."

When he spoke like that all my anger disappeared. That softness, that desire to make him happy because he was afraid of something in life (perhaps it was of death) enveloped me. It was because of this desire that I had married him. I vaguely understood then that he was afraid of something in this house, and that he wanted an ally. I was to be that ally. I knew because, although I had been in Kirkland Revels less than half an hour, I was catching that fear.

"Friday's still in his basket," I said.

"I'll take him outside." He opened the basket and Friday jumped out, barking his pleasure to be free. There was a knock and I turned sharply for the sound did not come from the door by which we had entered. I noticed then that there were two doors in this room.

A voice in a broad Yorkshire accent said: "Hot water, master."

The door was shut before I had a chance to see the owner of the voice.

"That's the old powder-closet," said Gabriel, indicating the door. "I use it for my ablutions. You'll find it useful. Lock both doors before you disrobe. One of the servants might come in."

He fastened the leash on Friday. "You don't want to lose yourself on your first evening, Friday," he said. And when he had gone I went into the powder-closet and there I saw the big hip-bath, the cans of hot water, the soap and towels. A big

46

mirror in an ornate gilded frame was fixed to the wall, and attached to this frame were two gilded candlesticks in which candles burned.

I looked at myself in the mirror. My eyes appeared to be more green than usual, and I found that they quickly strayed from my reflection and were looking over my shoulder, probing the shadowy corners of the powder-room.

Old houses in twilight. . . . Was it possible that in such places the presence of those long dead lingered?

What ridiculous thoughts for a sensible young Yorkshire woman to entertain.

I took off my costume and began to wash the stain of travel from my person. To-morrow, in daylight, I should laugh at my fancies.

We dined that night in a pleasant room on the first floor.

Gabriel had explained that on ceremonial occasions dinner was served in the hall. That was because the hall had been used for that purpose when the house had been built. " The refectory table down there is as old as the house itself. But we have a small and more comfortable dining-room for the family," he added.

It was a large room by Glen House standards ; the curtains were drawn when I entered and there were candles on the table. I could see that living here was going to be a somewhat formal affair.

There were six of us at dinner. This was the family. Ruth and Luke I had already met. I now encountered Gabriel's father, Sir Matthew Rockwell, and his aunt, Miss Sarah Rockwell ; they both seemed very old, being in their eighties.

As soon as I met Sir Matthew I began to feel happier because he was quite obviously pleased to see me. He had been very tall but stooped a little ; his hair was plentiful and quite white ; his face was ruddy but too much of the port wine shade to be healthy ; and his blue eyes, embedded so deeply in folds of flesh that they had almost disappeared, were bright—one might say jaunty.

" Gabriel's lucky to have such a beautiful wife," he said. Surely this was flattery for I was not beautiful and could not seem so even to old men of eighty. He kept my hand in his and then kissed it lingeringly. I guessed that he was not too old for gallantry ; he gave the impression that he had enjoyed his life and hoped the young members of his family would follow his example.

47

"You must sit beside me," he said. "I want to look at you and hear you tell me what you think of your new family."

So I sat beside him at the dinner table and every now and then he would lean towards me and pat my hand.

Aunt Sara was quite different although I recognised the Rockwell features and fairness. Her blue eyes were vacant and she had an air of strain as though she were desperately trying to understand what was going on about her and could not quite catch up with it all.

I imagined her to be even older than her brother.

"Sarah," shouted Sir Matthew, "this is my new daughter."

Sarah nodded and gave him a smile that was sweet in its innocence. I wished I had met these older people first. Then I should have felt I was being warmly welcomed.

"What is your name?" she asked.

"Catherine," I told her.

She nodded; and whenever I looked up, I found her eyes upon me.

Sir Matthew wanted to hear about our meeting and the suddenness of our decision to marry. I told him about Friday.

"Gipsies," he said. "They can be brutal to their animals. I won't have them on my land. I must say it was a lucky day for Gabriel when he rode that way."

Luke said: "He was always going away . . . riding off . . . and we never knew when he was coming back."

"Why not?" said Gabriel. "It's the way to take a holiday. I hate making plans. You anticipate the pleasures of getting away and it invariably disappoints. No. Go as the spirit moves you . . . that's my motto."

"And look how well it turned out!" pointed out Sir Matthew, smiling at me.

"I must show Claire my tapestry. She'd like to see it," said Sara.

There was a brief silence. Then Ruth said quietly: "This is Catherine, Aunt. Not Claire."

"Of course . . . of course . . ." murmured Sara. "Are you interested in tapestry, dear?"

"I admire it, but I don't excel at it. I'm not very handy with my needle."

"I should think not," retorted Sir Matthew. "You don't want to strain those fine eyes of yours." He leaned towards me, his hand caressing mine. "My sister is a bit forgetful. She wanders at times into the past." He grimaced. "No longer young . . . like myself alas!"

48

They talked of the house, of the country surrounding it, of the stables—which I was glad to hear were well stocked—of their neighbours, friends, county hunts and life generally in Kirkland Moorside ; and I felt then that they were doing their best to make me welcome, and that perhaps it was the strangeness of Gabriel which had made me doubt this in the beginning.

Ruth said that before the end of the week there would be a dinner party to celebrate our marriage, and that she would have arranged it for this evening had there been time.

"There are certain people you must meet," she said. "They will be most eager to meet *you*."

"Whom do you propose to ask?" Gabriel put in quickly.

"Well . . . Simon, I suppose. After all, he's part of the family. We shall have to ask Hagar too, but I doubt whether she'll come. And I thought perhaps the vicar and his wife, and of course the Smiths."

Sir Matthew nodded. Then he turned to me. "We want you to feel at home, my dear, without delay."

I thanked him and when the meal was over Ruth, Sara and I retired to a nearby drawing-room, leaving the men to their port. I was glad that they did not leave us long, for I felt uncomfortable with Gabriel's sister and aunt.

Gabriel came to my side immediately and remarked that I looked tired.

"No doubt it has been a busy day," murmured Ruth. "We shall all understand if you retire early."

I said good night to the members of my new family and Gabriel and I went up to our room at the top of the house.

Friday came out of his basket to greet us as we entered the room. It was clear that he, too, was finding it difficult to adjust himself to his new surroundings.

"Well," said Gabriel, "the worst is over. You've met the family."

"Not all, apparently."

"The rest are on the fringe. These are the ones you'll have to live with. Before we retire I want to show you the view from the balcony."

"Oh yes . . . your balcony. Where is it?"

"At the end of our corridor. Come now."

He put his arm about me and we left the room and went to the end of the corridor where there was a door. He opened this and we stepped out on to the balcony. The moon was high in the sky and it shone its light on the scene about us. I saw the Abbey ruins like a great ghost of its former self. I saw the dark river winding through the grassland and the black hump of the bridge, and beyond, away in the distance, the shadowy outline of the moor.

"It's beautiful," I breathed.

"When I'm away from here I dream of this view."

"I'm not surprised."

"Every night I come and look. I always have done since I was a child. It was a fascination for me." He looked down suddenly. "Two of my ancestors threw themselves over parapets—not this one. There are three others in the house."

I felt a shiver run along my spine and I looked down into the dimness below.

"We're at the top of the house," said Gabriel. "It was certain death to leap over on to the flagstones below. The only two suicides in our history . . . and both chose the same method."

"Come along in," I said. "I'm tired."

But when we entered the room I felt my fear returning. Those moments on the balcony had done that, those chance words of Gabriel's. I was certainly strung up, which was unusual for me. But all would be well to-morrow, I promised myself.

During the next two days I explored the house and the surrounding country. I was fascinated—at times enchanted, at times repelled. I enjoyed being in the house during the day-time, and I was continually losing my way in it; but when dusk fell—I am ashamed to admit—the habit of looking furtively over my shoulder when I was alone persisted.

I had never stayed in such a large or ancient house; when one was alone the present seemed to merge into the past; it was because so much of the furniture had been in the house for centuries and one could not get away from the idea that this was exactly how it had looked hundreds of years ago, when other footsteps, other voices had been heard, other figures had made those long shadows on the walls.

It was absurd to be influenced by such fancies when the people in the house were normal enough; I had them all clearly docketed in my mind within those first days: Sir Matthew, jolly old squire fond of good food, wine and women, a typical country squire of this or any other century; Aunt

Sarah, the spinster who had always lived at home, somewhat innocent, remembering the birthdays, the triumphs and failures of every member of the family, and only now that she was growing old forgetting to whom they had happened and thinking now and then that Gabriel's new wife was her sister-in-law, Claire, long dead wife of Sir Matthew; there was Ruth who had been mistress of the house since her mother had died, and naturally enough mildly resented the intruder; there was Luke, a young man absorbed in his own affairs as most young men were. A normal family similar to those which were to be found in many households throughout the country.

I had tried to make myself pleasant and I was sure I was succeeding. Ruth of course was the most difficult to reassure: I did want her to know that I had no intention of ousting her from her position. Heaven knew this house was large enough for us to live our separate lives in. Sir Matthew was master of the house and she was his daughter, who had been mistress of the place since she came of age, had continued to live here after her marriage, and naturally had remained when she became a widow. I wanted her to know that I considered she had more right to be the châtelaine of Kirkland Revels than I had.

She told me of the dinner party she was planning, and I candidly replied that she must go ahead with her plans, for I had come from a very small household and had done no housekeeping, having but a short while before my marriage been at school.

This seemed to please her and I felt happy.

During the first morning Gabriel was with his father; I guessed there were certain business matters concerning the estate which had to be discussed, particularly as Gabriel had been away from home so long. I assured him that I was well able to take care of myself.

I planned to take Friday for a walk, for I was eager to explore the country and in particular to have a look at the Abbey ruins. But on my way downstairs I met Luke. He grinned at me in a friendly way and stooped to have a word with Friday. Friday was delighted to be taken notice of and there was no doubt that he took a fancy to Luke right from the first.

" I like dogs," Luke told me.

" You have none?"

51

He shook his head. "Who'd look after them when I am away? I was often away . . . at school, you know. Now I'm in the transistory period. I have left school and shall shortly be going to Oxford."

"Surely there are plenty of people to look after a dog while you're away?"

"I don't see it. If you have a dog it's your dog and you can't trust anyone else to look after it. Have you seen the house yet?" he asked.

"Not all of it."

"I'll take you on a conducted tour. You ought to know it. You'll get lost if you don't. It's so easy to take the wrong turning. Shall I show it to you?"

I was anxious to be friends, and I felt it was best to accept his invitation. Moreover, I was eager to see the house, so I decided the walk could wait until the tour was over.

I had no idea of the size of the house. I reckoned there must be at least a hundred rooms. Each of the four parts which made up that rectangle of stone was like a house in itself, and it certainly was easy to lose oneself.

"The story goes," Luke told me, "that one of our ancestors married four wives and kept them in separate houses; and for a long time none of them knew of the existence of the other three."

"It sounds like Bluebeard."

"Perhaps the original Bluebeard was a Rockwell. There are dark secrets in our history, Catherine. You've no idea what a family you've married into!"

His light eyes regarded me with amusement which was not untinged with cynicism; and I was reminded of Gabriel's decision not to tell the family that he was going to marry me. Of course they regarded me as a fortune-hunter, for not only would Gabriel inherit this house, but also the means which would enable him to live in such a place, as well as the title which, as the only son of his baronet father, would be his when the old man died.

"I'm beginning to learn," I told him.

I went through those rooms in a state of bewilderment—there were so many, and all had the high windows, the lofty ceilings often decorated with exquisite carving, the panelled walls, the furniture of another age. I saw the great cellars, the kitchens, where I met some of the servants who also seemed to eye me with a certain suspicion; I saw the other three balconies so like that near our own room; I examined the massive stone pillars which supported them, and the faces of gargoyles which seemed to grimace at me from everywhere.

"How fond they seemed to be of these devils and grotesques," I said.

"They were to scare off intruders," Luke told me. "You must admit they're somewhat scarifying. 'Keep off,' they seem to be saying. 'The devils of Kirkland will get you if you don't look out.'"

"Surely they sometimes wanted to *welcome* visitors," I murmured lightly.

"We must have been an inhospitable crowd, sufficient unto ourselves perhaps."

When we reached the gallery he took me round, explaining who the subjects were. There was the first Sir Luke who had built the place, a fierce-looking gentleman in armour. There was Thomas, Mark, John, several Matthews and another Luke.

"We always have biblical names," he said. "It's a feature of the family. Always Matthew, Mark, Luke and John, Peter Simon, anything you can think of . . . even down to the Angel Gabriel. I often call him Angel, though he doesn't like it much. I think that was going a bit too far. A nice down-to-earth Mark or John would have been so much better. Now that Sir Luke . . . he died young. He jumped over the balcony in the west wing."

I stared at the young man in the picture; they were all so lifelike, those pictures, that the lips seemed to move as I watched.

"And that," went on Luke, "Is John who, about a hundred years after, decided he'd die the same way. He jumped over the balcony in the north wing. Strange, isn't it. Although I think he got the idea from that Luke."

I turned away. This talk made me feel uneasy. I was not sure why.

As I moved towards a woman in a feathered Gainsborough type hat, I heard Luke's voice at my elbow. "My great-great-great-grandmother. Only I'm not sure of the number of greats." I went on walking along the gallery.

"Oh, and here's your father-in-law himself," he added.

A younger Sir Matthew looked back at me; his flowing cravat was the essence of elegance as was his green velvet jacket; his complexion was ruddy, rather than port wine, his eyes slightly bigger than they were now, and I was sure that

I had not been mistaken when I had judged him to have been something of a rake in his day. And beside him was a woman whom I knew to be his wife; she was beautiful in a frail way and there was an expression of resignation on her face. Gabriel's mother, I thought, who had died soon after his birth. And there was a picture of Gabriel himself, looking young and innocent.

"You'll be beside him," said Luke. "You'll be captured like the rest and held prisoner on canvas . . . so that in two hundred years' time the new lady of the house will come to look at you and wonder about you."

I shivered, and was conscious of a great desire to escape from him, to get out of the house, if only for half an hour, because the talk of suicides had oppressed me.

"Friday is impatient for his walk," I said. "I think perhaps that I should take him now. It is very good of you to have taken so much trouble to show me everything."

"But I have not shown you *everything*! There is a great deal more for you to see."

"I shall enjoy it more another time," I replied firmly.

He bowed his head. "When," he murmured, "it will be my pleasure to continue with our tour."

I went down the staircase and, half-way, turned to look back. Luke was standing by the portraits watching me, looking as though he had but to step up into one of those frames to become one of them.

The rest of the day I spent with Gabriel. We went for a ride in the afternoon, right out on to the moors; and when we came back it was time to change for dinner, and the evening was spent like the previous one.

Before we retired for the night Gabriel took me out to the balcony, and as he stood for a while admiring that superb view I remarked that I had not yet visited the Abbey ruins and decided that I would do so the next day.

During the morning which followed, Gabriel was again with his father and I wandered off with Friday; this time I went to the Abbey.

As I approached those ancient piles I was struck with wonder. It was a sunny morning; and here and there the stone glistened as though it had been set with diamonds. I could have believed that this was not a ruin, for the great tower was intact and so was the wall which was facing me; it was not until I came close that I realised that there was no roof but the sky. The Abbey nestled in the valley close to the river and I guessed that it would be more sheltered from the storms than the Revels was. Now I saw clearly the high Norman tower, the ancient buttresses and the nave which, like the tower, was almost intact, apart from the fact that there was no roof. I was surprised at the vastness of the ruins and I thought how interesting it would be to make a plan of the Abbey and try to rebuild it in the imagination. Friday was running to and fro in great excitement as though he shared my emotions about the place. Here, I told myself, was a shell; yet there were enough stones to indicate which parts were the kitchens for instance, the cloister, the nave, the transept, the monks' quarters.

It was necessary to tread warily, for here and there stones jutted dangerously out of the ground. I lost Friday for a moment and was immediately conscious of a panic which was quite ridiculous; equally so was my relief, when after I had called to him, he came running back to me.

I wondered from what part of the Abbey the stones had been taken to build the house. I wanted to learn something of the history of this house and the family to which I now belonged. I laughed at myself. There was so much I did not know about my own husband. Why was he so secretive with me? Why was there this constant feeling that he was hiding something from me?

I sat down on a ridge of stones, obviously all that was left of a room of some sort—the monks' dorter, I hazarded—and I told myself then that I had not thought enough of Gabriel since I had arrived here. Naturally Gabriel would be full of odd fancies; he was a young man who was afflicted with a disease of the heart which threatened his life. It was for that reason that he was moody. He was afraid of death—and I had thought it was something in the house, something in these old ruins which had disturbed him! How should *I* feel if Death were round the corner, waiting for me? That was something which one could not imagine until it happened to one.

I would make Gabriel happy. Moreover, I would not accept the inevitability of death as he seemed to. I would take such care of him that he would live on.

Friday's barking startled me out of my daydream. I called: "Friday! Friday!"

And as he did not come to me I went to look for him.

I found him in the hands of a strange man; he was

struggling and, if he had not been so expertly held, he would have bitten those hands which imprisoned him.

"Friday!" I called. Then the man who held him turned to look at me. He was of medium height and I was struck by his brilliant dark eyes and olive complexion.

He released the dog when he saw me and, taking off his hat, bowed. Friday ran to me, barking furiously and, as I came forward, stood between me and the stranger as though to protect me.

"So the dog is yours, madam," said the man.

"Yes, what happened? He's usually so friendly."

"He was a little annoyed with me." I noticed the flash of very white teeth in that dark face. "He didn't understand that I probably saved his life."

"How was that?"

He turned and pointed to what I saw now was a well.

"He was perilously perched on the edge, looking down. If he had decided to explore farther, that would have been the end of him."

"Then I have to thank you."

He inclined his head, "This was the monks' well. It's deep—and probably not very sweet down there."

I peered over into the darkness. I was looking down the narrow well, to what might have been water at the bottom.

"He's rather inquisitive," I said.

"I should put him on a lead when you bring him here again. And you will come here again, won't you? I can see this place intrigues you. You have a look in your eyes which betrays your interest."

"Surely everyone would be interested."

"Some more than others. May I introduce myself? I believe I know you. You are Mrs. Gabriel Rockwell, are you not?"

"But how did you know?"

He spread his hands and smiled again; it was a warm, friendly smile. "A simple deduction. I knew you were due to arrive and, as I know almost everyone in these parts, I put two and two together and tried to guess."

"Your guess was correct."

"Then welcome to our community. My name is Deverel Smith. Doctor. I am at the Revels almost every day, so we should have met sooner or later."

"I have heard you mentioned."

"Pleasantly, I hope?"

"Very much so."

"I'm an old friend of the family as well as the doctor; and of course Sir Matthew and Miss Rockwell are no longer young. They both need my services rather frequently. Tell me, when did you arrive?"

I told him and he listened gravely. I thought there was a foreign look about him but his name was as English as it could be; I supposed he seemed so dark because of the extreme fairness of my new relations.

He said: "I was going to call at the Revels to-day. Shall we walk back together?"

We did so and he made me feel that I had found a new friend.

He talked familiarly of the family, and when he spoke of Gabriel there was an anxious note in his voice. I knew what that meant and I wanted to speak to him about Gabriel's health, but I refrained from doing so. Later, I promised myself. He would be easy to talk to.

He told me that he had been invited to dine at the house on Saturday. "My daughter and I," he added.

I was astonished that he should have a daughter old enough to be invited to a dinner party. He saw my surprise and I liked him no less because he appeared to be pleased by it. I had thought he was somewhere in his mid-thirties, but decided he must be older than that.

"I have a seventeen-year-old daughter," he said. "She enjoys parties. My wife is not well enough to attend them, so she and I go together."

"I shall look forward to meeting her."

"Damaris is looking forward to meeting you." He smiled.

"Damaris! That is an unusual name."

"You like it? It's from the Bible. Just a brief mention . . . but it's here."

I remembered what Luke had said about biblical names, and I wondered if it was a custom in this part of the world to take names from the Bible. I was about to mention this; then I remembered that Madame la Directrice had said that my impetuosity often verged on bad manners, so I restrained myself.

We went into the Revels together. The doctor sent one of the servants to tell Ruth he had arrived; and I went up to my room.

I wore a white gown on the night of the dinner party. It

was the only real evening dress I possessed, and I told myself that if entertaining at the Revels was going to be on a lavish scale. I should have some new clothes. The dress was of white chiffon and lace, very simple, as became a young woman. I had no qualms about it because I knew that the few clothes I had were perfectly cut and would appear elegant in any company. I did my hair in the coronet style which Gabriel liked so much; and I was waiting for him to come in and dress, for time was passing.

As he did not come, I wondered whether he was still out and I went on to the balcony to see if he were in the grounds. He was nowhere in sight, but I heard the sound of voices coming from the porch.

I was about to call out and ask if Gabriel was there when I heard a deep masculine voice say: " So I gather, Ruth, you have not taken to our little bride?"

I drew back, feeling the hot colour rush into my cheeks. I knew that listeners are said never to hear good of themselves. Fanny had told me that often enough ; but how difficult it is, when you overhear yourself being discussed far from flatteringly, to refrain from listening.

" It's early yet," answered Ruth.

There was a laugh. " I've no doubt she found our Gabriel easy prey."

I did not hear Ruth's reply to that, but the voice went on: " Why did you let him stray so far from home? He was bound to find some little fortune-hunter sooner or later."

I was furiously angry. I wanted to lean over the balcony and tell whoever was speaking to come out where I could see him ; I wanted to tell him that I had had no idea of Gabriel's position when I had married him.

I stood still, my eyes blazing. Then he stepped backwards a little, and by leaning over the parapet I saw him. His hair was light brown and he seemed excessively broad. There was a resemblance to the Rockwells there, but it was faint. He stepped forward suddenly into the house and was lost to view. I hated him, whoever he was.

I was trembling as I went back to our bedroom. Gabriel was already there. He was out of breath and had clearly been hurrying.

" I forgot the time," he said. " I shall have to look sharp. Where have you been? Why, you're dressed already."

It was on the tip of my tongue to tell him what I had heard, but I changed my mind. It would upset him and he was breathless now. No, I would fight my own battles; I should have to teach this relative, whoever he was, a lesson. So I helped Gabriel dress and when we went down I met my enemy.

He was Simon Redvers, the cousin; he looked less broad when seen on the level. He was very tall, a fact I had not fully realised looking down at him.

Gabriel introduced me, and when he took my hand those cynical eyes looked straight into mine and I knew exactly what he was thinking. His eyes were light brown and his skin deeply bronzed; his mouth was smiling slightly but his eyes were not. I knew my own were flashing with anger, for I had never found it easy to restrain my feelings and I could not get the sound of his words out of my ears.

"How do you do?" he said.

"I am well, thank you," I answered.

"I suppose I should congratulate you."

"Pray do not, unless you wish to."

He was faintly amused, and I could not resist saying: "I believe we have met before."

"I am certain we have not."

"You may not have been aware of the meeting."

"If it had taken place, I am convinced, I should remember."

I matched my smile with his. He was puzzled and he said: "It is the Rockwell resemblance, no doubt. You'll find it again and again in these parts."

I guessed he was referring to the amorous proclivities of his ancestors, and I thought this indelicate so I turned away.

There was, fortunately, a diversion created by the arrival of Dr. Smith and his daughter.

The doctor was already a friend. He came over to me and greeted me warmly. I was pleased to give my attention to him, but the girl who accompanied him immediately claimed it, and, I imagine, that of everyone in the room.

Damaris Smith was one of the loveliest creatures I had ever seen. She was of medium height and very dark—her hair smooth and silky with that blackness which has a sheen of blue in it, like a bird's wing. Here eyes were black, long and languorous, her skin olive; and the shape of her face was a perfect oval; her lips were delicately formed yet sensuous; her teeth white; her nose almost aquiline, giving dignity as well as beauty. But it was not merely her face which caught and held the attention. It was her slim, lissome body also; all her movements were full of grace. She was a joy to look at.

Dressed in white, as I was, she wore a gold belt about her tiny waist and in her ears were gold creole ear-rings.

There was silence as she entered—the silence which was homage to her beauty.

I asked myself: Why did Gabriel marry me when there was such a goddess on his very doorstep?

The effect she had on everyone was apparent. Her father obviously adored her, for his eyes rarely left her; Luke, I imagined, was less nonchalant than usual; Simon Redvers seemed to watch her almost speculatively. Already I disliked him intensely, seeing in him a type I could never tolerate. He would be a man to scorn sentiment; he would be practical in the extreme; he would be unimaginative, believing everyone else looked at life with the same calculating gaze; there was great virility there. His personality was overpowering so that it dominated the company in its masculine way as Damaris's beauty did in the feminine. Sir Matthew's admiration was apparent; but then he admired all women, it seemed; and during the dinner party he divided his attention between myself and Damaris.

Damaris herself I did not fully understand; she was a quiet person who had a smile for everyone and did not seek in the least to call attention to herself, which was, of course, unnecessary. The first impression she gave was that she was merely an innocent girl; I don't know what made me feel that that smooth, rather expressionless perfection was a mask.

The dinner was in honour of Gabriel and myself, and our health was drunk. Apart from the family there were the Smiths, Simon Redvers, the vicar and his wife and two other local people, neighbours, I gathered, rather than great friends.

I was asked what I thought of the house and the countryside, and Simon Redvers wanted to know how it compared with that part from which I had come. I answered that when not at school I had lived as close to the moor as they did, so that the change was not very great. I believe a note of asperity came into my voice when I addressed the man, that he noticed it and it amused him.

He, who was sitting next to me at dinner, leaned to me and said: " You must have your portrait painted so that it can be added to those in the gallery."

" Is that necessary?"

" Indeed, yes. Have you not seen the gallery? All the

masters of Kirkland Revels are painted and hung with their wives beside them."

"There's plenty of time for that."

"You'll make a good subject."

"Thank you."

"Proud . . . strong . . . determined."

"So you read character?"

"When it is there for me to see."

"I had no idea that I had such a legible face."

He laughed. "It's unusual in one so young. Don't you agree that as one grows older fate . . . life . . . whatever you call it . . . is like a mischievous artist, gradually etching the lines of betrayal?" He gazed along the table; I refused to follow his gaze, but looked down at my plate. I though his manners too candid, and I wanted him to know this. "I believe you doubt my word," he insisted.

"I believe what you say to be true, but is it not a little embarrassing—even impertinent—to test the theory on the present company?"

"You'll discover that I'm a blunt Yorkshireman; and they are not noted for their tact."

"Why speak of the future? I have already made the discovery."

I saw the smile touch his lips again; I thought it rather a brutal smile. He enjoyed baiting me because I was a worthy opponent. At least I had the satisfaction of knowing that, even if he did consider me a fortune-hunter, he did not find me a simpering one. I came to the conclusion in that moment that he had a grudging admiration for me, partly because he believed I had endeavoured to catch Gabriel, as he would put it, and had achieved my object. There was a ruthlessness in him which would always admire success.

I said impulsively: "You are Gabriel's cousin, or second cousin, are you not? Yet how unlike him you are! You are absolute opposites."

He gave me that cool, appraising smile again. I was telling him that I did not like him; and he was retaliating by implying that I would not have caught him as I had caught Gabriel. As if I should have wanted to! As if there had been any "catching" in our marriage!

"Talking of faces," he said, "you've looked at the gallery. What a splendid example of the revelations of physiognomy. You can see old Sir John who went on fighting for his King to the fury of Cromwell. He lost us the Revels for a while, that

one. You can see his obstinate idealism in his face. Then
there's Sir Luke, the gambler who nearly gambled away our
inheritance. And then there's that other Luke, and John . . .
the suicides. If you look long enough you can read their
histories in their faces. Take that Luke, for instance. You see
the weakness of the mouth. You can imagine him, finding
life too difficult and standing there on the west balcony, and
suddenly . . . over . . ."

I realised then that the others at the table had become
silent and were listening to Simon.

Sir Matthew leaned forward and patted my arm. "Don't
listen to my nephew," he said. "He's telling you about our
disreputable ancestors. Simon's annoyed because he's a Rockwell on the distaff side . . . and the Revels is not for him."

I saw that inscrutable gleam in Simon's eyes and said:
"I dare say you have a pleasant residence of your own."

"Kelly Grange!" Sir Matthew almost spat out the words.
"The Redvers family were always jealous of the Revels." He
pointed to Simon. "His grandfather married one of my sisters
but she wouldn't stay away from the Revels. She was always
coming back and bringing first her son, then her grandson,
with her. Don't see you here so often now, Simon."

"I must remedy that," said Simon; and he was smiling
ironically at me.

There was a deep chuckle from Sir Matthew which seemed
to shock the vicar and his wife.

So the conversation progressed and, in spite of my dislike
of my neighbour at the dinner table, I was a little sorry when
it was over; I enjoyed a battle, and I was enjoying mine with
him—although it was merely one of words. I told myself that
I particularly disliked those people who were ready to be
critical before they knew the truth. I was sure Simon Redvers
was one of these.

After dinner the ladies retired to the drawing-room and I
tried to get to know Damaris; but it was not easy; she was
pleasant, but so reserved that she made little effort to help
with the conversation, and I decided that a blank mind lay
behind that lovely face. I was pleased when the men joined
us; and when Simon Redvers kept at Damaris's side—rather
to the chagrin of Luke—I was glad and gave myself up to
conversation with the vicar, who told me how the grounds of
the Revels were used for the church annual garden party and
that he and his wife were trying to arrange to do a miracle
play or pageant in the Abbey ruins next Midsummer Night's

eve. He hoped that I would support his endeavours, and I told him that I should be delighted to do all I could.

It was shortly after dinner that Sir Matthew was taken ill. He lay back in his chair, his face a deeper purple than usual. Dr. Smith was immediately at his side, and with the help of Simon and Luke took Sir Matthew to his room. The incident naturally broke up the party, but when Dr. Smith rejoined us he told us that Sir Matthew would be all right. He was going back to his home for leeches. Sir Matthew always insisted on being bled in such a manner as his father had before him.

" He'll be about again in a day or so," the doctor assured us before he left.

But the party spirit had gone and we sat on talking desultorily.

When Gabriel and I retired it was about eleven-thirty. He put his arms about me and told me that I had been a success and he was proud of me.

" I'm not sure that I was very popular with everybody," I said.

" Who could fail to be charmed?"

" That cousin of yours for one."

" Oh, Simon! He was born a cynic. He is jealous. He'd throw away Kelly Grange for the Revels any day. You wait till you see the Grange. It is not half the size of the Revels— it's an ordinary old manor house."

" I don't understand why his desire for the Revels should affect his attitude to me."

" Perhaps he's jealous of me for more reasons than one."

" How absurd!"

At that moment Friday ran to the door and began barking furiously while he leaped at the door as though he would break it down.

" What on earth's the matter with him?" I cried.

Gabriel had turned pale. " Someone's out there," he whispered.

" It's evidently someone Friday doesn't like." I turned to Friday. " Be quiet, Friday."

But Friday for once ignored me; he continued to bark and jump frienziedly up at the door.

I picked him up and opened the door. " Who's there?" I called.

There was no answer, but Friday was struggling out of my arms.

" Something has disturbed him," I said. " I'm going to

put him on his lead. I don't want him jumping over the balcony."

Still holding him I went back to the room for his lead and slipped it on; and when I set him down he tugged at it with all his might.

He dragged me along the corridor, but before we reached the balcony door he leaped at another to the left of it. I tried this and it opened easily. It was a large empty cupboard, and Friday ran into it and began sniffing around.

I opened the balcony door, and there was no one on the balcony either.

" You see, Friday," I said. " It's nothing. What is it that's bothering you?"

I returned with him to the bedroom. Gabriel had his back to me as I entered the room. When he turned I saw how pale he was; and a terrible thought came to me then: he was afraid of what was out there and he had let me go alone. Was the man I had married a coward?

It was a horrible thought which I discarded almost as soon as it entered my head.

" Much ado about nothing," I said lightly.

Friday appeared completely to have satisfied himself; when I took him off the lead, he leaped into his basket and curled up there.

As I prepared myself for bed I wondered what Gabriel had been so disturbed about.

Then I remembered the conversation at dinner and I asked myself whether Gabriel had thought it was a ghost prowling out there. The balcony certainly had a morbid attraction for him.

But in a house like this fancies came easily.

It was late during the next afternoon when I discovered that Friday was missing. I remembered then that I had not seen him since the morning. It had been a busy morning, for the guests of the previous night all paid duty calls to give conventional thanks.

I saw Simon Redvers ride up on a magnificent grey horse, and I decided to stay in my room until he had left; I did not see him leave and was afraid that I should find he was staying to luncheon; however, when I went down he had gone. Dr. Smith and Damaris had ridden over in his brougham— the doctor to see how Sir Matthew was after his attack,

Damaris to pay her duty call. With all the guests arriving it seemed like a continuation of the party.

It was just before dinner when I began to be anxious about Friday's absence.

Dinner was a solemn meal that evening and there was little conversation. Sir Matthew was still in his room and I guessed that everyone was worried on his account although they assured me that such turns were frequent.

When the meal was over and there was still no sign of Friday, I was really alarmed. I went up to our room; his basket, with the folded blanket, was neat and had clearly not been used by him. Was it possible that he was lost?

I wondered if he had been stolen, and when I thought of the ill-treatment he had received at the hands of the gipsy woman I felt sick with worry. It was possible that there were gipsies not far from Kirkland Moorside, for the moor was always an attraction to them.

I slipped on a light coat and went downstairs, intending to ask Gabriel to come with me to look for him, but as I could not find him I went out alone, calling Friday as I did so.

I found my footsteps wandering towards the Abbey. At any other time I might have found it awe-inspiring; on this evening my thoughts were all for Friday.

I kept calling his name, straining my ears for an answering bark. There was nothing.

It was an uncanny experience to stand there among those ruins . . . alone. It had been a glorious day and there were signs of a fine day to follow. The old saying came into my head: Red sky at night, shepherd's delight.

Then suddenly the fear came to me. I felt that I was not alone; that through those narrow slits, which had once been windows, eyes watched me. The glow from the sky touched the stones so that they looked rosy; and the ridiculous fancy came to me that life was being breathed into them.

I did not know what had happened to me, but I expected to hear the chanting of monks as they walked down the nave. I felt my heart hammering as I looked up at the arches through which I glimpsed the blood-red sky. I imagined that somewhere, not far distant, I heard a stone dislodged and, following that, a footstep.

"Who's there?" I called; and the hollow sound of my own voice startled me.

I looked about me. There was nothing but those piles of

stones, those half-walls, those rectangles of brick within which the grass grew. Here a community of men had lived long ago and I could almost believe that I was moving back in time, that the half-walls would become walls in their entirety, that a roof would appear to shut out the sky and this nineteenth century.

I began to call Friday again, and I noticed that it had become considerably darker than when I had first entered the ruins. Evening skies change rapidly, and the red was now streaked with grey. The sun had disappeared and soon darkness would descend upon me . . . and the Abbey.

I tried to leave by the way I had come—at least I thought it was the way I had come, but after a few minutes I realised that I was in a section of the ruins which I had not visited before. I saw part of a staircase, leading down to darkness; I turned and hurried away; I tripped over a ridge of stone and only saved myself in time. I had a horrible fear of breaking an ankle and being forced to spend the night here . . . a prisoner. I began to feel faint at the thought of it.

This was most unlike myself. What is this? I demanded. Nothing but bricks and grass. Why be afraid? But what was the use? I *was* afraid.

I blundered on. My one thought, my great desire, was to escape from the ruins of Kirkland Abbey.

It was only now that I had lost my way that I became fully aware of the vastness of the place; and there was a time during that nocturnal adventure when I thought I should never find my way out of the maze of stone. With every passing second the light was fading and I was so anxious to get away from the place that I panicked and lost my sense of direction.

At length when I did escape I came out on the far side of the Abbey and it was now between me and the house.

Nothing would have induced me to go back the way I had come, which would have been difficult in any case, for I should have lost myself in that pile of stones. I ran on swiftly until I found a road. This I took and, guessing my direction, I hurried on, now and then breaking into a run.

As I came to a clump of trees through which the road wound, a figure emerged and for a moment I knew terror. Then it took on a familiar shape and a voice I knew said: "Hallo! Have you got the devil at your heels?"

The note of mockery in that voice set annoyance swamping my fear.

"I lost my way, Mr. Redvers," I said. "But I think I'm on the right road now."

He laughed. "You are, but I can show you a short cut . . . if you'll allow me."

"Doesn't this road lead to the house?"

"It does . . . eventually. But if you cut through the trees here you come out about half a mile nearer. Will you allow me to escort you?"

"Thank you," I said stiffly.

We walked side by side and he fitted his step to mine.

"How did you come to be out alone at this hour?" he asked.

I told him that my dog had been out all afternoon and evening, and I was anxious.

"You shouldn't wander too far alone," he reproved me. "You see how easy it is to lose yourself."

"Had it been day I should easily have found the right road."

"But it was not day. As for the dog, doubtless he has found a little companion somewhere. Dogs will be dogs."

I did not answer him; we had come through the trees and I saw the house. In five minutes we were there.

Gabriel, Ruth, Luke and Dr. Smith were in the grounds. They were all looking for me. The doctor had come in to see Sir Matthew and had heard that I had disappeared.

Gabriel was so anxious that he was almost angry with me for the first time in our lives.

I breathlessly explained that I had been looking for Friday, had got lost among the ruins and met Simon Redvers on the way back.

"You shouldn't have gone out alone at dusk," said Dr. Smith gently.

"One of us would have gone with you!" Luke reproved me.

"I know," I said and smiled with relief because I was so happy to be back. I turned to Simon Redvers. "Thank you, Mr. Redvers," I went on.

He bowed ironically. "Such a pleasure," he murmured.

"Has Friday come home?" I asked Gabriel.

He shook his head.

"He'll turn up to-morrow," Luke put in.

"I do hope so," I answered.

Gabriel put his arm through mine. "There's nothing else we can do to-night. And you look exhausted. Come along in."

They all seemed to be watching us. I turned and said: "Good night."

There was an echoing answer as Gabriel drew me into the house.

"I've never seen you look so white and tired," he told me. "I thought I should never get back."

He laughed and put his arm about me. He said suddenly: "Wasn't that honeymoon of ours wonderful. But it was very short. We ought to have a longer one. I've often thought I'd like to go to Greece."

"'The Isles of Greece, the Isles of Greece! Where burning Sappho loved and sung,'" I quoted, and my voice had a high pitch to it. Although I was worried about Friday, I was very relieved to be safe, which seemed unaccountably foolish.

"I'm going to tell them to bring you some hot milk. It'll make you sleep." said Gabriel.

"Gabriel, I can't stop wondering about Friday."

"He'll turn up. You go to your room and I'll go to the kitchen to tell them to bring that milk."

I went on up, thinking how gentle he was, how considerate to the servants. They had so many stairs in a house of this nature to contend with.

When I reached our room, the first thing I noticed was Friday's empty basket and I felt very unhappy.

I went into the corridor and called him once more. I tried to comfort myself that he was hunting rabbits. It was a favourite pastime of his and I had known him forget everything when pursuing it. It might be that in the morning he would come home.

I did realise there was nothing more I could do that night, so I undressed and got into bed.

So exhausted was I that I was almost asleep when Gabriel came in. He sat by the bed and talked about our trip to Greece he seemed really excited about it. But soon one of the servants came in with my milk on a tray.

I did not really want it but I drank it off to please Gabriel, and in a few minutes I fell into a deep sleep.

I was awakened by a banging on my door. Reluctantly I awoke; rarely had I slept so deeply. I sat up in bed to find Ruth standing in the room. Her eyes looked enormous, her face was the colour of white paper.

"Catherine," she was saying. "Wake up! Wake up, *please*!" And I knew something terrible had happened.

I looked for Gabriel but there was no sign of him.

"It's Gabriel," said Ruth. "You must prepare yourself for a shock."

"What . . . has happened to Gabriel?" I asked as though I found the greatest difficulty in getting out the words.

"He is dead," she said. "He has killed himself."

I did not believe her. I felt as though I was struggling out of a fantastic world of dreams.

Gabriel . . . dead? It wasn't possible. Why, only a short while ago he had sat by my bed watching me drink my milk, talking of our trip to Greece.

"You'll have to know," she said, looking at me steadily; and was it with a hint of accusation in her eyes? "He threw himself over the parapet of the balcony. One of the grooms has just found him."

"It can't be true."

"You'd better get dressed," she said.

I stumbled out of bed; my limbs were trembling; one thought kept hammering in my brain. This is not true. Gabriel did not kill himself.

Chapter 3

So within a week of my coming to Kirkland Revels tragedy had struck the house.

I do not clearly remember the sequence of events of that day, but I can recall the numbness which took possession of me, the certainty that something inevitable had taken place, something which had threatened me, warned me from the moment I entered the house.

I remembered lying on my bed during that first morning. Ruth had insisted that I should, and it was at this time that I learned what a forceful character she had. Dr. Smith came and gave me a sedative; he said it was necessary, and I slept until the afternoon.

I joined them in the room which was known as the winter parlour . . . one of the smaller rooms on the first floor which looked onto the courtyard and which was so-called because during the winter it could be kept warmer and more cosy than those rooms which were less sheltered. The entire family was there: Sir Matthew, Aunt Sarah, Ruth, Luke; and Simon

Redvers had joined them. I was conscious of the gaze of everyone as I entered.

"Come here, my dear," said Sir Matthew. "This is a terrible shock to us and especially to you, my dear child."

I went to him because I trusted him more than any of the others; and when I sat down beside him, Aunt Sarah came over and, taking the chair on the other side of me, placed her hand over mine and kept it there.

Luke had walked to the window. He was saying tactlessly: "It was exactly like the others. He must have remembered them. All the time we were talking of them, he must have been planning . . ."

I said sharply: "If you mean Gabriel committed suicide, I don't believe it. I don't believe it for a moment."

"This is so terrible for you, my dear," murmured Sir Matthew.

Aunt Sarah came a little closer and leaned against me. There was a faint odour of decay about her .

"What do you believe happened?" she asked; and her blue eyes were bright and eager with curiosity.

I turned away from her. "I don't know," I cried, "I only know he didn't kill himself."

"My dear Catherine," said Ruth sharply, "You're over-wrought. We all have the utmost sympathy for you, but . . . you knew him such a short time. He is one of *us* . . . all his life he has belonged to us. . . ."

Her voice broke, but I did not believe she was sincerely sorry. And I thought: The house will pass to Luke now. Are you pleased about that, Ruth?

"Last night he talked about the holiday we should have," I insisted. "He talked of our going to Greece."

"Perhaps he didn't want you to guess what he planned," suggested Luke."

"He couldn't deceive me. Why should he talk of going to Greece if he were planning to . . . do that!"

Simon spoke then. His voice sounded cold and seemed to came from a long distance. "We do not always say that which is in our minds."

"But I knew . . . I tell you, I knew . . ."

Sir Matthew had put a hand to his eyes and I heard him murmur: "My son, my only son."

There was a knock on the door and William entered.

He looked at Ruth and said: "Dr. Smith is here, madam."

"Then bring him in," Ruth answered.

And in a few moments Dr. Smith came in. His eyes were sympathetic, and it was to my side that he came.

"I cannot express my grief," he murmured. "And I am concerned for you."

"Please don't be," I replied. "I have suffered a great shock . . . but I shall be all right." I heard myself give a slightly hysterical laugh which horrified me.

The doctor laid his hand on my shoulder.

"I'm going to give you a sedative for to-night," he said. "You'll need it. Then when you wake up there'll be a night between you and all this. You'll be one step away from it."

Aunt Sarah spoke suddenly in a high, rather querulous voice: "She doesn't believe he killed himself, Doctor."

"No . . . no . . ." soothed the doctor. "It's hard to credit it. Poor Gabriel!"

Poor Gabriel! It seemed like an echo in that room, and it came from more than one of those present.

I found myself looking at Simon Redvers. "Poor Gabriel!" he said, and there was a cold glitter in his eyes as they met mine. I felt I wanted to shout at him: Are you suggesting that I had anything to do with this? Gabriel was happier with me than he had ever been in his life. He told me so repeatedly.

But I said nothing.

Dr. Smith said to me: "Have you been out to-day, Mrs. Rockwell?"

I shook my head .

"A little walk in the grounds would do you good. If you would allow me to accompany you, I should be glad."

It was clear that he had something to say to me alone, and I rose at once.

"You should wear your cloak," Ruth put in. "There's a chill in the air to-day."

A chill in the air, I thought; and a chill in my heart. What would happen next? My life seemed suspended between Glen House and Kirkland Revels and the future was like a thick fog all about me.

Ruth had rung the bell and eventually a servant appeared with my cloak. Simon took it from the maid and wrapped it about me. I looked over my shoulder and tried to read what I saw in his eyes, but that was impossible.

I was glad to escape from that room and be alone with the doctor.

We did not speak until we had left the house and were

walking in the direction of the Abbey. It was difficult to believe that it was only the night before that I had lost my way.

"My dear Mrs. Rockwell," said Dr. Smith, "I could see that you wished to get away from the house. That was one reason why I suggested this walk . You feel bewildered, do you not?"

"Yes," I said. "But there is one thing of which I am certain."

"You think it impossible that Gabriel killed himself?"

"Yes, I do."

"Because you were happy together?"

"We were happy together."

"I think it may have been because Gabriel *was* happy with you that he found his life intolerable."

"I do not understand you."

"You know that his health was precarious."

"He told me that before we married."

"Ah, I thought perhaps he might have kept it from you. His heart was weak and he might have died at any moment. But you knew that."

I nodded.

"It's a family weakness. Poor Gabriel, it struck him young. I had a conversation with him only yesterday about . . . his weakness. I am wondering now whether this had something to do with the tragedy. May I be frank with you? You are very young but you are a married woman, and I am afraid I must speak with candour."

"Please do."

"Thank you. I was struck from the first by your good sense and I rejoiced that Gabriel had chosen so wisely. Yesterday Gabriel came to me and asked me some questions about . . . his married life."

I felt a flush rise in my cheeks and said: "Pray tell me what you mean."

"He asked me if the state of his heart made it dangerous for him to indulge in marital relations."

"Oh!" My voice sounded faint and I could not bring myself to look at the doctor. We had reached the ruins and I stared up at the Norman tower. "And . . . what was your answer?"

"I told him that in my opinion he would take a considerable risk if such relations did occur."

" I see."

He was trying to read my thoughts, but I would not look at him. What had happened between me and Gabriel should, I decided, be our secret. I felt embarrassed to be involved in such a discussion and, although I reminded myself that this man was a doctor, the discomfort persisted. But I could see what he was driving at, and he had no need to explain ; but he did.

" He was a normal young man, apart from this weakness of the heart. He was proud. I realised when I warned him that I was giving him a shock—but I did not understand then how deeply it had affected him."

" And you think that this . . . warning . . . decided him?"

" It seems to me a logical deduction. What . . . is your opinion, Mrs. Rockwell? In the past, has there been between you . . . er . . ."

I touched a fragment of broken wall, and my voice was as cold as the stones as I said : " I do not think that what you told my husband would have made him wish to end his life."

The doctor seemed satisfied with that answer. He laughed lightly but without mirth. " I should not have liked to think that any words of mine . . ."

" You need have no qualms," I answered. " What you said to Gabriel was what any doctor would have said."

" I believe it may have been a reason . . ."

" Do you mind if we turn back?" I asked. " It seems to have grown colder."

" Forgive me. I should not have brought you out. You feel cold because of the shock you have suffered. I'm afraid I've behaved brutally to you, discussing this . . . indelicate matter . . . just when . . ."

" No, you have been kind to me. But I am shocked . . . and I cannot believe that only this time yesterday . . ."

" Time will pass. Believe me, I know what I'm talking about. You are so young. You will go away from here . . . at least I suppose you will. . . . You won't stay shut away here, will you?"

" I do not know what I shall do. I have not thought about it."

" Of course you have not. I was saying that you have your life before you. In a few years' time this will seem like a bad dream."

" Some bad dreams one never forgets."

"Oh come, you must not be morbid. You are so close to tragedy that it overwhelms you. You will feel a little better to-morrow, and a little better every day."

"You forget I have lost my husband."

"I know, but . . ." He smiled and laid his hand on my arm. "If there is anything I can do to help you . . ."

"Thank you, Dr. Smith. I shall remember your kindness."

We had returned to the grounds and walked across the front lawns in silence. As we approached the house I looked up at the balcony and pictured what might have happened . . . Gabriel, sitting on my bed, talking of the holiday we would have, making me drink my hot milk and then, when I slept, coming quietly out on to the balcony and letting himself fall. I shivered. "I don't believe it; I can't believe it."

I did not realise that I had spoken aloud until Dr. Smith said: "You mean you don't want to believe it. Sometimes the two are synonymous. Do not fret, Mrs. Rockwell. I hope you will look on me as something more than the family doctor. I have been on terms of close friendship with the Rockwells for years, and you are now a member of that family. So do please remember that if you need my advice at any time, I shall be very happy to give it."

I scarcely heard him; I thought the faces of the devils looked gleeful, those of the angels sad.

As I went in a feeling of desolation came over me, and I said quickly: "Friday is still missing."

The doctor looked blank and I realised that he had probably not heard of the dog's disappearance, for in view of what had happened who would have thought to tell him?

"I must find him," I went on.

I left and hurried to the servants' hall to ask if Friday had been seen. No one had seen him. I went through the house calling him.

But there was no response.

So I had lost Gabriel and Friday . . . together.

At the inquest the verdict was that Gabriel had taken his life while temporarily insane, in spite of my insistence that we had been planning to go to Greece. Dr. Smith explained that he had been suffering from a weakness of the heart which depressed him. It was his opinion that his marriage had brought home to him the magnitude of his infirmity and the consequent depression had forced him to act as he had done.

This seemed to be considered an adequate reason and the verdict was given without demur. I was present at the inquest although Dr. Smith had advised me against going.

"You will only distress yourself further," he said. Ruth agreed with him. But I had quickly recovered from my shock and I found a certain resentment mingling with my sorrow. Why, I kept asking myself, were they all so certain that Gabriel killed himself?

I answered that myself How else could he have died? By accident? I tried hard to think of how it could have happened. Could he have leaned too far over the parapet and fallen? Was that possible?

It must be possible, because it was the only reasonable explanation.

Over and over again I tried to picture it. Suppose he went on to the balcony as he so frequently did. Suppose something below caught his attention. Friday! I thought excitedly. What if Friday had appeared down there and he called to him and in his excitement leaned over too far?

But they had already passed their verdict and they would not have believed me. They would have called me a hysterical bride.

I had written to my father to tell him of Gabriel's death, and he came to the funeral. I had been pleased when I heard that he was coming, believing that he would have some comfort to offer me. Childishly I had expected that my trouble might bring us closer together; but as soon as I saw him I realised how foolish I had been. He was as remote as ever.

He sought an opportunity to speak to me before we left for the church, but I was conscious all the time that to him it was a painful duty.

"Catherine," he asked. "what are your plans?"

"Plans!" I echoed blankly, for I had not considered my future. I had lost the only two who had loved me—for as each day passed I began to despair of finding Friday—and I could think of nothing but my loss.

My father seemed a little impatient. "Yes, yes. You'll have to decide what you're going to do now. I suppose you could stay here or come back. . . ."

I had never felt quite so lonely in the whole of my life. I kept thinking of Gabriel's solicitude for me, his eagerness to be with me every minute of the night and day. I thought:

If only Friday would suddenly come bounding up to me, leaping into my arms, I might have something to plan for.

I said stonily: "I have made no plans so far."

"Perhaps it's early yet," he replied in his weary voice, "but if you should want to come back, you must of course."

I turned away from him; I could not trust myself to speak.

How melancholy it was when the hearse and carriages arrived with the plumed horses and velvet palls and the mutes dressed in black from head to foot. Gabriel was buried in the Rockwell vault in which lay so many of his ancestors. I wondered if those others were there—the two who had died in the same way.

I returned with the rest of the family to the house and we solemnly drank wine and ate the funeral meats which had been prepared for us. I felt a stranger in my widow's weeds. I was so pale that I looked like a ghost, and there seemed no colour in my face except that of my vivid green eyes. Surely mine was a most extraordinary fate—to be a bride and widow in less than two weeks.

My father left immediately after the funeral saying that he had a long journey ahead of him and adding that he would expect to hear from me what my plans were for the future. Had he shown me in some small way that he really wanted me, I should have been eager to go back with him.

I was drawn to Sir Matthew, who had lost all his jauntiness since the tragedy. He was very kind to me and made me sit beside him when all the mourners, who were not members of the family, had gone.

"How do you feel, my dear," he asked me, "in this house full of strangers?"

"I do not feel anything but a numbness now, an emptiness," I told him.

He nodded. "If you wish to stay here," he said, "you would always be welcome. This was Gabriel's home and you were Gabriel's wife. If you want to go away, I shall understand, but I should be very sorry."

"You are kind to me," I said, and those words of kindness brought the tears, which till now I had not been able to shed, to my eyes.

Simon had come to stand beside me. He said: "You will go away from here. What is there for you? It is so dull in the country, is it not?"

"I came from the country," I said.

"But after those years in France."

" I am surprised that you remember so much of my affairs."

" I have a very good memory. It is the only good thing about me. Yes, you will go away. You will be more free than you were . . . more free than you have ever been before." He changed the subject abruptly. " Those weeds become you."

I felt there was something behind his words, but I was too weary and too obsessed with thoughts of Gabriel to give him much of my attention.

I was glad when Luke came over to us and began to talk of other matters.

" It doesn't do to dwell on all this," he said. " We've got to forget. We've got to go on living."

I thought I detected a certain glitter in his eyes. He was, after all, the new heir. Was his grief for Gabriel rather superficial?

I was trying to hold off frightening notions which were creeping into my mind. I did not really believe that Gabriel had had an accident on the balcony. I did not believe that he had deliberately killed himself.

But what else was there to believe?

When Gabriel's will was read I learned that he had left me, although not rich, comfortably off. I had an income which would make me independent. This was a surprise because, although I had known that Kirkland Revels would pass to Gabriel on his father's death, together with an income adequate for its upkeep, I had not realised that he had so much money of his own.

The fact of my new affluence cheered me a little, and this was only due to the promise of freedom which it held out.

A week passed and I was still at the Revels, each day hoping for the return of Friday even though the days passed without sign of him.

I knew that the family were waiting for me to come to a decision as to whether or not I was going to stay, and I found it difficult to make up my mind. This house was of great interest to me ; I felt that there was so much I did not know and only by staying could I discover it. I had a right to live here ; I was Gabriel's widow. His father clearly wanted me to stay and, I believed, so did Aunt Sarah ; but I thought Ruth would have been relieved to see me go. I wondered why. Was it because she did not care to have another female in the house, or was there some other reason? As for Luke, he was friendly in a breezy manner; but I had a notion that he did not care either way. He was immersed in his own affairs, and try as he might he could not hide his new importance. He was the heir of Kirkland Revels and, in view of Sir Matthew's age and infirmity, it could not be many more years before he was its master.

The Smiths were frequently at the house now, and when the doctor visited Sir Matthew—which he did each day—he invariably made a point of seeing me too. He was always kind and solicitous; he made me feel as though I were a patient, and, during that unhappy time when I mourned for Gabriel and Friday. He seemed to be concerned about my health.

"You have suffered a great shock," he told me, "perhaps greater than you realise. We must see that you take care of yourself."

He was giving me that solicitude which I had sought in vain from my father, and I began to wonder whether one of the reasons why I lingered on at the house was because of Dr. Smith, for it seemed that he understood my grief and loneliness as no one else did.

Damaris often drove over with her father, always cool, always serene and beautiful. I could see that Luke was in love with her but it was impossible to know what her feelings for him were. She was inscrutable. If Luke had his way he would marry her, but they were both so young at present and I doubted whether Sir Matthew or Ruth would allow Luke to marry for some time. And who knew what could happen in three, four or five years?

I had a feeling that I was marking time. I had not recovered from that strange numbness which had come to me when I heard I was a widow, and I could make no plans until I was free of it. If I left Kirkland Revels, where should I go? Back to Glen House? I thought of those dark rooms made bright only by the filtering of light through the Venetian blinds. I thought of Fanny's pursed lips and my father's "bad turns." No, I was not eager to return to Glen House; yet I was not sure that I wanted to stay at the Revels. What I wanted was to clear away this ignorance which shut me in like a fog. I believed if I could do that I should understand . . . what?

I walked each day and my footsteps always seemed to lead me to the Abbey. I had found in the Revels library an old plan of the place as it must have been before the 1530's and the Dissolution, and it took my mind from morbid thoughts to attempt to reconstruct the old building on those ruins. The plan was a great help and I was able to identify certain landmarks. I was excited when I came upon what must have been the chapel of nine altars, the monks' dorter, the gate-house, the kitchens and the bakehouses. I also discovered the fish-ponds. There were three of these, a grassy bank separating them from each other.

I wondered whether Friday had fallen into one of these and been drowned. Impossible. They could not be very deep and he would swim to the bank. Nevertheless I called him whenever I came to the Abbey, which I knew was foolish even as I did it ; but I could not bear to face the fact that he was gone for ever. I must continue to hope.

I remembered the day when I had first seen Dr. Smith at this spot and he had said that Friday ought to have been brought here on a lead. As soon as I had recovered sufficiently from the shock of Gabriel's death, I had gone to the old well to look for Friday, but there was no sign of him there.

One day returning from my walk I took a new route and consequently arrived at the back of the house instead of the front, so I entered through a door I had not hitherto used. I was in the east wing of the house—a part with which I was not yet familiar. All the wings, I discovered, were almost identical with each other, except that the main staircase which led down to the hall past the minstrels' gallery was in the south wing.

I mounted a flight of stairs to the third floor, knowing that there were communicating corridors between the wings, and I thought I should easily find my way to my own apartments. But this was not so, for I found myself in a maze of corridors and I was not sure which was the door which communicated with the south wing.

I hesitated because I was afraid I might walk into someone's private room.

I knocked at several doors, opened them and found a bed-room or a sitting-room, a sewing-room, but not the corridor I was looking for.

I could either retrace my steps, leave the house and enter by the front door, or continue my search. I decided on the latter realising that it was the only thing to do, for how could I be sure that I would find my way out of such a maze?

In desperation I tried more doors, only to be disappointed.

At length when I knocked on one a voice said: "Come in."
I entered and Aunt Sarah was standing so close to the door
that she startled me and I jumped back.

She laughed and put out a thin hand with which she
clutched my sleeve.

"Come in," she said. "I've been expecting you, my dear."

She ran round me as I entered—she seemed more nimble
than she was when with the rest of the family—and quickly
shut the door as though she was afraid I would try to escape.

"I know," she said, "you've come to see my tapestries.
That's it, isn't it?"

"I should greatly enjoy seeing your tapestries," I told her.
"Actually I lost myself. I came in by the east door. I have
never done that before."

She shook a finger at me as though I were a naughty child.
"Ah, it's easy to lose your way . . . when you don't know.
You must sit down."

I was not sorry to do so because I was quite tired from my
walk.

She said: "It was sad about the little dog. He and Gabriel
went together. Two of them . . . lost. That is sad."

I was surprised that she remembered Friday, and felt at a
loss with her, because it was perfectly obvious that at times
her mind wandered, that she flitted from past to present in a
manner which was disconcerting; but there were occasions
when she was capable of unexpected clarity.

I noticed that the walls of this large room were hung with
tapestry, all exquisitely worked in bright colours; I was looking at it in fascination when she noticed this and chuckled
with pleasure.

"That's all my own tapestry," she said. "You see what
a large space it covers . . . but there is so much more to be
done. Perhaps I shall fill every bit of the walls . . . unless I
die. I am very old. It would be sad if I died before I had
finished all I had to do." The melancholy expression was
replaced by a dazzling smile. "But that is in the hands of
God, is it not? Perhaps if I ask Him in my prayers to let me
have a little longer, He will. Do you still say your prayers,
Claire? Come and look at my tapestry . . . come closer.
And I will tell you all about it."

She had taken my hand; her fingers were restless and
moved continually; they felt like claws.

"It's exquisite work," I said.

"You like it? Claire, you didn't work hard enough at

80

yours. I have told you many times that it is easy . . . easy
. . . if you persevere. I know you had a great deal to do. You
used to say that Ruth was such a wilful little thing. Mark was
good though . . . and then there was a new one coming . . ."

I said gently: " You have forgotten, Aunt Sarah. I am
not Claire. I am Catherine, Gabriel's widow."

" So you have come to see my tapestry, Catherine. It is
time you did. I know you will like it . . . you more than any."
She came close to me and peered into my face. " You will
figure in my tapestry. I shall know when the time has come."

" I?" I asked, bewildered.

" Here. Come close. Look. Do you recognise this?"

" It's the house . . ."

She laughed gleefully and pulled me away from the tapestry
I was studying, drawing me towards a cupboard which she
pulled open. Stacks of canvases fell out. She picked them up
laughing. She no longer seemed like an old woman, her movements were so agile. I saw that there was a cupboard within
the cupboard, and this she opened to disclose skein upon skein
of silks of all colours.

She stroked them lovingly. " I sit here and I stitch and
stitch. I stitch what I see. First I draw it. I will show you
my drawings. Once I thought I should be an artist and then
I did my tapestry instead. It is so much better, do you not
think so?"

" The tapestry is lovely," I told her. " I want to look at it
more closely."

" Yes, yes."

" I want to see that one of the house. It is so real. That is
the exact colour of the stones."

" Sometimes it is not easy to find the right colours," she
said, her face puckering.

" And the people . . . why, I recognise them."

" Yes," she said. " There is my brother . . . and my sister
Hagar, and there is my niece Ruth and my nephew Mark—
he died when he was fourteen—and Gabriel and Simon, and
myself . . ."

" They are all looking at the house," I said.

She nodded excitedly. " Yes," she said, " we are all looking at the house. Perhaps there should be more looking at
the house. . . . You should be there now. . . . But I do not
think you are looking at the house. Claire didn't look either.
Neither Claire nor Catherine."

I was not sure what she meant and she did not explain,

but went on: "I see a great deal. I watch. I saw you come. You didn't see me."

"You were in the minstrels' gallery."

"You saw me?"

"I saw someone."

She nodded. "From there you see so much . . . and are not always seen. Here is the wedding of Matthew and Claire."

I was looking at a picture of a church which I recognised as that of Kirkland Moorside; there were the bride and groom, the latter recognisable as Sir Matthew. It was astonishing how she had managed to convey a likeness with those tiny stitches. She was undoubtedly an artist.

"And Ruth's marriage. He was killed in a hunting accident when Luke was ten. Here it is."

Then I realised that here on the walls of this room was Rockwell history as seen through the eyes of this strange woman.

She must have spent years of her life recapturing these events and stitching them on to canvas.

I said: "You are a looker-on at life, Aunt Sarah."

Her face puckered again and she said almost tearfully: "You mean I haven't lived myself . . . only through others. Is that what you mean, Claire?"

"I am Catherine," I reminded her.

"Catherine," she said, "I have been happy looking on. See, I have this gallery . . . this tapestry gallery . . . and when I am dead people will look at it and they will know more of what happened to us than they can know from the picture gallery. I am glad I did my tapestry pictures instead of portraits. Portraits have little to tell."

I walked round that room and I saw scenes from the life of Kirkland Revels—I saw Ruth's husband being carried on a stretcher from the hunting field, and the mourners about his bed. I saw the death of Mark, and in between each of these scenes was a picture of the house and those recognisable figures gazing at it.

I said: "I believe that is Simon Redvers, among those who look at the house."

She nodded. "Simon looks at the house because it could be his one day. If Luke were to die as Gabriel died, then the Revels would be Simon's. So you see he is looking at the house too."

She was studying me intently and from the pocket of her gown she took a small note-book; and while I watched she sketched a figure. She managed to suggest myself by a few deft strokes of her pencil.

"You are very clever," I said.

She looked at me sharply and asked: "How did Gabriel die?"

I was startled. "They said at the inquest . . ." I began.

"*You* said he did not kill himself."

"I said I did not believe he could have done it."

"Then how did he die?"

"I do not know. I only sense within me that he could not have done it."

"I sense things within me. You must tell me. We must discover. I must know for my picture."

I looked at the watch pinned to my blouse. It was a gesture which meant that I must be going.

"I shall soon have finished the one I am working on. Then I shall want to start it. You must tell me."

"What are you working on now?' '

"Look," she said, and she drew me across the room to the window.

There on a frame was the familiar picture of the house.

"You have done that one before."

"No," she said, "this is different. There is no Gabriel to look at the house now. Only Matthew, Ruth, Hagar, myself, Luke, Simon . . ."

I felt stifled suddenly by the room and the effort of trying to catch at her innuendoes. She was indeed a strange woman, for she managed to give the impression of innocence and wisdom . . . almost simultaneously.

I had had enough of symbols. I wanted to get to my room and rest.

"I lost my way. Tell me how I can get back to the south wing."

"I will show you." She was like an eager child trotting at my side, as she opened the door and we went into the corridor.

I followed her and when she opened another door I went through in her wake to find myself on a balcony similar to that of the tragedy.

"The east balcony," she said. "I thought you would like to see it. It is now the only one over which no one has fallen to death."

There was a strange curve on her lips which might have been a smile.

"Look over," she said. "Look over. See how far down it

is." She shivered. And I felt her little agile body pressing me against the parapet. For a horrible moment I thought she was trying to force me over.

Then she said suddenly: "You don't believe he killed himself. You don't believe it."

I drew away from the parapet and moved towards the door. I felt relieved to step into the corridor.

She went on ahead of me and in a short time she had led me to the south wing.

She had now become like an old woman again and I imagined that the change came when she left the east for the south wing.

She insisted on accompanying me to my own rooms even though I told her I now knew the way.

At the threshold of my room I thanked her and told her how I had enjoyed seeing the tapestries. Her face lighted up; then she put her fingers to her lips.

"We must find out," she said. "Don't forget. There's the picture to do."

Then she smiled conspiratorially and went quietly away.

It was a few days later when I made my decision.

I was still using the rooms in which I had lived with Gabriel and I found little peace in them. I was sleeping badly —something that had never happened to me before; I would fall asleep as soon as I went to bed but in a few minutes I would awake startled as though someone was calling me. On the first few occasions I thought that this was indeed so and got out of bed to see who was outside my door. After a few times I was convinced that it was some sort of nightmare. I would doze and be startled again; and so it went on until the early hours of the morning when I would be so exhausted that I actually slept.

It was always the same dream—someone calling my name.

Sometimes it seemed to be Gabriel's voice calling Catherine. At others it was the voice of my father calling Cathy. I knew I had been dreaming and that this was due to the shock I had suffered.

Outwardly I could seem calm enough, but inwardly I was beset by misgivings. Not only had I lost my husband but, if I had to accept the verdict that he had killed himself, I could only think that I had never really known him.

If only Friday had been with me I could have been happier.

They were the two I had loved, and to have lost them both together was a double tragedy.

There was no one at the house with whom I could make a real friendship. Each day I asked myself: Why do you stay here? And the answer was: Where would you go if you left?

I was wandering among the Abbey ruins one golden afternoon calling Friday as I did now and then, when I was startled by the unmistakable sound of footsteps.

Even in daylight I could be overawed by the place and it says a great deal for the state of my nerves that I should not have been entirely surprised to see the figure of a black-robed monk emerge from the cloister.

Instead I saw the contemporary and sturdy figure of Simon Redvers.

" So you still hope to find your dog," he said, as he came towards me. " Don't you think that if he were here he would lose no time in coming home?"

" I suppose so. It was rather foolish of me."

He looked surprised—to hear me admit my folly, I supposed. He had an idea that I was a very self-opinionated young woman.

" Strange . . ." he mused, " that he should have disappeared the day before . . ."

I nodded.

" What do you think happened to him?" he asked.

" He was either lost or stolen. Nothing else would have kept him away."

" Why do you come here looking for him?"

I was silent for a while, because I was not entirely sure why I did. Then I remembered the occasion when I had met Dr. Smith here, and how he had told me that I should not bring Friday to the ruins unless I did so on a lead.

I mentioned this to Simon.

" He was thinking of the well," I added. " In fact, he said Friday was in danger of toppling over. He stopped him in time. That was when I first met Dr. Smith. It was one of the first places I went to when I was looking for Friday."

" I should have thought the fish-ponds might have been more dangerous. Have you seen them? They are worth a visit."

" I think every part of these ruins is worth a visit."

"They interest you, do they not?"

"Would they not interest anyone?"

"Indeed not. They are so much a part of the past. So many people have no interest in the past . . . only in the present, or in the future."

I was silent and after a while he went on: "I congratulate you on your serenity, Mrs. Catherine. So many women in your position would have been hysterical; but then I suppose with you it was different. . . ."

"Different?"

He smiled at me and I was aware that there was no real warmth in that smile.

He shrugged his shoulders and went on almost brutally: "You and Gabriel—well, it was no *grande passion*, was it . . . at least on your side."

I was so angry that I was unable to speak for a few seconds.

"Marriages of convenience are as one would expect them to be, convenient," he continued in what I can only call an insolent tone. "It was a pity though that Gabriel took his life before the death of his father . . . from your point of view, of course."

"I . . . I do not understand you," I said.

"I am sure you do. Had he died after Sir Matthew, so much of that which he inherited from his father would have been yours. . . . Lady Rockwell instead of plain Mrs. . . . and there would have been other compensations. It must have been a great blow to you, and yet . . . you are the perfectly composed yet sorrowing widow."

"I think you are trying to insult me."

He laughed, but his eyes flashed angrily. "I looked on him as my brother," he said. "There are only five years between us. I could see what you had done to him. He thought you were perfect. He should have enjoyed his illusion for a little longer. He would not have lived very many years."

"What are you talking about?"

"Do you think I accept his death . . . just like that? Do you think I believe that he killed himself because of his weak heart? He had known about that for years. Why did he marry and then do this thing? Why? There has to be a reason. There always has to be a reason. Following so soon after his marriage, it is logical to believe that it had something to do with that event. I could see what he thought of you. I could imagine the effect disillusion would have on him."

"What do you mean by disillusion?"

"That you would know better than I. Gabriel was sensitive to a degree. If he discovered that he had been married . . . not for love . . . he would think life was no longer worth living, and so . . ."

"This is monstrous! You seem to think that he found me in the gutter, that he lifted me out of squalor. You are quite mistaken. I knew nothing of his father's precious house and title when I married him. He told me none of these things."

"Why did you marry him? For *love*?" He seized me suddenly by the shoulders and put his face close to mine. "You were not in love with Gabriel. Were you? Answer me." He shook me a little. I felt my fury rising against him, against his arrogance, against his certainty that he understood all.

"How dare you!" I cried. "Take your hands off me at once!"

He obeyed and laughed again. "At least I've shaken you out of your serenity," he said. "No," he added, "you were never what I should call in love with Gabriel."

"It may be," I answered curtly, "that your knowledge of such an emotion is slight. People who love themselves so deeply, as you evidently do, are rarely able to understand the affection which some are able to give to others."

I turned from him and walked away, my eyes on the ground, wary of any jutting stone which might trip me.

He made no attempt to follow me, for which I was grateful. I was trembling with rage.

So he was suggesting that I had married Gabriel for his money and the title which would eventually go with it; worse still, he believed that Gabriel had discovered this and that it had driven him to take his life. So in his eyes I was not only a fortune-huntress but a murderess.

I left the ruins behind me and hurried towards the house. Why had I married Gabriel? I kept asking myself. No, it was not love. I had married him for pity's sake . . . and perhaps because I had longed to escape from the gloom of Glen House.

In that moment I wanted nothing so much as to finish with this phase of my life. I wanted to put the Abbey, the Revels and the whole Rockwell family behind me for ever. Simon Redvers had done this to me, but I could not help wondering whether he had whispered his suspicions to the others and that they believed him.

As I entered the house I saw Ruth; she had come from the garden and carried a basket full of red roses, which reminded me of those which she had put in our room on our return from the honeymoon, and how pleased Gabriel had been with them. I thought of his pale delicate face flushed with pleasure, and I could not bear to remember Simon Redvers's hideous insinuation.

"Ruth," I said on impulse, "I've been thinking about my future. I don't think I should stay here . . . indefinitely."

She inclined her head and looked at the roses instead of me.

"So," I went on, "I will go back to my father's house while I make my plans."

"You know you always have a home here, if you wish it," she replied.

"Yes, I know. But here there is this unhappy memory."

She laid her hand on my arm. "We shall all have that, but I understand. You came here and almost immediately it happened. It is for you to decide."

I thought of Simon Redvers's cynical eyes and my anger threatened to choke me.

"I have decided," I said. "I shall write to my father to-night telling him I am coming. I expect to leave before the end of the week."

Jemmy Bell was at the station to meet me, and while we drove to Glen House through those narrow lanes, and when I caught a glimpse of our moors, I could almost believe that I had dozed on the journey home from school and had imagined all that had happened to me between then and now.

It was so like the other occasion. Fanny greeted me while Jemmy took the trap round to the stables.

"Still thin as a rake," was Fanny's greeting; and her lips were tight and self-congratulatory; I knew she was thinking: Well, I didn't hope for much from that marriage.

My father was in the hall, and he embraced me, a little less absentmindedly than usual.

"My poor child," he said, "this has been terrible for you."

Then he put his hands on my shoulders and drew back to look at me. There was sympathy in his eyes and I felt that for the first time there was a bond between us.

"You're home now," he said. "We'll look after you."

"Thank you, Father."

Fanny cut in with: "Warming-pan's in your bed. There's been mist lately."

I realised that I was receiving an unusually warm welcome.

When I went up to my room, I stood at the window looking out to the moor, and was poignantly reminded of Gabriel and Friday. Why had I thought I could forget in Glen House more easily than I could at Kirkland Revels!

I slipped into the familiar pattern. There were meals with my father, when we both sought to find a topic for conversation. He did not speak very often of Gabriel, being determined, I was sure, not to raise the painful subject. So we were both delighted when those meals were over.

Two weeks after my arrival he went away again and came home melancholy. I felt I could not endure to live much longer in this house.

I rode and walked and once made my way to the spot where I found Friday and Gabriel, but the memory was now so painful that I decided I would not ride that way again. I must stop thinking of Gabriel and Friday if I were ever to be completely at peace again.

I think it was on that day that I made up my mind to rearrange my life. I was after all a young widow with some means. I could set up a house, engage a few servants and live a completely different life from that which I had lived with my father or my husband.

I wished that I had some real friend to advise me. If Uncle Dick had been at home I should have been able to confide in him. I had written to him to tell him that I was now a widow, but letters between us would always be inadequate.

I toyed with the idea of taking a sea trip. I might arrange to meet him in some port and tell him all that had happened to me. But even while I was considering this idea a possibility had occurred to me which excited me and made me feel that all the plans which had half formed in my mind would be cast aside if this were indeed true.

I was in an agony of doubt while I told no one of my suspicions. Several weeks passed and then I visited our doctor.

I shall always remember sitting there in his consulting-room with the sun streaming through and the certainty that the story of my encounter with Gabriel and Friday was not ended, even though they might no longer play their parts in it.

How can I express my emotions? I was about to undergo a wonderful experience.

He was smiling at me, because he knew my story and believed that this was the best possible thing that could happen to me.

"There is no doubt," he told me. "You are going to have a child."

All the rest of that day I hugged my secret to myself. My own child! I was impatient with the months of gestation which must ensue. I wanted my child . . . now.

My whole life was changed. I no longer brooded on the past. I believed that this was the consolation which Gabriel was giving me, and that nothing had been in vain.

It was when I was alone in my room that I remembered that, as this was Gabriel's child as well as mine, if it were a boy he would be the heir to Kirkland Revels.

Never mind, I told myself. There is no need for him to look at that inheritance. I have enough to give him. The Rockwells need never know that he is born. Let Luke take everything. What did I care?

But the thought tormented me. I did care. If I had a son I was going to call him Gabriel, and everything that I could give him must be his.

Next day during luncheon I told my father the news. He was startled, and then I saw the colour come to his face so that it was pale pink—with pleasure, I believed.

"You are happier now," he said. "God bless you. This is the best thing that could happen to you."

I had never known him so talkative. He said that I must inform the Rockwell family immediately. He knew of the precarious state of Sir Matthew's health and I guessed he thought it would be awkward if Luke inherited his grandfather's title when it should really belong to my unborn son—if it was a son I carried.

I caught his excitement, and I went at once to my room and wrote to Ruth.

It was not an easy letter to write because Ruth had never been very friendly towards me and I could well imagine the consternation the news would cause her.

My letter was stilted but it was the best I could do.

Dear Ruth,

I am writing to tell you that I am going to have a child. My doctor has just assured me that there is no doubt of this, and I thought I should let the family know that there will shortly be a new member of it.

I hope Sir Matthew has recovered from his attack.

I am sure he will be delighted to hear that there is a possibility of his having another grandchild.

I am in excellent health and I hope you are the same. I send my very best wishes to all.

Your sister-in-law,

Catherine Rockwell

Ruth's reply came within two days.

Dear Catherine,

We are surprised and delighted by your news.

Sir Matthew says that you must come at once to the Revels because it is unthinkable that his grandchild should be born anywhere but here.

Please do not refuse his request that you should do so. He will be most unhappy if you do ; and it is an old tradition with us that our children should be born in the house.

Please let me know by return when I may expect you. I will have everything ready for you.

Your sister-in-law,

Ruth

There was also a letter from Sir Matthew. The handwriting was a little shaky but the welcome was indeed warm. He had missed me, he said ; and there was nothing which could have delighted him more at this sad time than my news. I must not disappoint him. I must come back to Kirkland Revels.

I knew he was right. I had to go back.

Ruth and Luke drove to Keighley Station to meet me.

They greeted me with outward pleasure, but I was not at all sure that they were pleased to see me. Ruth was serene, but Luke, I thought, had lost a little of his breeziness. How did it feel, I wondered, to think yourself heir to something you must always have coveted, only to find that an intruder might be on the way? It depended, of course, on how strong was your covetousness.

Ruth made solicitous inquiries about my health while we drove to the house. I was filled with emotion as we left the moors and came to the old bridge, as I caught a glimpse of the Abbey ruins and the Revels itself.

We alighted and went through the portico, and I felt that the faces of the devils looker smug and evil, as though they were saying to me: Did you think you had escaped us?

But I felt strong as I entered the house. I had someone to love, to protect, and because of that someone the emptiness had gone from life and I was ready to be happy again.

Chapter 4

When I entered the house Matthew and Sarah were waiting for me. They both embraced me and handled me with such care that I might have been a piece of porcelain; which made me smile.

"I don't break, you know," I said, and that started everything on the right note.

"Your news . . . your wonderful news!" murmured Sarah, wiping her eyes, although I saw no tears.

"This means so much to us all," Sir Matthew told me. "It is a great consolation."

"We've been telling her that," Ruth put in. "Haven't we, Luke?"

Luke smiled with a return of his camaraderie. "Have we, Catherine?" he asked.

I avoided answering by smiling at him.

"I expect Catherine is tired and would like to go to her room," said Ruth. "Shall I have tea sent up, Catherine?"

"That would be nice."

"Luke, ring for one of the maids. Come along, Catherine. Your trunk has already gone up."

Sir Matthew and Sarah followed Ruth and myself up the stairs.

"I've put you on the first floor of the south wing," Ruth explained. "You won't want too many stairs, and this is a very pleasant room."

"If you don't like it," Sir Matthew said hurriedly, "you must tell us, my dear."

"How kind you are!" I murmured.

"You could come near me." Sarah's voice was high-pitched with excitement. "That would be very nice . . . very nice indeed."

"I think the room I have chosen will be most suitable," said Ruth.

We passed the minstrels' gallery and went up the staircase to the first floor. We then went along a short corridor in which were two doors. Ruth opened the second of these to disclose my room.

It was an almost exact replica of that which I had shared with Gabriel, even to the powder closet, and I saw from the windows, which gave me a view of the lawns and of the Abbey, that it was in a similar position although two floors below.

"It is very pleasant," I said; I looked at the decorated ceiling from which cherubs, encircling the chandelier in the centre, looked down upon me. My bed was a four-poster as were almost all in the house, I believed; there were blue silk curtains about it, and these matched those of blue damask at the windows. My carpet was blue. There was an enormous fireplace, a wardrobe and several chairs besides an oak chest over which hung a brass warming-pan. There was a red glow in the highly polished brass which came from a bowl of red roses, put there I guessed by Ruth.

I smiled at her. "Thank you," I said.

She inclined her head in acknowledgement, but I could not help wondering whether she was really pleased to see me or would have been happier if, when I had left the Revels, I had gone out of her life for ever. I was sure her welcome could not be wholehearted because of what the birth of a son to me would mean to Luke. She adored Luke, I was fully aware of that; and now that I was to be a mother myself I understood how ambitious one could become on one's children's behalf, and I felt no resentment against Ruth even if she did towards me.

"This should be convenient for you," she went on quickly.

"It is kind of you to take so much trouble."

Sir Matthew was beaming at me. "*You* are going to be put to a lot of trouble for us," he told me. "We are delighted . . . delighted. I've told Deverel Smith he's got to keep me alive by hook or by crook—by potions or spells—to see my new grandson."

"You have determined on the sex."

"Of course I have, my dear. Haven't a doubt of it. You were meant to be the mother of boys."

"I want you to come and see my tapestries, Hagar, my dear," murmured Sarah. "You will, won't you? I'll show you the cradle. All Rockwells use that cradle."

"It will have to be overhauled within the next months,"

Ruth put in practically. "And this is Catherine, Aunt Sarah."

"Of course it's Catherine," said Aunt Sarah indignantly. "We're good friends. She so liked my tapestry."

"I expect she would like to rest now."

"We must not tire her," agreed Sir Matthew.

Ruth nodded towards Aunt Sarah significantly, and Sir Matthew took his sister's arm.

"We shall be able to talk to her when she is rested," he said; and, smiling once more at me, he led his sister away.

Ruth sighed as the door shut on them. "I'm afraid she's becoming rather a trial. Her memory's so up and down. Sometimes she'll reel off all the dates of our births without an effort. It seems absurd that she can't remember to which of us she's talking."

"I suppose that happens when one grows older."

"I hope I escape that. There's a saying, 'Those whom the gods love die young.' Sometimes I think it's true."

I immediately thought of Gabriel. Was he loved by the gods? I did not think so.

"Please don't talk of dying," I said.

"I'm sorry. How silly of me. That tea should be along soon. I expect you need it, don't you?"

"It will be refreshing."

She went to the bowl of roses and began rearranging them.

"They remind me . . ." I began; and she looked at me interrogatively, so I had to go on. ". . . of those you put in the room when I first arrived here."

"Oh . . . I'm sorry. That was thoughtless of me I suppose." I guessed she was thinking that they would have to be careful in future, that when a tragedy had happened it was necessary to be very tactful to avoid bringing back memories.

One of the maids came in with the tea; she bobbed a curtsy to me and I said, "Good afternoon, Mary-Jane."

Mary-Jane set the tea down on a table by the window and I thanked her.

"Mary-Jane will be your personal maid," Ruth said. "She will answer your bell."

I was pleased. Mary-Jane was a rather tall, fresh-faced young woman who I was sure would be honest and conscientious. Because I showed my pleasure she allowed me to see hers, and I believed I had a friend in the house.

Ruth went over to the tray. "She has brought two cups," she said. "Shall I join you?"

"Please do."

"Then you sit down, and I'll bring yours to you."

I took the chair near the bed because I did not wish, at this moment, to look out of the window. I kept thinking of Gabriel and telling myself that anyone looking out of this window at the time of his accident would have seen him falling.

Ruth handed me the cup of tea ; then she brought a footstool and made me rest my feet.

"We're going to watch over you," she said, "all of us."

But I thought how cold her eyes were and that the note of friendship in her voice seemed forced.

Here I go! I thought. No sooner do I come to this house than my fancies grow. "We are going to watch over you." It could be ambiguous.

She went to the table by the window and sat down there. She talked of what had been happening during my absence. Sir Matthew had recovered from his attack, but he was getting too old for attacks nowadays, and Deverel Smith was worried. "Last week," she said, "he stayed all night. He's so good. He gives himself to his patients quite selflessly. There was no need for him to stay. We could have called him. But he insisted."

"Some doctors are very noble," I agreed.

"Poor Deverel, I don't think his home life is very happy."

"Really? I know little about his family."

"Damaris is the only child. Mrs. Smith must be a great trial to him. She is supposed to be an invalid. I would call her a hypochondriac. I imagine she indulges in illness as a way of attracting attention to herself."

"Does she never go out?"

"Rarely. She is supposed to be too ill. I imagine that the doctor has made his profession his whole life because of the state of his domestic affairs. Of course he dotes on Damaris."

"She is so very beautiful. Is her mother like her?"

"There is a resemblance, but Muriel was never half as beautiful as her daughter."

"If she were half as beautiful she would be extremely attractive."

"Yes, indeed. I'm so sorry for Damaris. I planned to give a ball for her, and for Luke too. But of course now that we are in mourning that is out of the question . . . for this year at least.

"She is fortunate to have such a good friend in you."

"We are fortunate to have such a good doctor. Would you care for more tea?"

"No, thank you. I have had enough."

"I expect you want to unpack. Would you care for me to send Mary-Jane along to help you?"

I hesitated. Then I said I would; and she went out and shortly afterwards Mary-Jane appeared with another of the maids who took the tea-tray away, leaving Mary-Jane with me.

I watched Mary-Jane kneeling by my trunk taking out my clothes.

"I shall have to buy some new clothes soon," I said. "These will not fit me."

Mary-Jane smiled. "Yes, madam," she said.

She was about my height and it occurred to me that she might like some of my clothes when I grew too large for them. I would give them to her.

"You look pleased, Mary-Jane."

"It's t'news, madam. And I'm right glad to see you back."

There was no doubt of her sincerity, and it made me happy.

The house was beginning to have an odd effect on me; I had only been in it an hour or so and I was already looking round for friends . . . and enemies.

"It'll be a long time to wait," I said.

"Yes, madam. My sister's expecting. Hers will be born in five months' time. We're hoping for a boy . . . though if it's a girl, reckon we won't fret about that."

"Your sister, Mary-Jane? So you have a family."

"Oh yes, madam. Etty's husband works up at Kelly Grange, and they've a fine cottage on t'estate. At t'lodge, madam, and all their firewood free. It's her first. . . . I get down to see her when I can."

"I'm sure you do. You must let me know how she gets on. We have something in common, Mary-Jane."

She smiled. "Time was, our Etty got terrible scared. The first . . . that's what it is. But they both was scared. . . . Jim as well. First she's scared she's going to die; then she wonders whether the baby's going to be a wreckling. Yes, scared our Ett was, that when t'baby was born it 'ud be short of something. But Jim asked the doctor to see her and he put her right. He was wonderful to her. He's a wonderful man . . . the doctor."

"Dr. Smith?"

"Oh . . . aye. He's kind. Don't care nowt whether you be gentry or poor folk. He said: 'Don't you fret, Mrs. Hardcastle—baby won't be a wreckling or now't like it. There's every sign it'll be bonny.' That set our Ett to rights."

"We are fortunate," I said, "to have such a good doctor to look after us."

She smiled. And I felt happier at the sight of her, shaking out my clothes and hanging them in the wardrobe. With her not uncomely person and her bright Yorkshire good sense, she brought normality into the room.

After dinner that first evening we were all assembled in one of the sitting-rooms on the first floor—not far from my own room—when Dr. Smith was announced.

"Bring him up," said Ruth; and as the door closed on the servant, she said to me: "He comes at all times. He's so attentive."

"He fusses too much," grumbled Sir Matthew. "I'm all right now."

As Dr. Smith came into the room he was, I was sure, looking for me.

"I'm so pleased to see you, Mrs. Rockwell," he said.

"You know the reason why she's returned, eh?" Sir Matthew asked.

"Indeed I do. I prophesy that by the end of the week there won't be one person in the village who doesn't know it. I can assure you that it makes me happy . . . very happy."

"You are not alone in that," said Sir Matthew.

"We are going through the nursery together," announced Sarah like a young child who had been promised a special treat.

"In fact," put in Luke—and was his voice mildly sardonic? —"we are preparing to join in the chorus while Catherine sings the Magnificat."

There was a slightly shocked silence at this irreverence, but Dr. Smith said quickly: "We must take great care of Mrs. Rockwell."

"We are all determined to do that," Ruth assured him.

The doctor came over to me and took my hand briefly in his. There was a certain magnetism about this man, of which I think I had been aware before, but which now struck me forcibly. He was outstandingly handsome in his dark way, and I knew that he was capable of deep feeling. I guessed that, disappointed in his marriage as he must be, he sublimated his desires for a wife's affection in his devotion to his patients.

I noticed that Sir Matthew, although complaining of his over-zealousness, was nevertheless pleased to see him, and it was clear to me that the old man felt comforted by his presence. I remembered what Mary-Jane had said of his kindness to her sister. The people of this neighbourhood perhaps should thank that unsatisfactory wife of his since his devotion to their needs was the stronger because of her.

" I know you are so fond of riding," he said, " but I don't think I should indulge in it too frequently . . . not after this month at any rate."

" I won't," I promised.

" You'll be a good and sensible young lady, I am sure of that."

" Have you been visiting Worstwhistle to-day?" asked Ruth.

" I have," said the doctor.

" And it has depressed you. That place always does." Ruth turned to me. " Dr. Smith gives his services free, not only to patients who cannot afford to pay, but to this . . . hospital."

" Oh come," cried the doctor, laughing, " don't make a saint of me. Someone has to look in on those people now and then . . . and don't forget if I have poor patients here I also have rich ones. I fleece the rich to help the poor."

" A regular Robin Hood," said Luke.

Dr. Smith turned to Sir Matthew. " Well, sir," he said, " I'm going to have a look at you to-day."

" You think it's necessary?"

" I think that since I am here . . ."

" Very well," said Sir Matthew rather testily, " but first of all you must join us in a toast. I'm going to have some of my best champagne brought up from the cellars. Luke, ring the bell."

Luke did so and Sir Matthew gave the order.

The wine was brought, the glasses filled.

Sir Matthew filled his glass and cried: " To my grandson." He put his arm about me while we all drank.

Very soon after that the doctor went with Sir Matthew to his room and I went to mine. Mary-Jane, determined to be a real lady's maid, was turning down the bed for me.

" Thank you, Mary-Jane."

" Is there anything else you'll be wanting, madam?"

I did not think there was, so I said good night to her, but as she went to the door I called: " By the way, Mary-Jane, do you know a place called Worstwhistle?"

She stopped short and stared at me.

"Why, yes, madam. It's some ten miles off on the way to Harrogate."

"What sort of place is it, Mary-Jane?"

"It's the place where mad people go."

"Oh, I see. Good night, Mary-Jane."

The next morning I was awakened by Mary-Jane, who came in to draw the curtains and bring my hot water.

It was comforting to wake up and see her pleasant face. She was looking a little shocked because there had been no need to draw the curtains as I had pulled them back before getting into bed; and I had opened the window. Mary-Jane shared the belief that night air was "dangerous."

I told her that I always slept with my window open, except in the depth of winter; and I was sure that she had decided I should need a great deal of looking after.

I took my bath in the powder-room and went along to the first-floor dining-room for breakfast. I felt quite hungry. Two mouths to feed now, I reminded myself, as I took eggs, bacon and devilled kidneys from the chafing dish on the sideboard.

I knew the routine. Breakfast was taken between eight and nine, and one helped oneself.

I rang for coffee and when it was brought to me I was joined by Luke. Later Ruth appeared and solicitously asked if I had had a good night and liked my room.

Had I any plans for the day? they wanted to know. Luke was going to Ripon and would be delighted to buy anything I needed. I thanked him and told him that I should need things, but I had not yet decided what.

"There's plenty of time before the happy event," he said; and his mother murmured his name indulgently, because she thought it was somewhat indelicate to refer to the birth of my child. I did not mind. It was something I wanted to think of continually.

I told them that I would take a little walk during the morning; I was longing to have a look at the Abbey again.

"The place appeals strongly to you," remarked Luke. "I believe it's the main reason why you wanted to come back here."

"It would interest anyone," I answered.

"You must not exhaust yourself," Ruth warned me.

"I feel very fit, so I don't think there's any danger of that."

"All the same you have to remember to take care."

The conversation turned to the affairs of the neighbourhood: the effort of the vicar to raise money for the upkeep of the church, the bazaars and jumble sales he was organising for this purpose, the ball which a friend was giving and which we could not attend as we were in mourning.

The sun streamed through the windows of that pleasant room and there was certainly nothing eerie about Kirkland Revels that morning. Even the Abbey, which I visited a few hours later, appeared to be nothing but a pile of ruins.

So that was a pleasant walk. I felt serene, ready to accept the theory that Gabriel had killed himself because of his illness. It seemed strange that I should feel more contented to believe that, but I did; perhaps it was because I was afraid of the alternative.

I came back though the Abbey ruins. It was very quiet—peaceful was the word to describe it this morning. This was merely a shell; the brilliant sunshine falling on to the grass floors, exposing the crumbling walls, defied that sense of the supernatural. I thought back to the evening when I walked here and panicked, and I laughed at my folly.

Luncheon was a quiet meal which I shared with Ruth and Luke, Sir Matthew and Aunt Sarah taking theirs in their rooms.

Afterwards I went to my room and began making out a list of things I should need. It was early, yet I was so impatient for the birth of my child that I could not wait. While I was thus engaged there was a knock on my door, and when I called, " Come in," Sarah stood on the threshold, smiling as though we were a pair of conspirators.

" I want to show you the nursery," she said. " Will you come with me?"

I rose without reluctance, for I was eager to see the nursery.

" It's in my wing," she went on. " I often go up to the nursery." She giggled. " That's why they say I'm in my second childhood."

" I'm sure they don't say that," I told her, and her face puckered a little.

" They do," she said. " I like it. If you can't be in your first childhood, the next best thing is to be in your second."

" I should love to see the nurseries," I said. " Please show me now."

Her face was smooth and happy again. " Come along."

We mounted the staircase to the top floor. I felt an involuntary tremor as I passed that corridor which led to our old

100

room and the front of the house, for my memories of Gabriel and Friday, which I was constantly trying to suppress, were as vivid as they had ever been; but Aunt Sarah did not seem to notice my mood; she was intent on leading me into the east wing and the nursery.

I was struck once more by the change in her as we entered her section of the house; she seemed almost girlish and very happy.

"Right at the top," she murmured, as she led the way up a short flight of stairs. "The schoolroom, the day nursery, the night nursery, Nanny's quarters and those of the under-nursemaid." She opened a door and said in a hushed voice: "This is the schoolroom."

I saw a large room with three windows, all of which were fitted with window-seats; the slightly sloping ceiling told me that we were immediately below the roof. I found my eyes fixed on the windows which had bars across them in accordance with nursery tradition. My child would be safe up here.

There was a large table close to one of the windows and beside it a long form. I went over to this table and saw the cuts and scratches on it; it must have been used by many generations of Rockwells.

"Look," cried Sarah. "Can you read that?"

I leaned forward and saw the name Hagar Rockwell carved there with a penknife.

"She always put her name on everything," Sarah laughed on a gleeful note. "If you went through this house peering into cupboards and such places you would see her name. Our father said she ought to have been the boy instead of Matthew. She used to bully us all . . . especially Matthew. She was annoyed with him for being the boy. Of course if she had been the boy . . . she would be here now, wouldn't she? . . . and Simon would have been . . . But perhaps that's not exactly right . . . because he's a Redvers. Oh dear, it's a little complicated, is it not? But she was not the son, and so it was Matthew."

"Hagar is Simon Redvers's grandmother?" I asked.

Sarah nodded. "She thinks the world of him." She came close to me. "She'd like to see him here . . . but she won't now, will she? There's the child . . . and there's Luke too . . . both before Simon. The child first. . . . I shall have to get some more silks."

"You're thinking that my child will make his appearance on your tapestries."

101

" Are you going to call him Gabriel?"

I was astonished, and I wondered how she had guessed my thoughts. She was studying me, her head on one side; now she looked infinitely wise as simple people sometimes do.

" It may not be a boy," I said.

She merely nodded as though there was no doubt of it.

" Little Gabriel will take big Gabriel's place," she said. " Nobody can stop him, can they?" Her face puckered suddenly. " *Can* they?" she repeated.

" If the child is a boy he will take his father's place."

" But his father died. He killed himself . . . they said so. Did he kill himself?" She had caught my arm and held it tightly. " You said he didn't. Who did? Tell me, please tell me."

" Aunt Sarah," I said quickly, " when Gabriel died I was distraught. Perhaps I did not know what I said. He must have killed himself."

She dropped my arm and looked at me reproachfully.

" I'm disappointed in you," she said, pouting. Then her mood changed at once. " We all sat at that table. Hagar the cleverest of us all—and the eldest—so you see it would have been best. . . . Then Simon would have been. . . . Our governesses did not like her though. They all liked Matthew. He was the favourite. All women liked Matthew. I was the stupid one. I could not learn my lessons."

" Never mind," I soothed. " You could draw beautifully; and your tapestry work will be here for years and years after we are all dead."

Her face lightened. Then she began to laugh. " I used to sit here, Matthew there . . . and Hagar at that end of the table. Our governess was always at the other end. Hagar said she should sit at the head of the table because she was the eldest. She could do everything . . . except drawing and needlework. I beat her there. Hagar was a tomboy. You should have seen her on horseback. She used to ride to hounds with our father. She was his favourite. Once she climbed up to the window nearly at the top of the Abbey tower. She could not get down and they had to send two of the gardeners with ladders. She was sent to her room for a whole day on bread and water; but she did not care. She said it was worth it." She came close to me and whispered: " She said: ' If you want to do something, do it and then think about paying for it afterwards—and if you've done it, you must not mind what you have to pay for it.' "

"She was a forceful character, your sister Hagar."

"Our father liked to take her round the estate with him. He was sorry when she married John Redvers. Then the trouble started with Matthew. He was sent down from Oxford. There was a young woman there. I remember that day. The girl came here to see Father. I watched them from where they couldn't see me; I heard it all."

"From the minstrels' gallery," I said.

She giggled. "They did not think to look up there."

She sat down at the table in that place which she had occupied to learn her lessons; and I knew that the reason for her youthfulness in this part of the house was due to the fact that here she relived her youth. I was sure that all her memories of the past would be flawless; it was only in the present that she was uncertain whether she was talking to Catherine or Claire, Gabriel's or Matthew's wife.

"Trouble," she brooded, "always trouble about women. He was well into his thirties before he married, and they went more than ten years without a child. Then Ruth was born. All that time Hagar thought it would be *her* son Peter who'd be master of Revels. Then Mark and Gabriel were born. Poor little Mark! But there was still Gabriel left. Then Luke was born . . . so you see Hagar was not happy about that." She rose from the table. She took me to the cupboard and showed me the marks on the wall there. There were three lines marked with the initials H. M. and S.

"Her Majesty's Ship," I murmured.

"Oh no," said Sarah earnestly. "Hagar, Matthew and Sarah. Those were our heights. Matthew shot up past her after that, and then Hagar wouldn't measure any more. I want to show you the night and day nurseries."

I followed her from the schoolroom and with her explored that part of the house which had been the children's domain through the centuries. I noticed with satisfaction that all the windows were barred. In the day nursery was a great oak chest, and this Sarah opened. In here were stored the Rockwell christening robes and she brought them out reverently for my inspection.

They were beautifully made of white silk and lace which I guessed were priceless.

"I must examine them," she said. "I may have to mend part of the lace. The last time they were used was for Luke. That's nearly eighteen years ago. He was not a good baby. None of our babies were good babies. I shall take these to my room. I shall allow no one to touch them except myself. I shall have them ready for you when you need them."

"Thank you, Aunt Sarah."

I looked at the watch pinned to my bodice and saw that it was four o'clock.

"It's tea time," I said. "I had no idea. How quickly the time passes when one is interested!"

She did not answer me; she was clutching the christening robe to her breast, and I believed that in her imagination she was already nursing the baby—or perhaps some other baby from the past—Ruth, Mark, Gabriel or Luke.

"I am going down to tea," I told her; but she did not answer me.

It was some days later when Ruth came to my room with a letter.

"One of the servants from Kelly Grange brought this over," she said.

"For me?" I asked, astonished.

"Undoubtedly for you. 'Mrs. Gabriel Rockwell'—it says it distinctly on the envelope."

Ruth was smiling as though she were amused when she handed this to me, and as she did not attempt to go I murmured, "Excuse me," and read it.

It was formal; almost like a command.

If Mrs. Gabriel Rockwell will call at Kelly Grange on Friday at 3.30 Mrs. Hagar Rockwell-Redvers will be pleased to receive her.

Because I had already crosed swords with Mrs. Hagar Redvers's grandson, I was prepared to do so with her. I flushed faintly with annoyance.

"A royal command?" asked Ruth with a smile.

I passed the invitation to her.

"It's characteristic of my Aunt Hagar," she said. "I really believe she's of the opinion that she is head of the family. She wants to inspect you."

"I have no intention of being inspected," I retorted rather sharply. "The inspection in any case would be rather useless at this stage."

"She's very old," said Ruth apologetically. "She's older than my father. She can't be far off ninety. You have to go carefully with her."

I said quickly: "I have decided that I shall not go to call on Friday."

Ruth shrugged. "The servant's waiting," she said. "My aunt will expect a reply."

"She shall have that," I answered; and sat down at my writing-table and wrote:

Mrs. Gabriel Rockwell regrets that she is unable to call on Mrs. Hagar Rockwell-Redvers at Kelly Grange on Friday at 3.30.

Ruth took the note from me. She was clearly amused.

I stood at my window watching the messenger from Kelly Grange ride away, and I thought: So it is from his Grandmother that he gets his arrogance.

Early the following week I was on the front lawn when Simon Redvers rode up to the house.

He leaped from his horse, lifted his hat to greet me, then shouted to one of the grooms as though he were the master of this house and its servants.

"Mrs. Catherine," he said, "I am pleased to find you at home because it was to see you that I have ridden over from the Grange."

I had not seen him since my return and I thought he looked larger, and more arrogant than ever. I endeavoured to look as dignified as possible as I said: "Pray tell me what your business is with me."

As soon as his horse was taken from him he came towards me; he was smiling almost ingratiatingly.

"May I say that it is a great pleasure to see you here again?"

"You may say it if you wish to."

"You are still angry with me.'

"I have not forgotten certain remarks you made to me before I left."

"Do you harbour resentments then?"

"If they are as insulting as those you made, yes."

"I am sorry about that because I have come to apologise."

"Indeed!"

"Mrs. Catherine, I am a forthright Yorkshireman, and you are a Yorkshire woman, and therefore forthright also. We are no dandified southerners to wrap up our thoughts in pretty phrases. I cannot pretend to possess the manners and style of a gentleman of London."

"I am sure it would be useless for you to make such a pretence."

He laughed. "You have a sharp tongue, Mrs. Catherine."

I was not altogether displeased by his method of addressing me. I found Mrs. Rockwell formal, and naturally I did not wish him to use my Christian name alone.

"I can only hope that it will be a match for yours on those occasions when we are obliged to meet."

"I hope those occasions will be many, and that while we sharpen our tongues we shall also sharpen our wits."

"What did you wish to say to me?"

"I wished to ask your pardon for certain unmannerly remarks I made at our last meeting. I have come to offer my congratulations, and to wish you good health and happiness."

"So you have changed your mind concerning me?"

"I hope I shall not do that, because I always admired you. But I sincerely ask your pardon. May I explain my feelings? Let us say that I was angered by the loss of one who was as my brother. I am the type who loses control of his tongue in anger, Mrs. Catherine. One of my less worthy traits, of which I fear there are many."

"Then let us say no more of the incident."

"So you will forgive and forget?"

"Forgiveness is so much easier to grant than forgetfulness. I promise you the first. The second . . . I hope will come."

"You are gracious, Mrs. Catherine, beyond my deserts. Now I am going to ask a favour of you."

"Ah!" I said.

"Not for myself," he added hastily, "but for my grandmother. She has asked you to visit her."

"It was scarcely a request."

He laughed. "You must forgive her methods. She is used to authority. It is a great grief to her that she has not seen you, and it would give her much pleasure if you would pass over the manner of her asking and remember that she is a very old lady, rarely able to leave the house."

"Did she send you to give this second command?"

"She has no idea that I have come. She was hurt by your refusal of her invitation and I am going to ask you to allow me to take you there to-morrow. I will drive over for you and take you to her. Will you allow me to do this?"

I hesitated.

"Oh come," he urged. "Remember she is old; she is lonely; she is greatly interested in the family and you are now a member of it. Please say yes. Please, Mrs. Catherine."

He suddenly seemed attractive; his eyes, screwed up against

the sunlight had lost their boldness; I noticed his strong teeth which looked very white against his sun-bronzed skin. He was a little like Gabriel without any of Gabriel's delicacy; and as I looked at him I found myself relenting.

He saw the change in my mood immediately. " Oh, thanks," he cried, and his face was creased in smiles such as I had not seen there before. He's really fond of that old grandmother, I thought; and I almost liked him because he was fond of someone other than himself.

He went on exuberantly: " You'll like her. You can't fail to do so. And she will like you . . . though she may be a little chary of showing it at first. Like you, she's a strong character."

This was the second time a man had refered to my strength, and I felt weakened suddenly. There was even a prickle in my eyes which suggested tears.

I was horrified at the idea of shedding tears, particularly before this man!

I said hurriedly to hide my embarassment: " Very well. I will come."

" That's wonderful. I shall call for you to-morrow at two o'clock. I am now going back to tell her that you have agreed to call and see her."

He did not wait for any more. He was shouting to the groom and seemed to have forgotten me.

Yet I liked him for it; and liking him, I was prepared not to dislike his grandmother, which previously I am afraid I had made up my mind to do.

The next day Simon Redvers called at the Revels promptly at two o'clock; he came in a phaeton drawn by two of the handsomest horses I had ever seen. I sat beside him during the journey which was under two miles.

" I could have walked," I said.

" And deprived me of the pleasure of taking you?" The mocking note was back in his voice, but the antagonism between us had considerably lessened. He was pleased with me because I had agreed to see his grandmother, and as his obvious affection for her had softened me towards him, we could not hate each other so wholeheartedly.

Kelly Grange was a manor house which I guessed to be less than a hundred years old—very modern when compared with the Revels. It was of grey stone and surrounded by fertile land. We drove up to a pair of massive wrought-iron gates through which I saw an avenue of chestnut trees. From the lodge a woman, who was clearly with child, came out to open the gates for us.

Simon Redvers touched his hat in acknowledgment and she bobbed a curtsy.

I smiled, and her eyes rested on me with speculation.

" Now I wonder," I said as we drove on, " if that could be Mary-Jane's sister."

" It's Etty Hardcastle. Her husband works on the land for us."

" Then it would be. Mary-Jane is my personal maid and she has told me of her sister."

" In a place like this, you find everyone is related to everyone else. There! What do you think of the Grange? A pale shadow, eh, of the Revels."

" It's very attractive."

" It has its points. Kelly Grange can offer you more in the way of comfort than the Revels, I do assure you. Wait until the winter and compare them. Our great fires keep the house warm. There are many draughty spots in the Revels. You'd need all the coal of Newcastle to keep that place warm in the winter."

" It is so much easier with a smaller place."

" Yet we are not exactly cramped. However, you shall see for yourself."

The wheels crunched on a gravel drive and soon we had drawn up before the front porch, on either side of which were marble statues of women, decently draped, holding baskets in which geraniums and lobelias had been painted. There was a long marble seat on each side of the porch.

The door was opened by a parlourmaid before we had reached it and I guessed that she had heard the sound of wheels in the drive. As we alighted, and the coachman drove off in the phaeton, I imagined this house full of servants all alert to anticipate Simon's needs.

We went into a tiled hall from which rose a wide staircase. The house was built round this hall, and, standing in it, one could look up to the roof.

It was a large house of its kind but it seemed small and intimate when compared with the Revels.

Simon turned to me. " If you will wait here a moment, I will go and tell my grandmother that you have arrived."

I watched him mount the stairs to the first-floor gallery, knock at a door and enter. In a few minutes he appeared and beckoned. I went up.

Simon stood aside for me to pass him and said with a certain amount of ceremony which may have held its mockery—I was not entirely sure of this—" Mrs. Gabriel Rockwell!"

I entered. It was a room crowded with heavy furniture; thick plush curtains as well as lace ones were held back by ornate brass fittings. There was a table in the centre of the room as well as several occasional tables; there was a horse-hair sofa, a grandfather-clock, many chairs, cabinets containing china, a whatnot, an epergne filled with white and red roses.

But all this I took in at a glance, for it was the woman in the high-backed chair who demanded my attention.

This was Hagar Redvers, Rockwell-Redvers as she called herself, the autocrat of the schoolroom who had remained an autocrat all her life.

It was evident that she was tall, although she was sitting down; her back was very straight; her chair was no soft and comfortable one, but had a hard carved wood back; her white hair was piled high on her head and on it was a white lace cap. There were garnets in her ears and her dress of lavender-coloured satin was high at the throat where a lace collar was held in place by a garnet brooch to match the stones in her ears. An ebony stick with a gold top leaned against her chair; I gathered she needed it when she walked. Her eyes were bright blue; another version of Gabriel's eyes, but there was none of Gabriel's gentleness there; there was none of his delicacy in this woman. Her hands, resting on the carved wooden arms of the chair, must have been beautiful in her youth; they were still shapely, and I saw diamonds and garnets there.

For a few seconds we took the measure of each other. I, being conscious of a faint hostility, held my head a little higher than I normally should have done, and perhaps my voice held a trace of haughtiness as I said: " Good afternoon, Mrs. Rockwell-Redvers."

She held out a hand as though she were a queen and I a subject. I had a feeling that she expected me to go down on my knees before her. Instead I coolly took the hand, bowed over it and relinquished it.

" It was good of you to come this afternoon," she said. " I had hoped you would come before."

"It was your grandson who suggested that I should come this afternoon," I told her.

"Ah!" her lips twitched a little, I fancied, with amusement. "We must not keep you standing," she said.

Simon brought a chair for me and set it before the old lady. I was very close to her and facing what light could come through the lace curtains; she had her own face in shadow and I felt that even in this small way they had sought to place me at a disadvantage.

"You are no doubt thirsty after your drive," she said, her keen eyes seeming to search through mine into my mind.

"It was a very short one."

"It is a little early for tea, but on this occasion I think we will not wait."

"I am quite happy to wait."

She smiled at me, then turned to Simon. "Ring the bell, grandson."

Simon immediately obeyed.

"We shall have much to say to each other," she went on, "and what more comfortable way of saying it than over a cup of tea?"

The parlourmaid whom I had seen before appeared, and the old lady said: "Dawson, tea . . . please."

"Yes, madam."

The door was quietly shut.

"You will not wish to join us, Simon," she said. "We will excuse you."

I was not sure whether she used the word royally or whether she meant that we should both prefer him not to be with us; but I did know that I had passed the first small test and that she had unbent slightly towards me. My appearance and manners evidently did not disgust her.

Simon said: "Very well. I'll leave the two of you to become acquainted."

"And be ready to drive Mrs. Rockwell back to the Revels at five o'clock."

Simon surprised me by his acquiescence. He took her hand and kissed it and, although even then there was a certain mockery in his manner, I could see how she enjoyed this attention and that, although she tried to, she could not retain her autocratic manner with him.

We did not speak until the door closed on him; then she said: "I had hoped to see you when you were at the Revels previously. I was unable at that time to come to see you and

I did not invite you because I felt certain that Gabriel would bring you to see me in due course. I am sure he would have done so had he lived. He was always conscious of his duty to the family."

"I am sure he would."

"I am glad that you are not one of those stupid modern girls who faint when any difficulty presents itself."

"How can you know these things on such a short acquaintance?" I asked, because I was determined that she should treat me as an equal, as I had no intention of giving her the reverence she seemed to demand.

"My eyes are as sharp as they were at twenty. They have a great deal more experience to help them along than they had then. Moreover, Simon told me how admirably calm you were during that distressing time. I am sure you are not one of those foolish people who say: We must not talk of this or that. Things exist whether we talk of them or not; so why pretend they don't by never mentioning them? Indeed, hiding the truth and making mysteries of straightforward events is the way to keep them alive. Do you agree?"

"I think there may be occasions when that is true."

"I was pleased when I heard you had married Gabriel. He was always rather unstable. So many of the family are, I'm afraid. No backbone, that's the trouble."

I looked at her erect figure and I permitted myself a little joke. "You evidently do not suffer from that complaint."

She seemed rather pleased. "What do you think of the Revels?" she asked.

"I found the house fascinating."

"Ah! It is a wonderful place. There as not so many like it left in England. That's why it is important that it should be in good hands. My father was very capable. There have been Rockwells, you know, who almost ruined the place. A house . . . an estate like that needs constant care and attention if it is to remain in good repair. Matthew could have been better. But a squire in his position should have dignity. There was always some woman. That's bad. As for Gabriel . . . he was a pleasant creature but weak. That was why I was gratified when I heard he had married a strong young woman."

The tea arrived and the parlourmaid hovered. "Shall I pour, madam?" she asked.

"No, no, Dawson. Leave us."

Dawson went away and she said to me: "Would you care

to take charge of the tea-tray? I suffer from rheumatism and my joints are a little stiff to-day."

I rose and went to the table on which the tray had been set. There was a silver kettle over a spirit lamp, and the tea-pot, cream jug and sugar bowl were all of shining silver. There were cucumber sandwiches, thin bread and butter, a seed cake and a variety of small cakes.

I had the feeling that I was being set yet another task to ascertain if I could perform this important social activity with grace. Really, I thought, she is an impossible woman; and yet I liked her in spite of herself and myself.

I knew that my colour was heightened a little, but apart from that I showed no sign of perturbation. I asked how she liked her tea and gave her the requisite amount of cream and sugar, carrying her cup over to her and setting it on the marble and gilt round table by her chair.

"Thank you," she said graciously.

Then I offered her the sandwiches and bread and butter, to which she helped herself liberally.

I kept my place behind the tea-tray.

"I hope you will come to see me again," she said, and I knew that her feelings for me were similar to mine for her. She had been prepared to be critical but something in our personalities matched.

I vaguely wondered whether in about seventy years' time I should be just such an old lady.

She ate daintily and heartily and she talked as though there was so much to say that she feared she would never say half she wanted to. She encouraged me to talk too and I told her how Gabriel and I had met when we had rescued Friday.

"Then you heard who he was, and that must have been pleasant for you."

"Heard who he was?"

"That he was an extremely eligible young man, heir to a baronetcy, and that in due course the Revels would be his."

Here it was again—the suggestion that I had married Gabriel for money and position. My anger would not be controlled.

"Nothing of the sort," I said sharply. "Gabriel and I decided to be married before we knew a great deal about each other's worldly position."

"Then you surprise me," she said. "I thought you were a sensible young woman."

"I hope I am not a fool, but I never thought it was necessarily sensible to marry for money. Marriage to an incompatible person can be most unpleasant . . . even if that person is a rich one."

She laughed and I could see that she was enjoying our encounter. She had made up her mind that she liked me; what shocked me a little was that she would have liked me equally well if I had been a fortune-hunter. She liked what she called my strength. How they admired that quality in this family! Gabriel had been looking for it and found it in me. Simon had presumed that I had married Gabriel for his money. I wondered whether he also would have thought no less of me for that. These people expected one to be shrewd and clever—sensible, they called it. No matter how callous, as long as you were not a fool, you were to be admired.

"So it was love," she said.

"Yes," I answered defiantly, "it was."

"It is a mystery which has not been solved."

"Perhaps you will solve it."

I was surprised to hear myself say: "I hope so."

"You will if you are determined to."

"Do you think so? Surely there have been unsolved mysteries although many people had devoted their time and energy to the discovery of the truth."

"Perhaps they do not try enough. And now you are carrying the heir. If your child is a boy, that will be the end of Ruth's hopes for Luke." She sounded triumphant. "Luke," she went on, "will be another Matthew; he is very like his grandfather."

There was the briefest of silences and then I found myself telling her how I had seen the schoolroom at the Revels with her initials in the cupboard and scratched on the table, how Aunt Sarah had conducted me there and given me a glimpse of the old days.

She was interested and willing enough to talk of them.

"It's years since I have been up to the nurseries. Although I pay a yearly visit to the Revels—at Christmas—I rarely go all over the house. It's such an effort to go anywhere nowadays. I am the eldest of the three of us, you know. I'm two years older than Matthew. I made them all dance to my tune in those days."

"So Aunt Sarah implied."

"Sarah! She was always a scatterbrain. She would sit at

113

the table twirling a piece of hair round and round until she looked as though she had been dragged through a hedge backwards . . . dreaming, always dreaming. I believe she's becoming quite simple in lots of ways."

"She's very alert in others."

"I know. She was always like that. I used to be at the house every day in the first years of my marriage. My husband never got on with my family. I think he was a little jealous of my feeling for them."

She smiled reminiscently and I could see that she was looking back through the years, seeing herself as the wilful, headstrong girl who had always managed to have her own way.

"We met so few people," she said. "We were very isolated here in those days. That was before the railways came; we visited the county people and there was no other family into which I could marry but that of the Redvers. Sarah didn't marry at all . . . but perhaps she would not have done so whatever her opportunities. She was born to dream her life away."

"You missed the Revels very much after you left to marry, I said, replenishing her cup and handing her the cakes.

She nodded sadly. "Perhaps I should never have left it."

"It seems to mean so much to the people who've lived in it."

"It'll mean a great deal to you one day perhaps. If your child is a boy he will be brought up at the Revels, brought up to love and revere the house. That's tradition."

"I understand that."

"I am certain the child will be a boy. I shall pray for it." She spoke as though even the Deity must obey her commands, and I smiled. She saw the smile and she smiled with me.

"If it were a girl," she went on, "and Luke were to die . . ."

I interrupted in a startled way: "Why should he?"

"Some of the members of our family enjoy longevity; others die young. My brother's two sons were extremely delicate in health. If Gabriel had not died in the manner he did he could not have lived many more years. His brother died at an early age. I fancy I see signs of the same delicacy in Luke."

The words startled me; and as I looked across at her I thought I detected a gleam of hope in her eyes. I was imagining this. She had her back to the light. I was letting my thoughts run on.

Luke and my unborn child, if it is a boy, will stand between Simon and the Revels. By the way she spoke of the Revels and of Simon I knew they meant a good deal to her . . . perhaps more than anything else in her life.

If Simon were the master of the Revels, then she would return there to spend her last days.

I said quickly as though I feared she would read my thoughts: "And your grandson's father . . . your son . . . was he also delicate?"

"Indeed no. Peter, Simon's father, was killed while fighting for his Queen and country in the Crimea. Simon never knew him; and the shock killed his mother, who never really recovered from his birth. She was a delicate creature." A faint scorn came into her voice. "It was not a marriage of my making. But my son had a will of his own. . . . I would not have had him otherwise, although it led him into this disastrous marriage. They left me my grandson."

"That must have been a great consolation to you."

"A great consolation," she said more gently than I had heard her speak before.

I asked if she would have more tea; she declined and as we had both finished she said: "Pray ring for Dawson. I do not care to see used cups and plates."

When the tea things had been taken away she began to talk about Luke. She wanted to know my impressions of him; did I find him attractive, amusing?

I found this embarrassing, for I was not sure what I really thought of Luke.

"He is very young," I replied. "It is difficult to form an opinion of young people. They change so quickly. He has been pleasant to me."

"The doctor's beautiful daughter often visits the house, I believe."

"I have not seen her since my return. We have so few visitors now that we are a house of mourning."

"Of course. And you are wondering how I hear so much of what goes on at the Revels. Servants make excellent carriers of news. My gatekeeper's wife has a sister at the Revels."

"Yes," I said, "she is my maid, a very good girl."

"I am glad she gives satisfaction. I am pleased with Etty. I see a great deal of her. She is about to have her first child and I have always taken an interest in our people. I shall see that she has all that she needs for her confinement. We always send silver spoons to babies born on the Kelly Grange estate."

"That's a pleasant custom."

"Our people are loyal to us because they know they can trust us."

We were both surprised when Simon arrived to take me back to the Revels. The two hours or so I had spent with Hagar Redvers had been stimulating, and I had enjoyed them.

I think she had too, for when she gave me her hand she was even gracious. She said: "You will come and see me again." Then her eyes twinkled and she added, "I hope." And it was as though she recognised in me one who could not be commanded. I knew she liked me for it.

I said I would come again with pleasure and should look forward to the visit.

When Simon took me home we did not say very much; but I could see he was rather pleased by the way things had gone.

During the next weeks I walked a little, rested a good deal, lying on my bed in the afternoons reading the novels of Mr. Dickens, Mrs. Henry Wood and the Brontë sisters.

I was becoming more and more absorbed in my child and this consoled me. Sometimes I would feel afresh the sorrow of Gabriel's death, and the fact that he would never know his child seemed doubly tragic. And each day, it appeared, there would be something to remind me poignantly of Friday. We had taken so many walks in the grounds about the house, and when I heard the distant bark of a dog, my heart would begin to beat fast with hope. I made myself believe that one day he would come back. Perhaps this was because I could not bear to believe that—as in the case of Gabriel—I should never see him again.

I tried to take an interest in the life of the neighbourhood. I had tea with the vicarage family; I went to church and sat in the Rockwell pew with Ruth and Luke. I felt that I was settling in as I had not begun to do while Gabriel was with me.

Sometimes I would be taken to the nurseries by Sarah— she never seemed to tire of taking me there. I was introduced to the family cradle which was a beautiful piece of workmanship on rockers and was about two hundred years old. Sarah was making a blue padded coverlet for it, and her needlework was exquisite.

I visited Hagar once more and we seemed to grow even closer; I assured myself that I had found a good friend in her.

We did no entertaining at Kirkland Revels on account of being in mourning, but close friends of the family visited us now and then. Damaris came, and I was certain that Luke was in love with her, but I was not at all sure of her feelings for him. I wondered idly whether Damaris had any feelings. I had noticed that even with her father she seemed sometimes unresponsive, although she was docile enough. I wondered whether she had any real affection, even for him.

The doctor was often in and out of the house, to keep an eye on Sir Matthew and Sarah, he said; not forgetting Mrs. Rockwell, he would add, smiling at me.

He made out a little schedule for me. I was not to walk too far, I must give up riding. I must rest whenever I felt so inclined; and take hot milk before going to bed.

One day when I had gone for my morning walk, I was about a mile from the house when I heard the sound of carriage wheels behind me and turning saw the doctor's brougham.

He instructed his man to pull up beside me.

" You've tired yourself," he accused me.

" Indeed I have not. And I am nearly home."

" Please get in," he said. " I'm going to give you a lift back."

I obeyed, protesting that I was not in the least tired. In fact, he looked much more tired than I, and in my somewhat forthright manner I told him so.

" I've been up to Worstwhistle," he said. " That always tires me."

Worstwhistle! The mention of that place saddened me. I thought of those people with their poor clouded minds, shut away from the world. How good he was to give his services to such a place!

" You are very good to go there," I told him.

" My motives are selfish, Mrs. Rockwell," he answered. " These people interest me. Besides they need me. It is a pleasant thing to be needed."

" That is so, but it is good of you all the same. I have

117

heard from others how you comfort them, not only with your medical skill but with your kindness."

"Ha!" He laughed suddenly and his white teeth flashed in his brown face. "I have a great deal to be thankful for. I'll tell you a secret about myself. Forty years ago I was an orphan . . . a penniless orphan. Now it is a sad thing in this world to be an orphan, but to be a penniless orphan, my dear Mrs. Rockwell, that is indeed a tragedy."

"I can well believe it."

"I might have been a beggar . . . standing by the road shivering with cold, driven to frustration by hunger, but life was good to me after all. As I grew up it became the dream of my life to heal the sick. I had no hope of attaining my ambition. But I caught the notice of a rich man and he was good to me. He educated me, he helped me to realise my ambition. But for that rich man, what should I have been? Whenever I see a beggar by the roadside, or a criminal in his prison, I say to myself: There but for the grace of that rich man go I. Then I give myself to my patients. Do you understand me?"

"I do not know . . ." I began.

"And now you think a little less of me because I am not quite a gentleman, eh?"

I turned on him fiercely. "I think you are a very great gentleman," I said.

We had reached the Revels and he murmured: "Then will you do me a favour?"

"If it is in my power."

"Take great care of yourself . . . even greater care."

I was taking tea with Hagar Redvers, and she was talking— as she loved to—of her childhood and how she had ruled the nursery at the Revels, when suddenly that overcrowded room seemed to close in on me and I could no longer breathe. Something happened to me, and I was not quite sure what it was.

The next thing I remembered was that I was lying on the horsehair couch and smelling salts were being thrust beneath my nose.

"What . . . happened?" I asked.

"It's all right, my dear." That was Hagar's authoritative voice. "You fainted."

"Fainted! I . . . But . . ."

"Don't disturb yourself. I think it is a fairly common

occurrence at this stage. Now lie still. I have sent for Jessie Dankwait. I have the utmost confidence in her."

I tried to rise, but those strong old hands sparkling with garnets and diamonds held me down.

" I think, my dear, you walked too far. This journey is becoming too much for you. You must be driven here next time."

She was sitting in the chair beside the sofa. She was saying: " I remember how I fainted when my son was on the way. It is such a horrible feeling, is it not. But it is surprising how, as the time progresses, one becomes accustomed to all the little inconveniences. Do you feel like some refreshment, my dear? I did wonder if a little brandy might be useful. But I think we should wait for Jessie Dankwait."

It could not have been much more than fifteen minutes later when Jessie Dankwait came into the room. I judged her to be in her middle forties; her face was rosy, her expression pleasant; her black bonnet, trimmed with jet beads which danced in rather a jolly fashion as she moved, was tied under her chin with black ribbons; on her gaberdine cloak jet also glistened. Beneath the cloak she wore a black dress and a very clean white starched apron.

I quickly discovered that she was the midwife who lived on the Kelly Grange estate, and as Hagar ruled over that estate like a queen over her kingdom, the midwife behaved as though she were a subject. I subsequently discovered that if any of the mothers were unable to pay her, Hagar paid for them. Jessie also acted as nurse, for she had received a certain amount of training in all branches of nursing.

She prodded me and questioned me and spoke knowledgeably about my condition. She came to the conclusion that everything was as it should be and that what I had experienced was natural enough considering the time of my pregnancy.

She thought that a cup of hot sweet tea was what I needed; and there was nothing to fear.

When she had left, Hagar ordered that a pot of tea should be made, and while I was drinking a cup of it, she said: " You could not do better than engage Jessie when your time comes. I know of none so good in the neighbourhood; that is why I employ her. She has more successful cases than any other midwife I have ever known. If I had been able to employ her for my daughter-in-law she would have been here to-day."

I said I thought it was an excellent idea, for I had been wondering what arrangements I should make.

"Then that's settled," said Hagar. "I shall tell Jessie to hold herself in readiness. It would be an excellent idea if you kept her at the Revels for a week or so beforehand. That is always wise."

It appeared that my affairs were being taken out of my hands, but I did not care. The change in my body seemed to be changing my character. I experienced a certain lassitude as I lay on that horsehair sofa listening to Hagar making plans for my future.

Jessie had not left the house, and when Hagar sent for her, before I left, to tell her that I had decided to use her services, she was delighted.

"Jessie will call on you regularly at the Revels," declared Hagar. "And you must take her advice. Now someone shall drive you back. And when you get there you should rest."

Simon was not at home, so one of the grooms drove me back. Ruth came out in some surprise when she saw how I had returned, and I hastily told her what had happened.

"You'd better go straight up and rest," she said. "I'll have dinner sent up to you."

So I went up and Mary-Jane came to me to make me comfortable; and I let her chatter on about her sister Etty, who some months back had fainted in just the same way.

I looked forward to a leisurely evening, reading in bed.

Mary-Jane brought up my dinner, and when I had eaten it she came back to tell me that Dr. Smith wanted to see me. She decorously buttoned my bed-jacket up to my neck and went out to say that I was ready for the doctor.

He came into my room with Ruth, and they sat near the bed while he asked questions about my faint.

"I understand it's nothing to worry about," I said. "Apparently it's the normal occurrence at this stage. The midwife told me."

"Who?" asked the doctor.

"Jessie Dankwait. Mrs. Redvers has the utmost faith in her. I have engaged her for the great occasion and she will be coming to see me from time to time."

The doctor did not speak for a while. Then he said: "This woman has a very good reputation in the neighbourhood." He leaned towards the bed smiling at me. "But I shall satisfy myself as to whether she is practised enough to take care of you," he added.

They did not stay long and after they had gone I lay back

luxuriously. It was a pleasant feeling to know that all was being taken care of.

It was two weeks later, when my peaceful existence was shattered, and the horror and doubts began.

The day had been a glorious one. Although we were in mid-September, the summer was still with us and only the early twilight brought home the fact that the year was so advanced.

I had passed the day pleasantly. I had been along to the church with Ruth, Luke and Damaris to take flowers to decorate it for the harvest festival; they had not allowed me to do any of the decorating, but had made me sit in one of the pews watching them at work.

I had sat back, rather drowsily content, listening to the hollow sound of their voices as they talked together. Damaris, arranging gold, red and mauve chrysanthemums on the altar, had looked like a figure from the Old Testament, her grace and beauty never more apparent. Luke was helping her—he was never far from her side—and there was Ruth with bunches of grapes and vegetable marrows which she was placing artistically on the sills below the stained-glass windows.

It was an atmosphere of absolute peace—the last I was to know for a long time.

We had tea at the vicarage and walked leisurely home afterwards. When night came I had no premonition that change was near.

I went to bed early as was now my custom. The moon was nearly full and since I would have the curtains drawn back, it flooded my room with soft light, competing with the candles.

I tried afterwards to recall that evening in detail, but I did not know at that stage that I should have taken particular note of it; so looking back it semed like many other evenings.

Of one thing I was certain—that I did not draw the curtains on either side of my bed, because I had always insisted that the curtains should not be drawn. I had told Mary-Jane of this and she bore me out afterwards.

I blew out my candles and got into bed. I lay for some time looking at the windows; in an hour or so I knew that the lop-sided moon would be looking straight in at me. It had awakened me last night when it had shone its light full on my face.

I slept. And . . . suddenly I was awake and in great fear, though for some seconds I did not know why. I was aware of a cold draught. I was lying on my back and my room was full of moonlight. But that was not all that was in my room. Someone was there . . . someone was standing at the foot of my bed watching me.

I think I called out, but I am not sure; I started up and then I felt as though all my limbs were frozen and for several seconds I was as one turned to stone. If ever I had known fear in my life I knew it then.

It was because of what I saw at the foot of my bed . . . something which moved yet was not of this world.

It was a figure in a black cloak and cowl—a monk; over the face was a mask such as those worn by torturers in the chambers of the Inquisition; there were slits in the mask for the eyes to look through, but it was not possible to see those eyes though I believed they watched me intently.

I had never before seen a ghost. I did not believe in ghosts. My practical Yorkshire soul rebelled against such fantasies. I had always said I should have to see to believe. Now I was seeing.

The figure moved as I looked. Then it was gone.

It could be no apparition, for I was not the sort of person to see apparitions. Someone had been in my room. I turned to follow the figure but I could see nothing but a dark wall before my eyes. So dazed was I, so shocked, that it was a second or so before I realised that the curtain on one side of my bed had been drawn so that the door and that part of the room which led to it were shut off from my view.

Still numb with shock and terror I could not move until suddenly I thought I heard the sound of a door quietly closing. That brought me back to reality. Someone had come into my room and gone out by the door; ghosts, I had always heard, had no need to concern themselves with the opening and shutting of doors.

I stumbled out of bed, falling into the curtain which I hastily pushed aside. I hurried to the door, calling: "Who was that? Who was that?"

There was no sign of anyone in the corridor. I ran to the top of the stairs. The moonlight, falling through the windows there, threw shadows all about me. I felt suddenly alone with evil and I was terrified.

I began to shout: ' Come quickly. There is someone in the house."

I heard a door open and shut; then Ruth's voice: "Catherine, is that you?"

"Yes, yes . . . come quickly. . . ."

It seemed a long time before she appeared; then she came down the stairs wrapping a long robe about her, holding a small lamp in her hand.

"What happened?" she cried.

"There was something in my room. It came and stood at the bottom of my bed."

"You have had a nightmare."

"I was awake, I tell you. I was awake. I woke up and saw it. It must have wakened me."

"My dear Catherine, you're shivering. You should get back to bed. In your state . . ."

"It came into my room. It may come again."

"My dear, it was only a bad dream."

I felt frustrated and angry with her. It was the beginning of frustration, and what could be more exasperating than the inability to convince people that you have seen something with your eyes and not with your imagination?

"It was not a dream," I said angrily. "Of one thing I am certain, it was not a dream. There was someone in my room. I did not imagine it."

Somewhere in the house a clock struck one, and almost immediately Luke appeared on the landing above us.

"What's the commotion?" he asked, yawning.

"Catherine has been . . . upset."

"There was someone in my room."

"Burglars?"

"No, I don't think so. It was someone dressed as a monk."

"My dear," said Ruth gently, "you've been going to the Abbey and letting yourself get imaginative there. It's an eerie place. Don't go there again. It obviously upsets you."

"I keep telling you that there was actually someone in my room. This person had drawn the curtain about my bed so that I shouldn't see his departure."

"Drawn the curtain about your bed? I expect Mary-Jane did that."

"She did not. I have told her not to. No, the person who was playing this joke—if it was a joke—drew it."

I saw Ruth and Luke exchange glances, and I knew that they were thinking I was obsessed by the Abbey; clearly I was the victim of one of those vivid nightmares which hang about when one wakes and seem a part of reality.

"It was not a dream," I insisted fervently. "Someone came into my room. Perhaps it was meant to be a joke . . ."

I looked from Ruth to Luke; would either of them play such a stupid trick? Who else could have done it? Sir Matthew? Aunt Sarah? The apparition which had flitted across my room, quietly closing the door after it, must have been agile.

"You should go back to bed," said Ruth. "You should not let a nightmare disturb you."

Go back to bed. Try to sleep. Perhaps to be awakened by that figure at the bottom of my bed! It had merely stood there this time and looked at me. What would it do next? How could I sleep peacefully again in that room?

Luke yawned. Clearly he thought it strange that I should wake them because of a dream.

"Come along," said Ruth gently and, as she slipped her arm through mine, I remembered that I was in my night-dress and presented an unconventional sight to the pair of them.

Luke said: "Good night," and went back to his room, so that I was left alone with Ruth.

"My dear Catherine," she said as she drew me along the corridor, "you really are scared."

"It was . . . horrible. To think of being watched while I was asleep, like that."

"I've had one or two alarming nightmares myself. I know the impression they leave."

"But I keep telling you, I was not asleep."

She did not answer as she threw open the door of my room. The current of air disturbed the drawn bed curtain; and I remembered the draught I had felt, and I was certain then that someone had crept silently into my room, and drawn the curtain along one side of the bed before taking a stand there at the foot of it.

All human actions. Some person in this house had done this to me.

Why should this person wish to frighten me, knowing of my condition?

"You see," I said, "the curtain is drawn at the side of the bed. It was not like that when I went to sleep."

"Mary-Jane must have done it."

"Why should she come back after I had said good night to her, to draw a curtain which I had expressly asked should not be drawn?"

Ruth lifted her shoulders.

"Lie down," she said. "Why, you are cold. You should have put something on."

"There wasn't time. I didn't think of it in any case. I was after . . . whoever it was. I thought I might catch a glimpse of the way it went. But when I came out there was nothing . . . nothing. I wonder if . . . it's still here . . . watching . . . listening . . ."

"Come, lie down. It can't be here because it was part of your dream."

"But I know when I am awake and when I'm asleep."

"I'm going to light your candles. You'll feel better then."

"The moon is so bright. I do not need candles."

"Perhaps it is better not to light them. I'm always afraid of fire."

She drew back the bed curtains and sat by the side of the bed.

"You will be cold," I said.

"I don't like to leave you while you are so disturbed," she replied.

I was ashamed to ask her to stay, and yet I felt afraid. But I was so convinced that what I had seen was no apparition that I was certain, if I locked my door on the inside, it could not come again to my room.

"I'm all right," I said. "I don't need company."

She rose smiling. "It is not like you to be afraid of dreams."

"Oh dear! Why can't you believe me? I *know* it was not a dream," I told her. "Someone is playing a trick on me."

"A dangerous trick . . . on a woman in your condition."

"It is someone who gives no thought to my danger."

She lifted her shoulders and the gesture was disbelieving.

"I am sorry to have disturbed you like this," I said. "Please go back to your room."

"If you are sure . . ."

I got out of bed and reached for my dressing-gown.

"Where are you going?" she asked.

"To lock the door when you have gone. If I lock that and the one which leads to the powder-room, and the door of the powder-room which opens on to the corridor. I shall feel safe."

"If you can only feel safe like that you must, but, Catherine, who in this place would do such a thing? You must have been dreaming."

125

" So I could believe," I said, " but for the fact that I felt the draught from the door and heard it shut, and the apparition had had the foresight to draw that curtain on one side of my bed. I should think apparitions are rarely so practical."

I was losing a little of my fear. It was strange that a human enemy was much less alarming than a supernatural one.

I had not then begun to ask myself the all-important question: Why?

" Well, I will say good night," Ruth said. " If you are sure . . ."

" I am all right now."

" Good night, Catherine. If you should have any more . . . alarms, remember I am not very far away . . . only on the next floor. And Luke is near too."

" I'll remember."

When she had gone I locked the door after her and made sure the door of the powder-room which opened on to the corridor was also locked on the inside.

I went back to bed, but not to sleep. I should not be able to sleep until daylight.

I turned the question over and over in my mind. Who had done this, and why? It was no ordinary practical joke. The person who had done this had meant to terrify me. I was not the sort of woman to be easily terrified, but the most strong-minded must be upset by seeing such a vision at the foot of their bed. And I was a woman, known to be pregnant.

I felt the menace then. Someone was plotting evil. It might be only indirectly aimed at me because of the precious burden I carried.

One prospective master of the Revels had died violently ; was something being plotted against another?

That was the beginning of my period of terror.

Chapter 5

I awoke soon after six o'clock the next morning, rose and unlocked my door ; then I returned to bed and fell asleep to be awakened by Mary-Jane at my bedside with a breakfast-tray.

" Mrs. Grantley said you should have a rest this morning," she told me.

I started out of a deep sleep, remembering the horror of the previous night; I must have stared at Mary-Jane for she looked slightly alarmed. In those first moments of waking I had half expected her to turn into a black-clad apparition.

"Oh . . . thank you, Mary-Jane," I stammered.

She propped me up with pillows and helped me on with my bed-jacket. Then she placed the tray on my knees.

"Is there anything else, madam?"

She was unlike herself, almost anxious to get out of the room. As she went I thought: Good heavens, has she heard already!

I sat up, sipping my tea. I could not eat. The whole thing had come back to me vividly in all its horror; I found that my eyes kept straying to the foot of my bed.

Realising it was no use trying to eat, I put aside the breakfast-tray and lay back thinking about last night, trying to assure myself that I had imagined it all. The draught . . . the bed curtain. . . . Had I walked in my sleep? Had I opened the door? Had I myself drawn the bed curtain? "Gabriel," I murmured, "did *you* walk in your sleep?"

I was trembling, so I hastily pulled myself together.

There was a logical explanation of my horrific adventure. There was always a logical explanation, and I had to find it.

I got out of bed and rang for hot water. Mary-Jane brought it and set it in the powder-room. I did not speak to her in my usual friendly way. My mind was too full of what had happened on the previous night and I did not want to talk about that with her . . . or anyone . . . just yet.

While I was finishing dressing there was a knock on my door and when I called, "Come in," Ruth entered. She said: "Good morning, Catherine," and looked at me anxiously. "How are you feeling this morning?"

"A little weary."

"Yes, you look it. It *was* a disturbed night."

"For you too, I'm afraid. I'm sorry I made such a fuss."

"It doesn't matter. You were really scared. I'm glad you did waken me . . . if it helped at all."

"Yes, it did help. I had to talk to somebody . . . real."

"The best thing we can do is to try to forget it. I know how that sort of thing can hang about, though. I think Deverel Smith ought to give you something to make you sleep to-night. You'll feel all the better for a good night's sleep."

I was not going to argue with her any more, because I could see it was useless. She had made up her mind that I had been the victim of a nightmare, and nothing would change it.

I said: "Thanks so much for sending up my breakfast."

She grimaced. "I saw Mary-Jane taking the tray away. You didn't eat much of it."

"I had several cups of tea."

"You have to take care, remember. What do you plan to do this morning?"

"Perhaps a little walk."

"Well, I shouldn't go too far and . . . don't mind my saying this, Catherine. . . . I should keep away from the Abbey for a while."

A faint smile curved her lips; it might have been apologetic. I was not sure, for Ruth only seemed to smile with her lips.

She left me and I went downstairs on my way out. I felt I wanted to get away from the house. I wished that I could ride out on to the moors, but I had given up riding and had curtailed my walking considerably.

As I came down to the hall Luke was coming in. He was in riding kit and looked surprisingly like Gabriel so that for a moment as he stood in shadow I could believe he was Gabriel. I gave a little gasp—my nerves had certainly been affected by what had happened and I seemed to be expecting to see strange things.

"Hallo," he said. "Seen any more hobgoblins?"

He grinned and his careless unconcern gave me a twinge of alarm.

I tried to speak lightly. "Once was enough."

"A hooded monk!" he murmured. "Poor Catherine, you were in a state."

"I'm sorry I disturbed you."

"Don't be sorry. Any time you need assistance, call me. I've never been attracted to monks anyway. All that fasting, hairshirts, ceilbacy and so on. . . . Seems to me so unnecessary. I like good food, fine linen and beautiful women. There's nothing of the monk about me. So if you want any help in tackling them, I'm your man."

He was mocking me, and I had come to the conclusion that the best way to treat the affair was lightly. My own opinions would not change, but it was no use trying to force them on others.

He and his mother were persisting in the belief that I had experienced a particularly terrifying nightmare. I would not seek to change that opinion. But nevertheless I was going to find out who in this house had played such a cruel trick on me.

"Thank you," I said, trying to speak as lightly as he had. "I'll remember that."

"It's a pleasant morning," he said. "A pity you can't ride. There's just that nip of autumn in the air to make riding a pleasure. However, perhaps before long . . ."

"I'll manage without," I told him; and as I passed him his smile was enigmatic and I had a feeling that he was picturing me as I had looked in my dishabille the night before. I remembered then that Hagar Redvers had said he was like his grandfather, and Sir Matthew had an eye for women.

I passed out into the open air. It was wonderful what fresh air could do. My fear evaporated and as I walked among the beds of chrysanthemums and Michaelmas daisies I felt capable of tackling any menace that might present itself.

If you believe that was a human being playing a trick, I told myself, all you have to do is search your room and the powder-room before retiring and lock doors and windows. Then if you are disturbed by apparitions you will know that they are of the supernatural class.

This was a test of my belief. It was, I reminded myself, all very well to be brave on a fresh bright morning like this, but how should I feel when darkness fell?

I was determined to test myself, to prove that I really did believe that some human being had played that trick on me.

I returned to the house for luncheon, which I took with Ruth and Luke. Luke made a reference to my "nightmare" and I made no contradiction of the term. That lunch was very like others; I fancy Ruth seemed relieved. She said I looked better for my walk, and it was true that I did eat well for I found I was hungry after having had no breakfast.

When I rose from the luncheon table William came into the dining-room with a message from Sir Matthew. He would like to see me if I could spare the time to visit him.

I said I would go at once if he was ready.

"I will take you to his room, madam," William told me.

He led me up the staircase to a room on the first floor which was not far from my own. I was beginning to learn where the family had their apartments. They lived mainly in the south wing: Sir Matthew on the first floor, where I now had my room, Ruth and Luke on the second; and the third, of course, was where I had lived with Gabriel during the short time we had been together in the house. Sarah was the only member of the family who occupied rooms other than in the south wing. She clung to the east wing where the nurseries were. The rest of the house was not being used at this time, but I was told that in the past Sir Matthew had entertained lavishly and that the Revels had often been filled with guests.

The kitchens, bakehouses and sculleries were on the ground floor and an extension of the south wing. The servants' sleeping quarters were on the top floor of the west wing. I had not seen them but Mary-Jane had told me this. So few people in such a large house!

I found Sir Matthew sitting up in bed, a woollen bed-jacket buttoned up to his neck and a nightcap on his head. His eyes twinkled as I came towards him.

" Bring a chair for Mrs. Gabriel, William," he said.

I thanked William and sat down.

" I hear you had a disturbed night, my dear," he said. " Nightmare, Ruth tells me."

" It's over now," I said.

" Frightening things, nightmares. And you ran out of your room on your bare feet." He shook his head.

William was hovering in the next room which, I presumed, was a dressing-room. The door was open and he would hear all that was said. I had a vision of the servants discussing the night's disturbance, and I wished to change the subject.

" And how are you to-day?"

" All the better for seeing you, my dear. But I'm a sad subject. I'm old and the body gets worn out in time. Now you are young, and we cannot have you upset. . . ."

" I shall not be scared in future," I said quickly. " It was the first time anything like it had happened. . . ."

" You have to take care now, Catherine, my dear."

" Oh, yes, I'm taking care."

" I heard nothing of all this."

" I'm so pleased. I should hate to think I had disturbed you too."

" I don't sleep well but when I do it's like the sleep of the dead. You'd have to shout somewhat loudly to awaken me. I'm glad I've seen you, my dear. I wanted to satisfy myself that you were your bright and beautiful self again." He smiled jauntily. " It was only for that reason that I asked you to come and see me in this state. What do you think of me, eh . . . poor old fellow in a nightcap!"

" It's quite becoming."

130

" Catherine, you are a flatterer. Well, my dear, remember you are a very important member of the family now."

" I do remember," I said. " I shall do nothing that would be harmful to the child."

" I like your outspoken ways, my dear. God bless you; and thank you for coming and saying a few kind words to an old man."

He took my hand and kissed it, and as I went out I was still aware of William in the dressing-room.

The whole house knows, I thought; and I wondered why Aunt Sarah had not been to see me. I should have thought she would have wanted to talk about the affair.

I went to my room but I could not settle there, and I thought of the servants' talking together; and it occurred to me that the story would soon reach the ears of Hagar and Simon Redvers. I felt disturbed at the idea of their hearing a version other than my own. I cared very much for the good opinion of Hagar and I believed that she would be very scornful of anything fanciful.

I decided then that I would go and see her and tell her exactly what had happened, before her opinions were coloured by other people's views.

I set out and walked over to Kelly Grange; it was three o'clock when I arrived.

Dawson took me into a small room on the ground floor and said she would tell Mrs. Rockwell-Redvers that I was there.

" If she is resting," I said, " please do not disturb her. I can wait awhile."

" I will inquire, madam," Dawson replied.

In a few minutes she returned with the message that Mrs Rockwell-Redvers would see me at once.

She was sitting in her high-backed chair as she had been on the occasion when I had first seen her. I took her hand and kissed it as I had seen Simon do—that was a concession to our friendship. I was no longer afraid that she would treat me with haughtiness. We now accepted each other as equals, and that meant that we could be quite natural together.

" It is good of you to call," she said. " Did you walk?"

" It is such a short distance really."

" You don't look as well as you did when I last saw you."

" I did not sleep very well."

" That is bad. Have you seen Jessie Dankwait?"

"This has nothing to do with Jessie Dankwait. I wanted to tell you about it before you heard it from another quarter. I wanted you to hear my version."

"You are over-excited," she said coolly.

"Perhaps. But I am calmer than I have been since it happened."

"I want very much to hear about it. Please tell me."

So I told her what had occurred, omitting nothing.

She listened. Then she nodded almost judicially.

"It is quite clear," she said, "that someone in the house is trying to alarm you."

"It seems such a foolish thing to do."

"I would not call a thing foolish if there is a reasonable motive behind it."

"But what motive?"

"To scare you. Perhaps to ruin your hopes of producing a child."

"This seems a strange way to go about it. And who . . ."

"It may be the beginning of a series of alarms. I think we must be on our guard against that."

There was a tap on the door. "Come in," she called and Simon entered.

"Dawson told me that Mrs. Catherine was here," he said. "Have you any objection to my joining you?"

"I have none," said his grandmother. "Have you, Catherine?"

"But . . . no."

"You don't sound very sure," he said, smiling at me.

"It is because we were discussing something which Catherine came here to tell me. I have no idea whether she would wish you to bear it."

I looked at him—and I thought I had never seen anyone so vital, so much a part of the present time. He radiated practical common sense. I decided that I wanted him to hear my version of the affair before anyone else's.

"I have no objection of his hearing what has happened."

"Then we'll tell him," said Hagar and proceeded to do so. It was a considerable comfort that she told him the story as I had told it to her. Never once did she say, "Catherine thinks she saw," or "Catherine believed it was," but always Catherine saw and it was. How grateful I was for that.

He listened intently.

"What do you think of it?" Hagar asked when she had finished.

"Someone in the house is playing tricks," he said.

"Exactly," cried Hagar. "And why so?"

"I imagine it could concern the heir who will in due course make his appearance."

Hagar gave me a triumphant look.

"It was a terrifying experience for poor Catherine," she said.

"Why did you not make an attempt to catch the trickster?" asked Simon.

"I did," I retorted indignantly. "But by the time I had recovered myself he had gone."

"You are calling it 'he.' You have some reason to believe the creature is of the masculine gender?"

"I don't know. But one must call it something. *He* comes more naturally than *she*. He was very quick; he must have been out of the door and along the corridor in a very short time, and then . . ."

"And then where did he go?"

"I don't know. If he had gone downstairs I must have seen him. He could never have run down the stairs and across the hall in time. I can't imagine how he went along the corridor so swiftly."

"He must have gone into one of the rooms there. Did you look?"

"No."

"You should have done."

"Ruth appeared then."

"And Luke came later," said Hagar significantly.

"Did Luke appear to have been rushing about?"

"You suspect Luke?" I asked.

"I merely wonder. It must have been someone in the house, I suppose. If the idea was to frighten you, it must have been either Ruth, Luke, Matthew or Sarah. Did you see them all?"

"Not Matthew, nor Sarah."

"Ah!"

"I cannot imagine either of them running about the house in the night dressed up as a monk."

Simon leaned towards me. He said: "The Rockwell family are all a little crazy about their traditions." He smiled at Hagar. "Everyone," he added. "I wouldn't trust any one of them where the old Revels is concerned, and that's a fact. They're living in the past half of the time. Who could help it in that old fortress? It's not a house. It's a mausoleum.

Anyone who lives there for any length of time is likely to get strange ideas."

" And you think I have!"

" Not you. You're not a Rockwell simply because you married one. You're a forthright Yorkshire woman who'll blow a blast of common sense into the stuffy old place. You know what happens to the dead when they are exposed to fresh air, don't you? They moulder and crumble away."

" I'm glad you don't think I imagined all this, because that is what they are all trying to pretend I did. They call it a nightmare."

" Naturally the trickster would want that put about."

" I shall pretend for him next time."

" He won't play the same game twice. You can be sure of that."

" He won't get an opportunity to. I intend to lock my doors to-night."

" But he may try something else," warned Simon.

" I'm ready for tea," said Hagar. " Ring for Dawson, and the three of us will have it together. Then, Simon, you must drive Catherine back to the Revels. She walked one way, and there and back is too far."

The tea was brought and once again I presided over the teacups.

I was feeling almost normal now ; the comfort I drew from these two astonished and delighted me. They believed in me ; they refused to treat me as a hysterical subject ; and that was wonderful.

I wanted that tea-time hour to go on and on.

Hagar said as she stirred her tea : " I remember once Matthew played a trick on me. Strangely enough he came into *my* bedroom. Really, it must have been something like your affair. I had my curtains drawn about the bed. It was mid-winter, I remember. . . . Christmas-time. The snow was deep outside and the east wind was driving a blizzard. We had a few people in the house . . . those who had arrived before the bad weather started. We thought they would have to stay with us well beyond the Christmas holidays unless there was a thaw. We children had been allowed to watch the ball from the minstrels' gallery. It was a wonderful sight . . . the dresses and the decorations. Well, that wasn't the point. We children had had too much plum pudding, I dare say, because we grew rather quarrelsome . . . at least Matthew and I did. Poor Sarah never joined in our quarrels.

"To get to the point, I had been discussing our ancestors and Matthew was wishing that he could wear those wonderful plumed hats and lace collars as they did in the days of the Cavaliers. I said: 'Like Sir John! Don't say you want to be like him in the least little bit.' 'But I do want to be exactly like Sir John,' Matthew said. 'I hate Sir John,' I cried. 'I *like* Sir John,' he answered. Then he twisted my arm and I made his nose bleed. I shouted that Sir John was a coward."

She laughed and her eyes sparkled at the memory. "You see, Catherine, Sir John was the master of Kirkland Revels at the time of the Civil War. Marston Moor had gone to Cromwell and Fairfax, and Prince Rupert was on the run. Sir John was naturally a Royalist and he went on declaring he'd hold the Revels against Cromwell or die in the attempt. Never should the Revels pass out of the Rockwells' hands. But when the Parliamentarians came into Kirkland Moorside he disappeared . . . he and everyone in the house. Just imagine the soldiers coming into the Revels. They would have hanged him on one of his own oaks if they had found him. But he just disappeared. It's been one of the mysteries of our house . . . how he and his household managed to disappear at the moment the Roundheads entered Kirkland Moorside. They took away all the valuables with them too. They were brought back after the Restoration. But I told Matthew that John was a coward because he did not stay and fight but walked out and calmly handed over the Revels to the enemy. Matthew didn't agree with me. Anything would have done to quarrel about on that day. Sir John happened to be the cause."

She stirred her tea thoughtfully and the haughtiness left her face as she looked back into the past.

Then she went on: "And so Matthew decided to play a practical joke with me as his victim. I was awakened to see the curtains of my bed divided, and there was a face drawn into a hideous scowl under a plumed hat. A voice hissed: 'So you are the one who dared call me a coward! You will regret that, Hagar Rockwell. I am Sir John and I've come to haunt you.' I was startled out of my sleep and for a few seconds I really did think my careless words had brought our ancestor from the tomb. Then I recognised Matthew's voice and I saw his hand clutching a candle. I leaped out of bed and grabbed the hat. I rammed it down on his head, boxed his ears, and threw him out of my room."

She laughed again ; then she looked at me apologetically. "It reminded me, although it was really so different."

"Where did he find the plumed hat?" I asked.

"There are lots of clothes put away in chests in the house. It was probably right out of period. I remember we were both put on bread and water and confined to our rooms for a day for disturbing our governess."

"The difference is that you caught your intruder," said Simon. "I wish we could discover who this monk really is."

"At least," I put in, "I shall be on my guard for the future."

Simon changed the subject and I found myself talking of the affairs of the neighbourhood: The home farm which was attached to the Grange and which he managed, and the smaller homesteads on the estate of which he would one day be the landlord. It was clear that he and Hagar felt deeply about the Kelly Grange estate, but in a different way from that worship of a house which I imagined obtained at the Revels. I had never heard the Rockwells discuss their tenants in the same way, and I was sure that Sir Matthew would not greatly care whether a man had been hurt when ploughing or that his wife was expecting a child again.

Hagar might look back on the traditions of the past but she had her keen eyes on the present. She might long to be mistress of the Revels and for Simon to be its master, but that did not mean she was indifferent to the Kelly Grange estate. Far from it. I believed that she would have liked to unite the two.

As for Simon he was so much the practical man; a house would never mean more to him than the stones of which it was built; the tradition in his opinion, I was sure, should be made to serve man, not man tradition.

There was so much about him that angered me, for I could never forget his hinting that I was a fortune-hunter, but on that day I needed his clear cold common sense, and I was grateful for it.

So those two gave me the strength and courage I badly needed. I knew that when I was alone in my room that night I should remember them and their belief in me, and it would help me to believe in myself.

He drove me back at five o'clock and, as I heard him drive off and turned to go into the house in which the first shadows of evening were beginning to fall, I felt my courage begin to ebb.

But I kept thinking of those two and as I mounted the stairs to my room I did not once look over my shoulder to see if I was being followed, although I wanted to.

Matthew, Luke and Ruth seemed to watch me rather furtively through dinner; as for Sarah, she had made no mention of the affair, which surprised me. I managed to appear quite normal.

After dinner Dr. Smith and Damaris called to take wine with us. I was sure that Ruth had sent for him, telling him what had happened, for when Damaris and Luke were whispering together, Ruth drew Sir Matthew aside—Aunt Sarah had already retired—and the doctor said to me: "I hear there was a little trouble last night."

"It was nothing," I said quickly.

"Ah, you have recovered from it," he said. "Mrs. Grantley thought she ought to tell me. I have made her promise, you know, to keep an eye on you."

"There was no need to tell you this."

"A nightmare, was it? That was what Mrs. Grantley called it."

"If it had been merely a nightmare I should not have left my room and awakened others. In my opinion it was not a nightmare."

He glanced at the rest of the company and whispered: "Could you tell me all about it?"

So once more that day I told the story.

He listened gravely, but made no comment.

"You may not sleep very well to-night," he said.

"I think I shall."

"Ah, you are a young lady of such sound good sense."

"I propose to lock my doors so that there is no possibility of the joker's coming into my room. Then I shall feel perfectly safe."

"Wouldn't you like a sleeping draught?"

"It will not be necessary."

"Take it in case. You don't want two bad nights running. I've got it here with me."

"It's unnecessary."

"There's no harm in having it at hand. Put it by your bed. Then if you can't sleep . . . take it and in ten minutes you'll be in a deep and restful sleep."

I took the small bottle and slipped it into the pocket of my gown.

"Thank you," I said.

"You needn't fear," he told me with a smile. "You won't become an addict after one dose, believe me. And I want you to have good nights . . . plenty of rest and good plain

137

food. So don't think you're being brave by refusing to take the draught. Think of the rest and relaxation you need . . . for the little one."

"You are very attentive, Dr. Smith."

"I am very anxious to look after you."

So when I retired that night I put the sleeping draught by my bed as I had promised. Then I searched my room and locked the doors. I went to bed; but I did not sleep as readily as I had believed I should. I would doze and start out of my sleep, my gaze going immediately to the foot of my bed.

I was by no means a hysterical subject, but I had received a violent shock and even the calmest of people cannot expect to recover immediately.

One of the clocks in the house was striking midnight when I took Dr. Smith's draught. Almost immediately I sank into a deep restful sleep.

Within a few days I had completely recovered from my shock, but I was still watchful. Nothing else of a similar nature had happened, but each night I locked my doors and was now sleeping normally without those distressing sudden awakenings to stare about the room, looking for an apparition.

The household had ceased to refer to the incident, and I guessed that in the servants' hall they had decided that it was one of the queer things which happen to women who are expecting a child.

But I was no less determined to discover who had been disguised as the monk and, as I brooded on it one morning, I remembered that Hagar had said there had been clothes of all kinds in various chests about the house. What if in one of the chests there was a monk's robe? If I could find such a thing I should be on my way to solving the mystery.

There was one person who might be helpful in this respect. That was Sarah—and I decided to go along and see her.

It was after luncheon, at which she did not appear, when I made my way to her apartments in the east wing.

I knocked at the door of her tapestry room, and I was pleased when she called to me to come in.

She was delighted that I should come to see her without being asked.

"Ah," she cried, creeping round me and standing with her back to the door as she had the first time I had come here, "you've come to see my tapestry."

"And *you*," I answered.

138

That pleased her. "It's coming along nicely," she said, leading the way to the window-seat on which was the blue satin coverlet she was making for the cradle. "Nearly finished," she said, spreading it out for me to see.

"It's exquisite."

"I was afraid," she said.

"Afraid?"

"If you'd died it would have been such a waste of time."

I looked astonished, and she said: "You were in your bare feet. You might have caught your death."

"So you heard about it?" I said.

"I've used such a lot of my blue silks."

"What did you think about . . . my fright?"

"All that work would have been in vain."

"Who told you about it?"

"But it would have done for some other baby. There are always babies." Her eyes widened and she went on: "Perhaps Luke's. I wonder if Luke will have *good* babies?"

"Please don't talk about my child as though it will never be born," I said sharply.

She recoiled as though I had struck her.

"It made you angry," she said. "People are angry when they are frightened."

"I'm not frightened."

"Are you angry?"

"When you talk like that about my baby."

"Then you're frightened, because angry people are really frightened people."

I changed the subject. "The coverlet is lovely. My baby will like it."

She smiled, well pleased.

"I went to see your sister a few days ago. She told me about a Christmas-time when Matthew dressed up."

She put her hand to her mouth and began to laugh. "They quarrelled so," she said. "She made his nose bleed. It went all over his jacket. Our governess was cross. They had nothing but bread and water for a whole day. He'd dressed up, you see . . . to frighten her. . . ." She looked at me, her brows puckered; I could see that she was struck by the similarity of the incidents. "What are you going to do, Hagar? What are you going to do about . . . the monk?"

I did not remind her that I was Catherine. Instead I said: "I want to see if I can find the clothes."

"I know where the hat is," she said. "I was there when he found it."

"Do you know where the monk's robe is?"

She turned to me, startled. "Monk's robe? I never saw it. There is no monk's robe. Matthew found the hat and he said he was going to frighten her when she was asleep. It was a hat with such a lovely feather. It's still in the chest."

"Where is the chest?"

"You know, Hagar. In that little room near the schoolroom."

"Let us go and look at it."

"Are you going to dress up and frighten Matthew?"

"I'm not going to dress up. I merely want to see the clothes."

"All right, she said. "Come on."

So she led the way. We went through the schoolroom and past the nurseries till we came to a door at the end of a corridor. She threw this open. There was a smell of age as though the place had not been ventilated for years. I saw several large chests, some pictures stacked against the walls, and odd pieces of furniture.

"Mother changed the Revels when she came here," mused Sarah. "She said we were overcrowded with furniture. She put some here . . . and some in other places. . . . It's been here ever since."

"Let us look at the clothes."

I saw that there was a film of dust on everything, and I looked intently about me, for if anyone had been at these chests recently would they not have left some mark in the dust?

I saw an imprint on the top of a chest which was Sarah's, and she was now ruefully looking at her hands.

"The dust," she said. "No one's been in here for a very long time. Perhaps not since we were children."

It was not easy to lift the lid, as the thing was not only heavy but stiff ; but we managed between us.

I looked down at the garments which were there. Gowns, shoes, cloaks, and there was the hat itself on which Sarah seized with a cry of triumph.

She put it on her head and she looked as though she had stepped right out of the picture gallery.

"Hagar must have had a fright," I said.

"Hagar wouldn't be frightened long." She was looking at me intently. "Some people are not frightened for long.

For a while they are and then . . . they stop being frightened. You are like that, Hagar."

I was suddenly conscious of the stuffiness of the attic, of the strangeness of the woman who stood before me, whose childlike blue eyes could be so vague and yet so penetrating.

She had bent over the chest and brought out a silk pelisse which she wrapped around her. The hat was still on her head.

"Now," she said, "I feel I am not myself. I am someone else . . . someone who lived in this house long long ago. When you wear other people's clothes perhaps you become like them. This is a man's hat though and a woman's pelisse." She began to laugh. "I wonder, if I put on the monk's robe, whether I should feel like a monk."

"Aunt Sarah," I said, "where *is* the monk's robe?"

She paused as though thinking deeply and for a moment I thought I was on the road to discovery. Then she said: "It is on the monk who came to your bedroom, Catherine. That's where the monk's robe is."

I began taking clothes from the chest, and as I could not find the robe I gave my attention to the smaller trunks and ransacked them. When I could not find what I sought I felt deflated. I turned to Sarah, who was watching me earnestly.

"There are other chests in the house," she said.

"Where?"

She shook her head. "I hardly ever leave my part of the house."

I felt the faintness coming over me again; the room was so airless, so confined; it smelt of dust and age.

What did Sarah know? I asked myself. Sometimes she seemed so simple, at others so knowledgeable.

Did she know who had come to my room in the guise of a monk? I wondered if it had been Sarah herself.

As this feeling became stronger I wanted to get away, back to my own room. I wondered what would happen to me if I fainted in this room among all these musty relics of the past, as I had in Hagar's house.

"I must go now," I said. "It has been interesting."

She held out her hand to me as though I were an acquaintance who had made a formal call.

"Do come again," she said.

Gabriel and Friday were constantly in my thoughts. I was still hoping that one day Friday would come back to me.

I simply could not bear to think that he was dead. But there was one matter which surprised me; although I remembered so vividly the occasion of my meeting with Gabriel, I had to concentrate to remember exactly what he looked like. I reproached myself for this because in some ways it seemed disloyal; and yet, deep in my secret thoughts, I knew that although we had been husband and wife, Gabriel and I had been almost strangers in some respects. Each day some revealing action had betrayed to me the fact that I had a great deal to learn about him. I told myself that this was due to an innate reticence in his nature. But was this so? I had been fond of Gabriel; I had missed him deeply; but what did I miss? Was it a friend rather than a lover?

Now I carried Gabriel's child and I believed that when I held my baby in my arms I should be happy. Already I loved my child and the force of my emotion was teaching me that the feeling I had had for Gabriel was shallow compared with this new love. I longed for the spring as I never had before because, with the coming of spring, my baby would be born. But there were many dark days between me and that happy time.

The weather had set in damp and, even when the rain ceased, the mist was with us. It crept into the house like a grey ghost, and shut out the view from the windows. I liked to walk whenever possible, and I did not mind the rain for it was not cold yet and was that gentle damp which came from the south and which put a soft bloom on the skin. I felt very well, only impatient of the dragging of time.

I was delighted when I noticed for the first time the lines of green in the brown fields on the Kelly Grange land. The young wheat was pushing through the earth: the promise of a new year and a reminder that spring was on its way. My baby was due to be born in March and this was November. Four more months to wait.

I had been over to Kelly Grange to see Hagar, and Simon had driven me back. We no longer talked of the monk incident, but I had not ceased to be watchful; and there were occasions when I woke in the night startled from some vague dream and hastily lighted a candle to make sure that I was alone in my room.

My feelings towards Simon were undergoing a change and this was the result of my friendship with his grandmother. Hagar always welcomed me and if she did not say how pleased she was to see me—she was after all a Yorkshire woman and therefore not given to demonstrations of affection—I was certainly made aware of her pleasure in my company. And when I was with her the conversation invariably turned to Simon. I was reminded again and again of his many virtues. I believed I understood him; he was blunt even to the extent of tactlessness; there was a hardness in his nature which I imagined no one but his grandmother had ever penetrated; but he radiated practical common sense; he liked undertaking difficult tasks, which most people would find impossible, and proving that they weren't—all part of the arrogance, of course, but admirable in its way. He was not uninterested in women. Hagar hinted at certain entanglements. Not that he had suggested marriage with any of these women. Hagar saw nothing immoral in this: a liaison would not have been nearly as shocking to her as a *mésalliance*.

"He has far too much sense for that!" she said. "When he marries he'll marry the right woman. He'll see to that."

"Let us hope," I retorted, "that she whom he considers right will be able to apply the same adjective to him."

Hagar looked startled. I think it astonished her that anyone should not see this grandson of hers as she did. Which showed, I told myself at the time, that even the most sensible people had their weaknesses. Hagar's was undoubtedly her grandson. I wondered what his was. Or if he had any at all.

Still, I should always be grateful to him for believing my version of what I saw in my bedroom that night, and I was less cool with him than I had been before that happened.

I said good-bye to him and went straight up to my room.

It was late afternoon and in half an hour or so the darkness would descend upon us. There were shadows on the stairs and in my room, as I opened the door I felt that horrible sense of evil which I had experienced when I opened my eyes and saw the monk.

This was perhaps a slight matter to arouse my feelings, but it was reminiscent: the curtains were drawn about my bed.

I walked straight to them and drew them back. I was half expecting to see the monk there, but of course there was nothing.

I looked hastily round the room and went into the powder-closet. There was no one there.

I rang the bell and very soon Mary-Jane appeared.

"Why did you pull the curtains about my bed?" I demanded.

Mary-Jane stared at the bed. "But . . . madam . . . I didn't . . ."

"Who else would have done that?"

"But, madam, the curtains are *not* drawn about your bed."

"What are you suggesting? That I imagined they were? I have just drawn them back."

I looked at her fiercely and she recoiled from me.

"I . . . I did now't to 'em. You've always said that you didn't want them drawn. . . ."

"Who else would have been here?" I asked.

"No one else, madam. I always do your room myself as Mrs. Grantley said I should."

"You must have drawn them," I said. "How otherwise could they have been drawn?"

She backed away from me. "But I didn't, madam. I didn't touch them."

"You've forgotten. You must have forgotten."

"No, madam, I'm sure I didn't."

"You did," I answered unreasonably. "You may go now."

She went, her face stricken. The relationship between us had always before been so pleasant, and it was unlike me to behave as I had done.

When she had gone I stood staring at the door and Sarah's words came back to me. "You're angry because you're frightened."

Yes, that was it. The sight of the drawn curtains had frightened me. Why? What was so strange about drawn curtains?

The answer to that was simple. It was because I had been reminded of that other terrifying occasion.

After all anyone might have drawn the curtains . . . to shake out the dust, say . . . and then forgotten them and left them drawn. Why could not Mary-Jane have admitted to that?

Simply because that had not been the case. Mary-Jane had not drawn the curtains. She would have remembered if she had, because I had always insisted that I would not have them drawn about the bed while I slept.

I was trembling slightly. I was thinking of it all again, that sudden waking in the night . . . that awful apparition and then turning to pursue, only to be faced by a wall of blue silk. It had reminded me, that was all, and it had frightened me. But I was already asking myself whether it was possible that I was not forgotten, that the weeks of peace were now over and new terrors were being devised for me.

I had been angry because I was afraid; but I had no right to turn that anger against Mary-Jane.

I felt very contrite and went at once to the bell. Mary-Jane came immediately in answer to my summons, but her bright smile was missing and she did not meet my eye.

"Mary-Jane," I said, "I'm sorry."

She looked at me in surprise.

"I had no right to say what I did. If you had drawn the curtains you would have said so. I'm afraid I was over-wrought."

She looked expectant and still bewildered. Then she said: "Oh . . . madam, it's of no account."

"It is, Mary-Jane," I insisted. "It was unjust, and I hate injustice. Go and bring the candles. It's growing dark."

"Yes, madam." She went out of the room happier than when she had left it a few minutes before.

By the time she came back with the candles I decided to be frank with her. I was anxious that she should not think that I was the sort of woman who vented her anger on other people when she was suffering from some personal irritation. I wanted her to know the reason.

"Put them over the fireplace, and on the dressing-table. That's much brighter. The room looks different already. Mary-Jane . . . when I saw those bed curtains drawn I was reminded of that occasion. . . ."

"I remember, madam."

"And I thought someone was playing another trick. So I wanted it to have been you who drew them. That would have been such a comforting explanation."

"But it wasn't, madam, I couldn't say it was if it was'nt."

"Of course you couldn't. So I'm left wondering who did it . . . and why."

"Anyone could have come in, madam. You don't lock the doors during the day."

"No, anybody could have done it. But . . . perhaps it's not important. Perhaps I'm too sensitive. It may be due to my condition."

"Our Etty isn't quite like she used to be, madam."

"I believe women are often so."

"Yes. She used to like to hear Jim sing. He's got quite a voice, Jim has. But now she can't abide it; she can't bear what she calls noise of any sort."

"Well, that's how we are, Mary-Jane. It's as well to be prepared for our strangeness. I've a dress here which I thought might do for you. I can't get into it any more."

I brought out a dark green gabardine dress trimmed with red and green tartan, and Mary-Jane's eyes glistened at the sight of it.

"Why, madam, it's grand. And it's sure to fit."

"Then take it, Mary-Jane. I'd like you to have it."

"Oh, thank you, madam."

She was a gentle creature. I believe she was as pleased that the pleasantness of our relationship had been restored as she was to have the dress.

When she had gone I felt that some of her pleasure remained behind her. I caught a glimpse of my reflection in the looking-glass. I looked young, and my green eyes were brilliant. Candlelight is always so flattering.

But even as I looked I found I was peering beyond my own reflection; I was trying to probe the shadows in the room. I was expecting some shape to materialise behind me.

Fear had come back.

That night I slept badly. I kept waking to stare about my bed. I kept fancying that I heard the swish of silk. But I was mistaken. The curtains remained as I had left them and I saw no more apparitions in my room.

But who had drawn the curtains? I did not want to ask, for fear of attracting the suspicious glances again. But I was on the alert.

It was only a few days later when it was discovered that the warming-pan was missing from my room.

I had not noticed that it was gone, so could not say exactly how long it had been absent from its place on the wall over the oak chest in my bedroom.

I was sitting up in bed while Mary-Jane brought my breakfast-tray to me. I had taken to having breakfast in bed on Dr. Smith's orders, and I must say that I was ready enough to indulge myself in this way, because, on account of the disturbed nights I was having, I almost invariably felt delicate in the mornings.

"Why, Mary-Jane," I said, my eyes straying to the wall, "what have you done with the warming-pan?"

Mary-Jane set down my tray and looked round. Her astonishment was obvious.

" Oh, madam," she said, " it's gone."

" Did it fall or something?"

" That I couldn't say, madam. I didn't take it away."

She went over to the wall. " The hook's still there, any road."

" Then I wonder who . . . I'll ask Mrs. Grantley. She might know what has happened to it. I rather liked it there. It was so bright and shining."

I ate my breakfast without giving much thought to the warming-pan. At that stage I did not realise that it had any connection with the strange things which were happening to me.

It was that afternoon before I again thought of it. I was having tea with Ruth and she was talking about Christmas in the old days and how different it was now—particularly this year when we were living so quietly on account of Gabriel's death.

" It was rather fun," she told me. " We used to take a wagon out to bring the yule log home; and there was the holly to gather too. We usually had several people staying in the house at Christmas. This time it can't possibly be more than family. I suppose Aunt Hagar will come over from Kelly Grange with Simon. They generally do, and stay two nights. She's almost certain to manage that journey."

I felt rather pleased at the prospect of Christmas, and wondered when I could go into Harrogate, Keighly or Ripon to buy some presents. It seemed incredible that it was only last Christmas when I was in Dijon. Rather lonely those Christmases had been because most of my companions had gone home to their families and there were usually no more than four or five of us who remained at the school. But we had made the most of the festivities and those Christmases had been enjoyable.

" I must find out if Aunt Hagar will be able to make the journey. I must tell them to air her bed thoroughly; last time she declared we were putting her into damp sheets."

That reminded me. " By the way," I said, " what has happened to the warming-pan which was in my room?"

She looked puzzled.

" It's no longer there," I explained. " Mary-Jane doesn't know what has become of it."

" Warming-pan in your room? Oh . . . has it gone?"

" So you didn't know. I thought perhaps you'd given orders for someone to remove it."

She shook her head. "It must have been one of the servants," she said. "I'll find out. You may be needing it when the weather turns, and we can't expect this mildness to continue long now."

"Thanks," I answered. "I'm thinking of going into Harrogate or Ripon soon. I have some shopping to do."

"We might all go together. I want to go, and Luke was saying something about taking Damaris in to do some Christmas shopping."

"Do let us. I should enjoy that."

Next day I met her on the stairs, when I was on the point of going out for a short walk because the rain had ceased for a while and the sun was shining.

"Going for a walk?" she asked. "It's pleasant out. Quite warm. By the way, I cannot discover what happened to your warming-pan."

"Well, that's strange."

"I expect someone moved it and forgot." She gave a light laugh and looked at me somewhat intently, I thought. But I went out and it was such a lovely morning that I immediately forgot all about the missing warming-pan. There were still a few flowers left in the hedgerows such as woundwort and shepherd's purse, and although I did not go to the moor I thought I saw in the distance a spray of gorse, golden in the pale sunshine.

Remembering instructions, I curtailed my walk, and as I turned back to the house I glanced towards the ruins. It seemed quite a long time since I had been to the Abbey. I knew I could never go there now without remembering the monk, so I stayed away, which showed, of course, that my protestations of bravery were partly false.

I stood under an oak tree and found myself studying the patterns on the bark. I remembered my father's telling me that the ancient Britons used to think that marks on the trunk of the oak were the outward signs of the supernatural being who inhabited the tree. I traced the pattern with my finger. It was easy to understand how such fancies had grown. It was so easy to harbour fancies.

As I stood there I heard a sudden mocking cry above me, and looked up startled, expecting something terrifying. It was only a green woodpecker.

I hurried into the house.

When I went to the dining-room that evening for dinner

I found Matthew, Sarah and Luke there; but Ruth was absent.

When I entered they were asking where she was.

"Not like her to be late," said Sir Matthew.

"Ruth has a great deal to do," Sarah put in. "And she was talking about Christmas and wondering which rooms Hagar and Simon would want if they came for a short holiday."

"Hagar will have the room which was once hers," said Matthew. "Simon will have the one he has always had. So why should she be concerned?"

"I think she's a little worried about Hagar. You know what Hagar is. She'll have her old nose into every corner and be telling us that the place is not kept as it was when Father was alive."

"Hagar's an interfering busybody and always was," growled Matthew. "If she doesn't like what she sees here, then she can do the other thing. We can manage very well without her opinions and advice."

Ruth came in then, looking slightly flushed.

"We've been wondering what had become of you," Matthew told her.

"Of all the ridiculous things . . ." she began. She looked round the company helplessly. "I went into . . . Gabriel's old room and noticed something under the coverlet there. What do you think it was?"

I stared at her and felt the colour rushing to my cheeks, and I was fighting hard to control my feelings, because I knew.

"The warming-pan from your room!" She was looking straight at me, quizzically and intent. "Whoever could have put it there?"

"How extraordinary!" I heard myself stammer.

"Well, we've found it. That's where it was all the time." She turned to the others. "Catherine had missed the warming-pan from her room. She thought I'd told one of the servants to remove it. Who on earth could have put it into the bed there?"

"We ought to find out," I said sharply.

"I asked the servants. They quite clearly knew nothing about it."

"Someone must have put it there." I heard my voice rise unnaturally high.

Ruth shrugged her shoulders.

" But we must find out," I insisted. " It's someone playing these tricks. Don't you see . . . it's the same sort of thing as the curtains being drawn."

" Curtains?"

I was annoyed with myself because the drawing of the bed curtains had been a matter known only to the one who had done it, and Mary-Jane and myself. Now I should have to explain. I did so briefly.

" Who drew the curtains?" screeched Sarah. " Who put the warming-pan in Gabriel's bed? And it was your bed, too, wasn't it, Catherine. Yours and Gabriel's."

" I wish I knew!" I cried vehemently.

" Someone must have been rather absent-minded," said Luke lightly.

" I don't think it was absent-mindedness," I retorted.

" But, Catherine," put in Ruth patiently, " why should anyone want to pull your bed curtains about your bed or remove the warming-pan?"

" That's what I should like to know."

" Let's forget all about it," said Matthew. " That which was lost is found."

" But why . . . why . . . ?" I insisted.

" You are getting excited, my dear," whispered Ruth.

" I want to know the explanation of these strange things which are happening in my room."

" The duckling is getting cold," said Sir Matthew. He came to me and slipped his arm through mine. " Never mind about the warming-pan, my dear. We shall know why it was moved . . . all in good time."

" Yes," said Luke, " all in good time." And he kept his eyes on my face as he spoke, and I could see the speculation there.

" We'd better start," said Ruth, and as they sat down at the table I had no alternative but to do the same ; but my appetite had deserted me. I kept asking myself what the purpose was behind these strange happenings which seemed in some way to be directed towards me.

I was going to find out. I must find out.

Before the month was out we were invited to the vicarage to discuss the last-minute plans for the imminent " Bring and Buy Sale."

" Mrs. Cartwright always gets the wind in her tail at such

times," said Luke. "This is nothing to the June garden fête or her hideous pagents."

"Mrs. Cartwright is an energetic lady," said Ruth, "possessing all the qualities to make her an excellent wife for the vicar."

"Does she expect me to go?" I asked.

"Of course she does. She'd be hurt if you didn't. You will come? It's only a short walk, but if you like we can drive there."

"I feel perfectly fit to walk," I said quickly.

"Then we'll go along. It's an excellent opportunity for you to meet some of our neighbours. Now that we're in mourning, the vicarage rather than the Revels has become the centre of our village. In the past, meetings were held here."

We set out about ten-thirty, and in a quarter of an hour had arrived at the vicarage, a pleasant grey stone house close to the church. We joined one or two people going in the same direction and Ruth introduced me. I was studied with a certain amount of curiosity because they all knew that I was the wife whom Gabriel had married somewhat hastily and whom he had left pregnant after two weeks of marriage.

They were summing me up, which I accepted as normal in the circumstances. I expected there were some of them who believed that shortcomings in myself may have been the reason for Gabriel's death.

Mrs. Cartwright, whom I had of course already met, was a large, somewhat florid woman with a powerful personality. She assembled us all in her drawing-room, which seemed small but only because I was accustomed to the rooms at the Revels, and here morning coffee with biscuits was being served by a maid.

I was conducted to the window from which I could see the churchyard. I could just make out the Rockwell vault with the wrought-iron work above it, and my thoughts immediately went to Gabriel.

When all the guests were present Mrs. Cartwright addressed us in her booming voice and told us of the need for speed. The sale must be in time to give people opportunities of buying their Christmas presents at it. "So please ransack your attics, and any little *objet d'art* will be appreciated. Perhaps it is something which you no longer value. That does not mean that no one else will. Please try to bring in your offerings before the day. It does give us time to decide how to price them. And on the day . . . do come and buy. Remember it is for the good of the church, and the roof does need attention. As you all know, there's death watch beetle up there in the rafters. I know you will help. But the need is immediate, ladies. Has anyone any suggestions?"

There were some, and Mrs. Cartwright considered them and asked for counter opinions. It was all very business-like and I admired our vicar's wife for her energy.

When the business of the meeting had been settled she came and sat in the window with me and told me how glad she was to see me there.

"It is wonderful to see you looking so well and to know that there is to be an addition to the family. I know that Sir Matthew is delighted . . . absolutely delighted. It is a comfort to him in the circumstances. . . ." She was one of those women who carry the whole of a conversation for the sheer joy of talking, and a better talker than a listener, I discovered. "Such a great deal of work to be done. The people here are so good . . . so helpful . . . but between ourselves they are rather slow in taking action . . . if you know what I mean. One has to prod . . . prod . . . to get anything done. This sale of work will not produce half the profit unless it takes place well before Christmas. I do hope you will be able to bring us a little something . . . and you will come and buy, won't you? Some little thing . . . just anything. . . . More than one, of course, if you have it. Anything . . . but the more valuable the better. Forgive me for begging so persistently."

I said it was in a good cause and I would see what I could find. "I have a brooch of turquoises and pearls . . . very small."

"Ideal! How generous of you. And to-morrow . . . could we have it then? I'll send someone for it."

"It's a little old-fashioned."

"No matter. It will be wonderful. I am so pleased that you have come. You are going to be such a help to us . . . particularly when . . . well, at the moment of course you are feeling less energetic than you will later. I can talk of these matters with feeling. I have six of my own. Ah yes, it is hard to believe, is it not? And the youngest is nineteen. He's going into the Church. I'm glad one of them is. I was beginning to be afraid. . . . As I was saying, you'll be so helpful later, I know . . . with the pageant. I do want a pageant in the ruins this summer."

"Have you had one before?"

"Five years ago was the last. Of course the weather was

tragic. Rain, rain, rain. That was July. I think we might choose June this year. July *is* a wet month really."

"What sort of pageant was it?"

"Historical. It must be historical . . . with such a setting. The costumes were excellent."

"We were lent some from the Revels and we made others. We were helped considerably from the Revels with the Cavaliers, but we made our own Roundheads. They were easy to do."

"Yes, I suppose they would be. So you started with the Civil War, did you?"

"Good heavens, no! We went back to before the Dissolution. It was the only thing to do with that wonderful setting all ready for our use. It was most effective. People said that on that day it was as though the Abbey was no longer a ruin."

I tried to keep the note of excitement out of my voice. "So some of the players were dressed as monks."

"Indeed yes. Many of them. They all played many parts . . . you know. A monk in one scene was a gay cavalier in another. It was necessary, you know. We haven't enough players. The men are so difficult and shy! There was many a female monk on that day, I do assure you."

"I suppose their costumes were easy to make."

"The simplest really. Just a black robe and a cowl . . . so easy to make it really effective, and against the grey ruins, I really think that part was the most successful."

"It must have been. After all, there was the Abbey to help."

"How wonderful that you should be so interested. I'm certainly going to try a pageant this year. But June . . . mind you. July is definitely a wet month."

Ruth was trying to catch my eye, and I rose. I felt I had made an important discovery and I was very pleased that I had decided to come to the vicarage this morning.

"It's time we went," said Ruth, "if we're not to be late for luncheon."

We said good-bye to Mrs. Cartwright and started for home.

I found it difficult to make conversation. I kept saying to myself: Somebody who played the part of a monk in the pageant five years ago had a monk's costume which still exists to-day. The person who came into my bedroom used it.

How could I find out who had played a monk in the

pageant five years ago? Who, in our household, that is to say. It could only be Ruth, I guesed. Luke would have been too young. But would he? Five years ago he would have been twelve years old. He was probably tall for his age. Why should he not have played the part of a monk? Sir Matthew and Aunt Sarah would have been too old. That left Ruth and Luke.

I said: " Mrs. Cartwright was talking to me about the pageant. Did you play a part in it?"

" You don't know Mrs. Cartwright very well if you think she would let any of us escape."

" What part did you play?"

" The King's wife . . . Queen Henrietta Maria."

" Just that part and no other?"

" It was an important part."

" I only asked because Mrs. Cartwright said that some people played several parts since she was short of players."

" Those would be the people who had small parts."

" What about Luke?"

" He was well to the fore. He was in and out of everything . . ."

Luke! I thought; and I remembered that it had been some time before he had appeared on that night; he had plenty of time to take off the robe and put on a dressing-gown. He must have been very quick getting up to the second floor but he was young and active.

And the bed curtains and the warming-pan? Why not? He was the one who would have had every opportunity. My doubt was becoming almost a certainty. Luke was trying to terrify me; he was trying to kill my child before it was born. Obviously Luke was the one who had most to gain from the death of my child.

" Are you feeling all right?" It was Ruth at my side.

" Oh yes . . . thanks . . ."

" Were you whispering to yourself?"

" Oh no. I was thinking of Mrs. Cartwright. She's very talkative, is she not?"

" She certainly is."

The house was now in view and we were both looking towards it. My eyes went, as they always did, to that south parapet from which Gabriel had fallen. There was something different about it. I stared and Ruth was staring too.

" What is it?" she said, and she quickened her pace.

There was something dark on the parapet; from this distance it looked as though someone was leaning over it.

"Gabriel!" I think I must have said it aloud because Ruth at my elbow said: "Nonsense! It can't be. But what . . . But who?"

I began to run; Ruth was beside me restraining me and I could hear my breath coming in great gasps

"Something's there," I panted. "What . . . is it . . . ? It looks . . . limp. . . ."

Now I saw that whoever was there was wearing a cloak and the hood of the cloak and part of the cloak itself was hanging over the parapet. It was impossible to see the rest.

"She'll fall. Who is it? What does it mean?" cried Ruth as she ran ahead of me into the house. She could go so much faster than I; I found it difficult to get my breath but I hurried after her as quickly as I could. Luke appeared in the corridor. He looked at his mother and then turned to stare at me, labouring up behind.

"What on earth's happened?" he asked.

"There's someone on the parapet," I cried. "Gabriel's parapet."

"But who . . . ?"

He had started up the stairs ahead of me and I went after him as fast as I could.

Ruth appeared on the stairs and there was a grim smile about her lips. She was holding something in her hand which I recognised as a blue cloak which belonged to me—a long winter cloak designed to shut out the winds; there was a hood attached to it.

"It's . . . mine," I gasped.

"Why did you hang it over the parapet like that?" she demanded almost roughly.

"I . . . But I did no such thing."

She and Luke exchanged glances.

Then she murmured: "It was made to look exactly like someone leaning over . . . about to fall. It gave me quite a shock when I saw it. It was such a silly thing to do."

"Then who did it?" I cried. "Who is doing all these silly cruel things!"

They were both looking at me as though they found me very odd, as though certain doubts they had concerning me were being confirmed.

I had to find out the meaning of these strange happenings.

155

I was becoming nervous, continuously watching for the next. They were such stupid tricks—except of course the appearance in my bedroom of the monk. If they had intended to alarm me they could not have chosen anything more calculated to do so. But these minor irritations. . . . What did they portend? Luke and Ruth seemed to have made up their minds that I was eccentric—but perhaps that was too kind a word. I was aware of them watching me on every occasion. It was unnerving.

I did think of going to see the Redverses and telling them everything, but I was growing so distrustful of everyone that I was not even sure of Hagar. As for Simon, he had taken my view of the monk incident, but what would he think of the bed curtains, warming-pan and cloak?

There was something sinister behind this and I had to find out what it was. I wanted to do so by myself because of this distrust which was stirring in me and which seemed to be directed against every person who was connected with the Revels.

The very next day I set out to call on Mrs. Cartwright. What she had to say about the pageant the day before had seemed important and I wondered whether I could glean more from her.

Besides the turquoise brooch I found an enamel box which I had had for years and had no particular use for, so I took this along as well.

I was fortunate to find her in. She was effusive in her welcome and expressed great pleasure in the brooch and box.

" Ah, Mrs. Rockwell, this is kind of you. And to save me the trouble of sending! I can see you are going to be a great help to us. Such a comfort. I am sure these lovely things of yours will fetch a good price. And if you would like a preview I'll be only too delighted to show you." She looked at me slyly as though she thought this was my reason for coming.

I hesitated. I had no wish to arouse suspicions and I felt that since these strange happenings were taking place it was very necessary for me to have a reason for everything I did.

" Well," I began.

She interrupted conspiratorially: " But of course. And why not. You deserve it. It's an excellent way of doing one's Christmas shopping, particularly when it is not quite so easy to get about. I think people who help us *should* have special privileges. . . . Have a look round and then perhaps you will drink a cup of coffee with me?"

I said there was nothing I should like better; so she took me into a small room where the articles were set out and I selected a scarf pin, a snuff box and a Chinese vase. She was delighted with me not only as a bringer but as a buyer, and I felt that had put her in a good mood for confidences.

As soon as we were drinking coffee together in her drawing-room I turned the conversation to pageants. That was easy. It was a subject very near to her heart.

"And do you really propose to put on a pageant this summer?"

"I shall do my utmost."

"It must be very interesting."

"It is indeed, and *you* must have a prominent part. I always thought that members of our leading family should. Don't you agree?"

"But yes," I said. "Have they always been amenable? I mean do they always take part in these affairs?"

"Oh yes, they have always been what I should call a *dutiful* family."

"I'd like to hear about the pageant. I suppose Mrs. Grantley and Luke would take parts."

"They did last time."

"Yes, Mrs. Grantley was telling me. She was the wife of Charles I."

"Yes, we did a big Civil War scene. That was because the Revels was actually occupied by the Parliamentarians. It's wonderful luck that they didn't destroy the place . . . the vandals! But then all the valuables had been hidden away."

"That must have been exciting. Where were they hidden?"

"Now, my dear Mrs. Rockwell, that's something your family might know more about than I do. It is a mystery though, I believe."

"And you did that scene in the pageant?"

"Not exactly . . . we just had the advance of the Round-heads, you know, and the occupation. Then we had the restoration of the family with the restoration of the king . . . linking up, you see, Rockwell history and England's history."

"And you showed the Abbey before the Dissolution. That must have been very interesting."

"Indeed it was, and I propose to do that again. I mean

157

it is essential. And of course it gives everyone an opportunity to play a small part."

"It must have been most impressive to see all those black-robed figures about the place."

"It was indeed."

"Luke was only a boy then—too young, I suppose, to play much of a part."

"Oh no, not at all. He was most enthusiastic. He was one of our best monks. He was almost as tall as a man then. The Rockwells are a tall family, as you know."

"You have an excellent memory, Mrs. Cartwright. I do believe you remember the parts which everyone played."

She laughed. "Amongst our immediate neighbourhood, of course. But this pageant was quite a big thing and we had people from all around playing parts; and of course that was good because it brought in spectators."

"How many monks did you use?"

"A great number. Almost everyone had to be pressed into service. I even tried to get Dr. Smith."

"Did you succeed?"

"No. It was his day for going to . . . that institution, and then of course he said he had to be on duty in case he was called somewhere."

"And his daughter?"

"She had a part of course. She was the little Charles. She looked wonderful in velvet breeches with her long hair. She was too young for it to seem immodest, and the 'When did you last see your father?' scene was most affecting."

"She couldn't play a monk?"

"Indeed not. But I shall never forget her Prince Charles. Everyone was splendid. Even Mr. Redvers—and no one could say acting was his line."

"Oh, what part did he play?"

"He was merely a monk, but he did join in."

"How . . . interesting."

"Will you have more coffee?"

"Thank you, no. That was delicious. But I should be going back now."

"It *was* so good of you to come, and I *do* hope the purchases will be satisfactory."

We parted with mutual thanks and as I walked home I felt bemused.

I was sure I had solved the mystery of the costume. Some person had used a pageant costume in which to frighten me.

Luke had had one at some time. Did he still possess it? Simon had had one too. Yet he had not mentioned this when I had told him of my experience.

At first I decided that I would discuss the matter of the costumes with Hagar and then I hesitated, because if I did so, Simon would hear of it; and I was not sure that I wanted Simon to know that I had discovered so much.

It seemed ridiculous to suspect Simon, for how could he possibly have been in the house at the time? And yet I had to remind myself that he was next in succession to Luke.

It was alarming to feel that I could trust no one, but that was exactly how I did feel.

So when I called to see Hagar the next day I said nothing of the cloak incident, although I longed to discuss it with someone. Instead I tried to keep the conversation on everyday matters and I asked Hagar if there was any Christmas shopping I could do for her. I told her that I hoped to go into one of the towns with Ruth and perhaps Luke, and if I did so I would be happy to execute any of her commissions.

She pondered this and eventually made a list of things which she would like me to get for her; and while we were discussing this, Simon came in.

"If you'd like to go to Knaresborough," he said, "I can take you. I have to drive in on business."

I hesitated. I did not really believe he would have tried to frighten me, and yet I reminded myself he had not liked me in the beginning; it was only because of my friendship with his grandmother that we were brought together. I was unaccountably depressed because I felt it was only reasonable not to place him outside suspicion. If he could really be trying to harm someone in my position he must be the exact opposite of the man I had been sure he was. Still, I was determined not to trust him.

My hesitation amused him. It had not occurred to him that I suspected him of villainy, only that I feared to offend the proprieties.

He said with a grin: "Ruth or Luke might like to come with us. If they'll come, perhaps you would deign to."

"That would be very pleasant," I replied.

And it was eventually arranged that when Simon went to Knaresborough he should take Luke, Damaris and myself with him.

The day was warm for early December. We left soon after

159

nine in the morning and planned to be back by dark, which was of course soon after four.

As we sat together in the carriage, Luke and Simon appeared to be in high spirits; and I found myself catching them; Damaris was quiet, as usual.

It occurred to me that whenever I was away from the house I recaptured my old common sense. I ceased to believe that there was anything for me to fear. At least, I could assure myself, there was nothing with which I could not cope. I could believe, as I listened to Luke's bright conversation, that he had played these tricks on me to tease me. As for the first, he now probably realised he had gone too far, and that was why he was amusing himself with things like warming-pans. He always regarded me in a slightly sardonic way. How foolish I had been to be afraid. I had merely been the victim of youthful high spirits.

That was my mood as we drove into Knaresborough.

I knew the town slightly from the past and it had always delighted me. I thought it was one of the most interesting and charming old towns in the West Riding.

We drove to an inn where we had some light refreshment, and afterwards separated, Simon to do the business which had brought him here, Luke, Damaris and I to shop, having arranged to meet in two hours' time at the inn.

Very soon I had lost Luke and Damaris, who, I presumed, had wandered off while I was in a shop because they wanted to be alone together.

I made the purchases Hagar had commissioned and a few for myself, and then, as I had almost an hour to spare, I decided that I would explore the town, something I had never before had an opportunity to do.

It was very pleasant to be there on that bright December afternoon. There were few people about and as I looked at the gleaming river Nidd and those steep streets of houses with their red roofs, at the ruined castle with its fine old keep, I felt invigorated, and I wondered how I could such a short time ago have been so frightened.

As I made my way to the river I heard a voice behind me calling, " Mrs. Catherine," and, turning, I saw Simon coming towards me.

" Hallo, have you finished your shopping?"

" Yes."

He took his watch from his pocket. " Almost an hour before our rendezvous. What do you propose to do?"

"I was going to wander along the river bank."

"Let's do it together."

As he took my parcels and walked beside me, two things struck me—one was the strength which radiated from him, the other was the loneliness of the river bank.

"I know what you want to do." he said. "You want to try your luck at the well."

"What well?"

"Haven't you heard of the famous well? Haven't you ever visited Knaresborough before?"

"Once or twice with my father. We did not visit the well."

He clicked his tongue mockingly. "Mrs. Catherine, your education has been neglected."

"Tell me about the well."

"Let's find it, shall we? If you hold your hand in the water, then wish and leave it to dry you will get your wish."

"I am sure you do not believe such legends."

"There's a great deal you don't know about me, Mrs. Catherine; although of course that's something else you haven't realised."

"I am sure you are the most practical person and never wish for that which can't reasonably be yours."

"You once told me that I was an arrogant man. Therefor you doubtless think I regard myself as omnipotent. In that case I might wish for anything and believe I have a chance of getting it."

"Even so you would realise that you had to work for what you wanted."

"That might be so."

"Then why bother to wish, when work would suffice?"

"Mrs. Catherine, you are in the wrong mood for the Dripping Well. Let us for once cast out common sense. Let us be gullible for once."

"I should like to see the well."

"And wish?"

"Yes. I should like to wish."

"And will you tell me if it comes true?"

"Yes."

"But don't tell me what you have wished, until it comes true. That is one of those conditions. It has to be a secret between you and the powers of darkness . . . or light. I'm not sure which it is in this case. There's the well, and there

161

is Mother Shipton's Cave. Did your father tell you the story of Old Mother Shipton?"

"He never told me stories. He talked to me very little."

"Then it looks as though I must explain. Old Mother Shipton was a witch and she lived here . . . oh, about four hundred years ago. She was a love child, the result of union between a village girl and a stranger who persuaded her that he was a spirit possessed of supernatural powers. Before the child was born he deserted her, and little Ursula grew up to be a wise woman. She married a man named Shipton and so became 'Old Mother Shipton.'"

"What an interesting story. I've often wondered who Old Mother Shipton was."

"Some of her prophecies came true. It is said that she foretold the fall of Wolsey, the defeat of the Armada and the effect the Civil War would have on the West Riding. I used to remember some of her prophecies; there's a rhyme about them.

> *Around the world thoughts shall fly*
> *In the twinkling of an eye . . .*

I used to know the whole thing and chant it to my grand-mother's cook until she chased me out of the kitchen. I made it sound like an evil prophecy intended for her alone. I remember:

> *Under water men shall walk*
> *Shall ride shall sleep shall talk,*
> *In the air men shall be seen . . .*

and it ends:

> *The world then to an end shall come*
> *In Nineteen hundred and Ninety-one.*

"We have some years left to us then?" I said, and we were laughing together.

Now we had reached the Dripping Well.

"It's a magic well," he said. "It's known also as the Petrifying Well. Anything which is dropped in this well will eventually become petrified."

"But why?"

"It has nothing to do with Mother Shipton, although I don't doubt some people would like to say it has. There's magnesian limestone in the water. It's actually in the soil and gets into the water which drips through and down into the well. You must let the water drip on to your hands and wish. Will you go first or shall I?"

"You first."

He leaned over the well and I watched the water, which was seeping through the sides of the well, drip on to his hands.

He turned to me holding out a wet hand.

"I am wishing," he said. "If I leave this water to dry I cannot fail to get my wish. Now it's your turn."

He was standing close to me as I took off my glove and leaned over the well.

I was conscious of the silence all about us. I was alone in this spot and only Simon Redvers knew I was here. I leaned forward and the cold water—I was sure it was the coldest water I had ever known—dripped on to my hand.

He was immediately behind me and there came to me then a moment of panic. In my mind's eye I saw him not as he had been a few seconds before, but wrapped in a monk's robe.

Not Simon, I was saying to myself. It must not be Simon. And so vehement was my thought that I forgot any other wish than that.

I could feel the warmth of his body, so close was he, and I held my breath. I was certain then that something was about to happen to me.

Then I swung round. He stepped back a pace. He had been standing very near me. Why? I asked myself.

"Don't forget," he said. "It's got to dry. I can guess what you wished."

"Can you?"

"Not a difficult task. You whispered to yourself: 'I wish for a boy.'"

"It has turned cold."

"That was the water. It is exceptionally cold. That has something to do with the lime, I think."

He was staring beyond me and I was conscious of a certain excitement in him. At that moment a man appeared close by. I had not noticed his approach, but perhaps Simon had.

"Ah, trying t'well," said the man pleasantly.

"Who could pass by without doing so?" answered Simon.

"Folks come from far and wide to test t'well, and to see Mother Shipton's Cave."

"It's very interesting," I said.

"Oh, aye. Happen so."

Simon was gathering up my parcels. "You must make sure the water has dried on your hand," he told me; and I held it out before me as we walked along.

He took my arm in a possessive manner and drew me away from the well into those steep streets which led to the castle.

Luke and Damaris were waiting for us at the inn and we had a quick cup of tea and then drove home.

It was dusk when we reached Kirkland Moorside. Simon dropped Damaris at the doctor's house and then drove Luke and myself on to the Revels.

I felt dejected when I entered my room. It was because of these new suspicions which had come to me. I was fighting them, but they would not be dismissed. Why had I felt frightened at the side of the well? What had Simon been thinking as he stood beside me? Had he been planning something which the casual arrival of a stranger had prevented his carrying out?

I really was astonished at myself. I might pretend to scorn the powers of the Dripping Well, but I had made my wish involuntarily and I fervently hoped it would come true.

Please let it not be Simon.

Why should I care whether it was Luke or Simon?

But I did care. It was then that I began to suspect the nature of my feelings for this man. I had no tenderness for him, but I found that I felt more alive in his company than I did in that of any other person. I might be angry with him —I so often was—but being angry with him was more exciting than being pleasant with anyone else. I cherished his opinion of my good sense and I was happy because he admired good sense more than any other quality.

Each time I saw him my feelings towards him underwent a change, and I understood now that I was more and more under the spell of his personality.

It was since he had loomed so large in my life that I had begun to understand what my feelings for Gabriel had been. I knew that I had loved Gabriel without being in love with him. I had married Gabriel because I had sensed a need in him for protection, and I had wanted to give it; it had seemed so reasonable to marry him when I could give him comfort and he could provide me with an escape from a home which was beginning to affect me more than ever with its melancholy. That was why I had found it difficult to remember exactly what he looked like; that was why, although I had lost him, I could still look forward to the future with hopeful expectation. Simon and the child had helped to do that for me.

It had been a cry from the heart when I had wished at the well: Please, not Simon.

I had now become aware of a change in the behaviour of everyone towards me. I intercepted exchanged glances; even Sir Matthew seemed what I can only call watchful.

I was to discover the meaning of this through Sarah, and the discovery was more alarming than anything which had gone before.

I went to her apartments one day and found her stitching at the christening robe.

"I'm glad you've come," she greeted me. "You used to be interested in my tapestry."

"I still am." I assured her. "I think it's lovely. What have you been doing lately?"

She looked at me archly. "You would really like to see?"

"Of course."

She giggled, put aside the christening robe, and standing up, took my hand. Then she paused and her face puckered. "I'm keeping it a secret," she whispered. Then she added: "Until it's finished."

"Then I mustn't pry. When will it be finished?"

I thought she was going to burst into tears as she said: "How can I finish it when I don't know! I thought you would help me. You said he didn't kill himself. You said . . ."

I waited tensely for her to go on but her mind had wandered. "There was a tear in the christening robe," she said quietly.

"Was there? But tell me about the tapestry."

"I didn't want to show it to anyone until it was finished. It was Luke. . . ."

"Luke?" I cried, my heart beating faster.

"Such a lovely baby. He cried when he was at the font, and he tore the robe. All that time it hasn't been mended But why should it be, until there's a new baby waiting for it?"

"You'll mend it beautifully, I'm sure," I told her, and she brightened.

"It's *you*!" she murmured. "I don't know where to put you. That's why . . ."

"You don't know where to put me," I repeated, puzzled.

"I've got Gabriel . . . and the dog. He was a dear little dog. Friday! It was a queer sort of name."

"Aunt Sarah," I demanded, "what do you know about Friday?"

"Poor Friday! Such a good little dog. Such a *faithful* dog. I suppose that was why ... Oh dear, I wonder if your baby will be good at the christening. But Rockwell babies are never good babies. I shall wash the robe myself."

"What were you saying about Friday, Aunt Sarah? Please tell me."

She looked at me with a certain concern. "He was your dog," she said. "You should know. But I shan't allow anyone to touch it. It's very difficult to iron. It has to be gophered in places. I did it for Luke's christening. I did it for Gabriel's."

"Aunt Sarah," I said impulsively, "show me the tapestry you're working on."

A light of mischief came into her eyes. "But it isn't finished, and I didn't want to show it to anyone ... until it is."

"Why not? I saw you working on one before you'd finished it."

"That was different. Then I knew ..."

"You knew?"

She nodded. "I don't know where to put *you*, you see."

"But I'm here."

She put her head on one side so that she looked like a bright-eyed bird. "To-day ... to-morrow ... next week, perhaps. After that where will you be?"

I was determined to see the picture. "Please," I wheedled, "do show me."

She was delighted by my interest which she knew was genuine.

"Well, perhaps you," she said. "No one else."

"I'll not tell anyone," I promised.

"All right." She was like an eager child. "Come on."

She went to the cupboard and brought out a canvas, and held the picture close to her body so that I couldn't see it.

"Do let me see," I pleaded.

Then she reversed it, still holding it against her. Depicted on the canvas was the south façade of the house; and lying on the stones in front of it was Gabriel's body. It was so vivid, so real, that I felt a sudden nausea as I looked at it. I stared, for there was something else. Lying beside Gabriel was my dog Friday, his little body stiff as it could only be in death. It was horrible.

I must have given a startled gasp, for Sarah chuckled. My horror was the best compliment I could have given her.

I stammered: "It looks so ... real."

166

"Oh, it's real enough . . . in a way," she said dreamily. "I saw him lying there, and that was how he looked. I went down before they could take him away, and saw him."

"Gabriel . . ." I heard myself murmur, for the sight of the tapestry had brought back so many tender memories, and I could picture him more clearly than I had since the first days of my bereavement.

"I said to myself," Aunt Sarah continued, "that must be my next picture . . . and it was."

"And Friday?" I cried. "You saw him . . . too?"

She seemed as though she were trying to remember.

"Did you, Aunt Sarah?" I persisted.

"He was a faithful dog," she said. "He died for his faithfulness."

"Did you see him, dead . . . as you saw Gabriel?"

Again that puckered look came into her face. "It's there on the picture," she said at length.

"But he's lying there beside Gabriel. It wasn't like that."

"Wasn't it?" she asked. "They took him away, didn't they?"

"Who took him away?"

She looked at me questioningly. "Who did?" It was as though she were pleading with me to give her the answer.

"You know, don't you, Aunt Sarah?"

"Oh yes, I know," she answered blithely.

"Then please . . . please tell me. It's very important."

"But you know too."

"How I wish I did! You must tell me, Aunt Sarah. You see, it would help me."

"I can't remember."

"But you remember so much. You must remember something so important."

Her face brightened. "I know, Catherine. It was the monk."

She looked so innocent that I knew she would have helped if she could. I could not understand how much she had discovered. I was sure that she lived in two worlds—that of reality and that of the imagination; and that the two became intermingled so that she could not be sure which was which. People in this house underrated her; they spoke their secrets before her, not understanding that she had a mind like a jackdaw, which seized on bright and glittering pieces of information and stored them away.

I turned my attention to the canvas and, now that the

shock of seeing Gabriel and Friday lying dead was less acute, I noticed that the work had taken up only one side of the picture. The rest was blank.

She read my thoughts immediately, which was a reminder that her speculations—if speculations they were were those of a woman who could be astute.

"That's for you," she said; and in that moment she was like a seer from whom the future, of which the rest of us were utterly ignorant, was only separated by a semi-transparent veil.

As I did not speak she came close to me and gripped my arm; I could feel her hot fingers burning through my sleeve.

"I can't finish," she said peevishly. "I don't know where to put *you* . . . that's why." She turned the canvas round so that I could not see the picture and hugged it to herself. "You don't know. I don't know. But the monk knows. . . ." She sighed. "Oh dear, we shall have to wait. Such a nuisance. I can't start another until I finish this one."

She went to the cupboard and put the canvas away. Then she came back to peer into my face.

"You don't look well," she said. "Come and sit down. You'll be all right, won't you? Poor Claire! She died, you know. Having Gabriel killed her, you might say."

I was trying to shake off the effects of seeing that picture, and I said absently: "But she had a weak heart. I'm strong and healthy."

She put her head on one side and looked quizzically at me.

"Perhaps it's why we're friends . . ." she began.

"What is, Aunt Sarah?"

"We *are* friends. I felt it from the first. As soon as you came I said, 'I like Catherine. She understands me.' Now I suppose they say that's why . . ."

"Aunt Sarah, do tell me what you mean. Why should you and I understand each other better than other people in the house?"

"They always said I am in my second childhood."

A wild fear came into my mind. "And what do they say about me?"

She was silent for a while, then she said: "I've always liked the minstrels' gallery."

I felt impatient in my eagerness to discover what was going on in her muddled mind; then I saw that she *was* telling me and that the minstrels' gallery was connected with her discovery.

"You were in the minstrels' gallery," I said quickly, "and you overheard someone talking."

She nodded, her eyes wide, and she glanced over her shoulder as though she expected to find someone behind her.

"You heard something about me?"

She nodded; then shook her head. "I don't think we're going to have many Christmas decorations this year. It's all because of Gabriel. Perhaps there'll be a bit of holly."

I felt frustrated but I knew that I must not frighten her. She had heard something which she was afraid to repeat because she knew she should not, and if she thought I was trying to find out she would be on her guard against telling me. I had to wheedle it out of her in some way, because I was sure that it was imperative that I should know.

I forced myself to be calm and said: "Never mind. Next Christmas . . ."

"But who knows what'll have happened to us by next Christmas . . . to me . . . to *you*?"

"I may well be here, Aunt Sarah, and my baby with me. If it's a boy they'll want it brought up here, won't they?"

"They might take him away from you. They might put you . . ."

I pretended not to have noticed that. I said: "I should not want to be separated from my child, Aunt Sarah. Nobody could do that."

"They could . . . if the doctor said so."

I lifted the christening robe and pretended to examine it, but to my horror my hands had begun to shake and I was afraid she would notice this.

"Did the doctor say so?" I asked.

"Oh yes. He was telling Ruth. He thought it might be necessary . . . if you got worse . . . and it might be a good idea before the baby was born."

"You were in the minstrels' gallery."

"They were in the hall. They didn't see me."

"Did the doctor say I was ill?"

"He said 'Mentally disturbed.' He said something about it being a common thing to have hallucinations . . . and to do strange things and then think other people did them. He said it was a form of persecution mania or something like that."

"I see. And he said I had this?"

Her lips trembled. "Oh, Catherine," she whispered, "I've

liked your being here. I don't want you to go away. I don't want you to go to Worstwhistle."

The words sounded like the tolling of a funeral bell, my own funeral. If I were not very careful they would bury me alive.

I could no longer remain in that room. I said: " Aunt Sarah, I'm supposed to be resting. You will excuse me if I go now?"

I did not wait for her to answer. I stooped and kissed her cheek. Then I walked sedately to the door and, when I had closed it, ran to my own room, shut the door and stood leaning against it. I felt like an animal who sees the bars of a cage closing about him. I had to escape before I was completely shut in. But how?

I very quickly made up my mind as to what I would do. I would go and see Dr. Smith and ask him what he meant by talking of me in such a way to Ruth. I might have to betray the fact that Sarah had overheard them, but I should do my utmost to keep her out of this. Yet it was too important a matter to consider such a trifle.

They were saying, " She is mad." The words beat in my brain like the notes of a jungle drum. They were saying that I had hallucinations, that I had imagined I had seen a vision in my room ; and then I had begun to do strange things— silly unreasoning things and imagined that someone else did them.

They had convinced Dr. Smith of this—and I had to prove to him that he and they were wrong.

I put on my blue cloak—the one which had been hung over the parapet—for it was the warmest of garments and the wind had turned very cold. But I was quite unaware of the weather as I made my way to the doctor's house.

I knew where it was because we had dropped Damaris there on our way back from Knaresborough. I myself had never been there before. I supposed that at some time the Rockwells had visited the Smiths, and that in view of Mrs. Smith's illness, such visits had not taken place while I was at the Revels.

The house was set in grounds of about an acre. It was a tall, narrow house and the Venetian blinds at the windows reminded me of Glen House. There were fir trees in the front garden which had grown rather tall and straggly ; they darkened the house considerably.

There was a brass plate on the door announcing that this was the doctor's house, and when I rang the bell the door was opened by a grey-haired maid in a very well starched cap and apron.

"Good afternoon," I said. "Is the doctor at home?"

"Please come in," answered the maid. "I'm afraid he is not at home at the moment. Perhaps I can give him a message."

I thought that her face was like a mask, and remembered that I had thought the same of Damaris. But I was so over-wrought that everything seemed strange on that afternoon. I felt I was not the same person who had awakened that morning. It was not that I believed I was anything but sane, but the evil seed had been sown in my mind, and I defy any woman to hear such an opinion of herself with equanimity.

The hall seemed dark; there was a plant on a table and beside it a brass tray in which several cards lay. There was a writing-pad and pencil on the table. The maid took this and said: "Could I have your name, please?"

"I am Mrs. Rockwell."

"Oh!" The maid looked startled. "You wished the doctor to come to you?"

"No, I want to see him here."

"It may be an hour before he is here, I'm afraid."

"I will wait for him."

She bowed her head and opened a door, disclosing an impersonal room which I suposed was a waiting-room.

Then I thought that I was after all more than a patient. The doctor had been a friend to me. I knew his daughter well.

I said: "Is Miss Smith at home?"

"She also is out, madam."

"Then perhaps I could see Mrs. Smith."

The maid looked somewhat taken aback, then she said: "I will tell Mrs. Smith you are here."

She went away and in a few minutes returned with the information that Mrs. Smith would be pleased to see me. Would I follow her?

I did so and we went up a flight of stairs to a small room. The blinds were drawn and there was a fire burning in a small grate. Near the fire was a sofa on which lay a woman. She was very pale and thin, but I knew at once that she was Damaris's mother, for the remains of great beauty were there.

She was covered with a Paisley shawl and the hand which lay on that shawl looked too frail to belong to a living human being.

"Mrs. Rockwell of Kirkland Revels," she said as I came in. "How good of you to come to see me."

I took the hand but relinquished it as soon as I could; it was cold and clammy.

"As a matter of fact," I said, "I came to see the doctor. As he is not in I thought I would ask if you could see me."

"I'm glad you did."

"How are you to-day?"

"Always the same, thank you. That is . . . as you see me now. . . . I can only walk about this room and then only on my good days. The stairs are beyond me."

I remembered that Ruth had said she was a hypochondriac and a great trial to the doctor. But that was real suffering I saw on her face and I believed that she was more interested in me than in herself.

"I have heard that you are going to have a child," she said.

"I suppose the doctor has told you."

"Oh . . . no. He does not talk about his patients. My daughter told me."

"I have seen a great deal of her. She is so often at the Revels."

The woman's face softened. "Oh yes. Damaris is very fond of everyone at the Revels."

"And they of her. She is very charming."

"There is only one fault that can be found with her. She should have been a boy."

"Oh, do you think so? I hope for a boy but I shan't really mind if my child is a girl."

"No, I didn't mind—one doesn't oneself."

I was talking desperately to keep my mind off my own plight, and I suppose I was not really thinking much about her or her affairs, but I said: "So it was the doctor who cared."

"Most ambitious men want sons. They want to see themselves reproduced. It's a tragedy when they are disappointed. Please tell me, is anything wrong?"

"Why do you ask?"

"I thought you looked as though it might be so."

"I . . . I want to consult the doctor."

"Of course. You came here to do that, didn't you? I'm sure he won't be long."

172

"Let him come soon," I was praying. "I must speak to him. I must make him understand."

"Do you want to see him so very urgently?" she asked.

"Yes . . . I did."

"It's on your own account, of course."

"Yes."

"I remember when I was having my children, I was continually anxious."

"I didn't know you had more than one, Mrs. Smith."

"There is only Damaris living. I have made many attempts to have a son. Unfortunately I did not succeed. I bore two stillborn daughters and there were others whom I lost in the early stages of pregnancy. My last, born four years ago . . . born dead . . . was a boy. That was a very bitter blow."

Although I could not see her face clearly because her back was to the light, I was aware of the change in her expression as she said. "It was the doctor's wish that we should have a boy. For the last four years . . . since the birth of the boy, I have never been well."

I was in a hypersensitive state. Worried as I was about my own problem, I was aware that she, too, had a problem of her own. I felt a bond between us which I could not fully understand and which I felt she saw clearly but was uncertain of my ability to see. It was a strange feeling. I was already beginning to ask myself whether my imagination was betraying me. But as soon as such a thought came into my head I dismissed it.

I was myself—practical, feet on the ground. Nobody, I told myself fiercely—perhaps too fiercely—is going to tell me that I'm going out of my mind.

She spread her hands on the Paisley shawl with an air of resignation.

"One thing," she said with a little laugh, "there could be no more attempts."

Conversation between us flagged; I was wishing that I had remained in that impersonal waiting-room for the doctor's return.

She tried again. "I was very upset when I heard of your tragedy."

"Thank you."

"Gabriel was a charming person. It is hard to believe . . ."

"It is impossible to believe . . . what they said of him," I heard myself reply vehemently.

173

"Ah! I am glad you do not believe it. I wonder you don't go back to your family . . . to have your child."

I was puzzled, for I noticed that there was a little colour in her cheeks and I could see that the thin white hands were trembling. She was excited about something and I fancied she was wondering whether to confide in me. But I was watching myself, and I thought desperately: Am I always going to watch myself from now on?

"My child—if a boy—will be the heir of the Revels," I said slowly. "It's a tradition that they should be born in the house."

She lay back and closed her eyes. She looked so ill that I thought she had fainted, and I rose to look for the bell, but just at that moment Damaris came in.

"Mother!" she cried, and her face looked different because the masklike quality had left it. She looked younger, a lovely vital girl. I knew in that moment that she was very fond of the invalid. Her face changed as her gaze fell on me. "But Mrs. Rockwell! What . . . ? How . . . ?"

"I called on the doctor," I said, "and as I had to wait I thought I'd make use of the opportunity to see your mother."

"Oh, but . . ."

"Why, have I done something I shouldn't? I'm sorry. Are you not allowed to receive visitors?"

"It is the state of her health," said Damaris. "My father is very careful of her."

"He is afraid they will over-excite her . . . or what?"

"Yes, that is it. She has to be kept quiet." Damaris went to her mother and laid a hand on her brow.

"I'm all right, my darling," said Mrs. Smith.

"Your head's hot, Mother."

"Would you like me to go?" I asked.

"Please no," said Mrs. Smith quickly, but Damaris was looking doubtful. "Sit down, Damaris," she went on, and turning to me: "My daughter is over-anxious on my behalf."

"And I expect the doctor is," I said.

"Oh yes . . . yes!" Damaris put in.

"I know he must be because he is so kind to all his patients. I hear his praises sung wherever I go."

Mrs. Smith lay back, her eyes closed, and Damaris said: "Yes, yes. It is so. They rely on him."

"I hope he will soon be back," I said.

"I am sure he would have hurried back if he had known you were waiting for him."

Damaris sat down near her mother and began to talk. I had never heard her talk so much before. She talked of our trip to Knaresborough and the Christmas holiday; she talked of the " Bring and Buy " sale and other church activities.

It was thus that the doctor found us.

I heard his footsteps on the stairs and then the door was flung open. He was smiling but it was a different kind of smile from that which I usually saw on his face, and I knew that he was more disturbed than I had ever seen him before.

" Mrs. Rockwell," he cried. " Why, this is a surprise."

" I decided to make the acquaintance of Mrs. Smith while I was waiting."

He took my hand and held it firmly in his for a few seconds. I had a notion that he was seeking to control himself. Then he went to his wife's sofa and laid a hand on her brow.

" You are far too excited, my dear," he said. " Has she been exciting herself?"

He was looking at Damaris and I could not see his face clearly.

" No, Father." Damaris's voice sounded faint as though she were a little girl and not very sure of herself.

He had turned to me. " Forgive me, Mrs. Rockwell. I was concerned on two counts. On yours and that of my wife. You have come to see me. You have something to tell me?"

" Yes," I said, " I want to speak to you. I think it is important."

" Very well," he said. " You will come to my consulting room. Shall we go now?"

" Yes, please," I said; and I rose and went to Mrs. Smith's couch.

I took the cold clammy hand in mine and I wondered about her as I said good-bye. She had changed with the coming of her husband, but I was not sure in what way, for it was as though a shutter had been drawn over her expression. I believed he was going to scold her for exciting herself. She had the air of a child who had disobeyed.

Her welfare is his greatest concern, I thought; which is natural. He who is so kind to his patients would be especially so to her.

I said good-bye to Damaris and the doctor led the way down to his consulting room.

As he shut the door and gave me a chair at the side of the roll-top desk and took his own chair, I felt my spirits rise a little. He looked so benign that I could not believe he would do anything but help me.

"Now," he said, "what is the trouble?"

"Strange things have been happening to me," I burst out. "You know about them."

"Yes," he admitted. "Some you yourself have told me. I have heard of the rest through other sources."

"You know then that I saw a monk in my bedroom."

"I know that you thought you saw that."

"So you don't believe me."

He lifted a hand. "Let us say at this stage that I know that you saw it—if that comforts you."

"I don't want comfort, Dr. Smith. I want people to accept what I tell them as truth."

"That is not always easy," he said, "but remember I am here to help you."

"Then," I said, "there were the incidents of the bed curtains, the warming-pan and the cloak over the parapet."

"That cloak you are wearing," he said.

"So you even know that."

"I had to be told. I am, you know, looking after your health."

"And you believe that I have fancied all these things—that they did not really happen outside my imagination."

He did not speak for a moment and I insisted: "Do you? Do you?"

He lifted a hand. "Let us review this with calm. We need calm, Mrs. Rockwell. You need it more than you need anything else."

"I am calm. What I need is people who believe in me."

"Mrs. Rockwell, I am a doctor and I have had experience of many strange cases. I know I can talk to you frankly and intelligently."

"So you do not think I am mad?"

"Do not use such a word. There is no need to."

"I am not afraid of words . . . any more than I am afraid of people who dress up as monks and play tricks on me."

He was silent for a few seconds, then he said: "You are going through a difficult time. Your body is undergoing changes. Sometimes when this happens the personalities of women change. You have heard that they have odd fancies for things which they previously have been indifferent . . . ?"

"This is no odd fancy!" I cried. "I think I should tell you immediately that I am here because I know you have been discussing what you call my case with Mrs. Grantley and that you have both decided that I am . . . mentally unbalanced."

"You overheard this!" he said; and I could see that he was taken aback.

I had no intention of betraying Aunt Sarah, so I said: "I know that you have been discussing this together. You don't deny it."

"No," he said slowly, "that would be foolish of me, wouldn't it?"

"So you and she have decided that I am crazy."

"Nothing of the sort. Mrs. Rockwell, you are very excited. Now, before your pregnancy you were not easily excited, were you? That is one change we see."

"What are you planning to do with me . . . to send me to Worstwhistle?"

He stared at me, but he could not disguise the fact that the thought had been in his mind.

I was stricken with fury . . . and panic. I stood up but he was immediately beside me. He laid his hands on my shoulders and gently forced me back into my seat.

"You have misunderstood," he said, resuming his seat and speaking very gently. "This is a painful matter to me. I am very fond of the family at the Revels and their tragedies affect me deeply. Please believe that there is no question of your going to Wortwhistle . . . at this stage."

I took him up at once. "Then at what stage?"

"Please, please, be calm. Very good work is done at . . . that place. You know I am a regular visitor there. You have been overwrought for some weeks. You could not hide this from me."

"I have been overwrought because someone is trying to make me appear hysterical. And how dare you talk to me of that place! You must be mad yourself."

"I only want to help you."

"Then find out who is doing these things. Find out who had monks' robes at the pageant. We might discover who still has one."

"You are still thinking of that unfortunate incident."

"Of course I think of it. It was the beginning."

"Mrs. Rockwell . . . Catherine . . . I want to be your friend. You can't doubt that, can you?"

I looked into those dark brown eyes and I thought they were very soft and gentle.

"I became interested in you from the moment Gabriel brought you to the Revels," he went on. "And when your father came to the funeral I saw how matters stood between you. That touched me deeply. It made you seem so . . . vulnerable. But I am being too candid."

"I want to hear what you have to say," I insisted. "I want nothing held back."

"Catherine, I wish you would trust me. More than anything I want to help you through this difficult time. Damaris is not much younger than you, and when I have seen you together I have often wished that you, too, were my daughter. One of my dearest wishes was to be the father of a large family. But you are growing impatient with me. Let me say briefly that I have always felt towards you as I would towards a daughter, and I have hoped that you would confide in me, that I might be able to help you."

"The best way in which you could do that would be to find out who it was who dressed up as a monk and came to my bedroom. If you could find that person, I shall be in no need of help."

He looked at me sadly and shook his head.

"What are you suggesting?" I demanded.

"Only that I want you to confide your troubles in me . . . as you would to your own father." He hesitated and, shrugging his shoulders, added: "As you might have done to a father who was closer to you than your own. I would gladly protect you."

"So you think someone is threatening me?"

"Something is. It may be heredity. It may be . . ."

"I don't understand you."

"Perhaps I have said too much."

"No one is saying quite enough. If I knew everything that was in the minds of these people about me, I should be able to show you that you have misjudged me when you think me . . . unbalanced."

"But you believe now that I want to help you. You do, I hope, look on me as a friend as well as a doctor?"

I saw the anxiety in his eyes and I was deeply moved. He had noticed my father's indifference to me and in some way I had betrayed how that had hurt me. He had called me vulnerable. I had not thought of myself in that way before, but I was beginning to realise that it was exactly what I was. I had longed for the affection which had been denied me;

Uncle Dick had given it to me, but he was not here with me at this important crisis of my life. Dr. Smith was offering his sympathy and with it that particular brand of paternal devotion for which I had longed.

"You are very kind," I said.

A look of pleasure touched his features. He leaned forward and patted my hand.

Then he was suddenly very serious. "Catherine," he said, as though he were considering very carefully what he was saying, "a short time ago you told me that you wanted me to be absolutely frank. I have convinced you, haven't I, that I have your welfare at heart? I want you to know too that I owe a great debt to the Rockwell family. I am going to tell you something which is not generally known, because I want you to understand my deep devotion to the family of which you are now a member. You may remember I told you that I began my life as an unwanted child, a poor orphan, and that it was a rich man who gave me my opportunity to do the work I longed to do. That man was a Rockwell—Sir Matthew in fact. So you see I can never forget the debt of gratitude I owe to the family and to Sir Matthew in particular."

"I see," I murmured.

"He wants his grandson to be born strong and healthy. I long to make that possible. My dear Catherine, you must place yourself in my hands. You must take great care of yourself. You must let me take care of you. And there is one fact of which I believe you are ignorant; and I am now turning over in my mind whether or not I should tell you this."

"You must tell me. You must."

"Oh, Catherine, it may be when you have heard it, that you will wish I had not spoken. I am asking myself at this moment—as I have so many times—whether it is wiser to tell you or not."

"Please tell me. I don't want to be left in the dark."

"Are you strong enough to hear this, Catherine?"

"Of course I'm strong enough. The only thing I can't bear is lies . . . and secrets. I am going to find out who it is who is doing this to me."

"I am going to help you, Catherine."

"Then tell me what this is."

Still he hesitated. Then he said: "You must realise that

if I tell you, I do so because I want you to understand the need for you to listen to my advice."

" I will listen to your advice . . . only tell me."

Still he paused and it was as though he were seeking the right words.

Then suddenly they came rushing out. " Catherine, you know that I have for some years made a habit of visiting Worswhistle."

" Yes, yes."

" And you know what Worstwhistle is."

" Yes, of course I know."

" I am in a very trusted position there and I have access to the records of patients. As a medical man . . ."

" Naturally," I interrupted.

" A close relative of yours is in that institution, Catherine. I do not think you know of this . . . in fact I am sure you do not. Your mother has been a patient at Worstwhistle for the last seventeen years."

I stared at him; I felt as though the walls of the room were about to collapse upon me; there was a rushing in my ears. It seemed to me that this room with its roll-top desk, this man with the gentle eyes, were dissolving and in their place was a house made dark, not because the Venetian blinds were always drawn, but because there was always there an atmosphere of brooding tragedy. I heard a voice crying in the night: " Cathy . . . come back to me, Cathy." And I saw him, my tragic father, going off regularly each month and coming back dispirited, sad, melancholic.

" Yes," went on the doctor. " I fear it is so. I have never met your father but I am told that he is devoted to his wife, that he pays regular visits to the institution. Sometimes, Catherine, she knows who he is. Sometimes she does not know him. She has a doll which at times she knows to be a doll; and at others she thinks it is her child . . . you, Catherine. At Wortwhistle all that can be done for her is done . . . but she will never leave the place. Catherine, you see what I mean? Sometimes the seed is passed on. Catherine, do not look . . . so stricken. I am telling you that we can care for you . . . that we can help you. That's what I want to do. I am only telling you this so that you will put yourself in my hands. Believe me, Catherine."

I found that I had buried my face in my hands and that I was praying. I was crying: " Oh, God, let me have dreamed this. Let it not be true."

He had risen and was standing by my chair; his arm was about my shoulders.

"We'll fight it, Catherine," he said. "We'll fight it together."

Perhaps the word "fight" helped me. It was a lifelong habit of mine to fight for what I wanted. I kept thinking of that vision I had had. The curtain had been pulled about my bed. Who had pulled it? There had been a draught from the door. I would not accept this theory that I was the victim of delusions.

He sensed the change in my mood. "That's the spirit, Catherine," he said. "You don't believe me, do you?"

My voice sounded firm as I said: "I know someone is determined to harm me and my child."

"And do you believe that I would be so cruel as to concoct this story about your mother?"

I did not answer. There were my father's absences from home to be explained. How could he have known of these? And yet . . . I had always been led to believe that she had died.

Suppose it were true that my mother was in that place—it was not true that my mind was tainted. I have always been calm and self-possessed. There had never been any signs of hysteria. Even now when I had been subjected to this terror, I believed that I had been as calm as anyone could hope to be in the circumstances.

I was as certain as I ever had been that whatever had happened to my mother, I had not inherited her insanity.

"Oh, Catherine," he said, "you delight me. You are strong. I have every hope that we will fight this. Believe me, it is true that your mother, Catherine Corder, has been in Worstwhistle for the last seventeen years. You accept that, don't you, because you know that I would not tell you this unless I had made absolutely sure. But what you won't accept is that you have inherited one small part of her insanity. That's going to help us. We'll fight this."

I faced him and said in a firm voice: "Nothing will convince me that I have imagined these things which have happened to me since I came to the Revels."

He nodded. "Well then, my dear," he said, "the thing for us to do is to find out who is behind this. Have you any suspicions?"

"I have discovered that several people possessed a monk's robe five years ago at the time of the pageant. Luke had one,

Simon Redvers had one. And both of them are in line to inherit the Revels."

He nodded. "If anyone has been deliberately seeking to harm you . . ." he murmured.

"They have," I answered vehemently. "They have."

"Catherine," he said, "you are exhausted by your emotions. I should like you to go home and rest."

I was aware how weary I was, and I said: "I should like to be at home. I should like to be in my room . . . alone to rest and think of all this."

"I would drive you back but I have another patient to see."

"I don't want them to know that I've been to see you. I want to walk home and go in . . . just as though nothing unusual has happened."

"And you want to say nothing of all this?"

"At present, yes. I want to think."

"You are very brave, Catherine."

"I wish I were wiser."

"You are wise too, I think. I am going to ask you to do me a favour; will you?"

"What is it?"

"Will you allow Damaris to walk back with you?"

"That is not necessary."

"You said you would take my advice, and this news of your mother has been a great shock to you. Please, Catherine, do as I say."

"Very well. If Damaris has no objection."

"Of course she will have none. She will be delighted. Wait here and I will go and fetch her. I am going to give you a little brandy first. Please don't protest. It will do you good."

He went to a cabinet and brought out two glasses. He half filled one and gave it to me. The other he filled for himself.

He lifted the glass and smiled at me over it.

"Catherine," he said, "you will come through all this. Trust me. Tell me anything you discover which you think is important. You know how much I want to help."

"Thank you. But I can't drink all this."

"Never mind. You have had a little. It will help to revive you. I am going to find Damaris."

He went and I was not sure how long I remained alone. I kept going over it in my mind: My father's leaving Glen

House and not returning until the following day. He must have stayed a night near the institution . . . perhaps after seeing her he had to compose himself before returning home. So this was the reason for that house of gloom; this was why I had always felt the need to escape from it. He should have warned me; he should have prepared me. But perhaps it was better that I had not known. Perhaps it would have been better if I had never known.

Damaris came into the room with her father. She was wearing a heavy coat with fur at the collar, and her hands were thrust into a muff. I thought she looked sullen and reluctant to accompany me, so I began to protest that I was in no need of companionship.

But the doctor said determinedly: "Damaris would like a walk." He smiled at me as though everything were normal and he had not almost shattered my belief in myself by his revelations.

"Are you ready?" asked Damaris.

"Yes, I am ready."

The doctor shook my hand gravely. He said I should take a sedative to-night as I was sleeping badly, implying to Damaris, I thought, that this was the reason for my coming. I took the bottle he gave me and thrust it into the inside pocket of my cloak; and Damaris and I set out together.

"How cold it is!" she said. "We shall have snow before morning if this continues."

The wind had whipped the colour to her cheeks and she looked beautiful in her little hat which was trimmed with the same fur as her muff.

"Let's go through the copse," she said. "It's a little longer but we shall escape the wind."

I was walking as though in my sleep. I did not notice where we went. I could only go over and over in my mind what the doctor had told me, and the more I thought of it the more likely it seemed.

We stopped in the shelter of some trees for a while for Damaris said she had a stone in her boot which was hurting her. She sat on a fallen tree-trunk and removed the boot, shaking it and then putting it on again. She grew red trying to do the buttons up.

Then we went on, but the boot was still hurting her and she sat down on the grass while the operation was repeated.

"It's a tiny piece of flint," she said. "This must be it."

183

And she lifted her hand to throw it away. "It's amazing that such a little thing could cause such discomfort. Oh dear, these wretched buttons."

"Let me help."

"No, I can do them myself." She struggled for a little while, then she looked up to say: "I'm glad you met my mother. She was really very pleased to see you."

"Your father seems very anxious about her."

"He is. He's anxious about all his patients."

"And she is, of course, a very special patient," I added.

"We have to watch her or she will overtax her strength."

I thought of Ruth's words. She was a hypochondriac and it was because of the doctor's life with her that he threw himself so wholeheartedly into his work.

But my mind was filled by one thought only as I stood there among the trees.

Was it true? I did not ask that question about my mother because everything fitted so well. I knew that must be true. What did I mean then? I had asked the question involuntarily: Am I like my mother? In doing so I had admitted my doubts.

Standing there in the woods on that December day I felt that I had come as near to despair as I had in my whole life. But I had not touched the very bottom yet. That was imminent but at that moment I believed that nothing worse could happen to me.

Damaris had buttoned her boot; she had thrust her hands into her muff and we were off again.

I was surprised when I found that we had come out of the trees on the far side of the Abbey, and that it was necessary to walk through the ruins to the Revels.

"I know," said Damaris, "that this is a favourite spot of yours."

"It was," I amended. "It is some time since I have been here."

I realised now that the afternoon was fading and that in an hour or so it would be dark.

I said: "Luke must take you home."

"Perhaps," she answered.

It seemed darker in the ruins. It was naturally so because of the shadows cast by those piles of stones. We had passed the fish-ponds and were in the heart of the Abbey when I saw the monk. He was passing through what was left of the arcade; silently and swiftly he went; and he was exactly as he had been at the foot of my bed.

I cried out: "Damaris! There! Look!"

The figure paused at the sound of my voice, and, turning, beckoned. Then he turned away and went on. Now the figure had disappeared behind one of the buttresses which held up what was left of the arcade; now it was visible again as it moved into the space between one buttress and the next.

I watched it, fascinated, horrified, yet unable to move.

I cried out: "Quick! We must catch him."

Damaris clung to my arm, holding me back.

"But there is no time to waste," I cried. "We'll lose him. We know he's somewhere in the Abbey. We've got to find him. He shan't get away this time."

Damaris said: "Please, Catherine . . . I'm frightened."

"So am I. But we've got to find him." I went stumbling towards the arcade, but she was dragging me back.

"Come home," she cried. "Come home at once."

I turned to face her. "You've seen it," I cried triumphantly. "So now you can tell them. You've seen it!"

"We must go to the Revels," she said. "We must go at once."

"But . . ." I realised that we could not catch him because he could move so much faster than we could. But that was not so important. Someone else had seen him, and I was exultant. Relief following so fast on panic was almost unendurable. Only now could I admit how shaken I had been, how frightened.

But there was no need to fear. I was vindicated. Someone else had seen.

She was dragging me through the ruins and the house was in sight.

"Oh, Damaris," I said, "how thankful I am that it happened then . . . that you saw."

She turned her beautiful, blank face towards me and her words made me feel as though I had suddenly been plunged into icy water.

"What did you see, Catherine?"

"Damaris . . . what do you mean?"

"You were very excited. You could see something, couldn't you?"

"But do you mean to say you didn't!"

185

"There wasn't anything there, Catherine. There was nothing."

I turned to her. I was choking with rage and anguish. I believe I took her arm and shook her.

"You're lying," I cried. "You're pretending."

She shook her head as though she was going to burst into tears.

"No, Catherine, no. I wish I had . . . How I wish I could have seen . . . if it meant so much to you."

"You saw it," I said. "I know you saw it."

"I didn't see anything, Catherine. There wasn't anything."

I said coldly: "So you are involved in this, are you?"

"What, Catherine, what?" she asked piteously.

"Why did you take me to the Abbey? Because you knew it would be there. So that you could say that you saw nothing. So that you could tell them I am mad!"

I was losing control, because I was thoroughly frightened. I had admitted my fear when I thought there was no longer reason to be afraid; and that was my undoing.

She was clutching at my arm but I threw her off.

"I don't need your help," I said. "I don't want your help. Go away. At least I've proved that you are his accomplice."

I stumbled on. I could not move very fast. It was as though the child within me protested.

I entered the house; it seemed quiet and repelling. I went to my room and lay on my bed, and I stayed there until darkness came. Mary-Jane came to ask if I wished to have dinner sent up to me; but I said I was not hungry, only very tired.

I sent her away and I locked the doors.

That was my darkest hour.

Then I took a dose of the doctor's sedative and soon I fell into merciful sleep.

Chapter 6

There is some special quality which develops in a woman who is to have a child; already the fierce instinct is with her. She will protect that child with all the power of which she is capable and, as her determination to do so increases, so it seems does that power.

I awoke next morning refreshed after the unbroken sleep

which the doctor's sedative had given me. The events of the previous day came rushing back to my mind, and even then I felt as though I were at the entrance of a dark tunnel it would be disastrous for me to enter, but into which I might be swept by the bitter blast of ill-fortune.

But the child was there, reminding me of its existence. Where I went there must the child go; what happened to me must have its effect on the child. I was going to fight this thing which was threatening to destroy me—not only for myself but for the sake of one who was more precious to me.

When Mary-Jane came in with my breakfast she did not see that anything was different, and I felt that was my first triumph. I had been terrified that I should be unable to hide the fear which had almost prostrated me on the previous day

"It's a grand morning, madam," she said.

"Is it, Mary-Jane?"

"A bit of a wind still, but any road t'sun's shining."

"I'm glad."

I half closed my eyes and she went out. I found it difficult to eat, but I managed a little. The sun sent a feeble ray on to the bed and it cheered me; I thought it was symbolic. The sun is always there, I reminded myself, only the clouds get in between. There's always a way of dealing with every problem, only ignorance gets in the way.

I wanted to think very clearly. I knew in my heart that what I had seen had been with my eyes, not with my imagination. Inscrutable as it seemed, there was an explanation somewhere.

Damaris was clearly involved in the plot against me; and what more reasonable than that she should be, for if Luke wished to frighten me into giving birth to a stillborn child, and Damaris was to be his wife, it was surely reasonable enough to suppose that she would work with him.

But it was possible that these two young people could plot so diabolical a murder, for murder it would be even though the child had not come into the world.

I tried to review the situation clearly and work out what must be done. The first thing that occurred to me was that I might go back to my father's house. I rejected that idea almost as soon as it came. I should have to give a reason. I should have to say: "Someone at the Revels is trying to drive me to the brink of madness. Therefore I am running away." I felt that it would be an admission of my fear, and if, for one moment, I accepted the view that I was suffering from hallucinations, I had taken the first steps on that road along which someone here was trying to force me.

I did not think at this time I could endure the solemnity, the morbid atmosphere of my father's house.

I had made my decision: I could never know peace of mind again until I had solved this mystery. It was therefore not something from which I could run away. I was going to intensify my search for my persecutor. I owed it to myself—and to my child.

I must now make a practical plan, and I decided that I would go to Hagar and take her into my confidence. I should have preferred to act alone, but that was impossible because my first step, I had decided, must be to go to Worstwhistle and confirm Dr. Smith's words.

I could not ask anyone at the Revels to drive me there so I must go to Hagar.

When I had bathed and dressed I set out immediately for Kelly Grange.

It was about half past ten when I arrived, and I went straight to Hagar and told her what the doctor had told me.

She listened gravely and when I had finished she said: Simon shall take you to that place immediately. I think with you that should be the first step."

She rang for Dawson and told her to send Simon to us at once. Remembering my suspicions of Simon I was a little anxious, but I realised that I had to get to Worstwhistle even if it did mean taking a chance; and as soon as he entered the room my suspicions vanished, and I was ashamed that I had ever entertained them. That was the effect he was beginning to have on me.

Hagar told him what had happened. He looked astonished and then he said: " Well, we'd better get over to Worstwhistle right away."

" I will send someone over to the Revels to tell them that you are taking luncheon with me," said Hagar; and I was glad she had thought of that because I should have aroused their curiosity if I had not returned.

Fifteen minutes later Simon was driving the trap, with me sitting beside him, along the road to Worstwhistle. We did not speak much during that journey; and I was grateful to him for falling in with my mood. I could think of nothing but the interview before me which was going to mean so much to me. I kept remembering my father's absences from home and the sadness which always seemed to surround him; and I could not help believing that there was truth in what the doctor had told me.

It was about midday when we came to Worstwhistle—a grey stone building which to my mind resembled nothing so much as a prison. It *was* a prison, I told myself—stone walls within which the afflicted lived out their clouded lives. Was it possible that my own mother was among those sad inhabitants, and that there was a plot afoot to make me a prisoner here?

I was determined that should never be.

Surrounding the building was a high wall and when we drew up at the heavy wrought-iron gates, a porter came out of the lodge and asked our business.

Simon told him authoritatively that he wished to see the Principal of the establishment.

"You have an appointment with him, sir?"

"It's of the utmost importance," Simon replied and threw the man a coin.

Whether it was the money or Simon's manner, I was not sure, but the gates were opened to us and we drove along a gravel drive to the main building.

A man in livery emerged as we approached and Simon dismounted and helped me down.

"Who'll hold the horse?" he asked.

The porter shouted and a boy appeared. He held the horse while we, with the man in livery, went towards the porch.

"Will you tell the Principal that we wish to see him immediately on a matter of great urgency?"

Again I was grateful for that authoritative arrogance which resulted in immediate obedience.

We were led through the porch into a stone-flagged hall in which a fire was burning; but it was not enough to warm the place, and I felt the chill. But perhaps it was a spiritual rather than a physical chill.

I was shivering. Simon must have noticed this for he took my arm and I found comfort in that gesture.

"Please to sit in here, sir," said the porter; and he opened a door on our right to disclose a high-ceilinged room with whitewashed walls, a heavy table, and a few chairs. "Your name, sir?"

"This is Mrs. Rockwell of Kirkland Revels, and I am Mr. Redvers."

"You say you had an appointment, sir?"

"I did not say so."

"It's usual to make one, sir."

"We are pressed for time and, as I said, the matter is urgent. Pray go and tell the Principal that we are here."

The porter retired, and when he was gone Simon smiled at me.

"Anyone would think we were trying to see the Queen." Then his face softened into a tenderness which I had never seen him give to anyone before except perhaps Hagar. "Cheer up," he said, "even if it's true, it's not the end of the world, you know."

"I'm glad you came with me, I hadn't meant to say that but the words slipped out.

He took my hand and pressed it firmly. It was a gesture which meant that we were not foolish, hysterical people and should be able to take the calm view.

I walked away from him because I did not trust my emotions. I went to the window and looked out, and I thought of the people who were held captive here. This was their little world. They looked out on the gardens and the moor beyond—if they were allowed to look out of windows—and this was all they knew of life. Some had been here for years . . . seventeen years. But perhaps they were kept shut away. Perhaps they did not even see the gardens and the moor.

It seemed that we waited a very long time before the porter returned. Then he said: "Come this way, will you, please."

As we followed him up a flight of stairs, and along a corridor, I caught a glimpse of barred windows and shivered. So like a prison, I thought.

Then the porter rapped on a door on which the word "Superintendent" had been painted. A voice said "Come in"; and Simon, taking my arm, drew me into the room with him. The whitewashed walls were bare; the oilcloth polished to danger point; and it was a cold and cheerless room; at a desk a man with a tired grey face and a resentful look in his eyes because, I presumed, we had dared invade his privacy without an appointment.

"Pray sit down," he said, when the porter had left us. "Am I to understand that your business is urgent?"

"It is of the utmost urgency to us," said Simon.

I spoke then. "It was good of you to see us. I am Mrs. Rockwell, but before my marriage I was Catherine Corder."

"Oh!" The gleam of understanding which came into his face was a blow which shattered my hopes.

I said: "You have a patient here of that name?"

"Yes, that is so."

I looked at Simon and, try as I might, I could not speak because my tongue had become parched, my throat constricted.

"The point is," went on Simon, " Mrs. Rockwell has only very recently heard that a Catherine Corder may be here. She has reason to believe that this may be her mother. She has always been under the impression that her mother died when she was very young. Naturally she wishes to know whether the Catherine Corder in this establishment is her mother."

"The information we have about our patients is confidential, as you will appreciate."

"We do appreciate that," said Simon. "But in the case of very close relatives would you not be prepared to give the information which was asked?"

"It would first be necessary to prove the relationship."

I burst out: "Before my marriage my name was Catherine Corder. My father is Mervyn Corder of Glen House, Glengreen, near Harrogate. Please tell me whether the patient you have here, who bears the same name as myself, is my mother."

The Superintendent hesitated; then he said: "I can tell you nothing except that we have a patient here of that name. It is not such an unusual name. Surely your father would supply the information you are seeking from me?"

I looked at Simon, who said: "I should have thought that such a close relation had a right to know."

"As I said, the relationship would first have to be proved. I do not think I could betray the trust placed in me by my patient's relations."

"Tell me," I cried wildly, "does her husband come to visit her regularly each month?"

"Many of our patients' relatives visit them regularly."

He surveyed us coldly and I could see that he was adamant. Simon was exasperated, but he could not move the Superintendent.

"Could I see . . . ?" I began.

But the Superintendent held up his hand in horror. "Certainly not," he said sharply. "That would be quite impossible."

Simon looked at me helplessly. "There's only one thing to do," he said. "You must write to your father."

"I think you are right in that," said the Superintendent, rising to imply that he had given us enough of his time. "Our patient has been placed here by her husband, but if he gives you permission to see her we should raise no objection, providing, of course, that she is well enough to receive you when you come. That is all the help I can give you."

He pulled the bell and the porter reappeared. We were led out to the waiting trap.

I felt frustrated as we drove away. Simon did not speak until he had put about a mile between us and the institution. Then he pulled up. We were in a lane over which the trees would make an arch of green in the summer; now we could see the blue-grey sky between the black branches, and the clouds being chased across it by the keen wind.

I did not feel the wind; nor, I imagine, did Simon.

He turned to me and slid his arm behind me, although not touching me.

"You're depressed by all this," he said.

"Do you wonder?"

"It wasn't altogether illuminating, was it?"

"Illuminating enough. They have a Catherine Corder there. He did tell us that."

"She may not be connected with you."

"I think it is too much of a coincidence if she should not be. I haven't told you, have I, that my father used to disappear at regular intervals. We did not know where he went. I used to think that he went visiting some—woman . . ." I laughed harshly. "I know now that he went to Worstwhistle."

"Can you be so sure?"

"Something tells me it is so. Dr. Smith, remember, has seen her records and he has told me that she is my mother."

Simon was silent for a few seconds and then he said: "It's not like you, Catherine, to despair."

I noticed that he had dropped the Mrs. and I knew intuitively that that was a sign of the change in our relationship.

"Would you not feel like despair if all this were happening to you?"

"The best way to fight something that frightens you is to go right up to it and look it in the face."

"I am doing that."

"Well, what is the worst that could happen?"

192

"That another Catherine Corder should be taken to that place. That her child should be born there."

"We'll not let it happen. Nobody could do that, could they?"

"Could they not? If the doctor was convinced that it was the best place for me?"

"It's all such nonsense. I never knew anyone so sane. You're as sane as I am."

I turned to him and said vehemently: "I am, Simon, I *am*."

He took my hands and, to my astonishment—for I had not until this moment thought him capable of such a gesture towards me—he kissed them, and I could feel the fervour of those kisses through my gloves.

Then he pressed my hand so tightly that I winced at the pain of his grip.

"I'm with you in this," he said.

I knew a moment of great happiness. I felt the strength of him flowing into my body, and I was grateful, so grateful that I wondered whether such gratitude must be love.

"Do you mean it?"

"Heart and soul," he answered. "Nobody shall take you where you don't want to go."

"The way things have been going alarms me, Simon. I'm looking this right in the face, as you said. And I am frightened. I thought I should fight it better by pretending not to be afraid, but pretence isn't going to help, is it? Ever since I saw the monk the first time, life has changed for me. I've been like a different person . . . a frightened person. I now know that all the time I've been wondering what is going to happen next. It has made me nervous . . . different, Simon, different."

"Anyone would feel so. There's nothing strange about that."

"You don't believe in ghosts, Simon, do you? If people say they see a ghost, you think they're lying or that they've imagined they saw something."

"I don't think that about you."

"Then you can only think that inside the monk's robe was a real person."

"Yes, I think that."

"Then I must tell you all the truth. Nothing must be held back." And I told him of the apparition I had seen in the Abbey when Damaris was with me, and how she had declared there had been nothing there. " I think that was the worst moment of all because then I began to doubt myself."

" We must assume that Damaris knows what's going on ; she must be a party to the plot."

" I am sure Luke wants to marry her, but does she want to marry Luke?"

" Perhaps she wants to marry the Revels," said Simon ; " and she couldn't do that, could she, unless the place was Luke's."

" You're helping me . . . you're helping me a lot."

" It's what I want to do more than anything."

" How can I thank you! "

His arm was round me now ; he drew me to him and kissed me lightly on the cheek. I could feel his cold face pressed against mine for a few seconds and the warmth which enveloped me surprised me.

" It is strange that I should look to you for comfort.".

" Not at all strange. We're two of a kind."

" Oh yes, you admire my common sense. You thought it was very clever of me to marry Gabriel . . . for his possessions."

" So you remember that."

" It is not the sort of thing one is likely to forget. I suppose you would not blame whoever it is who wants to drive me mad . . . if they succeed."

" I'd wring his neck . . . if I could find him."

" Then your attitude has changed."

" Not in the least. I didn't admire you for, as I thought, marrying Gabriel for what he could give you. I admired you for your sharp wits and your courage . . . which I knew were there."

" I am not being very courageous now."

" You are going to be."

" I must be, it seems, if I am to retain your good opinion."

He was pleased by the lightness which had crept into our conversation ; as for myself I was surprised that, with the burden of suspicion that was lying heavily upon me, I could indulge in it ; but it did me good—that much I knew.

" Yes," he repeated, " you are going to be. And I am here to help you."

" Thank-you, Simon."

He looked at me intently for a few seconds and I read in his looks the knowledge which he wished me to share. He and I were about to embark on a new relationship ; it was an exciting one; it would be one of stimulation to us both, of fierce disagreements and splendid accord. We were two of a kind. He had recognised that, as I did now. I knew what he was telling me, and I wanted to listen so much.

I went on: " There have been times when I did not know whom I could trust."

" You will trust me," he said.

" It sounds like a command." I smiled. " It often does when you make a statement."

" That is a command."

" And you think you have a right to command me?"

" Yes . . . in view of . . . everything, I do."

I did not want to move from this spot. I felt as though I had found a peaceful place in which to rest and be happy. Behind me lay that grim institution with its dark secrets; ahead of me the Revels and, somewhere not far distant, was my father's house. But here I was suspended between threats of disaster, and here I wanted to stay.

I believed in that moment that I was in love with Simon Redvers and he with me. It was a strange conclusion to arrive at at such a time in a cold country lane.

It did not seem strange to me that these strong emotions I felt were for Simon Redvers. In some way he reminded me of Gabriel; he was Gabriel without his weakness. When I was with Simon I understood what had made me hurry into that marriage with Gabriel. I had seen something to love and protect there, and that was what I needed; I had loved him in a way, for there are many kinds of love. Pity is love, I thought; the need to protect is love. But there was a deep and passionate love of which I knew nothing; I knew, though, that to love completely one must know every phase of loving, and that was the real adventure, to widen one's emotions, to discover their depths as the years passed.

But I was a long way from such an adventure. There was so much to be lived through first. I had to be delivered of a child and of my fear. And at this moment I could not peer very far into the mist which hid the future.

But Simon was with me, and such a thought, even at this time, could set my senses singing.

" Very well," I said, " I am ready to listen to your commands."

" Ready then. The first thing we're going to do is drive to an inn a mile along this road. There we are going to eat."

" I couldn't eat."

"You have forgotten that you suggested I should command."

"But the thought of food revolts me."

"There is a quiet little room just off the inn parlour where the host serves his special guests. I am always a special guest. His speciality is a pudding made with steak and mushrooms. It has to be tasted to be believed. We'll have a claret which he will bring from his cellar especially for us. I defy you to resist when you smell the aroma of mine host's speciality."

"I will come with you and watch you enjoy it."

He took my hand again, brought it half-way to his lips, then pressed it and smiled at me.

It was strange that I could be almost happy as we bowled along that road with the wind in our faces and the wintry sun trying to smile at us ; but I was.

I even ate a little of the special pudding ; and the claret warmed me.

Simon was practical as he always would be.

"Your next step," he said, "is to write to your father. You must ask him for the truth. But mind you, whatever the truth, we are not going to be downhearted."

"But suppose that is really my mother in that place?"

"Well, suppose it is."

"Let's look at it clearly, Simon. My mother in that place . . . and myself, according to some, seeing visions, doing strange things."

"We don't believe in the visions, do we?" he said gently.

"I don't. And how can I thank you and your grandmother for supporting me in this?"

"You don't have to thank us for having an opinion, Catherine. If we could only catch the monk in the act, that is all we should need to prove our case. It's my opinion that he's found some place in which to hide himself. We must try to discover it. Next week the Christmas festivities will begin, and my grandmother and I will spend two nights in the house. That may give us a chance to discover something."

"I wish it were this week."

"It will soon come."

"And if they try anything in the meantime . . . ?"

He was silent for a few seconds, then he said: "If you should see the monk again, tell no one. I believe he wants you to talk of what you have seen, but do not give him that satisfaction. Continue to lock your doors at night so that you can't be startled from your sleep. You haven't been, have

196

you, since you began to lock them? I think that's significant. In the meantime you will hear from your father—and you are not going to be distressed, whatever he has to tell you. I never did believe that we relied on our ancestors for what we are. We are in command of our own fates."

"I'll remember that, Simon."

"Yes, do remember it. What we are and what we become is in our own hands. Think of it like this: what is the population of England to-day? Some ten times what it was a few hundred years ago. Has it struck you that if we could trace our ancestors far back enough we must all be related in some way with each other. In all our families there have very likely been rogues and saints, madmen and geniuses. No, Catherine, each of us is an individual with his—or her—own life in his hands."

"You are philosophical," I said. "I had never thought that. I had thought you practical in the extreme, excelling in good, straightforward common sense, but without imagination and therefore without sympathy."

"That's the mask I wear. We all wear them, don't we? I'm tough; I'm shrewd; I'm a blunt man who doesn't mince his words. That's the outward me. Not a very attractive personality, you'll agree, as you did on our first meeting. Brash, determined that no one shall get the better of him— therefore he's going to start trying to get the better of everyone else. That's part of me . . . I don't deny it. I'm all of that. But perhaps I'm something else besides. A man's made up of many parts. . . ." He looked at me slyly. "And a woman is probably more complex still."

"Please go on," I said. "You're doing so much for me."

"All right. When you go back to the Revels how are you going to feel?"

"I don't know, except that it won't be so good as I feel here."

"No," he said. You're going to be afraid. You're going to hurry up the stairs, turning to see if you are being pursued; you're going to throw open the door of your room, and you're going to look anxiously about you to see if he's there. Then you're going to lock him out, but you won't lock out your fear completely, because it's there in your mind and with the darkness your fear will grow stronger."

"You are right, of course."

He leaned across the table and took my hand.

"Catherine, there is nothing to fear. There is never anything to fear. Fear is like a cage which prevents our escaping, but *we* make the bars of the cage ourselves. We see them as strong iron bars . . . unbreakable. They are not so, Catherine. We ourselves have the power to take those bars in our hands and break them. They can be strong; they can be flimsy; for we ourselves have made them what they are."

"You are telling me *I* have nothing to fear!"

"Nothing has really harmed you, has it. You have only been frightened."

"How can I know that it never will?"

"The motive, at least, is becoming clear to us. This person —or persons—is seeking to unnerve you. Your life is not in danger. If you were to die violently, following Gabriel, suspicions would certainly be aroused. No, it is the child who is threatened. This person's motive is to reduce you to such a state of fear that your chances of producing a healthy child are endangered. In view of Gabriel's death, it has to appear natural."

"And Gabriel's death . . ." I began.

"I am beginning to think that was the first act in the drama."

"And Friday?" I murmured, remembering then the night before Gabriel's death, when Friday had behaved strangely and insisted on going into the corridor. I told Simon of this. "There was someone there. Waiting. But for Friday it might have been that night. And then Friday disappeared."

He put his hand over mine. "We don't know how it happened," he said. "Let us concern ourselves with what lies ahead of us; we can only conjecture what happened in the past. If we can discover the identity of our monk, if we can catch him in his robe, then we can demand an explanation; and I have no doubt that we shall learn what part he played in Gabriel's death."

"We must find him, Simon."

"We must. But if you see him again, ignore him. Do not try to tackle him. Heaven knows what he might do. If there's anything in our conjectures about Gabriel, remember we may be dealing with a murderer. You must do as I say, Catherine."

"I will, Simon."

"And remember," he added, "you are not alone. We're fighting this . . . together."

We left the inn and he drove me back to the Revels. I was pleased because, although my visit to Worstwhistle had not

198

given me the satisfaction for which I had hoped, I no longer felt alone, and that was a wonderful comfort.

I wrote to my father and I believed that I should have the truth from him in a few days' time, because he would understand my need to know quickly; and when I had posted the letter I felt strengthened. Nothing unusual happened the next day, and during the following morning Dr. Smith came to the house.

He wanted to see me alone, and Ruth left us in the winter parlour together.

He looked at me almost tenderly as he came to the chair in which I was sitting. He laid his hand on the arm of the chair and said gently: " So you paid a visit to Worstwhistle."

" I wanted to be sure," I explained.

" Of course you did. And you satisfied yourself that I had been speaking the truth?"

" They would tell me nothing."

He nodded. " The Superintendent acted in the only way possible. Naturally he must respect the privacy of his patients and their relations. But you did discover that there was a patient of that name in the institution."

" Yes."

" Catherine, believe me. I am telling you the truth when I say I know that patient to be your mother. Your father, Mervyn Corder, visits her regularly each month. No doubt he thought he was wise in keeping this from you."

" If the patient in Worstwhistle is my mother, no doubt he did."

" I am glad to see you calmer, Catherine. If you had asked me, I would have taken you to Worstwhistle. You would have seen then that I could have done so much more for you than Simon Redvers could possibly do."

I was almost on the point of telling him that I had written to my father, but I did not do so. Simon had said that the two of us would solve the mystery together, and I wanted to keep this our secret matter.

Besides, there was little I hoped for from anything my father could tell me. It semed obvious that the Catherine Corder who was in Worstwhistle must be my mother.

" Perhaps later," the doctor was saying. " I will take you to the place and you might see her."

" Would that serve any useful purpose since I have never known her?"

"But you would like to see your own mother?"

"I doubt if she would know me."

"She has her lucid moments. There are times when she thinks she is young again and you are a baby. And there are other times when she is vaguely aware of what has happened to her."

I shivered. I was not going to tell him that I had a horror of entering that place; that I had a strange premonition that if I crossed that threshold again, I might become a prisoner there. If I told him that, he would listen with sympathy, but he would be telling himself that it was part of my overwrought condition which made me imagine that, as I imagined that I saw "visions."

I could not be so frank with him as I was with Simon. This was a further indication of my feelings for the latter. I told myself that I could trust no one—not even Dr. Smith—for I knew that he was ready to believe that I was in an unbalanced state. But it wasn't true that I trusted no one. I trusted Simon.

Christmas was three days away. The servants had decorated the hall with branches of holly and there was mistletoe too. I had heard some of the female servants giggling with the men as this was fixed up in the most appropriate places. I had seen the dignified William seize Mary-Jane and give her a resounding kiss under the pearly berries. Mary-Jane responded good-humouredly; it was all part of the fun at Christmas.

Then I received the letter. I was in the garden when I saw the postman coming towards the house. I had been looking out for him because I did not believe my father would keep me long in suspense.

And I was right. There was his handwriting on the envelope.

With wildly beating heart I hurried to my bedroom, and took the precaution of locking the doors before I opened the letter.

My dear Catherine, I read,

I was startled and shocked to receive your letter. I understand your feelings and, before you read any further, I want to assure you that the Catherine Corder who is now in Worstwhistle is *not* your mother, although she is my wife.

I had meant, of course, to tell you the truth on your

marriage, but I did not feel I could do so without consulting my brother, who is deeply concerned in this.

My wife and I were devoted to each other, and two years after our marriage we had a child—a daughter named Catherine. But this was not you. My wife adored our daughter and could scarcely bear the child out of her sight. She spent the greater part of her time in the nursery supervising everything concerned with her. We had a nurse, of course. She came to us with good recommendations, and she was affectionate, fond of children and efficient—when she was not under the influence of gin.

One day when my wife and I had been visiting friends, there was mist on the moor and we lost our way. We were two hours later than we had expected to be, and when we returned the damage had been done. The nurse, taking advantage of our absence, had become intoxicated; and while she was in this state she had decided to bath the baby. She put our child into a bath of scalding water. There was only one consolation—death must have been Almost instantaneous.

My dear Catherine, you who are about to become a mother will understand the grief which overtook my wife. She blamed herself for leaving the child in the nurse's care. I shared her grief, but hers did not grow less as time passed. She continued to mourn the child and I began to be alarmed when she gave way to accusations against herself. She would pace through the house wildly sobbing, wildly laughing. I did not know then what this tragedy had done to her.

I used to tell her that we would have more children. But I could see that the need to pacify her was urgent. And then your uncle Dick had this idea.

I know how fond you are of your Uncle Dick. He has always been so good to you. That is natural, Catherine, when the relationship between you is known. He is your father, Catherine.

It is difficult to explain this to you. I wish he were here so that he could do it himself. He was not a bachelor as he was thought to be. His wife—your mother—was French. He met her when he was in port for a spell at Marseilles. She came from Provence and they were married within a few weeks of their first meeting. They

201

were ideally suited and deeply regretted your father's long absences. I believe he had almost decided to give up the sea when you were about to be born. Strangely enough tragedy hit us both in the same year. Your mother died when you were born ; and that was not more than two months after we had lost our child.

Your father brought you to us because he wanted a settled home for you, and he and I believed at the time that having a child to care for would help to comfort my wife. You even had the same name. We had called our child Catherine after my wife, and your father—because you were coming to us—had decided that you should be Catherine too. . . .

I stopped for a few seconds. I was seeing it all so clearly ; events were fitting together neatly to make the picture.

I was exultant because that which I had feared was not true after all.

Then, projecting myself into the past, I seemed to remember her, the wild-eyed woman who held me tightly, so tightly that I cried out in protest. I thought of the man whom I had known as my father, living through those weary years, never forgetting the happiness he had shared with the woman in Worstwhistle, dreaming that he was back in those days of anguish, calling for her to return . . . not as she was now, but as she had been.

I was filled with pity for him, for her ; and I wished that I had been more tolerant of that gloomy house with its drawn blinds and the sunlight shut out.

I picked up the letter.

Dick thought that you would feel more secure with us than you could be with him. It was no life for a child, he said, with a father who was constantly away from home, particularly one who had no mother. He could not leave the sea now that your mother was dead ; he told me that he missed her more when he was ashore than when he was at sea, which was natural enough. So we let you believe that you were my daughter, although I often said to him that you would have been happier to know you were his. You know how devoted to your interests he always was. He was determined that you should receive part of your education in your mother's country and that was why you were sent to Dijon. But we wanted everyone to think of you as my child because I was sure in the beginning that your aunt would come to think of you as her own more readily that way.

If only it had worked! For a while we thought it would. But the shock had been too much for her to bear and it was necessary to send her away. When she had left we moved to Glen House. It seemed better to cut ourselves off from old associations, and there we were not far from her place of asylum . . .

How I wished I had known! Perhaps then I should have been able to do something to comfort him.

But the past was over and I was happy on that December morning because I was delivered of my fears.

Now I would set to work to discover who in this house was my enemy; and I would go to it with such a will that I could not fail.

My baby would be born in the early spring and I would never for a minute be parted from my child. Uncle Dick—no, my father, but I should never be able to call him that; he would always be Uncle Dick to me—Uncle Dick would come home.

I would watch over my child, and Simon would be there, and our relationship would develop as such relationships should, gradually budding, flowering, bearing fruit.

Yes, I was happy on that day.

It seemed as though the Fates had determined to be kind to me, for another incident took place on the very next day which could not fail further to raise my spirits.

During the previous day I had hugged the news to myself. I had my meals in my own room because, although I wanted to flourish the letter under the noses of Ruth, Luke, Sir Matthew and Aunt Sarah, I had decided that for a while I was going to keep this news to myself. Nothing could have strengthened me more. My fear had gone. I was certain that if I awakened to find the monk at the foot of my bed I should be quite calm. But I was determined to discover who the monk was, and I would do this because I was no longer hampered by terrible doubts.

Caution, I said to myself. For the time being no one must know.

Simon? I asked myself. Should I tell Simon and Hagar?

The wind was bitingly cold and I decided that if it snowed

I might do myself some harm, so I stayed indoors. I did think of sending a letter to them. But how could I be sure, absolutely sure, that it would not be intercepted?

The news could wait. In the meantime I would plan what I was going to do next.

It was after luncheon when Mary-Jane came to me in a state of excitement.

" It's our Etty, madam," she said. " Her time's come. . . . Two days before Christmas. We hadn't thought it would be till the New Year."

" You want to go and see her, don't you, Mary-Jane?"

" Oh well, madam. . . . Me Dad's just sent word. Me Mother's gone over there."

" Look, Mary-Jane, you go along and see how she's getting on. You may be able to help."

" Thank you, madam."

" There's a terrible wind blowing."

" Oh, I won't mind that, madam."

" Just a moment," I said. And I went to my wardrobe and brought out my heaviest cloak. It was the blue one which had been hung across the parapet. I put it about Mary-Jane and pulled the hood right over her head. " This will keep out the wind." I said. " It buttons right up, you see . . . and the cold can't penetrate."

" That's good of you, madam."

" I don't want you catching cold, Mary-Jane."

" Oh, madam . . . thank you." Her gratitude was indeed sincere. She went on rather shyly: " I'm . . . so pleased, madam, because you've seemed so much better this last day or so."

I laughed as I finished buttoning the cloak.

" I am better. So much better," I told her. " Go on now . . . and don't worry about getting back. Stay for the night if you want to."

It was about dusk when she returned. She came straight up to my room and I saw at once that she was deeply disturbed.

" Etty . . ." I began.

She shook her head. " The baby was born before I got there, madam. A lovely girl. Our Etty's all right."

" What's wrong, then?"

" It was when I was coming home. I came round by the Abbey. And I saw it, madam. It gave me a turn. You see, it was nearly dark . . ."

204

"You saw . . . what?" I cried.

"It, madam. The monk. It looked at me and it beckoned."

"Oh, Mary-Jane, how wonderful! What did you do? What did you do?"

"I stood for a second or two staring. I didn't seem as if I could move. I was struck all of a heap. Then . . . I ran. It didn't follow me. I thought it was going to."

I put my arms about her and hugged her. "Oh, Mary-Jane, I only needed this."

She looked at me in some astonishment, and I stood back to gaze at her.

She was about my height and the cloak was all-enveloping. She had been mistaken for me, because she was wearing my cloak, the well-known cloak which had been put over the parapet.

She was loyal; there was a bond between us; I knew that she looked upon me as the kindest mistress she had ever had. Ruth was too cold to win affection; Aunt Sarah too strange. Mary-Jane had enjoyed working for me because the relationship between us was warmer than that which usually existed between a maid and her mistress. I decided that I would take Mary-Jane into my confidence to some extent.

"Mary-Jane," I said, "what did you think it was? A ghost?"

"Well, madam, I don't rightly believe in such things."

"Nor do I. I believe that what is inside that monk's robe is no ghost."

"But how did it get into your bedroom, madam?"

"That's what I'm going to find out."

"And did it pull the curtains and take the warming-pan away?"

"I believe it did. Mary-Jane, for the time being will you please say nothing to anyone of what you have seen. Our monk thinks that it was I who was hurrying home through the Abbey ruins at dusk. He has no idea that it was you. I want to keep him in ignorance . . . for a while. Will you do this?"

"I always want to do as you say, madam."

Christmas morning dawned bright and frosty. I lay in bed happily reading my letters and greetings. There was one from the man whom I still thought of as my father. He sent me Christmas greetings and hoped that his previous letter had not upset me. A letter from my real father had arrived on the previous day and in this he told me that he hoped to be home in the spring.

That longed-for spring! Then I should have my child. What else? But I did not want to look beyond that. That was enough.

As I lay in bed my thoughts went back—indeed they were never far away—to the desire to discover the identity of the person who was trying to harm my child, and I went over the various monk incidents in detail, for those were the ones in which I was sure I should find the clue to the identity of my persecutor.

The monk had appeared in my room, sped along the corridor when I hurried after him, and then disappeared. The more I thought of this, the more excited I became. Was there some secret hiding-place in the gallery? The monk had been seen not only in the house but in the Abbey ruins. What if there was some connecting passage between the Abbey and the house? What if two people played the role of monk? What if Luke and Damaris had both worn the robe—Damaris, on the first night I had seen it, thus enabling Luke to appear in his dressing-gown on the second floor; Luke, when I was with Damaris in the ruins?

I remembered the old plan of the Abbey which I had seen when I first came to the Revels. It was somewhere in the library. If I could find some indication on that plan where a connecting passage could possibly be, I might have begun to solve the problem. I did possess two vital clues. There was the arcade in the ruins where the monk had been seen on two occasions—by Damaris and me and by Mary-Jane. I would study the plan very closely at that spot. And there was the minstrels' gallery in the house.

I was so excited, I could scarcely wait to dress.

Why should I?

I slipped on a robe and hurried down to the library. I had little difficulty in finding the plan. It was in a leather binding with a few details about the Abbey; the parchment roll on which these were written, was yellow with age.

As I took the roll and tucked it under my arm I heard a movement behind me and, turning sharply, I saw Luke standing in the doorway.

He was looking at me with that alertness which I had noticed in people's faces recently and which had once filled me with alarm but now had no power to hurt me.

"Why, if it isn't Catherine! Happy Christmas, Catherine . . . and a fruitful New Year."

"Thank you, Luke."

He was standing in the doorway barring my way. I felt embarrassed, not only because of what I was carrying but because I had only a robe over my nightdress.

"What's wrong, Catherine?" he asked.

"But nothing."

"You look as though you're afraid I'm going to gobble you right up."

"Then my looks are deceptive."

"So you really feel quite benevolent towards me on this Christmas morning?"

"Shouldn't one feel so towards the whole world on this of all mornings?"

"You're taking the words out of old Cartwright's mouth. We shall have to go and hear him preaching his Christmas sermon." He yawned. "I always feel I'd like to time him by stop-watch. I heard of someone doing that the other day. Some local bigwig. It's a fact. He'd go to church, set his watch . . . ten minutes' sermon and no more. . . . When the ten minutes were up he'd snap his fingers and that sermon had to stop—and it did, for the parson had his living to think of." His eyes narrowed and he went on: "I'm thinking of doing it myself one day, when . . ."

I looked at him sharply. I knew very well what he meant: when he was in command.

I felt uneasy even though the library was full of daylight.

"Well, what are you reading?" His firm fingers were on the leather case.

"Oh, it's just something I've seen in the library. I wanted to have another look."

He had taken the roll, in spite of my efforts to retain it, for I had to let it go; I could not indulge in a tug-o'-war here in the library for no apparent reason at all.

"The old Abbey again!" he murmured. "Do you know, Catherine, you've got an obsession for abbeys . . . monks . . . and such like."

"Haven't you?" I asked.

"I? Why should I? I was born here. We take all that for granted. It's the people who are new to the place who think it's all so marvellous."

He put the roll under my arm.

"Why, Catherine," he went on, "we're standing under the mistletoe."

Then he put his arms round me and kissed me quickly on the lips.

"Merry Christmas, Catherine, and a happy New Year!"

Then he stood aside and bowed ironically. I went past him with as much dignity as I could, and started up the stairs. He stood at the library door watching me.

I wished that he had not seen what I had been carrying. I wondered how much of my thoughts he had read. Luke bothered me. I didn't understand him; and I had the feeling that he was the one who resented my presence here more than any . . . he and Ruth together. If it were Ruth and Luke, I thought, it would be easier for them than anyone; and the fact that Damaris had lied as she did could mean that she had done so for Luke.

When I reached my room I got into bed again and studied the plan.

It was headed Kirkland Abbey with the date 1520, and as I looked at it, it was as though the place came alive under my eyes, as though walls were built up where they had decayed, as though roofs were miraculously replaced. There it was—a series of buildings which housed a community, sufficient unto itself, which had no need of outside resources, since it was completely self-supporting. It was so easy to picture it all. I realised that I had learned the topography of the Abbey fairly well. It was not that I had visited the place so much but my impressions had been so vivid. The central Norman tower was an excellent landmark. I traced it with my finger. The north and south transept, the sanctuary, the gallery, the chapter house, the monks' dorter. And the arcade, with its buttresses, where I had seen the monk, was that which led to the dining hall, to the bakehouses and malt-house. Then my eyes fell on the words: "Entrance to the cellars."

As there were cellars beneath the Abbey, there would almost certainly be tunnels connecting them with other underground chambers. Such a labyrinth was a feature of abbeys of the period. I knew this because I had read accounts of our well-known abbeys such as Fountains, Kirkstall and Rievaulx. I noticed with rising excitement that the cellars were on that side of the Abbey which was nearest to the Revels.

I was so intent that I did not hear a knock on my door, and Ruth had come in before I realised she was there.

She stood at the end of my bed in the spot where the monk had stood.

"Merry Christmas," she said.

"Thank you, and the same to you."

"You seem absorbed."

"Oh . . . yes." Her eyes were on the roll and I guessed she recognised it.

"How are you feeling?"

"Much, much better."

"That's good news. Are you going to get up? Our guests will be arriving very soon."

"Yes," I said, "I shall get up now."

She nodded; and her eyes went once more to the plan. I fancied she looked a little anxious.

By the time the family was ready to go to church, Simon and Hagar had still not arrived.

"They are usually here before this," said Ruth. "Perhaps something has happened to delay them. However, we shall go to church. We must be in our pew on Christmas morning."

Matthew and Sarah came down to the hall dressed for church. This was indeed a rare thing and I realised that I had very seldom seen either of them dressed for going out. The carriage would take them to the church and bring them back, and it was one of those traditions that their pew should be occupied on Christmas Day.

There was something which I was longing to do, and that was go to the Abbey and look for those cellars; and I wanted to do it when no one could follow me there. If only I could make some excuse for not going to church, I could be sure that for about two hours there would be no one to surprise me.

I should have liked to go to church with them and to have taken my place in the pew, for I was beginning to feel a fondness for the old traditions and a need of the peace which the Christmas service would give me. But I had a more imperative need—the protection of my child; and I decided to practise a little deception.

When they were stepping into the carriage I stood very still for a moment, putting my hands to my body.

Ruth said sharply: "What's wrong?"

"It's nothing, but I really don't think I shall go with you. The doctor said I should be very careful indeed not to over-tax myself."

209

"I'll stay behind with you," Ruth told me. "You should go to bed at once."

"No," I insisted. "Mary-Jane will help me. She is very good and understands perfectly."

"But I feel I should stay behind," said Ruth.

"Then if you feel that, I must come with you, for I am certainly not going to allow you to miss the Christmas service."

She hesitated. Then she said: "Well, if you insist. . . . What are you going to do?"

"Go to my room. . . . I do want to feel well for the rest of the day."

She nodded. Then she said to the groom: "Go and bring Mary-Jane to me . . . and quickly, or we shall be late for church."

Mary-Jane came hurrying out.

"Mrs. Rockwell doesn't feel well enough to accompany us to church," she said. "Take her to her room and look after her."

"Yes, madam," said Mary-Jane.

Ruth, satisfied, got into the carriage and in a few seconds they were driving away, while Mary-Jane and I went up to my room.

When we were there I said: "We are going out, Mary-Jane."

"But, madam . . ."

I knew I had to take Mary-Jane into my confidence to a greater extent. When the monk had appeared before her he had brought her into this mystery, and the fact that she had come straight to me and told me what she had seen, and had kept her promise to tell no one else, proved her to be an ally.

"I feel quite well," I said. "I should have liked to join the church party, but there is something else I have to do. We are going to the Abbey."

I made her wrap herself in the blue cloak, and I myself wore another of dark brown.

Then we set out for the Abbey.

I was anxious that we should lose no time, for I did not know how long our explorations would last and it was necessary that we should be back in the house before the church party returned.

"I have been looking at a plan of the Abbey," I told Mary-Jane. "I have it with me here. When we have seen the monk in the ruins he has been near one spot and that is close by the entrance to the cellars. Let us go there immediately."

" If we see the monk, what shall we do?" she asked.

" I don't think we shall this morning."

" I'd like to give him a piece of my mind. Gave me a turn, he did, even though *I'm* not expecting."

"I should hope not," I said; and we laughed together, rather nervously, I thought, because Mary-Jane realised as well as I did that we were not concerned with a mere practical joker and that there was a sinister implication behind all that had happened. "What we have to do," I told her, "is find out if there is some means of getting from the Abbey ruins into the house. We must remember that a long time ago certain valuables remained hidden for some years and probably members of the family too. You see, Mary-Jane, everything points to the fact that there is a secret entrance."

Mary-Jane nodded. "It wouldn't surprise me, madam. Why, this house is full of old nooks and crannies. Happen it's there somewhere if we could find it."

When we reached the ruins I felt slightly breathless—with excitement and exertion—and Mary-Jane slowed us down a little. "You've got to remember how it is with you, madam."

I did remember. I was determined to take the utmost care of myself. I thought then: there was never a child in need of as much care as this one; the danger which threatens it makes it so.

We went along the arcade from buttress to buttress as I had seen the monk do; and we came to what I knew to be the bakehouse and malt-house. Now we had reached the remains of a spiral staircase which I was sure must lead to the cellars. Having studied my plan so well, I knew that we had been working back towards the house, and this was a part of the ruins which was very likely the nearest to the Revels.

Warily I descended the stairs ahead of Mary-Jane, and at the bottom of them we came to two passages, both leading in the direction of the house. These had evidently been tunnels, and I felt disappointed that I saw them because they, like the nave and transepts, had only the sky for their roofs.

However, we each walked along one of these, that half-wall dividing us, and when we had gone about fifty yards they merged into one and we were in what could easily have been a dwelling-place. There were several large chambers, the remains of brick walls showing us where they had been divided. I suspected that this was the place where the valuables had been hidden at the time of the Civil War. In that case there must be some connecting link with the house. We had to find it.

We crossed these chambers and that seemed like the end of the ruins. I could see the Revels now, very close, and I knew that the part of it which contained the minstrels' gallery was immediately opposite us. I was excited, yet exasperated, for it appeared that we could go no farther.

Mary-Jane looked at me helplessly as though to ask what next. But I glanced at my watch and saw that if we did not return to the house we should not be back by the time the church party returned.

"We'll have to go," I said, " but we'll come again."

Mary-Jane in her disappointment kicked at several large stones which were propped against a crumbling wall. There was a hollow sound; but the significance of this did not occur to me until later, because my mind was on the conjectures which might arise if it were discovered that I had feigned indisposition in order to visit the ruins.

"Another time," I went on. " Perhaps to-morrow. But we must go now."

It was fortunate that we returned to the house when we did, for I had been in my room no more than a few minutes when Mary-Jane came to tell me that Dr. Smith was below and asking for me.

I went down at once.

"Catherine," he said, taking my hand in his and looking searchingly into my face, " how are you?"

"I am well, thank you," I answered.

"I was disturbed when I saw you were not at church with the others."

"Oh, I thought it would do me more good not to go to-day."

"I see. You merely felt you needed a rest. I was there with my daughter—and took the first opportunity of slipping out."

"But you would have known if I had been taken ill. Someone would have come for you."

"It's true I thought it must mean only some slight indisposition. Nevertheless I wanted to see you for myself."

"How attentive you are!"

"But of course I am."

"Yet I am not really your patient, you know. Jessie Dankwait is coming to the Revels in due course."

"I shall insist on being at hand."

"Come into the winter parlour," I said. "There is a good fire there."

We went into the parlour which looked charming, for holly decorated the walls, and the scarlet berries were particularly big and plentiful that year.

"Wasn't that your maid I saw when I arrived?" asked the doctor as we seated ourselves by the fire. "I believe she has a sister who has just had a baby."

"That is so. Mary-Jane was very excited on the day the child was born. She went to see her, and whom else do you think she saw?"

He was smiling as though he were very pleased to see me in such good spirits.

"You'll be surprised," I went on, "when I tell you that Mary-Jane saw the monk."

"She saw . . . the monk!"

"Yes. I had made her wear one of my cloaks, and she came home by way of the ruins. The monk was there and went through the same performance, beckoning her."

I heard his deep intake of breath. "Indeed!"

"I have told no one, but you must know, of course, because you suspected that I might be losing my mind, and I do want you to know that I am as balanced as I ever was. And there is something even more wonderful."

"I am eager to hear it."

"I have heard from my old home." I told him what my father had told me. He relaxed visibly. Then he leaned forward and grasped my hand warmly in his.

"Oh, Catherine," he said fervently, "this is indeed wonderful news. Nothing could have pleased me better."

"You can imagine how I feel."

"I certainly can."

"And now that Mary-Jane has seen the monk . . . well, everything is changed since that dreadful day when you told me . . ."

"I have been so anxious ever since. I could not make up my mind whether I had been right to tell you or whether I should have held my peace."

"I think you were right to tell me. It is better to have these matters brought into the open. You see, I have now been able to clear up all doubts."

He was suddenly very grave. "But, Catherine, you were saying that Mary-Jane saw the apparition. What does this mean?"

" That someone is threatening the life of my child. I must discover the identity of that person. At least I know of one who is involved."

I stopped and he said quickly: " You know of one who is involved?"

Still I hesitated for it was not easy to tell him that I suspected his daughter.

But he was insistent and I blurted out: " I'm sorry, but I have to tell you that Damaris is involved in this."

He stared at me in horror.

" She was with me when we returned to the house," I went on. " You will remember that you insisted she should accompany me. We saw the monk—and she pretended not to see him."

" Damaris!" he whispered, as though to himself.

" There was no doubt that she saw, yet she denied doing so. She must know who this person is who is trying to unnerve me. When she denied that she saw him, I knew at once that she was an accomplice."

" It can't be true! Why . . . why?"

" I wish I knew. But at least I have made some discoveries in the last few days. The trouble is that it is so difficult to trust anyone."

" That is a reproach and I believe I deserve it. You must believe me, Catherine, when I tell you that I suffered torment when I discovered there was a Catherine Corder in Worstwhistle, and her connection with you. I told the Rockwells— Sir Matthew and Ruth—because I considered it my duty to do so. I only wanted you to go there for a few days for observation. I had made no suggestion that you should go . . . in the ordinary way. I was thinking of what was best for you."

" It was such a blow when I heard my name mentioned in connection with the place."

" I know. But . . . this is becoming a nightmare. Damaris . . . my own daughter . . . to have played a part in it. There must be some mistake. Have you told anyone of this?"

" No, not yet."

" I think I understand your reasoning. The less you say of these matters the easier it will be to catch your enemy. But I am glad you have told me."

There was a knock on the door and William entered.

" Mrs. Rockwell-Redvers and Mr. Redvers have arrived, madam."

So the doctor and I went downstairs together to welcome Hagar and Simon to the Revels.

That afternoon Simon and I had an opportunity to talk together. The wind was still blowing from the north but the snow had held off.

The older members of the family were in their rooms resting. I did not know where Ruth and Luke were. Ruth had said that as I felt too unwell for church that morning I ought to rest before tea. I said I would do this, but I was restless in my room and I came out after ten minutes and went along to the winter parlour, where Simon was sitting thoughtfully by the fire.

He rose delightedly when I entered the room.

"You've been looking radiant since we arrived," he told me. "The change is remarkable. I'm sure something good has happened. You've discovered something?"

I felt myself flush with pleasure. Simon's compliments would always be genuine. That was his way—so I knew that I did look radiant.

I told him about the letter and Mary-Jane's adventure; and how we had gone on a tour of exploration that morning.

I was thrilled to see the way he received the news of my parentage. His face creased into a smile and then he began to laugh.

"There couldn't be better news for you, could there, Catherine," he said. "As for me . . ." He leaned towards me and looked into my face. "If you came from a line of raving lunatics I should still say you are the sanest woman I've ever met."

I laughed with him. I was very happy there in the winter parlour . . . the two of us sitting by the fire; and I thought: If I were not a widow, this might be considered a little improper.

"You told the doctor?" he said. "You were with him when we arrived."

"Yes, I told him. Like you, he was delighted."

Simon nodded.

"And about Mary-Jane?"

"Yes, I told him that too. But, Simon, I have decided not to tell anyone else . . . except your grandmother, of course. I want no one else to know just yet."

"That's wise," he said. "We don't want to put our monk on his guard, do we? How I wish he would appear at this moment; I should like to come face to face with him. I wonder if there's a chance of his putting in an appearance to-night."

"Perhaps there are too many people in the house. However, let us hope he does."

"I'd catch him, I'll guarantee."

"I believe you would."

Simon looked down at his hands and I noticed afresh how strong they were. I guessed he was thinking of what he would do to the monk if he caught him.

"I have a map of the Abbey," I said. "I've been trying to find another way into the house."

"Any luck?"

"None at all. I took Mary-Jane down to the ruins while the others were at church this morning."

"I thought you were supposed to be resting."

"I didn't say so. I merely said I wished to stay at home. The rest was presumed."

"The deceit of a woman!" he mocked me; and I was so happy in this friendship between us. "Now tell me," he went on, "what have you discovered?"

"Nothing for certain, but I believe it possible that some connecting passage exists."

"Why are you so sure?"

"Because of the way in which the monk appeared both in the house and in the Abbey ruins. He would have to keep his costume somewhere. Then he disappeared so neatly on the first night I saw him. I believe he has an accomplice."

"Damaris," he said.

I nodded. "Who might play the monk on certain occasions."

"It's possible."

"I have a suspicion that the way into this hiding-place is in the minstrels' gallery."

"Why?"

"Because that's the only place into which he could have disappeared on that first night."

"Good God!" he cried. "That's true."

"I feel certain that there is some way out of the house in the gallery there."

"Could there be . . . and the household know nothing about it?"

"Why not? The Roundheads lived here for some years and they didn't find it."

216

"What are we waiting for?" asked Simon.

He rose and together we made our way to the minstrels' gallery.

The gallery had always seemed an uncanny place because it was so dark. There were no windows up there, and the only light came from the hall. Heavy curtains hung on either side of the balcony. In the past the idea must have been for the musicians who played there to be heard and sometimes not seen.

On this afternoon it was dismal and eerie.

It was not large. It would hold an orchestra of ten men perhaps, but they would have been somewhat cramped. The back wall was hung with tapestry which had clearly not been moved for years. Simon went round tapping the walls, but he could only do so through the tapestry, which was not very helpful.

At one spot he found that the tapestry could be pulled aside, and my excitement was great when behind this we discovered a door. I held the tapestry back while he opened it, but it was only an empty cupboard which smelt damp and musty.

"He could have hidden in this cupboard until the hue and cry was over," said Simon, closing the door.

"But he came from the second floor."

"You mean Luke?"

"Well . . . I was thinking of Luke," I answered, letting the tapestry fall into place.

"H'm!" murmured Simon.

There was a sudden movement behind us ; we had had our backs to the door which led into the gallery, and we turned like two guilty people.

"Hallo," said Luke. "I thought the ghosts of the minstrels had returned to haunt us when I heard voices in here."

I fervently wished then that I could have seen his face.

"This gallery's not used enough," said Simon. "It reeks of age."

"It could scarcely accommodate a modern orchestra. At the last ball we gave we had the players on the dais in the hall."

"So much more effective to have them in the gallery," I heard myself say.

"Yes, playing the harpsichord or the sackbut or psaltery . . . or whatever they did play in the dim and distant past." Luke's voice sounded mocking. I thought: This morning he found me in the library. This afternoon it is the minstrels' gallery.

We all came out on to the stairs and Luke returned with us to the winter parlour.

There we sat by the fire idly talking together, but I felt that there was a wariness among us of which each of us was conscious.

Dinner that evening was to be served in the hall, for even though we were still in mourning Christmas was Christmas, and for centuries Christmas dinner had been eaten there.

The long refectory table had been dressed with taste. At intervals candles burned in candlesticks of pewter, shining a light on the gleaming cutlery and glass on the table, and sprigs of holly were strewn on the huge lace tablecloth. It would have seemed impossible not to be festive at such a table. Candles burned in their sconces on the walls and I had never seen the hall so brightly lighted. As I came down the stairs I thought: This is how it must have looked a hundred years ago.

I was wearing a loose tea gown of mole-coloured velvet with wide hanging sleeves which fell back from the elbows, and ruffles of lime-green lace at the neck. I had sent to Harrogate for it, and I felt I could not have had anything more suitable for my condition and this occasion.

It was the custom, Ruth had told me, to exchange gifts at the dinner table and I saw that brightly coloured packages were piled up at various places on the table. I saw that our names had been written on pieces of parchment and set in the places we were to take. We were fairly widely spaced at such a large table for there were only seven of us to dine, although after dinner several people would call on us, as Sir Matthew had said, to take wine. I knew that among these people would be Dr. Smith and Damaris, and Mr. and Mrs. Cartwright and some members of their family.

Ruth was already there talking to William who was busy at the wagon with two of the maids.

" Ah," she said as I came down, " are you feeling better?"

" I am feeling very well, thank you."

" I'm so glad. It would have been unfortunate if you had not felt well to-night. But if you should feel tired before everyone leaves, you must slip away. I'll make your excuses for you."

"Thanks, Ruth."

She pressed my hand; it was the first time I had felt any warmth from her. The Christmas feeling, I told myself.

Hagar was the next to arrive. I watched her sweep down the staircase, and although she had to walk with the aid of a stick she made a magnificent entrance. She was dressed in a velvet gown of heliotrope, a shade which was becoming to her white hair, and a style that had been fashionable twenty years before. I had never seen anyone with as much dignity as Hagar; I felt that everyone must be a little in awe of her, and I was glad that she and I had become such friends.

She was wearing an emerald necklace, ear-rings and a ring in which was a huge square-cut stone.

She put her cool cheek against mine and said: "Well, Catherine, it is pleasant to have you here with us. Is Simon down yet?" She shook her head in affectionate exasperation. "I am sure he is dressing under protest."

"Simon never did like what he calls dressing up for an occasion," said Ruth. "I remember he once said that no occasion was worth all the trouble."

"He has his opinions about such matters," agreed Hagar. "And here's Matthew. Matthew, how are you?"

Sir Matthew was coming down the stairs and I saw Aunt Sarah behind him.

Sarah was looking excited; she had put on a gown with rather extreme *décolletage*. It was of blue satin decorated with ribbons and lace and it had the effect of making her appear very young—but perhaps that was the excitement one sensed in her.

Her eyes went to the table. "Oh, the presents!" she cried. "Always the most fascinating part, don't you think, Hagar?"

"You will never grow up, Sarah," said Hagar.

But Sarah had turned to me: "You like the presents, don't you, Catherine. You and I have a lot in common, haven't we?" She turned to Hagar. "We decided that we had when . . . when . . ."

Simon came down the stairs then. It was the first time I had seen him dressed for the evening, and I thought that if he was not handsome he looked very distinguished.

"Ha!" cried Hagar. "So you have succumbed to custom then, grandson."

He took her hand and kissed it, and I watched the contented smile on her lips.

"There are times," he said, "when there is no alternative but to succumb."

We were standing together in that candlelit hall when suddenly we heard the sounds of a violin coming from the minstrels' gallery.

There was immediate silence and everyone was looking up. The gallery was in darkness but the violin went on playing, and the tune it played was one I knew well as "The Light of Other Days."

Hagar was the first to speak. "Who is it?" she demanded.

No one answered and the wail of the violin filled the hall.

Then Simon said: "I'll investigate."

But as he moved towards the staircase a figure appeared at the balcony. It was Luke, his long fair hair falling about his pale face.

"I thought it was appropriate to serenade you all on such an occasion," he called.

He began to sing in a very pleasant tenor voice and to accompany himself with the violin.

> "When I remember all
> The friends, so linked together,
> I've seen around me fall
> Like leaves in wintry weather;
> I feel like one,
> Who treads alone
> Some banquet hall deserted,
> Whose lights are fled
> Whose garlands dead,
> And all but he departed!"

When he had finished, he bowed, laid down his violin and shortly afterwards was running down the stairs to join us.

"Very effective!" murmured Simon dryly.

"You're like your grandfather," put in Hagar. "Fond of admiration."

"Now, Hagar," protested Sir Matthew with a laugh, "you were always hard on me."

"I have often said," Ruth put in affectionately, "that Luke should sing more and practise more with the violin."

We sat down at the table and, while William and the maids began to serve us, we looked at our presents. Sarah squealed with delight as a child might have done; the rest of us opened our gifts decorously and murmured conventional thanks to each other.

There was one present beside my place which held a certain significance. This bore the inscription, "A Happy Christmas from Hagar and Simon Rockwell-Redvers," in Hagar's bold handwriting. I wondered why they had given me a joint present and my heart sank a little because I imagined that Simon had had nothing for me and that Hagar had probably added his name to hers to hide this fact. But when I opened the box I stared in amazement, for it contained a ring. I knew that it was a valuable one and that it was not new. It was some family heirloom, I guessed—a ruby set in a circle of diamonds. I lifted it out of the case and looked from Simon to Hagar. Simon was watching me intently; Hagar was giving me the special smile which usually she reserved for Simon only.

"But this is too . . . too . . ." I stammered.

I was aware that the attention of all at the table was on me and the ring.

"It has been in the family for generations," said Simon. "The Redvers family, that is."

"But it's so beautiful."

"Oh, we did have some possessions, you know," said Simon. "The Rockwells didn't have everything."

"I didn't mean . . ."

"We know what you mean, my dear," said Hagar. "Simon is teasing. Slip it on your finger. I want to see if it fits."

It was too small for the middle finger on my right hand, on which I tried it first, but it fitted perfectly on the third finger.

"It looks becoming, does it not?" Hagar asked, glaring round at the rest of the company as though daring them to contradict her.

"It is such a beautiful ring," Ruth murmured.

"The Redvers seal of approbation, Catherine," murmured Luke.

"How can I thank you?" I said, looking at Hagar, for I could not look at Simon then. I knew that there was a significance about this and that everyone at the table was aware of it, although I was not . . . entirely. But I did know it was a very valuable present and that in giving it to me Simon and Hagar were proclaiming their affection for me; perhaps they meant to tell the person who was persecuting me that he had not only to deal with me but them also.

"By wearing it," Simon answered.

"It's a talisman," cried Luke. "Do you know, Catherine, while you wear that ring nothing can harm you. It's the old family tradition. There's a curse on it . . . no, sorry, a blessing, The genie of the ring will protect you from the powers of evil."

"Then it's doubly precious," I said lightly. "Since it not only preserves me from evil but is so decorative. I am so grateful to you for giving me such a lovely present."

"Puts the rest of our little gifts to shame, doesn't it," sighed Luke. "But always remember, Catherine, it is the spirit of the gift that counts."

"It is a good thing to remember," Hagar's voice boomed authoritatively.

Because I was afraid that I might betray the emotion this gift aroused in me, I decided to say no more before the others but to thank both Hagar and Simon privately; so I hastily turned to my soup which William had served, and by the time the turkey, with its chestnut stuffing, was being eaten I was conscious of a quiet peaceful pleasure.

The Christmas pudding was brought in—magnificent with it's wreath of holly round the base and the sprig stuck jauntily into the top. William poured the brandy over it and Sir Matthew at the head of the table set it alight.

"Last Christmas," said Sarah, "it was very different. The house was full of guests. Gabriel was sitting where you are sitting now, Catherine.

"Don't let's talk of sad things," said Matthew. "Remember this is the first day of Christmas."

"Christmas is a time for remembering," protested Sarah. "It's the time when you recall the departed."

"Is it?" said Ruth.

"Of course it is," cried Sarah. "Do you remember, Hagar, that Christmas when we joined the party for the first time?"

"I remember," said Hagar.

Sarah had leaned her elbows on the table; she was staring at the flaming pudding.

"Last night," she said, in a hollow voice, "I lay in bed thinking of all the Christmases of my life. The first one I remembered was when I was three. I woke up in the night and heard the music and I was frightened. I cried, and Hagar scolded me."

"The first of many a scolding from Aunt Hagar, I'm certain," said Luke.

"Someone had to take charge of the family," Hagar

222

answered serenely. " It might not have done you much harm, Luke, to have encountered a little more discipline."

Sarah was going on dreamily: " Right through them all I went until I reached last Christmas. Do you remember how we drank the toasts afterwards? There was a special one to Gabriel after his escape."

There was a silence of some seconds which I broke by asking: " What escape was that?"

" Gabriel's," said Sarah. " He might have been killed." She put her hand to her lips. " Just think if he had . . . he would never have met Catherine. You wouldn't be here with us to-day, Catherine, if he had died. You wouldn't be going to . . ."

" Gabriel never told me about this accident," I said.

" It was hardly worth mentioning," said Ruth sharply. " One of the walls in the ruins collapsed ; he was close by and there was a slight injury to his foot. It was nothing much . . . a matter of bruises."

" But," cried Sarah, her blue eyes flashing almost angrily, I thought, because Ruth was trying to make light of something which she thought important, " just by chance he saw what was about to happen. He was able to escape in time. If he hadn't seen it. . . . he would have been killed."

" Let's talk of something cheerful," said Luke. " It didn't happen. So that's that."

" If it had," murmured Sarah, there wouldn't have been any need to . . ."

" William," said Ruth, " Mrs. Redvers's glass is empty."

I was thinking of Gabriel, of the fear he had seemed to have of his home ; I remembered the cloud which had appeared during our honeymoon when he had discovered the coastal ruins which must have reminded him of Kirkland Abbey. Was the falling of the wall really an accident? Did Gabriel know that someone in the Revels was trying to kill him? Was that the explanation of his fear? Was that why he had married me—so that there would be two of us to fight against the evil which threatened? Had that evil caught up with Gabriel? If so, it meant that someone wanted his inheritance. That person must have been horrified when, after murdering Gabriel—and I had come to the conclusion now that Gabriel had been murdered—he found that there was another who might step into Gabriel's shoes: my child.

It was all so clear ; and there in the candlelit hall, while we were formally served with Christmas pudding, I realised as

223

I never had before the certainty that the person who had murdered Gabriel was now determined that my child should never be born, in case it should be a boy.

There was one way of making absolutely sure that I did not produce a son—and that was by killing me.

There had been no attempt on my life. No, as Simon had said, that would have been too suspicious in view of Gabriel's sudden and violent death. I began to see a pattern forming. I was in danger—acute danger—but I was no longer terrified as I had been. It was not danger which could frighten me so much as the fear that my mind was tainted and that I was imagining all the uncanny occurrences. How strange it was that this actual danger was far more tolerable than something which I might have conjured up in a distorted imagination.

I found myself looking at Luke. With his long fair hair falling about his pale face I thought he looked like a cross between an angel and a satyr. He reminded me of the figures which were carved on the stonework. There was a satanic gleam in his eyes as they met mine. It was almost as though he read my thoughts and was amused by them.

We drank toasts in champagne. My turn came and they all stood, their glasses lifted. I believed that one of those people who were drinking my health might at that very moment be planning to kill me, but it must not be a violent death—it would have to appear a natural one.

The meal over, the table was quickly cleared by the servants, and we were ready to receive our guests. There were more people than I had expected. Dr. Smith and Damaris were the first arrivals and I wondered what was happening to the doctor's wife and what she thought of being left alone on Christmas Day.

I asked Damaris and she said that her mother was resting. It was long past her time for retiring to bed and the doctor would not allow Christmas or anything else to interfere with her routine.

The Cartwrights came with several members of their family, including married sons and daughters and their families. That was the extent of the guests, and, like Sarah, I began to wonder about other Christmases—only I thought of Christmases in the future, not the past.

There was no dancing and the guests were conducted to a drawing-room on the first-floor; even the conversation was quiet. Everyone was remembering Gabriel on that day, because it was due to his death that the traditional entertaining had not taken place.

I found an opportunity of thanking Hagar for the ring. She smiled and said: "We wanted you to have it . . . both of us."

"It is very valuable. I must also thank Simon for it."

"Here he is."

Simon was standing beside us, and I turned to him. "I was thanking your grandmother for this magnificent ring."

He took my hand and studied the ring. "It looks better on her hand than it did in its case," he remarked to his grandmother.

She nodded and he continued to hold my hand for a few seconds, his head on one side, regarding the ring with a smile of satisfaction about his lips.

Ruth joined us.

"Catherine," she said, "if you want to slip away to your room I should do so. You mustn't tire yourself. That's the very thing we wish to avoid."

I did feel then so moved by new emotions that I wanted to go to my room, for there was a great deal I had to think about. Moreover, I knew that I should be resting.

"We shall be here to-morrow," Hagar reminded me. "We might go for a drive to-morrow morning—the three of us—unless you would like to come, Ruth?"

"I dare say people will be calling all the morning," said Ruth. "You know how it is on Boxing Day."

"Well, we shall see," said Hagar. "Good night, my dear. I am sure you are wise to retire. It must have been a long day for you."

I kissed her hand, and she drew me to her and kissed my cheek. Then I gave my hand to Simon. To my astonishment he bent down swiftly and kissed it. I could feel his kiss, hard and warm on my skin. I flushed faintly and hoped Ruth did not notice this.

"Slip away, Catherine," said Ruth. "I'll make your excuses to everybody. They'll understand."

So I slipped away, but when I was in my room I knew I could not sleep. I was too excited.

I lighted the candles and lay down on my bed. I turned the ring round and round on my finger. I believed that it was a ring which the Redvers family treasured and that it had been given to me because they wished to imply that they wanted me to be one of them.

I had been lying thus when the monk had come to my room and the strangeness had begun. I kept going over everything that had happened, right from the first, and I was conscious of an urgency. Time was short. Already I was easily tired and forced to leave the party before it was over. This mystery should be solved . . . and quickly solved.

If I could find that way into the house . . . if I could find the monk's robe. . . .

We had not really examined the minstrels' gallery thoroughly. We had found the cupboard, but we had not looked behind the tapestries on the walls. How long, I wondered, was it since that tapestry had been taken down?

I rose from my bed—I had not undressed—for I was filled with a great desire to have another look at the gallery.

I went along the corridor. I could hear the sound of voices and they were coming from the drawing-room on this floor ; quietly I descended the first flight of stairs to the minstrel's gallery. I opened the door and went in.

The only light came from the numerous wall candles in the hall. So it was dark and gloomy in the gallery and I told myself that I had been foolish to hope to discover anything in this poor light.

I leaned over the balcony looking down on the hall, of which I had a good view apart from that section immediately below.

And as I stood there the door opened and a shape loomed on the threshold. For a moment I thought it was the monk and, in spite of my belief that I wanted to see him, a shudder of fear ran through me.

But this was no monk. It was a man in ordinary evening dress and when he whispered: "Why . . . Catherine!" I recognised the voice of Dr. Smith.

He went on speaking very quietly. "What are you doing here?"

"I couldn't sleep."

He came into the gallery and we stood side by side near the balcony.

He put his fingers to his lips. "There is someone down there," he whispered.

I was surprised that he should consider that a matter for secrecy as there were so many guests in the house, and was about to say so, when he seized my arm and drew me closer to the balcony.

Then I heard voices.

"Damaris! We're alone at last." The sound of that voice gave me a pain which was almost physical. It was not only the words but the tone in which they were spoken which was so significant. For it was both tender and passionate, and only rarely had I heard that timbre in the voice. It was Simon who was speaking.

Then Damaris: "I am afraid. My father would not be pleased."

In these matters, Damaris, we do not please our fathers, but ourselves. . . ."

"But to-night he is here. Perhaps he is watching us now."

Simon laughed and at that moment they moved towards the centre of the hall. He had his arm about her.

I turned away, not wanting to look. I was afraid they might be aware of us. My humiliation would have been complete if Simon knew that I had looked on at his flirtation with Damaris.

As I walked towards the door of the gallery, the doctor was still beside me; and together we went up the stairs to the first floor. He seemed preoccupied, scarcely aware of me, and I had no doubt that he was very worried about his daughter.

"I shall forbid her to see that . . . philanderer!" he said.

I did not answer; I had clasped my hands together and touched the ring which but a short time ago had seemed to have such a significance.

"Perhaps it would be useless to forbid her," I suggested.

"She would have to obey me," he retorted; and I saw the veins, prominent at his temples. I had never known him so agitated before and that seemed to mark the depth of his affection for her. I warmed to him because such parental concern was exactly what I had so sadly missed during the absences of my real father.

"He is overbearing," I said, and my own voice was very angry. "I believe he would always find a way of getting what he wanted."

"I am sorry," said the doctor. "I am forgetting you. You should be resting, I thought you had retired to do that. What made you come to the gallery?"

"I couldn't sleep. I was too excited, I suppose."

"At least," he said, "this is a warning to us both."

"What made *you* come to the gallery?" I asked suddenly.

"I knew they were down there together."

"I see. And you would frown on a match between them?"

"A match! He would not offer her marriage. The old

lady has other plans for him. He'll marry *her* choice and it won't be my daughter. Besides . . . she is for Luke."

" Is she? She did not seem to think so to-night."

" Luke is devoted to her. If only they were older they would be married by now. It would be a tragedy if she were ruined by this. . . ."

" You do not think very highly of his honour."

" His honour! You have not been here long enough to know his reputation in the neighbourhood. But I am keeping you and it grows late. I shall be taking Damaris home immediately. Good night, Catherine."

He took my hand. It was the one on which was the Redvers ring.

I went to my room. I was so upset that I forgot to lock my doors that night. But there were no midnight visitors, and I was alone with my emotions.

That night I learned the true nature of these emotions, and I blamed myself for allowing them to become so strong, disguised as they were by the semblance of dislike. I had been angry with him because I thought he did not esteem me enough. I had been hurt because I wanted that esteem.

That night I learned that hatred grows out of the strength of one's own emotions ; and that when a woman comes close to hating a man she should be watchful, for it means that her feelings are deeply engaged.

He is a cheat, I told myself, as I tried to shut out the echo of his voice talking to Damaris. He is a philanderer who amuses himself with any female who is handy. I happened to be at hand. What a fool I am. And how we hate those who make us aware of our own folly. Hate and love. There are times when the two can run side by side.

Chapter 7

I did not sleep well that night and it must have been nearly morning when I was awakened by Mary-Jane. It was dark and she was carrying a lighted candle.

" Mary-Jane!" I said. "What is the time?"

" It's six o'clock, madam."

" But why . . . ?"

" I wanted to tell you yesterday, but with all the Christmas

228

preparations I didn't get a chance. I only found it yesterday. It was while we were getting the hall ready."

I sat up in bed and cried: "Mary-Jane, you have found the way out of the house?"

"I think so, madam. It is in the gallery . . . in the cupboard. There are two floorboards there with a gap between them, enough to get your fingers in. I thought there was something not usual about them so I put my fingers down and gripped one of the boards. It lifted up easy. Then I saw the great black space below, so I got a candle and looked down. There are some stairs leading down. That's all, madam. William was calling me then, so I let the board fall back and didn't say anything . . . thinking I'd come straight to you to tell you. But then I had to go to the kitchens and help and I couldn't get another chance, but I've been thinking about it all night."

"Mary-Jane," I said, "we must look into this."

"I thought you'd want to."

"There's no one up yet?"

"Only the servants, madam, and they're not in this wing. They'll be coming to do the hall in half an hour's time though."

"Well, we must move quickly," I said. "We're going to have a look at those stairs now."

"Shouldn't you dress yourself first, madam?"

"No, I can't wait," I said. "I'll put on my cloak over my nightgown."

So together Mary-Jane and I left my bedroom and quietly made our way to the minstrels' gallery. I was afraid all the time that Luke would suddenly appear, but Mary-Jane was with me, and it would be difficult for him to do me any harm.

I was excited, for this was the proof I needed. The only person in this house whom I could trust was Mary-Jane, and we were together in this.

The house was very quiet, and for that reason even my slippered tread seemed noisy. But we reached the gallery and no one appeared.

Mary-Jane very gently shut the door, and I held the candle while she opened the cupboard and showed me the floorboards. She knelt and lifted one of these up and, as she had explained, it came up easily; evidently it had been cunningly made to act as a trap-door.

I leaned over the aperture, holding the candle. I could see the flight of steps which she had told me about. I longed to go down there, but it would be necessary to take a short leap on to the top step and I dared not trust myself to do that.

But Mary-Jane was lithe and slim. I turned to her.

"You get through," I said. "And I'll hand you the candle. Just look round and tell me what you see down there."

She had turned a little pale, but she was the sort who would despise what she would call the gormless; and after that second's hesitation she lowered herself through the aperture and when she was standing on the steps I handed her the candle.

She said: "It seems like a big room down there. It's very cold."

"Just have a quick look round," I ordered. "Then we'll try to find the way in from the Abbey side."

There was silence for a while. I peered down. I could see her gingerly descending the stairs, and sharply I warned her to be careful.

"Oh aye," she assured me. "I'm safe on me feet, madam."

I heard her voice again when she had descended the steps. "I can see a light in the distance. That must be the way out. I'll just have a quick look."

My heart was beating madly. I wanted to be down there with her, but I dared not risk slipping on those stone steps. I glanced over my shoulder. I could not rid myself of the feeling that someone was watching us. But there was no one there; there was no sound at all in that silent house.

I heard a sudden call from Mary-Jane. "I've found something, madam."

"I can't see you now," I called. "Where are you?"

Her voice sounded faint. "The candle nearly went out, madam."

"Come back now, Mary-Jane. Bring what you've found if you can carry it."

"But, madam . . ."

"Come back," I said authoritatively.

Then I saw the candle again and breathed more freely.

Mary-Jane appeared on the steps; she was holding the candle in one hand and something under her arm. She handed the bundle up to me and I knew at once that it was the monk's robe. I took the candle from her and in a second or so Mary-Jane had scrambled through the aperture and was safe in the gallery.

"I was alarmed when you disappeared from sight," I said.

"I wasn't all that brave meself, madam, down there. Gave me the shivers."

"Why, you are cold, Mary-Jane."

"It's cold down there, madam. I found the robe though."

"Let's go along to my room. We don't want anyone to find us here."

We let down the floorboard of the cupboard and satisfied ourselves that it showed no signs of having been disturbed; and taking the robe with us we went back to my room.

When we were there Mary-Jane put the robe about her and I shuddered.

"Take it off," I said. "We must guard this. If anyone dare say that I've seen visions because my mind is disturbed, we can prove that it was not visions I saw."

"Shouldn't we tell someone? Shouldn't we show them the robe?"

The day before I should have said: "Yes. We will tell Mr. Redvers." But I could no longer say that. I no longer trusted Simon, and if I could not trust Simon I trusted nobody.

"We will say nothing of this for the moment, Mary-Jane," I said. "We have the evidence here. I will put it in my wardrobe and the door shall be locked so that no one can steal it."

"And then, madam."

I looked at the clock over the fireplace and saw that it was seven o'clock.

"You will be missed, if you stay here much longer. I will go back to bed. You will bring my breakfast in the ordinary way. I shall want very little to eat. Bring my hot water earlier. I want to think what I ought to do next."

"Yes, madam," she said.

And she left me.

Ruth came to my room to see how I was.

"You look exhausted," she said. "Yesterday was too much for you."

"I do feel tired," I admitted.

"I should stay in your room all day. I'll keep them away. Then perhaps you'll feel well enough to join us this evening. There will only be the family; and Simon and Hagar will be leaving early to-morrow morning. The carriage always comes for them sharp at nine-thirty on the day after Boxing Day."

"Yes. I should like to rest awhile," I said.

All that day I lay on my bed and thought about the events

231

which had led up to my discovery of the robe. I went over everything, beginning with my meeting with Gabriel and Friday. Gabriel knew there had been an attempt on his life in the ruins, and he was afraid. He had hoped that I would be able to help him—at least there would be two of us to fight whatever threatened him. Then there was the night before he died, when Friday had heard someone in the corridor. It would have been that night when Gabriel met his death, but for Friday. Friday had obviously been killed so that he could not again give the warning. Sarah knew this and had conveyed it on her tapestry. How much more did she know? So Gabriel had died and I had been of little interest to the murderer until it was disclosed that I was to have a child. The idea to make me seem mad must have come when Dr. Smith thought it his duty to tell the family that there was a Catherine Corder in Worstwhistle.

What a diabolical mind was behind that plot! I did not believe the idea was to send me to Worstwhistle, but to build up a case of insanity against me and then possibly stage my suicide before the child was born.

Why was I thinking of the plot in the past tense? It still existed. And when my would-be murderer discovered that his robe was missing, what would he do? Perhaps he would think there was need for prompt action.

I was undecided. Perhaps I should go back to Glen House. But how could I do this in secret? If I announced my intention I could expect immediate action. I was certain that I should not be allowed to leave this house.

I thought of them . . . Luke and Simon. I tried not to think of Simon. It was Luke, I told myself. It must be Luke. And Damaris was helping them.

Damaris! But had I not learned something last night of the relationship between Damaris and *Simon*!

My thoughts went round and round like a mouse in a cage. I had the robe; I should have been triumphant if I could have shared my knowledge with Simon.

But what could I ever share with Simon now?

I was wishing again, as I had wished when I let the water from the Knaresborough Well trickle on my hands: " Not Simon. Oh, please, not Simon!"

I joined the family at dinner. Simon was attentive and appeared anxious on my behalf and, although I had told myself that I would give no sign of my changed feelings towards him, I could not help a coolness creeping into my manner.

He was next to me at dinner, which we took in the hall as we had on the previous night.

"I am disappointed," he told me, "that I've had no opportunity of being with you to-day. I had planned that we should take a drive together . . . you, my grandmother and myself."

"Would not the weather have been too cold for her?"

"Perhaps, but she would not admit it. She, too, was disappointed."

"You should have made up a party with the others."

"You know that would not have been the same thing at all."

"Perhaps Damaris would have accompanied you."

He laughed, and lowered his voice. "I have something to tell you about that."

I looked at him interrogatively.

"Because," he added, "you obviously noticed. It is often necessary to go by devious ways to reach a certain goal."

"You are talking in riddles."

"Which is not inappropriate. We have a riddle to solve."

I turned away because I fancied Luke was trying to listen to our conversation; but fortunately Aunt Sarah was talking loudly about Christmases of the past, and although she was repeating what she had said yesterday she seemed determined that no one should miss a word.

After dinner we retired to the first-floor drawing-room, and there were no other visitors that night. I talked to Sir Matthew and would not leave his side, although I could see that Simon was growing exasperated with me.

I left the company early and had not been in my room more than five minutes when there was a knock on the door.

"Come in," I called, and Sarah entered.

She smiled at me conspiratorially and whispered as though to excuse the intrusion: "Well, you were interested. That's why . . ."

"What do you mean?" I asked.

"I've started to fill it in."

My thoughts immediately went to the half-finished piece of tapestry which she had showed me when I was last in her room. She was watching me and her face seemed suddenly full of knowledge.

"Can I see it?"

" Of course. That's why I came. Will you come back with me?"

I rose eagerly and when we were in the corridor she put her fingers to her lips. " Don't want anyone to hear us," she said. " They're still in the first-floor drawing-room. It's early yet . . . for a Boxing night. All very well for you to retire early. That's on account of your condition. But the others . . ."

We mounted the stairs and went through to her wing. It was very silent in this part of the house and I shivered—whether with cold or apprehension, I was not sure.

She led the way to her tapestry room, and she was now as excited as a child with a new toy which she wants to show off. She lighted several candles from the one she was carrying; then, setting that one down, she ran to the cupboard. She took out the canvas and held it in front of her as she had on another occasion. I could not see very clearly although it was obvious that the blank side had now been filled in with something. I picked up a candle and held it close to the canvas. Then I saw the outline of a drawing.

I looked closer. On one side were the dead bodies of Gabriel and Friday, and on the other a faint pencil drawing. This was of another building, and the effect was that of looking through barred windows into a room which was like a prison cell. In that cell was the vague outline of a woman who held something in her arms. I felt a thrill of horror as I realised this was meant to be a baby.

I looked into Sarah's face. Illumined as it was by the light of the candles, all shadows and lines seemed to be eliminated; she was rejuvenated—more than that; she seemed not quite human. I longed to know what secrets, what motives lay behind those calm eyes which could at times seem so simple, at others so wise.

" I suppose that figure is myself?" I said.

She nodded. " You saw the baby, did you? You see, the baby is born."

" But we seem to be in a sort of prison."

" I think it would feel like being in prison."

" Aunt Sarah, what would feel like being in prison?"

" There," she said. " That place."

I understood. " That's all cleared up," I explained. " It was all a mistake. The doctor made a mistake. There is no need to think of that any more."

" But it's here," she insisted. " It's here in the picture."

234

"That's because you don't know all that's happened."

She shook her head almost petulantly, and my apprehension increased. I knew she moved quietly about the house, listening from secret places; and then quietly in this room she recorded the family's history. The history of the Rockwells was the most important thing in her life. That was why she spent hours over her exquisite tapestry. Here in this room she was supreme, a sort of goddess looking on at the follies of her creatures; elsewhere she was of no account—merely poor Sarah, who was a little simple.

I was foolish to allow myself to be upset by the vague ideas which circulated in her wandering mind.

"In a prison," she murmured, "there has to be a jailor. I can see him. He's all in black, but he has his back to me and his hood makes it impossible to recognise him."

"The monk!" I spoke lightly for I could think of that creature without fear now.

She came up to me and looked into my face. "The monk is very near you, Catherine," she said. "The monk is waiting for you, waiting to catch you. You should not think the monk is not near . . . and coming nearer."

"You know who it is!" I accused her.

"It's a lovely night," she answered. "The stars are wonderful. There is frost in the air, and, Catherine, the view is beautiful from the balcony."

I drew away from her.

"You're right," I said. "It is cold here. I think I should go back to my room."

"Wait awhile, Catherine."

"I think I should go."

I went to the door but she had caught my robe and was clinging to it. I had begun to shiver again, but this time not with cold.

"The candle," she said. "You'll need one. Take mine."

Still holding my robe, she drew me into the room. She picked up one of the lighted candles and thrust it into my hand. I grasped it and, disengaging myself, hurried along the corridor, half expecting her to pursue me.

I was breathless when I reached the sanctuary of my room and my apprehension remained with me. I could not dismiss Sarah's ramblings from my mind because I was certain that there was some meaning hidden within them.

How uncertain I was on that night! I longed to confide in someone. When I was with Simon I could not help but trust him and I doubted my ability to resist him; I believed that if I told him what I had discovered and he gave me a plausible explanation, I should be only too glad to meet him half-way. Readily would I believe any story he could tell me if only it would exonerate him from the murder of Gabriel and from the attempted murder of me and my child.

I believed that night that I dared not listen to Simon. I had to remain aloof. For the first time I could not trust my own good sense. I was at the mercy of my feelings for this man. It was humiliating, and yet in a way it was exhiliarating, because love must always be like that. And I learned that night, if I had not known it before, that I was in love with Simon.

The next day Simon and Hagar left Kirkland Revels. I said good-bye warmly to Hagar, coolly to Simon. He was aware of my changed attitude and it seemed to amuse him. I thought: Can he really be as cynical as that?

When they had left I went to my room. I wanted to be quiet and formulate some plan. I knew that I must act quickly, because it might be that already the robe had been missed.

The only person in whom I could confide was Mary-Jane; and what could she do to help me? Still, at such a time it was a comfort to confide in anybody. I thought of going to Sir Matthew, showing him what I had discovered, and asking him to make up a party to explore the passage between the house and the Abbey. Ruth? Could I tell Ruth? I was not sure of Ruth and it would not have surprised me to learn that she—although not the prime mover in the plot against me—was not unaware of what was going on. Sarah? What sense could one hope to get from Sarah? And Luke . . . I still clung to my belief that Luke was my real enemy.

I could not make up my mind.

I was in my room trying to come to some decision when I noticed an envelope lying on the floor by the door. I hurried to it and picked it up. There was nothing written on it. I opened my door, hoping to find someone hurrying away, but there was no one there; the letter might have been quietly pushed under my door some minutes before I had noticed it.

I shut my door and slit the envelope. There was a single sheet of paper inside; and on it was written in a shaky hand-writing:

" Go back to your old home without delay. You are in imminent danger."

I stared at it. I did not know the handwriting and I wondered whether the shakiness was a method of disguising it, for the letter was unsigned and there was no address on the paper.

Who had pushed the letter under my door? And what did it mean? Was it yet another trick?

But there was something tangible about a piece of paper. No one could say I had imagined this.

I went to the window and looked out. Then my heart began to hammer wildly because I saw someone hurrying away from the house and I recognised her—Damaris!

I suspected Damaris of working against me. How could I do otherwise when she had been with me and had seen the monk, and then had declared she had not?

I looked back at the paper. I would not let myself believe that she was working with Simon in this. And yet the position was desperate. I must look at the facts ; I must face the truth. I had seen them together on Christmas night, and what had been implied by their words shocked me deeply. But I couldn't believe this of Simon. My common sense might try to insist that I did, but my ridiculous feminine emotions refused to be convinced.

Someone had sent Damaris to put that note under my door. Was it Luke? He could have done it himself. Dr. Smith? I looked again at the handwriting, and because I had seen his decided that those words could not in any circumstances have been written by him.

Then I remembered that occasion when I had called at his house. I thought of the sick woman, the wife who was such a disappointment to him that he threw himself so wholeheartedly into his work. The shaky handwriting might be that of a sick woman, a woman who was in some stress.

I put the paper into my pocket, wrapped myself in my heavy cloak and left my room. I paused on the stairs by the minstrels' gallery ; then I opened the door and looked inside, because I thought that someone might be hiding there.

There was no one.

I went down through the hall and out of the house.

There was a bitterly cold wind blowing but I was impervious to the weather. I hurried away from the house, looking back only once to see if I was being followed. I could see no one, but I felt that from every window eyes might be watching me.

237

I went on until I came to the doctor's house. It seemed more gloomy than it had on that other occasion. The Venetian blinds were all drawn and the wind whistled through the firs.

I rang the bell and the maid let me in.

"The doctor is not at home, Mrs. Rockwell," she said.

"I have come to see Mrs. Smith."

She looked surprised. "I will tell her you are here."

"Please tell her that I am very eager to see her on a matter of importance."

The maid went away almost reluctantly, while I wondered what I should do if Mrs. Smith refused to see me. I might ask for Damaris. I would insist on knowing whether it was she who had brought the note, why she had denied seeing the monk, what part she had played and was playing in this plot against me. I was determined to know the truth without delay.

In a few moments the maid returned.

"Mrs. Smith will see you," she said; and I followed her up the stairs to the room which I had visited once before.

I was astonished to see Damaris with her mother. She was standing by Mrs. Smith's chair, and it seemed as though she were clinging to her mother for protection. Mrs. Smith looked even more emaciated than when I had last seen her; her eyes were enormous and they seemed to burn with some deep purpose.

She said in a quiet voice: "Good morning, Mrs. Rockwell. It was good of you to call."

I went forward and took the hand she extended; and then the door shut on the maid and we three were alone.

"Why did you come here?" she asked quickly. "This is the last place you should come to."

I took the sheet of paper from my pocket and held it out to her.

"Have you shown this to anyone else?" she asked.

"To no one."

"Why . . . do you come here?"

"Because I believe you wrote that and sent it to me. I saw Damaris leaving the house."

There was silence.

Then I cried: "You did write it, didn't you?"

Damaris put her arm about her mother. "You must not be disturbed," she said. She looked at me almost defiantly. "You are making her ill."

238

I answered: "I think she can help me to find out who has been trying to make *me* ill."

"You must not fret, my darling," said Mrs. Smith to Damaris. "She has come here, and it was very unwise of her. But she is here now and I must do what I can."

"You already have . . ."

"If she would only take my advice!"

"What is your advice?" I demanded.

"Go away from here. Do not delay a moment. Return at once to your father's house to-day. If you do not . . . it will be too late."

"How do you know?"

"There is a great deal I know," she said wearily.

"Will you tell me this: Did you write that note?"

She nodded. "Because I know that you must get away if you wish to give birth to a child that will live?"

"How do I know that I can trust you?"

"What could I possibly gain by warning you?"

"Don't you see that I'm in the dark?"

"Yes, I do. You are headstrong. You will not take my advice and go. You want to solve mysteries. You are too bold, Mrs. Rockwell."

"Tell me what you know," I said. "You owe that to me."

"Mother!" gasped Damaris, and the mask dropped from her lovely face. I knew that she was terrified.

I took the thin, clammy hand. "You must tell me, Mrs. Smith," I said. "You know you must tell me."

"Unless I tell you everything you will never believe me. You will never understand."

"Then tell me everything."

"It is a long story. . . . It goes back many years."

"I am in no hurry."

"You are wrong. You should be in a great hurry."

"I shall not leave until you tell me."

"And if I can convince you that your child is in danger, that you are in danger, will you go to your father's house to-day?"

"If I think that necessary, I will."

"Mother," said Damaris, "you must not . . . you dare not."

"You are afraid still, Damaris?"

"So are you, Mother. We both are . . . as we always have been."

239

"Yes," said Mrs. Smith, "I am afraid. But I am thinking of the child . . . and of her. We cannot stand by and see that happen to her . . . can we, Damaris? We must not think of ourselves. . . . We must thing only of her now."

I was beside myself with impatience. "You must tell me," I said. "Come now."

Still she hesitated, then bracing herself as for a mighty effort, she began:

"I married against my family's wishes. You may think my story has nothing to do with this. I am merely trying to tell you how I happen to know . . ."

"Yes, yes." I cried.

She plucked at the blanket which was wrapped about her knees.

"I have a small fortune of my own. As you know, when a woman marries, her fortune becomes her husband's. He needed the fortune . . . so he married me. I had a great opinion of him. He was the dedicated doctor and I wanted to work with him. I wanted to help him . . . his patients loved him so. He was so self-sacrificing. But you see there were two doctors. There was the doctor who went among his friends and patients . . . such a charming man, so solicitous of others. And there was the doctor at home. They were two different men. He liked to play his part but we couldn't expect him to act all the time, could we, Damaris?"

Damaris murmured: "You must not . . . oh, you must not. When he hears . . ."

"You see," went on Mrs. Smith, "he believed himself to be not quite mortal like the rest of us. He had done brilliantly at his work and from such humble beginnings. I admired that at the start. But he soon tired of playing the part for me. That happened before Damaris was born. He was very angry that she was not a boy. He wanted a son, to be exactly like himself—which in his eyes meant perfect. Damaris quickly learned to understand him. Do you remember, Damaris, how you would be playing, somewhere happily forgetful . . . because children do forget and when they are happy for an hour they believe they have always been so. Then we heard his step in the hall; and you would come to me and cower beside me, remembering."

"He ill-treated you?" I asked.

"Not physically. That is not his way. But he hated me. ~~Why~~ should he do otherwise? He had wanted my money and ~~got~~ his. and after many attempts I had failed to give him a son, I was of little use to him. Those dreary years of sadness and terror . . . I cannot think how I have lived through them."

"So it is Dr. Smith who has tried to destroy me. Why . . . why?"

"I will tell you that too. I met his foster mother. She lives not far from here in a little cottage on the moors. He was brought to her when he was a baby. He was born to a gipsy girl who had forsaken her people for a while to work in the kitchens at the Revels. She was married to a gipsy named Smith; but when her child was born she did not want him and she deserted him. Sir Matthew took an interest in the girl. I do not know whether he was ever her lover, but that was what Deverel always believed. He believed that he was the son of Sir Matthew. Do you begin to understand now?"

"I begin to see some light," I said.

"And when Sir Matthew had him educated, and trained as a doctor he was certain of this. He married me, and our daughter was called Damaris because the Rockwells had always chosen names from the Bible for their children. But it was a son he wanted. He wanted to see a son of his in the Revels. And so . . ."

She turned to Damaris, who was crying quietly.

"I must tell her this," she soothed. "It is the only way. I should have told her before. But you know how we have always feared his anger."

"Please go on," I pleaded.

"After several miscarriages I was warned that I ought to have no more children . . . but he wanted a son. I tried again. There was no son. The child was born dead and I . . . well, I have been an invalid ever since. Imagine how he hates me! I cannot even give him a son. I think that he would have rid himself of me if it had not been for Damaris." She put out a hand and stroked her daughter's hair. "You see, he does not know how far she would betray him if he attempted to destroy me." She turned to Damaris. "You see, my darling, in some ways we have him in our power." Then to me: "It was four years ago that I did my best to bear him a son. Before that I was not strong but I was able to take my part in the life of the neighbourhood. I played a part in the pageant . . . only one of the monks, it was true. I still had my robe though . . . until a few months ago."

I caught my breath and said: "So it is yours, that robe?"

"Yes, it was mine. I had kept it. I am a little sentimental

about such things. It was a reminder to me of the days when I was not an invalid."

"Damaris helped him," I said accusingly. "She swore that she had seen nothing."

"I had to," whispered Damaris, with a sob in her voice. "He told me what I had to do. We always obeyed him. We dared do nothing else. I was to take you to the ruins . . . not too quickly . . . to give him time to get there before us. And then, when he appeared, I was to pretend I saw nothing. There is a way from the ruins into the house. He discovered it when he was a boy. So he appeared to you in the house as well."

Now that I had the vital facts, events began to fall into place. I saw how he had everything fitted so neatly. I was filled with a wild exultation, and the reason was that the wish I had made at the Knaresborough Well had come true. It was not Simon.

"Why . . . *why* . . . ?" I demanded.

"He was determined to live in the Revels one day. As the poor boy he had watched the guests come and go. He had seen the picnics in summer, the skating parties in the winter; he had looked through the windows at the balls. He was obsessed by the Revels because he believed that he was Sir Matthew's son and therefore belonged there. He was determined to get there one day, and he saw that the way to do so was through Damaris. She was to marry Luke."

"But how could he be sure of that?"

"My daughter has a rare beauty. I do not think Luke is unaware of it. They were thrown together always. It may have been that he would have found some way of insisting on that marriage. He discovered the secrets in people's lives and used them when he found it expedient to do so. He would have discovered some things perhaps which Sir Matthew would not want made known . . . or perhaps Mrs. Grantley. The marriage would have taken place. He was not unduly concerned about Gabriel. Gabriel was delicate; he himself diagnosed that weak heart—the same complaint of which his mother had died. Perhaps Gabriel's heart was sound; perhaps he was preparing the way to Gabriel's end . . . I do not know everything. But when Gabriel married you he became a menace. He feared what actually did happen—that you might have a child. He was determined that Gabriel must die, and you at that time were of little interest to him. So Gabriel . . . died."

"It is not difficult to imagine how," I said grimly. And I pictured it. Did he lure Gabriel on to the balcony, or did Gabriel go there as he had made a habit of doing? There was no Friday on that night to warn him of a sinister presence. And then as he stood there, a stealthy movement from behind, a hand over his mouth and his body lifted and sent hurtling over the balcony.

Suicide? It seemed a reasonable verdict.

She said: "We are wasting time. Believe me, there is nothing more I can do for you. I have helped you all I can. Go at once to your old home. There you will be safe."

"You know that he plans something?"

"We know that. He is angry. He does not take us into his confidence, but there are certain things we cannot help knowing. Something has happened to anger him."

I knew what that was. He had discovered that the robe had been removed. He was planning some immediate action against me. I thought of his coming into the minstrels' gallery on Christmas night, and I wondered what would have happened to me then if Simon and Damaris had not been in the hall.

I caught their nervous excitement. I knew I had to act promptly. I could not see how he could harm me now, because I had so much evidence against him, but I did not doubt that he was diabolically clever.

"Go at once," pleaded his wife. "Do not wait for anything. He may return here at any moment. If you found you . . . if he knew what we had told you. . . ."

"Yes," I agreed. "I will go at once. How can I thank you for telling me this? I know what it must have meant to you."

"Don't waste time in thanking us. Please go, and he *must* not see you leave this house."

So I went, and when I came through the fir trees to the gate I was trying to make up my mind what I should do.

I was not going to Glen House. I was going to Kelly Grange. But first I would return to the Revels because I was determined that I would take the monk's robe with me. I was not going to allow anyone in future to believe that I had suffered from hallucinations.

As I walked back to the Revels, I was in a state of great excitement. I was certain that the account I had heard was a true one. How could I doubt that sick woman? Her fear had been genuine. Besides, now that I knew who my enemy was it was easy to understand how he had been in a position to act as he did. I thought back to the very beginning . . . the occasion when Friday had warned us of an intruder and had insisted on being taken out to the corridor; the next day when he had been missing and I had gone to look for him and lost my way and been brought home by Simon, Deverel Smith had been present on our return. He could have heard Gabriel say that he was going to order some milk for me. He might have seen the maid bringing it up, and have explained to her that I was upset about the loss of my dog and he would slip a sedative into my milk. Such a possibility had not entered my mind; on that tragic morning none of us thought of anything but Gabriel's death. But this could have been the reason why I slept so quickly and so deeply.

Then how easy it was for him to slip in and out of the house; to pull the curtains about my bed, to remove the warming-pan, and to put my cloak over the balcony.

He could come by the secret entry and if he were seen, on the stairs, in the hall, he would always have a plausible answer. He had been worried about Sir Matthew . . . Sarah . . . and latterly myself, and had dropped in to assure himself that all was well.

And Simon? I had to face the truth. I believed that Damaris regarded her father's determination to marry her to Luke with repulsion; and what I had originally thought was an affection between her and Luke was merely Damaris's desire to please a father whom she feared, and Luke's natural interest in an attractive girl—and with one as beautiful as Damaris that interest would normally be intensified. But with Simon . . . it would be different; and I did not believe that any woman could be completely indifferent to the virile charm of Simon Redvers. Even I—down to earth and sensible person that I believed myself to be—could not.

I must not think of Simon. But Hagar was my friend. I could rely on her. So I was going to the Revels; I was going to take the monk's robe from my wardrobe and go with it to Kelly Grange. I would tell Mary-Jane to pack some of my things, and she could bring them over in the carriage later. I should walk because I was not going to let anyone but Mary-Jane know that I was leaving.

Those were my plans as I entered the Revels.

I rang my bell, and Mary-Jane came to my room.

"Mary-Jane," I said. "I am going at once to Kelly Grange. Pack some things that I shall need. I will send for you and them. But I propose to go immediately."

"Yes, madam," said Mary-Jane, here eyes wide with surprise.

"Something has happened," I told her. "I cannot stop to explain now. But I am going to leave this house at once."

As I spoke I heard the sound of carriage wheels, and I went to the window.

I saw Dr. Smith alight and, because I no longer saw him as the benevolent doctor, I felt myself tremble.

"I should be gone," I said. "I must leave at once."

I hurried out of the room, leaving a bewildered Mary-Jane staring after me; I went along the corridor, down the first flight of stairs; then I heard the doctor's voice; he was talking to Ruth.

"Is she at home?"

"Yes, I saw her come in only a few minutes ago."

"That is fortunate. I will go and get her now."

"What if she . . . ?"

"She will know nothing until I have her safely there."

My heart began to hammer uncertainly. He was already striding across the hall. I slipped into the minstrels' gallery quickly, thinking that I might hide myself there while he went on to my room. Then I should run out of the house and to Kelly Grange.

Ruth had remained in the hall and I wondered how I should get past her. Would she tell the doctor that I had run out of the house? If so, how long would it take him to catch up with me?

I quietly shut the door of the gallery and I immediately thought of the cupboard. If I could escape by way of the secret tunnel they would not catch me.

But even as I, my body bent so that I should not be seen from the hall, went towards the cupboard, the door of the gallery opened and he was standing there.

"Oh . . . hallo, Catherine." He was smiling the benign smile which had deluded me in the past.

I could say nothing for the moment; my voice had lost itself in my constricted throat.

"I came to call on you, and I saw you come in here as I started up the stairs."

"Good morning," I said and I felt that my voice sounded calmer than I had thought possible.

He stepped into the gallery and shut the door. When I glanced over the balcony I could see Ruth standing below.

"It's a fine morning," he went on. "I wanted you to come for a little drive with me."

"Thank you. I was just going out for a walk."

"But you have just come in."

"Nevertheless, I am just going out again."

He lifted a finger and there was something so sinister in that playful gesture that I felt a shudder run down my spine.

"You are doing too much walking, and you know I don't allow that."

"I am perfectly healthy," I answered. "Jessie Dankwait is pleased with me."

"The country midwife!" he said contemptuously. "A drive will do you good."

"Thank you, but I do not wish to go."

He came towards me and took my wrist; he held it tenderly yet firmly.

"I am going to insist to-day, because you are looking a little pale."

"No, Dr. Smith," I said. "I do not wish to go for a drive."

"But my dear Catherine" (his face was close to mine and his gentle, suave manner seemed more horrible than violence), "you are coming with me."

I tried to walk past him, but he caught and held me firmly. He took the robe from me and threw it on the floor.

"Give that to me and let me go at once," I said.

"My dear, you must allow me to know what is good for you."

I was filled with sudden panic. I called: "Ruth! Ruth! Help me."

I saw her start up the stairs, and I thanked God that she was at hand.

She opened the door of the minstrels' gallery; he was still holding me in a grip so firm that I could not extricate myself.

"I am afraid," he said to her, "that she is going to give us a little trouble."

"Catherine," said Ruth, "you must obey the doctor. He knows what's best for you."

"He knows what is best! Look at this robe. He is the one who has been playing those tricks on me."

"I fear," said the doctor, "that it is more advanced than I believed. I am afraid we are going to have trouble. It is a

246

mistake to delay too long in these matters. It has happened before in my experience."

"What diabolical plan have you in mind now?" I demanded.

"It is the persecution mania," murmured the doctor to Ruth. "Believing that they are alone against the whole world." He turned to me. "Catherine, my very dear Catherine, you must trust me. Have I not always been your friend?"

I burst out laughing and it was laughter which alarmed me. I was truly frightened now, because I began to see what he planned to do with me, and that Ruth either believed him or pretended to, and I was alone with them . . . and friendless. I knew the truth, but I had been a fool. I had told no one of my discovery. I could still do that. . . . But whom could I tell . . . these two whose plan was to destroy me? For Ruth, if not his accomplice, was no friend to me.

"Look," I said, "I know too much. It was you, Dr. Smith, who decided that my child should never be born. You killed Gabriel and you were determined to kill anyone who stood between Luke's inheriting the Revels . . ."

"You see," he said sadly, "how far advanced it is."

"I found the robe, and I know, too, that you believe you belong here. I know it all. Do you think that you can deceive me any more."

He had seized me firmly in his arms. I smelt a whiff of what might have been chloroform as something was pressed over my mouth. I felt as though everything was slipping away from me and I heard his voice, very faint, as though it were a long way off.

"I hoped to avoid this. It is the only way when they are obstreperous. . . ."

Then I slipped away . . . into darkness.

I have heard it said that the mind is more powerful than the body. I believe that to be so. My mind commanded my body to reject the chloroform even as it was pressed over my mouth. This was not possible, of course; that would have been asking too much, but as it began to affect my body my brain continued to struggle against it. I must not sink into unconsciousness. I knew that if I did I should wake up a prisoner, and that all the evidence which I had acquired would be destroyed and my protests called the aberrations of the mentally sick.

So even as my body succumbed, my mind fought on.

So it was that I was half conscious of being in that jolting carriage with the evil doctor beside me. And I summoned all my will power to fight the terrible drowsiness which was lulling me into a sense of utter forgetfulness.

I realised he was taking me to Worstwhistle.

We were alone in his brougham and the driver could not hear what was said. The swaying of the vehicle was helpful; the clop-clop of the horse's hoofs seemed to be saying: "Doom is at hand. Fight it. Fight it with all your might. There is still time. But once you enter that grim grey building . . . it will not be so easy to come out."

I would not enter. I would never let anyone be able to tell my child that once its mother had been an inmate of Worstwhistle.

"You should not struggle, Catherine," said the doctor gently.

I tried to speak but the effect of the drug was claiming me.

"Close your eyes," he murmured. "Do you doubt that I will look after you? There is nothing for you to fear. I shall come and see you every day. I shall be there when your child is born. . . ."

My mind said: "You are a devil. . . ." But the words did not come.

I was frightened because of this terrible drowsiness which was seeping over me, and which would not let me fight for my future and that of my child.

Subconsciously I knew that this had been his plan all along, to get me to Worstwhistle before my child was born, to attend to me there and make sure, if my child was a boy, that he did not live.

If I gave birth to a daughter or a stillborn child, then I should be of no more interest to him, because I should no longer menace Luke's accession to the Revels and the marriage with Damaris.

But, fight as I would, I could only remain in this half-conscious state. And I reserved my strength for the moment when the carriage wheels should stop and he would call strong men to help him bring another reluctant victim to that grim prison.

The carriage had drawn up.

We had arrived. I felt sick and dizzy, and only half conscious.

248

"Why, my dear Catherine," he said, and he put his arm about me; and once more I felt his gentle touch to be more hurtful than a blow, "you are unwell. Never mind. This is the end of the journey. Now you shall know peace. No more fancies . . . no more visions. Here you shall be cared for."

"Listen . . ." I began, and I seemed to drawl the words. "I . . . am not going in there."

He was smiling. "Leave this to me, my dear," he whispered. There was the sound of running footsteps and a man took his stand on one side of me; I felt him take my arm.

I heard their voices.

"She knows where she's going, this one . . ."

Then the doctor's voice: "They have their lucid moments. Sometimes it's a pity."

I tried to scream but I could not; my legs were buckling under me. I was being dragged forward.

I saw the great iron door swing open. I saw the porch with the name over it—the name which must have struck terror into a thousand hearts and minds.

"No . . ." I sobbed.

But they were so many; and I was so weak against them. I heard the sudden clatter of a horse's hoofs. Then the doctor said sharply: "Quickly! Get the patient inside."

And there was a note of fear in his voice to replace that gentle assurance which had been there before.

Then my whole being seemed to come alive again, and I realised that what seemed to make the blood run hot in my veins was hope.

A voice I knew well, a voice I loved, was shouting: "What the devil's all this!"

And there he was—the man whom I had failed to dismiss from my thoughts although I had tried—striding towards me; and I knew that he came like a knight of old, and that he had come to save me from my enemies.

"Simon," I sobbed; and as I fell forward I felt his arms about me.

I ceased to fight the lassitude then; I accepted the darkness.

I was no longer alone. Simon had come to stand beside me and fight my battle for me.

Chapter 8

So I did not enter Worstwhistle on that terrible day. Simon was there to prevent that. Mary-Jane had left the house with all speed while I was struggling in the minstrels' gallery, and had gone to Kelly Grange to tell what was happening, for she had overheard what the doctor had said about taking me away, and she knew enough to guess where.

So Simon had gone straight there and, although I was not able to see how he fought for my freedom, I knew it had happened.

He had faced Deverel Smith and had accused him on the spot of the murder of Gabriel. He had threatened the Superintendent with the loss of his post if he dared take me in merely on Dr. Smith's word. I could imagine the power of him as he fought the battle for my freedom and the life of my child.

Of course he won. Simon must always win. He was invincible when he determined on what he would have. I have grown to learn that, and I would not have it otherwise.

I often wonder what Deverel Smith had thought as he stood there knowing that his elaborate scheme had been foiled at the very last moment. Because, if once he had had me accepted in Worstwhistle as a patient whom he certified as of unsound mind, it would not have been easy to prove that I had not suffered from insanity, even if only temporarily.

But Simon had come.

He took me back to Kelly Grange, where Hagar was waiting for me, and I stayed there until my child was born.

That happened prematurely, which was not to be wondered at, but my Gabriel soon picked up and became a strong little boy. We doted on him—Hagar and I; and I think Simon did too, but he was determined to make a man of the boy and he rarely showed the softer side of his feelings. I did not mind, because I wanted Gabriel to be the kind of boy who would appreciate being treated as a man rather than a baby. I wanted my son to be strong.

But there were other happenings before the birth of Gabriel.

I often think of Deverel Smith, of his belief in himself, and

I am sure he saw himself as godlike, powerful beyond other men, of stronger intellect, of greater cunning. He had not believed that he could be defeated. He bore a grudge against life which he had determined to satisfy. He believed that he was the son of Sir Matthew and that no one should stand between him and his inheritance. If Gabriel was the legitimate son, he would reason, he was himself the elder son ; and so he eliminated Gabriel.

We never learned exactly how that happened ; and whether Gabriel was lured on to the balcony or went there of his own accord and was surprised there, will remain a mystery, but he killed Gabriel to make the way open for Luke, and when Luke had married Damaris he would have come to live at the Revels. In his subtle, sinister way, he would have been master of the Revels because he would have made himself aware of some weakness in the people who lived about him and used a subtle blackmail in order to dominate them.

That was his delight—to dominate. Ruth told me, much later, that he had discovered an indiscretion of hers. She had indulged in a love affair after the death of her husband which could have created a distressing scandal if it had become common knowledge. It was not that he had said: " If you do not support me I shall tell of this matter which you are so anxious ' to keep secret." But he had intimated that he was aware of it and in exchange for his silence he expected her support and an outward show of friendship. Subtly he had forced her to his side, and she had always made a show of welcoming him to the Revels and extolling his virtues whenever she had an opportunity.

Perhaps Deverel Smith had also held some sway over Sir Matthew. In any case he had no doubts about the support of both Sir Matthew and Ruth for a marriage between Luke and Damaris.

I have often wondered what would have happened in that household but for Simon. I should have been out of the way—I do not care to think even now of what my future would have been. But there at the Revels, I imagined him the master . . . holding his gentle but evil sway over them all.

But it was not to be so ; and how could he endure to see all that he had schemed for lost . . . because of one strong man?

How he must have hated Simon ; but Simon could return hate with hate. *He* would have no mercy and Deverel Smith knew it. When he stood facing Simon at the portals of Worstwhistle he must have realised that at last he faced an adversary stronger than himself.

So he died—as he had lived—dramatically. When Simon demanded a carriage to take me back to Kelly Grange—for he had galloped to Worstwhistle on one of his fleetest horses— and when it was brought for him and he had lifted me in and prepared to leave for Kelly Grange, Deverel Smith had already gone back to the Revels.

He went to the house and right to the top of the east wing, to that balcony which was the only one in the house from which a Rockwell had not fallen to his death. He threw himself over in a last defiant gesture, as though by so doing he proved to the world what he had always sought to prove to himself: he was of that family, and Kirkland Revels meant to him all that it ever could to any member of the family who had been born there and lived his life within its walls.

There is little else to say. Mrs. Smith—whose health improved after her husband's death—went away with Damaris, I heard later that Damaris made a brilliant marriage in London. Luke went up to Oxford and there collected several bad debts and became involved in some trouble with a young woman. That was all part of growing up, said Sir Matthew, who had done it all before him. Ruth had changed too. Her manner to me grew warmer and, though we should never be great friends, she was contrite because of her readiness to play the doctor's game, even though she was ignorant of his wickedest motives. Sarah remained—as she always had been—my good friend. Gleefully she told me she had completed the picture. I was there, with Gabriel and Friday, but I was in my own room at Kirkland Revels, not in a cell. She had wanted to warn me because she had known I was in imminent danger, but she had not realised that the monk and the doctor were one and the same, and this had baffled her. How happy she was now that the danger was past; she was as eager for the birth of my child as I was.

It was a wonderful day when Gabriel was born and it was known that he would live and that I should recover from my ordeal, which was a little more severe than it would have been owing to the upsets of the preceeding months. I remember lying with my child in my arms, experiencing that wonderful feeling of lassitude which I suppose is one of the most enviable feelings a woman can have. People had been coming to see me; and then, suddenly, there was Simon.

He had already told me that he had begun to suspect the doctor; and it was he who, after Deverel Smith's death, discovered the way into the secret chamber from the Abbey side. Mary-Jane and I had come near to finding it on that Christmas morning. Had we removed the stones which, in her exasperation, Mary-Jane had kicked, we should have disclosed the flight of steps leading down to the chamber in which she found the robe. We eventually learned that the passage connecting the house with the Abbey vaults had been constructed when the house was built. Considering the emergencies which could so easily arise, the proximity to the house of such an excellent hiding-place would have seemed too important to be overlooked.

It was some years later when, exploring the tunnels, I discovered a secret recess hidden by a pile of stones and, removing these, came on Friday's grave. I guessed then that Deverel Smith had poisoned him and buried him in this spot. There was nothing left but his bones.

Simon had come to the conclusion that the doctor's motive was to prevent my bearing a living child, so that Luke should inherit, and marry Damaris.

"For that reason," he had explained, "I paid attention to her. I knew she was not as interested in young Luke as she pretended to be, and I wanted to see the effect on her father if someone else began paying court to her."

"It sounds as good a reason as the other," I told him.

"What other?" he wanted to know.

"That she happens to be one of the most attractive women either of us can ever have seen."

He grinned at that and seemed pleased; and now that I know him well I understand that it was my jealousy that pleased him far more than Damaris's charms.

And when he stood looking at my son I saw the regret in his face, and I said: "What is it, Simon?"

Then he looked straight at me and said: "He's a grand chap, but there's one thing wrong with him."

"What's that, Simon?"

"He ought to be mine," said Simon.

That was a proposal of marriage, and it was for this reason that as I lay there with the child I experienced the happiest moment of my life which I had known up to that time.

All that spring and summer we made our plans. Because my son Gabriel would one day be master of Kirkland Revels, he should be brought up between the Revels and Kelly Grange, and this would mean that to some extent the two estates would be as one.

Uncle Dick came home and it was wonderful to accept the close relationship between us. He gave me away when, the following Christmas, I married Simon. And as we came down the aisle together I thought: And that is the end of the beginning.

Then I wondered what the future would hold for us and if in the years ahead we should weather the storms which must surely beset two such personalities as ours. Life perhaps would not be always calm between us. We both were headstrong, and neither of us meek.

But as we came out into the Christmas sunshine, my spirits were lifted. I knew there was nothing to fear, for there was love between us, and it is love which casts out fear.

Victoria Holt

The supreme writer of the 'gothic' romance, a compulsive storyteller whose gripping novels of the darker face of love have thrilled millions all over the world.

The Shivering Sands 30p
King of the Castle 30p
Mistress of Mellyn 30p
Bride of Pendorric 30p
Menfreya 30p
Kirkland Revels 30p
The Legend of the Seventh Virgin 30p
The Queen's Confession 40p
New in paperback July 1972:
The Secret Woman 35p

All available in Fontana Books

Victoria Holt also writes as

Jean Plaidy

'One of England's foremost historical novelists.'

Birmingham Mail

Murder Most Royal 35p
St. Thomas's Eve 30p
The Sixth Wife 30p
Royal Road to Fotheringay 30p
The Captive Queen of Scots 35p
The Wandering Prince 30p
A Health Unto His Majesty 30p
Here Lies Our Sovereign Lord 30p
Daughter of Satan 30p
The Thistle and the Rose 30p
The Spanish Bridegroom 30p
Gay Lord Robert 30p
Madame Serpent 35p
The Italian Woman 30p
Queen Jezebel 30p
Louis the Well-beloved 30p
The Murder in the Tower 30p

All available in Pan Books

Fontana Books

Fontana is best known as one of the leading paperback publishers of popular fiction and non-fiction. It also includes an outstanding, and expanding section of books on history, natural history, religion and social sciences.

Most of the fiction authors need no introduction. They include Agatha Christie, Hammond Innes, Alistair MacLean, Catherine Gaskin, Victoria Holt and Lucy Walker. Desmond Bagley and Maureen Peters are among the relative newcomers.

The non-fiction list features a superb collection of animal books by such favourites as Gerald Durrell and Joy Adamson.

All Fontana books are available at your bookshop or newsagent; or can be ordered direct. Just fill in the form below and list the titles you want.

FONTANA BOOKS, Cash Sales Department, P.O. Box 4, Godalming, Surrey. Please send purchase price plus 5p postage per book by cheque, postal or money order. No currency.

NAME (Block letters) _____

ADDRESS _____

_____

_____

While every effort is made to keep prices low, it is sometimes necessary to increase prices at short notice. Fontana Books reserve the right to show new retail prices on covers which may differ from those previously advertised in the text or elsewhere.